BEC
DR BELL

JOANNA NEIL

MIDWIFE, MOTHER...
ITALIAN'S WIFE

BY
FIONA McARTHUR

MILLS &
BOON®

This is your invitation to not one but two

ITALIAN WEDDINGS!

Turn the page to meet dreamy doc Nick Bellini
and delicious Dr Leon Bonmarito.
Two gorgeous Italians about to
sweep the women of their dreams off their feet!

BECOMING DR BELLINI'S BRIDE
by Joanna Neil

and

MIDWIFE, MOTHER…ITALIAN'S WIFE
by Fiona McArthur

BECOMING DR BELLINI'S BRIDE

BY
JOANNA NEIL

MILLS &
BOON

All the characters in this book have no existence outside the imagination of the author, and have no relation whatsoever to anyone bearing the same name or names. They are not even distantly inspired by any individual known or unknown to the author, and all the incidents are pure invention.

First published in Great Britain 2011
Harlequin Mills & Boon Limited,
Eton House, 18-24 Paradise Road, Richmond, Surrey TW9 1SR

© Joanna Neil 2011

ISBN: 978 0 263 88577 4

Harlequin Mills & Boon policy is to use papers that are natural, renewable and recyclable products and made from wood grown in sustainable forests. The logging and manufacturing process conform to the legal environmental regulations of the country of origin.

Printed and bound in Spain
by Litografia Rosés, S.A., Barcelona

Dear Reader

There cannot be many lovelier sights than the glorious sweep of the California coastline where it meets with the deep blue of the Pacific Ocean. I know that's where I longed to be when I wrote my story BECOMING DR BELLINI'S BRIDE.

Even more, I wanted to wander around the vineyards of the Carmel Valley, with their lush fruit hanging off the vines, just waiting to be picked.

This, I decided, was the perfect backdrop for a story of family secrets, yearnings, and the desire for the return of land held for generations by the Bellini family.

Of course those cherished dreams bring Nick Bellini into sparking conflict with lovely, idealistic Katie, who is fiercely protective of her father's holdings. Too bad his land once belonged to Nick's family!

And what of the heartache Katie endures when she discovers a long-held family secret…? Will Nick be the one to soothe and comfort her?

I hope you enjoy finding out how everything works out for Nick and Katie.

Joanna Neil

When **Joanna Neil** discovered Mills & Boon®, her life-long addiction to reading crystallised into an exciting new career writing Medical™ Romance. Her characters are probably the outcome of her varied lifestyle, which includes working as a clerk, typist, nurse and infant teacher. She enjoys dressmaking and cooking at her Leicestershire home. Her family includes a husband, son and daughter, an exuberant yellow Labrador and two slightly crazed cockatiels. She currently works with a team of tutors at her local education centre, to provide creative writing workshops for people interested in exploring their own writing ambitions.

Recent titles by the same author:

PLAYBOY UNDER THE MISTLETOE
THE SECRET DOCTOR
HAWAIIAN SUNSET, DREAM PROPOSAL
NEW SURGEON AT ASHVALE A&E

CHAPTER ONE

KATIE stood still for a moment, her green eyes slowly scanning the horizon. Her nerves were frayed. Perhaps taking time out to look around her at this part of the sweeping California coastline was just the medicine she needed right now.

She would never have believed she would find herself in such a beautiful place as this small, quiet town, with its charming cottages and quaint shops and general sleepy atmosphere. As for the bay, it was a wide arc of golden sand, backed by rugged cliffs and rocks, a striking contrast to the clear blue of the Pacific Ocean that lapped its shores. Beyond all that was the magnificent range of the Santa Lucia Mountains, lush and green, their slopes forested with redwoods, oaks and pine.

She drank in the view for a moment or two longer, absorbing the tranquillity of her surroundings. Then she pulled in a deep breath and turned away to walk along the road towards a distant building set high on a bluff overlooking the sea.

One way or another, it had been a difficult day so

far, and she could see little chance of things improving. She still had to meet with her father, and even though she had become used to seeing him over these last couple of weeks, it was always something of a strain for her to be with him.

'We'll have lunch,' he'd said, as though it was an everyday, natural occurrence.

'Okay.' She'd looked at him and his expression had been relaxed and easygoing. He seemed to genuinely want to meet up with her again. 'I have a half-day on Wednesday,' she told him, 'so that should work out well enough.'

And now he was waiting for her at the restaurant, sitting at a table on the open-air terrace, gazing out over the ocean. Katie guessed he was watching the boats on the horizon. He hadn't noticed her coming towards him, and she was glad of that. It gave her the chance to compose herself, as well as an opportunity to fix his image once more in her mind.

She studied him. He was not as she remembered from all those years ago, neither did he bear any resemblance to the pictures her mother had carefully stored in the photograph album. She guessed at one time he must have been tall and vital, a vigorous man, full of energy and ambition, but at this moment he appeared frail, a shadow of his former self. His body was thin, his face faintly lined, and his brown hair was faded, threaded through with silver strands.

'Hi, there…' Katie hesitated. She was still struggling with the idea of calling this man her dad. It went against the grain to use the word, considering that he was almost a stranger to her. Instead, she asked, 'Have you been waiting long? I'm sorry I'm a bit late. I was held up at work.'

'That's all right. Don't worry about it.' Her father smiled and rose carefully to his feet to pull out a chair for her. 'You look harassed. We can't have that, can we? Sit yourself down and take a minute or two to settle. Life's too short to be getting yourself in a tizzy.'

His breathing was wheezy and laboured, and Katie was concerned. She'd heard that he had been ill for some time, but his health seemed to have taken a downturn even in the few days since she had last seen him.

'Thanks.' She sat down quickly so that he could do the same. Then she gazed around her. 'It's lovely to be able to sit out here and enjoy the fresh air… And it's all so perfect…idyllic, with the tubs of flowers and all the greenery.'

'I thought you'd like it. The food's good, too.'

A waitress approached with menus, and Katie accepted hers with a smile, opening it up to look inside and study the contents. In reality, though, her mind was in a whirl and she was finding it difficult to concentrate, so that the text became a blur.

Her father signalled to the wine waiter and ordered a bottle of Cabernet Sauvignon, before turning back to Katie. 'Why don't you tell me what sort of a day you've had?' he suggested. 'It can't have been too good, by the looks of things. Are you getting on all right at the hospital? You've been there almost a week now, haven't you?'

She nodded. 'I'm really happy to be working there. The people are great...very friendly and helpful. I'm working in Paediatrics most of the time, but I also have a couple of days when I'm on call to deal with general emergencies if they arise locally. Mostly people will ring for an ambulance if there's an accident or medical incident, but if I'm nearer and it's likely to be something serious then I'll go out as a first responder. It's a good opportunity for me to keep up with emergency work, so I was glad with this job came up.'

Her father glanced at his menu. 'It sounds as though it's the kind of work you enjoy. It's what you were doing in England, in Shropshire, isn't it?'

'That's right.'

The wine waiter arrived, pouring a small amount of clear, red wine for her father to taste, before filling two glasses.

Katie took a sip of her drink, savouring the rich, fruity flavour. She sent her father a quick, searching glance. Somehow he always managed to get her to talk about herself. He very rarely revealed anything of his lifestyle, about what had brought him to where he was now.

'What about you?' she asked. 'Did you always have it in mind to come out here—was there something about Carmel Valley that drew you—or was it *someone* who led you to this place?'

'The company I worked for sent me out here,

initially,' he answered, placing his menu down on the table. He nodded towards the one she was holding. 'Have you decided what you'd like to eat yet? The filet mignon is always good.'

'Yes, I think I'll go with that. But I'd prefer the cold slices, rather than a steak, I think…with tomato, red onion and blue cheese.'

'And a Caesar salad?'

'That sounds good.'

He nodded. 'I'll grab the waitress's attention.' He studied her once more. 'So what's been happening to get you all flustered today? You've always been calm and collected whenever we've seen one another, up to now. Is it a problem at work?'

She shook her head. 'Not really… I mean, yes, in a way, I suppose.' She gave an inward sigh and braced herself. It didn't look as though he was going to give up on trying to tease it out of her, so she may as well get it off her chest.

'I saw a little boy at the clinic today,' she said. 'He was around four years old, and his mother told me he'd been unwell for some time. She hadn't known what to do because his symptoms were vague, and she put it down to the fact that he'd had a cold and sore throat. Only he took a sudden turn for the worse. When I examined him, his body was swollen with oedema, his blood pressure was high, and his heart was racing.'

Her father frowned. 'Seems that he was in a bad way, poor little chap.'

'Yes, he was. I had him admitted to the renal unit.

He was losing protein in his urine, and it looks as though his kidneys are inflamed.'

He winced. 'Definitely bad news. So, what will happen to him now?'

'They'll do tests, and give him supportive treatment. Probably diuretics to bring down the swelling, and he'll be put on a low-sodium, low-protein diet.'

She glanced around once more, looking out over the redwood deck rail to the ocean beyond. The sound of birds calling to one another mingled with the soft whoosh of surf as it dashed against the rocks below.

She looked back at him. 'What about you? You haven't told me much about yourself. Mum said that you worked in the import and export trade years ago—you had to travel a lot, she said.'

'Yes, I did. I suppose that's how I first became interested in the wine business.' He beckoned the waitress and gave their orders. After the girl had left, he said gently, 'This child you treated—he isn't the reason you're not quite yourself, is he? After all, you must have come across that kind of thing many times in the course of your work.'

She nodded, brushing a flyaway tendril of chestnut hair from her cheek. Her hair was long, a mass of unruly natural curls that defied all her attempts to restrain them. 'That's true.' She pressed her lips together, uneasy at having to revisit the source of her discomfort. 'I think he reminded me of a child I treated back in Shropshire...my ex-boyfriend's son, though he was much younger, only two years old. He had the same condition.'

'Ah...' He leaned back in his chair, a thoughtful expression crossing his face. 'So it made you think about the situation back home. I see it now. Your mother told me all about the break-up.'

She sent him a sharp glance. 'You've spoken to my mother?'

'I have.' He gave a faint smile. 'She called me... naturally, when she knew you would be coming out here, she wanted to make sure that you would be all right. A mother's protective instinct at work, I guess.'

Katie frowned, and began to finger her napkin. She wasn't at all pleased with her father knowing everything there was to know about her personal life. In many ways he was an unknown quantity as far as she was concerned, and yet it appeared he knew things about her that she would much rather had remained secret.

She was still trying to take it on board when a man approached their table. He was in his mid-thirties, she guessed, a striking figure of a man with dark, smouldering good looks that sent an immediate frisson of awareness to ripple along her spine. His clothes were superb. He was wearing an immaculate dark suit that had been expertly and, no doubt, expensively tailored, while his shirt was made from a beautiful fabric, finished in a deep shade of blue that perfectly matched his eyes.

Those eyes widened as he looked at Katie, and his

gaze drifted appreciatively over her, lingering for a while on the burnished chestnut curls that brushed her shoulders, before moving downwards to lightly stroke her softly feminine curves.

Katie shifted uncomfortably in her seat, trying to shake off the impact of that scorching gaze. She felt warm all over, and the breath caught in her throat. Suddenly, she was all too conscious of the closely-fitting blouse she was wearing, a pintucked design in delicate cotton, teamed with a dove-grey, pencil-slim skirt.

Getting herself together, she looked up, deciding to face him head on and return the scrutiny in full measure. He had a perfectly honed physique, long and lean, undoubtedly firm-muscled beneath all the civilised trappings. His hair was jet black, strong and crisply styled, cut short as though to tame it, but even so there was an errant kink to the strands. He had the dazzling, sensual good looks of an Italian-American.

His glance met hers and a glint of flame sparked in his blue eyes. Then he dragged his gaze from her and turned to her father.

'Jack,' he said, 'this is a pleasant surprise. It's good to see you.' He extended a lightly bronzed hand in greeting. 'I'd thought of dropping by the house in the next day or so, since you've not been looking too well of late. How are things with you?' His voice was evenly modulated, deep and soothing like a creamy liqueur brandy, and Katie's heart began to thump heavily in response. Why on earth was this man having such an effect on her?

'Things are fine, Nick, thanks.' Her father waved a hand towards Katie. 'You haven't met my daughter, Katie, have you?'

Nick looked startled. 'Your daughter? I had no idea...'

'No. Well...' Her father cut him short, his breath rasping slightly with the effort. 'It's a long story. She came over here from the UK just a fortnight ago.' He switched his attention to Katie. 'Let me introduce you,' he said. 'Katie, this is Nick Bellini. He and his family own the vineyard next to mine. He's in partnership with his father and brother.'

Katie frowned. So her father hadn't even told his friends that he had a daughter. Another small part of her closed down inside. Perhaps she had been hoping for too much. Coming out here might turn out to be the biggest mistake of her life so far.

'I'm pleased to meet you,' Katie murmured. She wasn't expecting him to respond with more than a nod, but he reached for her, taking her hand in his and cupping it between his palms.

'And I'm more than delighted to meet you, Katie,' Nick said, his voice taking on a husky, sensual note. 'I'd no idea Jack was hiding such a treasure.'

Katie felt the heat rise in her cheeks. There was nothing casual about his greeting. The way he was holding her felt very much like a caress and it was thoroughly unsettling. Her alarm system had gone into overdrive at his touch and it was way more than she could handle. As if she hadn't had enough problems with men.

As soon as it was polite enough to do so, she carefully extricated her hand. Over the last year she had worked hard to build up a shield around herself, had even begun to believe she was immune, and here, in less than two minutes, Nick Bellini had managed to shoot her defences to smithereens.

'I've a feeling I've heard the name Bellini somewhere before,' she murmured. 'In a newspaper article, I think. I just can't recall exactly what it was that I read.'

He gave her a wry smile. 'Let's hope it was something good.'

He gave his attention back to her father. 'I was hoping we could get together some time in the next week or two to talk about the vineyards. My father has drawn up some papers, and he'd appreciate it if you would look them over.'

Her father nodded. 'Yes, he mentioned them to me.' He waved a hand towards an empty chair. 'Why don't you join us, Nick...unless you have business to attend to right now? We've only just ordered.'

Katie's heart gave a disturbing lurch. She stared at him. What was her father thinking?

'Thank you.' Nick acknowledged the invitation with a nod. 'I'd like that, if you're quite sure I'm not intruding?'

He looked to Katie for an answer, but words stuck in her throat and she had to swallow down the flutter of uncertainty that rose in her. Why on earth had her father made the suggestion? They spent so little time together as it was, and there was so much she wanted to know, so many questions that still had to be answered. She needed to be alone with him, at least until she knew him better.

But what choice did she have? To refuse after Nick had shown his willingness to accept the invitation would be churlish.

Of course, Nick Bellini must have known all that. She nodded briefly, but sent him a glance through narrowed eyes.

He pulled out a chair and sat down, a half-smile playing around his mouth. She had the feeling he knew something of what she was going on in her mind, but if he had any real notion of her qualms he was choosing to ignore them.

'I came here to see the management about their wine cellar,' he said. 'After all, we might be able to tempt them into adding our new Pinot Noir to their collection—not strictly my job, but I like to keep in touch with all the restaurateurs hereabouts.' He paused as the waitress came to take his order.

'I'll have the teriyaki chicken, please, Theresa… with a side salad.' He gave the girl a careful, assessing look. 'You've done something different with your hair, haven't you?' His expression was thoughtful. 'It looks good. It suits you.'

'Thank you.' The girl dimpled, her cheeks flushed with warm colour.

Nick watched her as she walked away, and Katie observed him in the process. Did he respond like that to every woman who came his way? Were they all treated to a sample of his megawatt charm?

'Pinot Noir is a notoriously difficult wine to get right,' Jack said. 'But your father seems to have the Midas touch.'

Nick gave a fleeting smile. 'The key is to harvest the grapes in the cool of the evening and in the early morning. Then they're cold soaked before fermentation…and we use the whole berries for that process. Then, to reduce the risk of harsh tannins from the seeds and skins, they're pressed early.'

Jack nodded. 'Like I said, your father knows his business. Your vines are looking good again this year. It looks as though you'll have one of the best seasons yet.' He poured wine into a glass and passed it to Nick.

'We're hoping so.' Nick held the glass to his lips. 'Though you don't do too badly yourself. The Logan name is well respected around here…that's why we'd really like to make it part of the Bellini company.'

'It's a big undertaking.' Jack's features were sombre. 'I've worked hard to build up the business over the years. It's been my life's work.'

'Of course.' Nick tasted the wine, savouring it on his tongue before placing his glass down on the table. 'I'm sure my father will have taken all that into account.'

Katie frowned. It sounded as though the Bellinis were offering to buy out her father's company, but as usual Jack Logan was keeping his cards close to his chest. Was he thinking of selling up, or would he try to fend off their attempt at a takeover?

Nick turned towards Katie, as though remembering his manners. 'I'm sorry to talk shop...I expect this discussion of wine and grapes and company business must be quite boring for you.'

'Not at all.' Katie's expression was sincere. 'In fact I was really intrigued to learn that my father owns a vineyard, and I was actually hoping that one day soon I might get a chance to see it.'

'That won't be a problem,' Jack murmured. 'Just as soon as I get over this latest chest infection I'll take you on a tour. In the meantime, I'm sure Nick would be glad to show you around his place.'

'I'd be more than happy to do that,' Nick agreed, his gaze homing in on her. 'Maybe we could make a date for some time next week?'

'I... Possibly.' Katie was reluctant to commit herself to anything. She wasn't ready for Nick's full-on magnetism. Didn't she have enough to contend with right now, without adding to her troubles? 'I'll have to see how things work out at the hospital.'

'The hospital?'

Nick lifted a dark brow and Jack explained helpfully, 'Katie's a doctor...a paediatrician. She came out here to get a taste of California life and she's just settling into a new job.'

'Oh, I see.'

The waitress arrived with the meals just then, and Katie realised that she was hungry, despite her restless, slightly agitated frame of mind. Perhaps food would help to calm her down.

She tasted the thinly sliced beef. It was cooked to perfection, and the blend of tomatoes and cheese was sublime. She savoured the food, washing it down with a sip of red wine, and for a moment she was lost in a sweet oasis of serenity.

'So what was it that prompted you to come out here just now?' Nick asked. 'I mean, I guess you must have decided to come and see your father, but what made you choose to do it at this particular point in time?'

The peaceful moment was shattered in an instant. 'I... It just seemed to be the optimum moment,' she murmured. 'My contract back in Shropshire was coming to an end...and I'd heard that my father was ill. I wanted to see how he was doing.'

Nick studied her thoughtfully. 'There must have been more to it than that, surely? After all, Jack has suffered from lung problems for a number of years, and yet you haven't been over here to see him before this. Why now? Was it the job at the hospital that encouraged you to make the move?'

Katie frowned. Was that remark a faint dig at her because she hadn't visited her father in the last few years? What business was it of his, and who was he to judge? What did he know of their lives, of the torment she'd been through?

She made an effort to calm down. Perhaps she was being oversensitive...after all, the emotional distance between herself and her father was upsetting. It was a sore point that had festered over the years, and no one could really be expected to understand her inner hurt. And Nick was just like her father, wasn't he, probing into things she would sooner were left alone?

She said cautiously, 'The job was a factor, of course, and I suppose the idea of getting to know more of a different country held a certain appeal.'

Nick frowned. 'You could have taken a long-ish holiday, but instead you chose to come and live and work here. That must have been quite a big decision.'

Katie shrugged. 'Not necessarily.' She took a sip of her wine.

Jack shifted restlessly in his chair, as though he was impatient with the way the conversation was going. 'The truth is, Nick, Katie had a nasty break-up with a fellow back home in the UK. They'd been together for quite some time. Turns out she discovered he wasn't quite what he seemed, and she learned that he had a child by another woman. Katie still hasn't managed to get over it.'

He speared a piece of steak and held his fork aloft. 'So the long and the short of it is, she finished things with him, upped sticks and headed out here. Of course, he tried to stop her. He pleaded with her to stay with him, but she wasn't having any of it. The child was the one obstacle they couldn't overcome.'

He gave Nick a compelling stare, and Nick's eyes widened a fraction. An odd look of comprehension passed between the two men, as though somehow in that brief moment they had cemented some kind of masculine bond of understanding with one another.

Katie drew in a shocked breath. She felt as though she'd had the wind knocked out of her. Why was her father tittle-tattling her private business, especially to a man she'd only just met? Could things possibly get any worse? She was beginning to feel slightly nauseous.

'Well, that would certainly explain things.' Nick rested his fork on his plate. He studied her curiously, a faintly puzzled but sympathetic expression creasing his brow. 'I'm sorry. I imagine it must have come as a great shock to you,' he murmured. 'These things are very upsetting, of course, especially if it came out of the blue. He obviously meant a great deal to you, this man, if his fall from grace caused you to do something as drastic as to leave home and come out here. That must have been really difficult for you.'

He paused, looking at her, taking in the taut line of her jaw, and when Katie didn't respond, he added gently, 'But he was obviously very fond of you, too, and clearly he tried to explain his actions. I find it incredible that any man would do anything to cause you distress…but, in his defence, people do make mistakes, and I suppose all we can do is talk things through and try to understand how the situation came about.'

He hesitated once more, as though waiting for her to say something, but Katie stayed mute. She couldn't speak. Inside, she was a cauldron of seething emotions.

Perhaps her continuing silence had thrown him off balance because he added cautiously, 'It's not necessarily such a bad thing, fathering a child out of the confines of marriage…these things do happen sometimes. It's how people deal with the aftermath that probably matters most—they have to accept responsibility for their actions, and then perhaps we all need to take on board what's happened and move on.'

Katie took a deep breath and finally found her voice. 'So you've studied psychology along with wine production, have you, Mr Bellini?' Her gaze was frosty. 'I do appreciate you trying to help—I'm sure your theory has a good deal of merit, but, you know, I think I handled the situation the very best way I could.'

She stabbed at a slice of green pepper on her plate. 'Since I'd been with my fiancé for some three and a half years and, bearing in mind that his child was just two years old, I wasn't about to deal with his fall from grace lightly. I'm pretty sure we talked it through to the nth degree, and I have a very good idea of how the situation came about. I'm also in no doubt that James accepted full responsibility for his actions. For my part, I acknowledged totally what had happened…and I decided to move on.' Her green glance locked with his. 'That's one of the reasons why I'm here now.'

Nick looked as though he'd been knocked for six. 'It never occurred to me that any man would cheat on you,' he said in a preoccupied tone. 'I'd assumed the child was born before you met.' He held up his hands in a gesture of capitulation. 'Okay… I admit defeat. I was totally out of order. Clearly, it's none of my business and I was wrong to try to intervene.' He frowned. 'And you must call me Nick. I insist.'

Katie gave a crooked semblance of a smile. 'Perhaps it would be for the best if we change the subject?' She glanced at her father. He had started all this, but he seemed altogether indifferent to the havoc he had caused. He simply picked up the wine bottle and began to refill her glass.

'This is an excellent vintage,' he said. 'I'll order another bottle.'

Katie took a sip of wine. 'Tell me more about the vineyards,' she said, shooting a glance towards Nick. 'How much involvement do you have, if you're in partnership with your father and brother? Do you each have separate roles?'

'We do. I deal with the wine-making process rather than the growing side of things, whereas your father is more interested in aspects of cultivation. It's intensely important to get it right, if we're to produce a select variety of wines. You must let me show you the winery—I'm sure you would enjoy a visit. Maybe you could come along for a wine-tasting session?'

'Maybe.' She wasn't about to agree to anything.

'I'll give you a call some time and see if we can arrange a date.' Clearly, he wasn't about to give up, but by now Katie was well and truly on her guard.

From then on, they kept the conversation light. The meal progressed, and Katie tried to damp down her feelings of antagonism towards this man who had cut in on her time with her father. What did her father care about her sensibilities, anyway? Perhaps she was wasting her time trying to find out why he had left all those long years ago.

And as to Nick Bellini, she had made up her mind that she would steer clear of him…no matter how hard he tried to persuade her into another meeting. He had touched a nerve with his comments, leaving her unusually rattled, and, besides, she knew it was a matter of self-preservation to avoid him. He could turn on the charm as easily as igniting a flame. She had been burned once. She wasn't going to risk body and soul all over again.

CHAPTER TWO

'No, Mum, I really don't want to go and live with my father.' Katie frowned at the idea. 'He suggested it but, to be honest, it would be like living with a stranger. After all, we barely know one another... even after three weeks I still haven't really managed to fathom him out.'

She glanced around the medical office that she had begun to call her own and leaned back in her seat, beginning to relax. There were still some ten minutes of her coffee break left, more than enough time to sit and chat with her mother.

'These things take time, I suppose...' her mother said, 'but I think it was a wise decision to go over to California to see him. You would never have been comfortable with yourself if you hadn't gone to seek him out. I suppose we all need to discover our roots, if only to find out if there are some genetic characteristics that have been passed on.' Her tone was pensive. 'I know you're like your father in some ways—you know what you want, and once you've made up your mind, you go after it. That's why you've done so well with your medical training.'

Eve Logan was thoughtful for a moment or two, and Katie could imagine her at the other end of the line, mulling things over. 'It's a shame you couldn't find a place to stay that was nearer to the hospital, though,' Eve added. 'A half-hour drive to work every day doesn't sound too good, though I expect it could have been worse.' She hesitated. 'Anyway, how is your father? From what you said last week, it sounds as though he's more ill than we suspected.'

'He has breathing problems—he's suffering from what they call chronic obstructive pulmonary disease.' Katie had spoken to her father about his difficulties, and though he'd been reluctant to dwell on his problems, he'd at least opened up enough to give her a brief outline. 'He's taking a variety of medicines to keep it under control, but I don't think they're having the desired effect. I suspect his condition's deteriorating. He puts on a show of being able to cope, but I can see that it's a struggle for him sometimes.'

She paused. 'Anyway, you're right, it makes me even more glad that I decided to come out here when I did. No matter what I think about him, he's my father, and I feel as though I have to get to know him. Trouble is, every time we meet, he manages to sidestep my questions one way or another, or we're interrupted somehow.'

It still rankled that Nick Bellini had come along to disrupt her lunch with her father, though in truth she couldn't really blame him for that. He was an innocent bystander in all this, wasn't he, and how could he know what kind of relationship they had?

Still, he'd reached her in more ways than she could have imagined. Her father's business associate wasn't someone she would easily forget.

'That must be annoying,' her mother acknowledged. 'Still, you have plenty of time to build up some kind of relationship with him. You've signed a contract for a year, haven't you, so you don't have to rush things…and if, in the end, it doesn't work out, you can always come home. There'll always be a place here for you.'

'Thanks, Mum. That's good to know.' Katie's mouth made a rueful curve. She made it sound so easy, but the truth was, her mother was making a new life for herself back in Shropshire. She was going to marry Simon, a director of the pharmaceutical company where she worked, and they were very much wrapped up in one another right now. Katie wasn't going to do anything to intrude on that.

'Anyway,' she said, 'in the meantime, the scenery around here is fantastic, and with any luck I'll get to see the vineyard before too long. It's not as big as the Bellini vineyard next to it, but by all accounts it's quite impressive.'

'Bellini—I've heard that name,' her mother commented, an inflection of interest in her voice. 'There was an article about them in the Sunday supplement some time ago…all about the different varieties of wine they produce, as I recall. Apparently their land included your father's vineyard at one time—there was something about an Italian migrant seeing the potential for development at the turn of the last century and buying up as much acreage as he could afford. But as the generations went by there were financial problems and part of the land was sold off around 1980. As far as I know, your father didn't get into the business until some twenty or so years ago.'

'Well, he's made a success of it, by all accounts,' Katie murmured. Her mother's comments about the Sunday supplements had triggered a thought process in her mind, but she still couldn't remember what it was that she'd read about Nick Bellini. Some kind of high-society gossip that kept the Sunday papers occupied for a week or two, but annoyingly the gist of it had slipped her mind.

Her pager began to bleep, and she glanced at the small screen, quickly scanning the text message from her boss. 'I'm sorry, Mum,' she said, 'but I'll have to ring you back later. I have to go out on an emergency call. Someone's had a fall at a hotel nearby, and I need to go and see what the damage is.'

'All right, Katie, love. Take care of yourself. Remember I'm always here for you.'

'I will. Bye, Mum.'

Katie grabbed her medical bag and stopped by the reception desk on her way out. 'Divert any patients to Mike O'Brien, will you, Carla? I'm going out on a call to the Pine Vale Hotel.'

'I'll do that. No problem. You'll find the hotel just off the main road out of here.' The clerk gave her a wave as Katie disappeared through the wide front doors of the building.

Pine Vale Hotel was up in the hills, only a short drive from the hospital, and Katie reached it in good time. As she slid out of her car and took a look around, she was stunned by the magnificence of the building. White painted, it was a long, symmetrical edifice with two front extending wings at either end. It stood three storeys high, and there were large, Georgian-styled windows in abundance, with green painted shutters folded back. On the ground floor several sets of French doors were set back in archways, and Katie guessed the hotel must be flooded with light.

She wasn't wrong. Inside, the foyer reflected a quiet elegance, with traditional, comfy sofas that invited people to sit and take their ease. There were low, marble-topped tables and flower arrangements everywhere, adding glorious splashes of colour to delight the eye.

'Hello.' Katie introduced herself to the woman behind the desk. 'I'm Dr Logan. I understand you have a patient for me.'

'Oh, thank goodness you're here.' The woman, around thirty years old, with fair hair cut into a neat, gently curving bob, looked relieved. 'Yes, please come with me and I'll take you to her. The ambulance is on its way…the emergency services said they were sending a doctor out as well, as there might be a head injury, so I'm really glad to see you. I'm Jenny, by the way…Jenny Goldblum. I'm the hotel manager.'

Katie nodded acknowledgement. 'I was told that the lady fell in her room and appears to be semi-conscious—did anyone see the fall? It always helps to know the circumstances.'

Jenny shook her head. She pressed the button for the lift, and frowned as the door swished open. 'It isn't clear what happened. The maid found her when she went to clean the room. We think perhaps it had only just happened because a lady in the room next door had been speaking to Mrs Wyatt just a minute or so before.'

They stepped out of the lift on to the first floor, and Katie was ushered into a large, airy room, furnished in elegant style. There was a double bed with bedside units and an oak dresser to one side of the room, but at the far end, by the window, furniture had been arranged in a seating area. There was an oval oak coffee table and a couple of brocade-covered straight-backed chairs, along with armchairs uphol-stered in a matching fabric.

The patient, a woman in her fifties, was lying on the floor by the dresser. 'What's her first name?' Katie asked. 'Do you know?'

'It's Laura,' Jenny answered. 'She's staying here with her husband, but he went out earlier for a walk. We haven't been able to contact him yet.'

'Okay, thanks.'

The woman was being tended by one of the hotel staff members, but the girl moved aside as Katie ap-proached. A rug covered the area close by, and it looked as though this had been crumpled when Mrs Wyatt fell.

Katie went to kneel down beside the injured woman. 'Mrs Wyatt…Laura…I'm Dr Logan. Can you hear me? Are you able to answer me?'

Laura Wyatt mumbled something indistinct and Katie tried again. 'Do you feel pain anywhere, Laura?' she asked gently. 'Can you tell me where it hurts?'

Again there was a muffled reply, and Katie came to the conclusion that Mrs Wyatt was too dazed to answer properly. She began a swift initial examination, checking for any obvious injuries and finishing with a neurological check.

'Laura,' she said at last, 'I think you've broken your shoulder—I know that it must be very painful, so I'm going to give you an injection to help with that. Do you understand what I'm saying?'

Laura tried to speak, but whatever she was trying to say didn't come out right, and Katie went ahead and set up an intravenous line. 'We're going to get you to hospital just as soon as possible,' she told the woman. 'In the meantime, I'm going to try to make you more comfortable with a sling that will stop you moving your arm.'

It wasn't clear whether Laura understood or simply couldn't answer, but Katie went on with her examination, checking her patient's blood pressure and listening to her heart.

'What's happened here?' A familiar male voice disturbed Katie's quiet concentration, and she looked up to see with a shock that Nick Bellini had entered the room. 'Katie?' He frowned, studying her for a moment, then turned his attention to her patient. Mrs Wyatt was groaning faintly.

His expression became grim, his eyes an intense, troubled blue.

'Nick?' Katie queried, removing the stethoscope from her ears. What was he doing here? And why had he thought it would be all right to come barging in that way? 'You really shouldn't be in here,' she told him. 'I'm examining a patient.'

'Yes… I see that. I'm sorry for intruding, but you have to understand, I own this hotel… I came as soon as I heard… I'm very concerned that someone has been injured on the premises.' His glance went to the woman once more. 'How is she?'

Katie's eyes widened. He owned this beautiful place? Was there no end to the extent of his empire? She blinked, and then hurriedly dragged her mind back to the business in hand. 'She has a fractured shoulder. I'm sure you must be very worried,' she murmured. 'That's understandable…but this lady has a right to privacy. I think you should leave.'

His head went back, a lock of midnight hair falling across his brow. He seemed stunned by her words, as though it hadn't for an instant occurred to him that anyone would ever try to evict him from where he wanted to be. She waited, bracing herself and expecting an argument, but then he said briefly, 'You'll keep me informed?'

Katie nodded, and without another word he turned and strode out of the room.

She went back to treating her patient. Nick's intrusion had set her emotions in turmoil once more. She had thought she had seen the last of him, and yet here he had turned up when she'd least expected him. His presence had thrown her completely off balance, and now, perhaps because she'd just learned of his association with the hotel, there was a snippet of a newspaper headline running through her head… Something about an heiress…the daughter of a hotel magnate…and Nick Bellini.

She made an effort to push all thoughts of him to one side, and concentrated her attention on her patient, helping the woman to sit up. Then she put the immobiliser sling in place.

'That should keep you fairly pain free until they can take care of you at the hospital,' she said.

The paramedics arrived a few minutes later, and Katie went with them to oversee her patient's transfer to the ambulance. By this time Laura's husband had arrived, and he went along with her, sitting beside his wife and holding her hand.

Katie turned to go back into the hotel, only to find that Nick was right there by her side. She gave a startled jump. He seemed to tower over her, his body firm as a rock. She took a moment to gather herself together and then she gave him a fleeting once-over. He was turned out as faultlessly as ever, dressed in a perfectly tailored dark suit that made him every inch the businessman, a force to be reckoned with.

He looked at her. 'A fractured shoulder, you said. Was she able to tell you what caused her to fall? Was it possible that it could have been the rug in her room—might she have tripped?'

She frowned, walking back with him into the foyer of the hotel. 'Are you worried about liability?' she asked. 'Is that why you rushed over here?'

'First and foremost, I came to see how the lady was doing…but, yes, I have to think about the hotel's liability in this. We take every precaution, but if someone were to be hurt on the premises, it could lead to some very worrying consequences.'

'Well, unfortunately I can't really say what caused the accident. Mrs Wyatt was too dazed to give me any answers, I'm afraid. All I know is that she'll probably need to have shoulder replacement surgery—she fell heavily and it was a nasty injury.'

His mouth flattened as he absorbed that information. Then he said in an even tone, 'Do you have to rush on to another call, or would you have time to stay and have a drink with me?'

She hesitated. Part of her wanted to walk away and avoid getting involved with him any further than need be, but another bit of her recognised his concern. He was anxious for the woman's well-being, and as a hotel proprietor he must be all too conscious of the threat of litigation. Maybe it wouldn't hurt to stay for a while and talk things through with him.

'I don't have to be back at work—my surgery hours are finished for the day, but I'm still on call, so perhaps we should make it coffee rather than anything alcoholic?'

He smiled, his face relaxing for the first time, reminding her all too potently of that sizzling allure that had made her go weak at the knees the first time she'd met him. She had to keep a firm hold on herself. This man could annihilate her sense of security with just one look, and that wouldn't do at all. She'd been down that road, and from her experience it led to heartache…big time. Emotionally, James, her ex, had scarred her for life. She'd been blissfully unaware that he'd been cheating on her, and once his indiscretions had come to light it had torn the heart out of her.

'We'll go out on to the sun terrace,' he said. 'I'll have Jenny send us out a tray of coffee. Just give me a moment to catch up with her.' He lightly cupped Katie's elbow, as though to keep her close, and she stood still for a moment while he beckoned to Jenny. That light touch was like a searing brand on her soft flesh.

The hotel manager was waiting by the desk, talking to the receptionist, but she turned and came over immediately.

'Ask chef to make up a lunch tray, will you, Jenny? Dr Logan will be staying for a while. We'll be out on the terrace by the shrubbery.'

Jenny nodded. 'I'll do that.' She glanced at Katie. 'Is Mrs Wyatt going to be all right?'

'I hope so,' Katie answered. 'The shoulder will give her some problems for quite a while, but those can be dealt with. I'm more concerned about her lack of response. They'll have to do tests at the hospital.'

Jenny nodded and hurried away to find the chef. Nick ushered Katie across the foyer and lounge then out through wide glass doors onto a paved area that was set out with white-painted wrought-iron tables and chairs. The scent of roses filled the air, and Katie was struck by the mass of colour all around, shades of crimson, yellow and pink shrub roses, all vying for attention in the landscaped garden.

'It's really beautiful out here,' Katie murmured as they sat down at one of the tables. 'Everything I've seen so far is overwhelmingly luxurious. I had no idea that you had other interests aside from the vineyard.'

He smiled. 'This place has been in my family's possession for many years—as far back as I can re-member. I took it over when my father decided it was time to cut back on his commitments. I bought him out, rather than see it fall to outsiders.'

She gave him a considering look. 'The family name means a lot to you, doesn't it? You're very conscious of your heritage.'

He nodded. 'That's true. Generations of my family have lived in the valley since the end of the nineteenth century, and my great-great-grandfather worked im-mensely hard to make a go of his enterprise. I feel that we have a duty to secure the results of his labour for generations to come.'

Two waitresses came out on to the terrace just then and placed laden trays down on the table. On one there was a porcelain coffee pot, along with cups and saucers, cream and sugar. The other held an appetising selection of food, as well as plates and cutlery.

Nick began to pour coffee for both of them. 'It isn't just about my own heritage. At the same time I believe we have to give of our best to the local community. That's why what happened this morning concerns me so much. We hold a certain position of trust out here. People look to us to set standards.'

He offered her a plate and napkin. 'Please, help yourself to food.'

'Thank you. It looks delicious.' She gazed at the tempting choices before her. There was *prosciutto*, a dry-cured Italian ham, cut in paper-thin slices, along with sun-dried tomatoes, gnocchi and a crisp salad.

She added a little of each to her plate. 'I wish I could be of more help,' she said quietly, 'but until Mrs Wyatt recovers enough to tell us what happened, we can only wait for the test results to come back from the hospital and hope that they will give us some clue.'

'Was there any head injury?'

'Not that I could see. Of course, that doesn't always mean there's nothing to be concerned about. Any kind of extreme jolting movement within the skull can cause problems that might develop later.'

He tasted a portion of the ham. 'I'll go and see her just as soon as the doctors have had time to treat her shoulder. In the interim I've sent the under-manager along to the hospital to see if we can do anything to make her stay more comfortable.' He frowned. 'It's a dilemma. We generally make sure that the rugs in the rooms are in good condition, not easily rucked. If it was the case that she tripped, I'll have to think about having them removed.'

Katie glanced at him across the table. His concern seemed genuine, and she wondered if there was any comfort she could offer.

'It's always possible that she might have a health problem that caused her to fall—something quite un-related to the hotel. She might have suffered a dizzy spell, for instance.'

'Or a TIA, perhaps.'

Transient ischaemic attack... Katie gave him a considering look, and slid her fork into succulent, sauce-covered potato gnocchi, giving herself time to think. 'That's a definite possibility. Any restriction of the blood supply to the brain could cause a temporary loss of consciousness.'

'Or stroke-like symptoms.'

She nodded. 'It sounds as though you have some experience of the condition. Has someone in your family had problems with TIAs?'

'No, nothing like that.' His gaze meshed with hers. 'As it happens, I'm a doctor, like yourself. I suppose that's why I didn't think twice about rushing in on you when you were examining Mrs Wyatt. I'm so used to tending these medical emergencies that it didn't cross my mind to steer clear.'

She gave a soft gasp. 'I had no idea.' She studied him afresh, a small frown indenting her brow. 'I can't imagine how you find time to practise medicine when you have a vineyard and a hotel to run.'

He laughed. 'I guess it would be difficult if I tried to do all three…but the fact is, I have managers to do the day to day work for me. They let me know if any problems arise that need my attention—like today, for instance. Jenny called me. Otherwise, I make regular checks to make sure that everything's going smoothly, but for the most part I work in the emergency department at the hospital.'

Her eyes widened. 'That must take some dedication. After all, you could have chosen to stay in the valley and reap the benefits of years of grape cultivation. Your wines are internationally famous, according to my mother.'

'That's true. But I've always wanted to be an emergency physician. When I was a teenager, I saw one of my friends injured in a traffic accident. It was horrific…and for a while it was touch and go as to whether he would survive. Thankfully, he had the best surgical team looking after him, and he made it in the end. It left a huge impression on me. So, you see, I'm passionate about my work, and I can't think of anything else I'd rather do. After all, saving lives is a job that's definitely worthwhile. It gives me more satisfaction than I could ever get from gathering in the grape harvest.'

'I can see how you would feel that way but, then, I'm biased.' She gave a faint smile. 'I have to admit, though, there are times when I'm tempted to swap it all for the kind of life I see out here…lazy days in the sunshine, a trip down to the beach to watch the surfers ride the waves…but then I come back to reality. I couldn't give up medicine. It's part of me.'

He nodded, his glance trailing over her. 'I was surprised to see you here. I remember you said you were a paediatrician…but you did a pretty good job of taking care of Mrs Wyatt, as far as I could see. She didn't appear to be in any pain, there was an IV line already in place, and you had her on oxygen. No one could complain at the standard of treatment she received.'

'Let's hope not, anyway.' She guessed he was still thinking about the repercussions of that morning's accident, and how it might affect him as a proprietor. 'I do work as a paediatrician most of the time, but I'm on call two days a week. During my training, I specialised in both paediatrics and emergency, and I wanted to keep up my skills in both those fields. This job was ideal.'

'I can imagine it would be.' He smiled, his gaze slanting over her, and then he waved a hand towards a platter. 'Won't you try our Burrata cheese? I think you'll find it's out of this world.'

'Thanks.' She helped herself to one of the cheeses, a ball wrapped in mozzarella, giving it a springy, soft texture. As she bit into it, she savoured the buttery texture of the centre, a mixture of cream and shredded mozzarella. 'Mmm,' she murmured. 'It's like a little taste of heaven.'

He chuckled, his gaze moving over her, flame glimmering in the depths of his blue eyes. 'Your expression said it all.' His glance slid to the soft fullness of her mouth and lingered there. 'What I wouldn't give to have savoured that with you,' he said on a husky note. 'You have the lips of an angel...soft, ripe and exquisitely sensual.'

She stared at him, her green eyes widening in confusion. His words took her breath away, and a tide of heat rushed through her body. 'I... Uh...' She didn't know what to say to him. She wasn't prepared for his reaction and his comment was unexpected, disarming, leaving her completely at a loss.

Nervously, she swallowed the rest of her coffee then ran the tip of her tongue over her lips, an involuntary action to make herself feel more secure, to help her to know that all was as it should be, and he made a muffled groan.

'Don't...please...' he said, his tone roughened, his gaze darkening to reflect the deep blue of the ocean. 'That just adds to the torment.'

Katie's pulse began to thump erratically, and a torrent of heat rushed to her head. Panic began to set in. Why was he having this strange effect on her? Hadn't she come all the way out here to start afresh? She didn't want any entanglements, and yet Nick seemed to be constantly in her face, a powerful, authoritative man, someone it was hard to ignore. He wasn't like other men she had met, and she was finding she couldn't trust her instincts around him. At the first foray into dangerous territory she was conscious of the ground sliding out from under her feet. She couldn't let him do this to her.

She straightened, leaning back in her chair. 'Perhaps I should leave,' she said distractedly, her thoughts spiralling out of control. He was altogether too masculine, too hot-blooded for a girl like her. With just a word, a touch he had her senses firing on overdrive.

'Surely not?' he murmured. 'Please, stay a while longer.'

She shook her head. Her bewildered mind searched for options, rocketed from one impossible scenario to the next and collapsed in a panicked heap. 'I've probably spent way too much time here already,' she managed. 'It was good of you to offer me lunch. Thank you for that, but I should be on my way now.'

He reached out to her, laying a hand over hers when she would have drawn back from the table. 'Don't let me frighten you away, Katie. It's just that you shook me to the core the first time I met you, and that feeling hasn't gone away. You're really something special and I'd do anything to see you again.'

She gently pulled her hand out from under his. 'I'm sorry… It's not that I have anything against you, Nick, but I'm not in the market for relationships right now. I just… There are too many things going on in my life, too many changes I have to deal with.'

It was all too much for her. The business with James had hurt her deeply, made her guarded and uncertain, and now she was struggling to build a new life, trying to find her niche in a new job. She couldn't deal with any distractions right now, and she sensed that Nick was way more trouble than she could ever handle.

She pulled in a deep breath and stood up, pushing back her chair. 'Thanks again for lunch,' she said, hating herself for the slight tremor in her voice. 'It was delicious…but I really must go.'

He wasn't going to make it easy for her, though, she discovered. He came to stand beside her, his body so close to hers that she could feel the heat coming from him, could register the heavy thud of his heart-beat as he leaned towards her and slid an arm around her waist. Or was that her own heart that she could feel—that pounding, intense rhythm that warned of imminent danger? His hand splayed out over her rib cage, and her whole body fired up in response.

'That's such a shame,' he murmured. 'There is so much more I want to say to you. I could even show you around the hotel if only you would stay a little longer.'

She shook her head, steeling herself to resist the lure of his embrace. She couldn't allow herself to lean into the warmth of his long, hard body, no matter how great the temptation. 'I can't,' she murmured. 'I… I really ought to go back to the office and type up my notes while everything's fresh in my mind.' It sounded such a weak excuse, even to her ears.

'Such mundane tasks, when life could be so much more interesting.' He sighed, reluctantly giving in. 'If you're determined to go, you must at least let me walk you to your car.'

She nodded. 'Okay.' At least he was yielding to

her decision. Escape was within reach at last, and maybe soon the fog of indecision would lift from her mind…though it didn't help at all that he kept his arm around her as they headed back through the hotel.

Only when they reached her car did he let her go and finally she began to breathe a little more easily.

'I imagine you have to write up a report on Mrs Wyatt's accident,' he said on an even note, 'for the inquiry.'

'Yes.' She nodded. 'There'll more than likely be an official investigation. I gather any kind of accident on public premises causes the wheels to be set in motion.'

'Hmm…do you have any idea what will go in your report?'

She sent him a quick glance. 'I can only state the facts. Anything else would be pure conjecture.'

He considered that for a moment, a line indenting his brow. 'Yes, of course.' He pulled open the car door for her and held it while she slid into the driver's seat. 'I'd be interested in hearing the results of the tests.' He paused. 'Anyway, I expect we'll run into one another again before too long.

She nodded. 'I should think so.' He closed the door and she turned the key in the ignition, starting up the engine.

She frowned as an errant thought dropped into her mind. He'd asked about the report and what she might put in it…and for a good deal of the time while they had been eating he had been asking about the precise details of Mrs Wyatt's medical condition.

Was he worried about the outcome of the investigation and how it would affect the hotel?

Her report could sway things one way or the other. Was that the real reason he was making a play for her? Why would a man such as him be interested in her, after all, when no doubt he could take his pick of beautiful women? The thought disturbed her. She had to tread cautiously, and she couldn't take anything or anyone at face value these days, least of all Nick Bellini.

CHAPTER THREE

'I'M SURE I'd have been all right if we'd stayed at home,' Jack Logan said. His breath was wheezy, coming in short bursts, so that Katie frowned. 'There was no need for you to bring me to the hospital,' he added, struggling to gulp in air as he spoke. 'It's your day off. You shouldn't be tending to me.'

'You're ill,' she said firmly. 'And I'm your daughter, so of course I should be looking after you.' He was a proud man, not one to ask for help, and up to now she had been cautious about stepping in where she might not be wanted. Today, though, he had reached a point where medical intervention was imperative. 'You need to see a doctor right away so that we can get your medication sorted out. You can't go on like this. I won't let you.'

He didn't answer and she suspected his strength was failing fast. She wrapped an arm around him, supporting him as she led him to a chair in the waiting room. The emergency department was busy at this time of the day, just after lunchtime, but she hoped they wouldn't have too long to wait. Her father's breathing was becoming worse by the minute, and it was worrying her.

She paused awkwardly, scanning his features. 'You have your tablets with you, don't you...and your inhaler?'

'Yes.' He eased himself down on to the padded seat, dragging in a few difficult breaths and giving himself a minute or two to recover.

'Perhaps you should have a few puffs on the inhaler now. It might help a bit.' She watched as he fumbled in his pocket for the medication. 'Will you be all right for a minute or two while I go and have a word with the clerk on duty?'

He nodded. 'I'll be fine. I don't need to be here.'

She made a wry face and turned to walk over to the reception desk. He was stubborn and independent, but she wasn't going to let him get away with trying to bamboozle her. He was in a bad way, and he needed help...maybe even to be admitted to hospital.

She gave the clerk her father's details. 'He's gasping for breath and I believe he needs urgent treatment. His medication doesn't seem to be working properly.'

The clerk glanced over to where Katie's father was sitting. 'I'll see if we can have him looked at fairly quickly, Dr Logan. If you'd like to take a seat, I'll have a word with the triage nurse.'

'Thanks.' Katie went back to her father and sat down. 'We shouldn't have to wait too long,' she told him. 'Just try to relax.'

In fact, it was only a matter of minutes before they

were called to go into the doctor's room, and Katie was startled to see Nick coming along the corridor to greet them. He looked immaculate, as ever, with dark trousers that moulded his long legs, a crisp linen shirt in a deep shade of blue, and a tie that gave him a businesslike, professional appearance.

She hadn't expected to run into him so soon after their meeting at the hotel. It threw her, coming across him this way, and for a moment or two she wasn't sure how to respond.

'I didn't realise that you worked here,' she said, frowning. 'I'd somehow imagined that you worked at one of the bigger city hospitals.'

He smiled. 'I prefer this one. It has all the up-to-date-facilities, and I've been familiar with it since childhood. It's become like a second home to me.'

He lent her father a supporting shoulder. 'I'm sorry to see that you're having problems, Jack,' he murmured. 'We'll go along to my office where we can be more private.' He turned and called for a nurse. 'Can we get some oxygen here, please?'

'Of course.' The nurse hurried away to find a trolley, while Nick led the way to his office.

Nick waved Katie to a leather-backed chair by the desk, and then turned his attention to Jack.

'Let me help you onto the examination couch,' he said quietly, pumping the bed to an accessible height and assisting Jack into a sitting position, propped up by pillows. 'I see you have your inhaler with you. Is it helping?'

Jack shook his head. 'Not much.' He leaned back

against the pillows and tried to gather his breath. His features were drawn, his lips taking on a bluish tinge.

Nick handed him the oxygen mask and carefully fitted it over his nose and mouth. 'Take a few deep breaths,' he said. 'We'll soon have you feeling better, don't worry.'

Katie watched as Nick examined her father. He was very thorough, listening to his chest, taking his blood pressure and pulse and asking questions about the medication he was taking. All the time he was efficient, yet gentle, and she could see that he was a doctor who would put a patient's mind at ease whatever the circumstances. He set up a monitor so that he could check Jack's heart rate and blood oxygen levels. Katie saw that the results were way out of line with what they should be.

'Excuse me for a moment,' Nick murmured. 'I'm going to ask the nurse to bring a nebuliser in here. We'll add a bronchodilator and a steroid to the mix to reduce the inflammation in your airways, and that should soon make you feel a lot more comfortable.'

He went to the door and spoke to the nurse then returned a minute or two later, coming to stand beside the couch once more. 'Your blood pressure is raised,' he said, 'so I think we need to adjust your tablets to bring that down...and also perhaps we should question what's happening to bring that about.'

'I dare say I can give you an answer on that one,' Katie remarked under her breath. Her tone was cynical, and that must have alerted Nick, because he began to walk towards her, obviously conscious that she wouldn't want her father to hear.

'You know what's causing it?' he asked.

'I think so. You and your father have been pushing him to sell the vineyard, and he's worried about making the right decision. It's tearing him apart, thinking about giving up the one thing that has kept him going all these years.'

Nick raised dark brows. 'You're blaming my father and me?' He, too, spoke in a lowered voice.

'I am. Who else would I blame?' She returned his gaze steadily. 'His health is failing, yet you bombarded him with paperwork and tried to persuade him to hand it over. He was looking at the papers this morning when he was taken ill. The vineyard means everything to him, and you've set him a huge dilemma. I don't believe he's in any state to be dealing with matters such as this.'

'I hardly think you can lay the blame at our feet. Jack has been ill for a number of years, and his lung function is way below par. As to causing him any distress, all I can say is that if he didn't want to consider our offer, he only had to say so.' His eyes darkened. 'He's perfectly capable of making his own decisions.'

Katie stiffened. He hadn't added 'without his daughter's interference', but the implication was there, all the same.

The nurse appeared just then with a trolley, and Nick broke off to go and set up the nebuliser. 'Just try to relax and breathe deeply,' he told her father, his manner soothing. 'It'll take a few minutes, but your blood oxygen levels should gradually start to rise. In the meantime, I'm going to go and glance through your medical notes and see where we can make changes to your medication.' He halted as a thought had occurred to him. 'Katie's obviously concerned about you. Do you mind if I discuss your medical history with her, or is it something you would rather I kept private?'

Jack shook his head. 'That's fine. Go ahead. There's nothing to hide.'

'Okay.' Nick checked the monitor once more, before saying quietly, 'I'll also arrange an urgent appointment for you with your respiratory specialist.'

'Thanks,' Jack said. He looked exhausted and seemed relieved to be able to just lie back and let the drugs do their work.

Nick came back to the desk and glanced towards Katie as he sat down.

'He should start to feel better once his airways expand.' He accessed her father's medical notes on the computer, and then said quietly, 'You seem very concerned over this matter of the vineyard. Have you been out to see it?'

She nodded. 'He took me on a tour a few days ago. I was very impressed, completely bowled over by it, in fact. So much work has gone into making it what it is now. It's something to be proud of.' She looked at him through narrowed eyes. 'I can't see any reason why he would want to let it go.'

His mouth made a crooked shape. 'I'd say it was

possibly becoming too much for him to handle, but it's probably better if we leave off that discussion for a while. It isn't getting either of us anywhere, is it?'

She clamped her lips shut. Nick glanced at her briefly, and then said, 'Your father's heart is taking a lot of strain—the effect of years of lung disease.' He lowered his voice as he studied her. 'I wonder if you realise just how precarious his situation is becoming.'

She nodded, her mouth making a downward turn. 'I'd guessed. I suppose I just needed to have it confirmed.'

He checked the drug schedule for a moment or two on the computer, and then stood up and went back to her father. 'How are you feeling?' he asked.

'Much better.' Jack managed a smile. 'You've taken good care of me, as always. Thank you for that.'

'You're welcome. It's what I'm here for.' Nick glanced down at his chart. 'I want to prescribe some tablets to ease the workload on your heart, and I think we'll arrange for you to have oxygen at home. If you give me a few minutes, I'll go and see if the respiratory specialist is around. It's possible he might be able to come and see you while you're here, and that way we can finalise the details of your medication in one go.'

'Okay.' Jack nodded. 'I'm not going anywhere for a while.'

Katie could see that he was looking much better. 'The colour is coming back into your face,' she said, going over to him as Nick left the room. 'You had me worried there for a while.'

His glance trailed over her. 'You worry too much. Your mother was the same. I used to say to her, life's too short to be fretting about this and that. Seize the day—as they say. Make the most of it where you can.'

Katie's mouth flattened. 'I suppose that was back in the days when you were getting along with one another…before it all went wrong.'

'I… Yes…' He hesitated, shooting her a quick, cautious glance. 'It hasn't been easy for you, has it, Katie? We tried to make a go of things, you know, your mother and I, but there were problems… For one thing, my job took me away from home so much.'

Katie was unconvinced. 'Your job obviously meant more to you than we did, because one day you went away and never came back.' Even now, her heart lurched at the memory. 'Mum was devastated, and I could never understand why you left us that way. You were living thousands of miles from us. I was eight years old, and suddenly I'd lost my father, and my mother was in pieces. You disappeared from our lives. For a long time I thought I'd done something wrong and it was all my fault that you'd gone away.'

He frowned, his grey eyes troubled. 'I'm sorry, Katie. I should have handled things differently; I know that now.' He pulled in a deep breath. 'But your mother and I were going through a bad time, and the atmosphere was incredibly tense between us. There were lots of bitter arguments. Back then I thought it would be for the best if I stayed away. I thought it would be easier, less painful.'

She gave a short, harsh laugh. 'You were wrong. It might have been better for you, maybe, but as far as I was concerned a card here and there at birthdays and Christmas was hardly going to make up for the lack of a father. Did you really think it would? And as for presents that you sent—well, they were great but it just made me realise that you didn't even know me. I appreciated the gifts, but I couldn't help thinking that a visit would have been more to the point. But it never happened. I thought perhaps you didn't care.'

It was as though her words had cut into him like a knife. He caught his breath and seemed to slump a little, his features becoming ashen, and Katie looked on in dismay, a rush of guilt running through her. What was she thinking of, having this discussion with him in here, of all places? She had gone too far…way too far. He might have a lot to answer for, but he was ill, after all, and she was layering him with anxiety that could bring on respiratory collapse. She ought to have known better.

'That was thoughtless of me,' she said in an anxious voice. 'I didn't mean to do anything to aggravate your condition.'

'It's all right.' He paused, sucking in another breath. 'It was something I struggled with all the time—leaving you. I kept meaning to come back to see you, but somehow the longer I left it, the harder it became. I thought…if I came back to see you…'

he started to gasp, fighting against the constriction in his lungs '…you might be all the more upset if I left you once more. You were very young.'

Katie's expression was bleak. 'Let's not talk about it for the moment. You're ill, and we should concentrate on making you more comfortable. Keep the mask over your face. Take deep breaths and try to relax.'

'What's going on here?' Nick came into the room and hurried over to the bed. 'What happened?' He checked the monitor, and Katie could see that her father's heart rate and respiratory rate had increased to dangerous levels.

'It was… We were just talking. It's my fault,' she said in a halting tone. 'I said some things I shouldn't have said.' She had berated Nick for causing her father stress, and then she had done exactly the same thing, hadn't she?

She pressed her lips together. Wasn't this all part of the problem she had battled with since she had come out here? There was so much resentment locked up inside her, but none of it could gain release… not when her father was so ill. It was frustrating, an ongoing dilemma that could have no end. No matter what he had done, she would have to be inhuman to ignore his condition, wouldn't she?

'No, no…you mustn't blame yourself,' her father said, cutting in on her thoughts. 'It's only right that you should say what's on your mind. I let you down.'

Nick gave her a thoughtful glance. Perhaps he was

curious about what was going on between them, but he said nothing. Instead he checked the monitors once more and handed her father a couple of tablets and a drinking cup. 'Take these,' he said. 'They'll bring your blood pressure down and calm your heart rate. Then you need to rest.' He sent Katie a warning glance and her face flushed with heat.

'It isn't Katie's fault,' Jack said, after he had swallowed the tablets. 'The old ticker isn't what it used to be. There isn't much more that you doctors can do for me—you know it, and I know it.'

'I never give up on a patient,' Nick said, his tone firm. 'You'll be fine if you take things easy. Lie back and give the medicine time to take effect.'

They sat with her father for several more minutes, watching as his breathing slowly became easier.

'I feel much better now,' he said, after a while. 'I'll be okay.'

'Maybe, but you can stay where you are for a bit longer,' Nick told him. 'The specialist will be stopping by as soon as he's finished dealing with a patient. He'll sort out your medication and make sure that you're in a good enough condition to go home.'

His pager went off and he turned to Katie. 'I have to go and deal with an emergency that's coming in,' he said. 'Maybe we could meet up some time soon for coffee or dinner? I feel there are things we need to talk about.'

He was probably thinking of her father's illness, and she acknowledged that with a slight inclination of her head. 'Actually, I have the test results on Mrs

Wyatt, back in my office—the lady who fell and injured herself at your hotel. She gave me permission to share them with you, although I haven't had time to look at them properly yet. I suppose we should arrange a time to get together to talk about them.'

He nodded. 'Would it be too much of an imposition for you to come over to my beach house with them, say, later this afternoon? I have to be there because I have some people coming to do some work in the courtyard. Just say if it's a problem for you.'

She thought about it and then shook her head. 'It's not a problem. I'm off duty, and you don't live too far from my place.'

'That's great. I'll see you then.' He glanced towards her father. 'I'm glad you're feeling better, Jack. Take care. I'll see you again before too long, I expect.'

He left the room, and Jack sent Katie a questioning look. 'There was a problem at the hotel?'

She nodded and explained what had happened. 'I think he's worried in case the woman or her relatives decide to take it to court. They might try to say her fall was the fault of the hotel proprietor.'

He frowned. 'I can see how he would be worried. It won't simply be the effect this might have on trade at the hotel—the Bellinis have always taken pride in doing the right thing. Nick's father is ultra-traditional in that respect. Everything has to be done the proper way. He's a very private man, and he deplores any negative publicity.'

'I can imagine. But so far they've managed to keep

things quiet, and anyway there's a lot riding on the results of various tests that were carried out at the lab.'

'And now he wants you to take the results over to the house?' Jack sent her a thoughtful glance. 'Do I detect more than just a professional collaboration going on here?'

Katie's eyes widened at the question, and she gave a faint shrug of her shoulders. 'You heard what he said. It's just easier this way.'

She wasn't going to say any more on that score. Her father hadn't earned the right to intervene in her private life, had he? Besides, how could she possibly answer him when she didn't know for sure herself what had prompted the invitation? The deed had been accomplished before she'd had time to give it much thought.

Jack was frowning. 'I could see that he was interested in you from the outset…but you should be careful how you go, with him, Katie. I know you're still recovering from what went on back in the UK, and I wouldn't want to see you hurt all over again.'

He halted for a second or two to allow his lungs to recover. 'Nick Bellini's a law unto himself where women are concerned. They seem to fall for him readily enough, but he's never yet settled down with any of them. Don't go getting your heart broken over the likes of him. He's a fine doctor—he's kept an eye on me over the last few years, just because he was concerned for me—and he's a great businessman, a wonderful friend and associate, but he's lethal to the fairer sex.'

Katie frowned. He was only telling her what she'd already guessed. That newspaper headline that had been bugging her for the last few days suddenly swam into her head once more, and this time she could see it with perfect clarity. '*Tearful heiress Shannon Draycott leaves hotel under cover of darkness. Bellini tycoon declines to comment.*' There had been more. The article had said something about a broken engagement, and there had been a lot of conjecture, along with several interviews with friends of the young woman. They all painted a picture of a tragic heiress who had been left in the lurch.

'Well, thanks for warning me. I'll be sure to keep it in mind.'

Was Nick a man who was afraid of commitment, flitting from one woman to another? Katie was determined not to get involved with anyone like that ever again. She had been devastated when her relationship with James had ended. She had trusted him and believed they might have had a future together, but it had all gone terribly wrong, and now she would do everything she could to steer clear of any man who might cause her pain.

She studied her father. He was an enigma. He looked gaunt, with prominent cheekbones and dark shadows under his eyes, and something in her made her want to reach out to him and wrap her arms around him. It was confusing.

All those years he had stayed away, removing

himself from her life, and yet now he was acting like a protective father, as though her well-being was suddenly important to him. She couldn't quite work him out. For so long she had tried not to think about him at all. He had walked out on her and her mother and she couldn't forgive him for that…and yet now her emotions were torn.

Little by little, as she came to know him better, he was beginning to tug at her heartstrings. She didn't know how it had happened, but she felt sorry for him and in spite of herself she was worried about him. He looked so thin and wasted, and it occurred to her that he probably wasn't eating as well as he should.

As for Nick Bellini, she'd already learned to be wary of him, and she had to be grateful that her father had let her know what she was up against. Anyway, surely her fears were groundless? Her relationship with Nick was going to be strictly professional, wasn't it?

It didn't surprise her one bit to discover that he had the reputation of a compulsive heartbreaker.

A couple of hours later, Katie dropped her father off at his house and left him in the care of Libby, his housekeeper. 'I'll keep an eye on him, don't you worry,' the woman said, and Katie immediately felt reassured. Libby was kindly and capable looking, and Katie knew she was leaving him in good hands.

Then she set off for Nick's beach house. The scenery was breathtaking as she drove along, with the sun glinting on the blue Pacific Ocean and the rugged length of the coastline stretching out ahead of her.

Living here was like being dropped into a secluded corner of paradise, she reflected as she parked her car in Nick's driveway a few minutes later. She slid out of the car and looked around, gazing out over the bay and watching the surf form lacy white ribbons on the sand. Black oystercatchers moved busily amongst the rocks, seeking out mussels and molluscs with their long orange beaks.

'Katie, I'm glad you could make it,' Nick said, coming out of the house to greet her. 'I was on the upper deck when I saw you arrive.' His arms closed around her in a welcoming hug, and in spite of herself her senses immediately responded in a flurry of excitement. 'How's your father?' he asked.

'Much better.'

'I'm glad.'

His arms were warm and strong, folding her to him, and for a wild moment or two she was tempted to nestle against him and accept the shelter he offered. She could feel the reassuring, steady beat of his heart through the thin cotton of her top.

'It's good to see you,' he murmured, stepping back a little to look at her. 'I hope you didn't mind coming out here to visit me—it's just that I have to be at the house to oversee some work I'm having done out back, as I told you. The workmen are installing a hot tub in the courtyard.'

'That sounds like fun,' she said, easing herself away from him. She ran a hand over her jeans in a

defensive gesture, smoothing the denim. This closeness was doing strange things to her heart rate, and
it wouldn't do to have him see what effect he was
having on her. 'You certainly have the climate for it
out here.'

He smiled, his hand slipping to her waist as he
gently led her towards the house. 'I'm looking forward to trying it out. All those jets of water are supposed to make you feel really good, like a soothing
massage.' He grinned. 'Perhaps you might like to try
it with me some time?'

'I…uh…' She gave a soft intake of breath. 'I'd
have to think about that.' She blinked. The prospect
of sharing a hot tub with him was much more than
she could handle right then. In fact, she'd have to
know him a whole lot better before anything like
that ever happened.

He laughed softly. 'I'll take that as a definite
maybe,' he said. 'Let me show you around the
house.'

'Thank you. I'd like that.' She gazed at the beautiful building as they walked along the path. It was
multi-storeyed, with sloping roofs at varying levels,
the tiles a soft sandstone colour that contrasted
perfectly with the white-painted walls. There were
arched windows and glass doors, and there were
steps leading from a balconied terrace on the upper
floor, providing external access to the ground below.
Behind the whole edifice was a backdrop of green
Monterey pines, and in the far distance she could see

lush, forested mountain slopes. 'This is fantastic,' she murmured. 'It's a spectacular house.'

She turned to look back at the Pacific. 'I really envy you, living out here by the ocean. It must be lovely to look out over the water every day and gaze at the cliffs that form the bay.'

'It's very relaxing. I know I'm fortunate to be able to enjoy it.' He showed her into the house, and they stepped into a wide entrance hall whose pale-coloured walls reflected the light. The oak floor gleamed faintly.

He led the way into a room just off the hall. 'This is the lounge, as you can see. I tend to sit in here to read the paper or watch TV of an evening. It's a very peaceful room, and it looks out over the patio garden. And, of course, with the French doors it's handy for the courtyard…and, from now on, the hot tub, too,' he added with a grin.

She peered out through the open doors at the courtyard that was closed in on three sides by different wings of the building. The remaining side was made up of a decorative screen wall, providing a glimpse into the garden beyond. 'I can see the men are still working on it. It looks as though you have everything you need out there—a place to relax and enjoy the sunshine, a barbecue area, and all those lovely flowers and shrubs to enjoy. It looks like a little piece of heaven.'

She turned to gaze around the room. 'I like the pale-coloured furnishings in here, too. It just adds to the feeling of light.' Her glance took in glass shelves and a low table, before trailing over the sumptuous sofa and chairs. Pastel-coloured cushions added a delicate touch.

'I'm glad you like it,' he said, claiming her hand and leading her through an open doorway. 'Let me show you the kitchen, and I'll make us a drink. What would you like—coffee, tea? You could have iced tea, if you prefer. Or maybe you'd like something stronger?'

'Iced tea sounds fine, thanks.' She stopped to look around. 'Oh, this is lovely,' she said with a soft gasp. 'And it's such a large room, too.' The cupboards and wall units were all finished in the palest green, verging on white, and marble worktops gleamed palely in the sunlight that poured in through the windows. There were shelves filled with bright copper pans, and corner wall units with attractive ceramics on display.

'Well, it serves as a breakfast kitchen,' Nick explained, going over to the fridge. 'There's a separate dining room through the archway, but I tend to eat in here, mostly...or upstairs on the upper deck. I can look out over the ocean from there.'

'That sounds like bliss.'

He nodded, putting ice into two glasses and adding tea from a jug. 'It is. Would you like lemon and mint with this?' he asked, indicating the iced tea.

'Please. That would be good.'

He placed the two glasses on a tray, along with the jug of tea and a plate of mixed hors d'oeuvres. 'We'll take these upstairs and I'll show you the upper deck.

'It's great up there at this time of day, and you can see over the whole of the bay from the terrace.'

She followed him up the stairs, walking through a second sitting room and out through beautifully embellished glass doors onto the balcony terrace.

He was right. The view from the deck was fantastic, and Katie could even see the wildflowers that grew on the craggy slopes in the distance. He pulled out a chair for her by a wrought-iron table, and she sat down and began to relax.

Out here, there were tubs of yellow and orange California poppies, their silky petals moving gently in the faint breeze, and against the far wall, standing tall alongside a trellis, were spiky blue delphiniums. Hanging baskets provided even more colour, with exuberant displays of petunias.

'Help yourself to food,' he said, sliding a plate across the table towards her. 'I wasn't sure whether you would have eaten or not before you came.'

'Thanks.' She glanced at the food on display. There was pâté with crackers, honey-glazed chicken and a spicy tomato dip with tortilla chips. 'It looks delicious.'

He smiled. 'Not my doing, I'm afraid. I have food sent over from the hotel quite often. I don't always have time to cook.'

'I'm not surprised. You must spend the bulk of your time at the hospital, and even if you don't work on a day-to-day basis at the vineyard or the hotel, there must be a fair amount of organisational work to deal with. I expect you're the one who has to make the most important decisions, aren't you?'

He nodded. 'That's true. Things tend to crop up from time to time that need my attention—like this unfortunate episode with Mrs Wyatt.' He frowned. 'I went to see her, and I'm really pleased that she's looking a lot better than she was a few days ago.'

Katie smiled. 'Yes. I couldn't help noticing that you arranged for her to have a private room—the basket of fruit and the flowers you sent were a lovely touch. I know she appreciated them.'

'It was the least I could do.' He spread pâté onto a cracker and bit into it. 'People come to the hotel expecting to have a good time and live for a while in the lap of luxury. They don't want to find themselves being taken out of there by ambulance.'

'But you weren't obliged to pay anything towards her hospital care, were you?'

He shrugged. 'No, that's true. Her insurance company will pay for that…but I wanted to be certain she had the upgrade to make sure that she's comfortable, and, anyway, I count it as good customer relations.'

'Hmm. I can see that you take your role as hotelier seriously.' She dipped a tortilla chip into the fiery salsa sauce. 'You must be anxious to know what caused Mrs Wyatt to fall and break her shoulder. Would you like to hear the results of the tests?'

'Yes, definitely… I'm glad she said it would be all right for you to discuss them with me. Is it what we thought—a TIA?'

She nodded. 'It looks that way. The doctors

monitored her heart and discovered that she has atrial fibrillation—as you know, that kind of abnormal heart rhythm can sometimes cause clots to form in the blood vessels. They did a CT scan, along with blood tests, and found a narrowing of the arteries. The general feeling is that she probably developed a blood clot that temporarily disturbed the flow of blood to the brain. This most likely dissolved of its own accord, but it's possible that more will form as time progresses if she doesn't have treatment.'

'So presumably they have her on anti-thrombotic therapy? And they'll give her medication to counteract the abnormal heart rhythm?'

'That's right.' She took a sip of iced tea. 'It looks as though you're in the clear—or, should I say, the hotel's in the clear?' She smiled at him. 'That must be a huge relief to you.'

'Yes, it is. I can't tell you how badly I needed to hear that. It's great news. Lucky, too, for Mrs Wyatt, because now she gets to have the treatment she needs to put her back on the road to health.' He rested back in his seat, taking a swallow of iced tea and looking the picture of contentment. 'Thanks for telling me that, Katie. I'm really obliged to you for finding out all this information.'

He set down his glass and looked her over, leaning towards her. 'In fact, if I didn't think you'd take it amiss, I could kiss you for it.' He came closer, as though, having hit on the idea, he was ready to carry it through into immediate action, regardless of the consequences.

Katie flattened herself against the back of her chair, deftly foiling his attempt. 'I think you'd better give that one a miss,' she said, her green gaze meshing with his. 'It wouldn't do if every male doctor tried to kiss me whenever I presented them with good results, would it?'

His eyes narrowed. 'Have any tried?'

'Oh, yes. From time to time.'

'And succeeded?' He was frowning now, his blue eyes darkening.

'Maybe. Once or twice.' His expression crystallised into one of seething frustration, and she laughed softly. 'Sorry about that. I couldn't resist. You looked so put out.'

He gazed at her, totally nonplussed. 'You certainly got me going there,' he said, his mouth twisting. 'My fault. I should have known any number of men would want to try their luck with you. That goes for me, too. Somehow, ever since we first met, I've been hung up on getting to know you better...much better.'

She pulled a face. 'Well, I'm not sure that's such a good idea—not in the way you mean, at least.'

He studied her thoughtfully for a moment or two, his expression serious. 'He hurt you badly, didn't he—this man from back home? You must have been very much in love with him.'

'I thought I was,' she said awkwardly. 'I thought I knew him, but perhaps I was blind to his faults. He had a lot of charisma, and I believed he was saving it all for me. It turned out I was wrong.'

And wasn't Nick so very much like James? He had

that scintillating charm that could sweep a woman off her feet, and Katie was no exception. She had to be on her guard. No matter how hard he tried, she wasn't going to succumb to Nick's winning ways. Hadn't her father warned her about him?

'But let's not dwell on any of that,' she murmured. 'I'm here with you now, and we do have two things in common…our work and my father. Maybe it would be safer all round if we simply kept things between us on that level.'

'Hmm…maybe.' He sounded doubtful. His eyes were still dark, and there was a brooding quality to his expression.

Katie decided to plough on with her new diversionary tactic. She helped herself to some food and said quietly, 'Perhaps we should talk about what happened this morning—about your efforts to persuade my father to sell his land, and the effect it's having on him. Maybe we need to clear the air on that score. You know I'd sooner you put an end to any attempt at making a deal. Anyway, I have the feeling he's not at all sure about going ahead with it.'

Nick frowned. 'He hasn't said as much to me… and while there's a chance he'll concede to us, we're bound to keep trying. It would mean a lot to my father to bring the vineyard back into our keeping. My great-great-grandfather bought the land at the turn of the century, but a parcel of it was sold off some years back when the family fell on hard times. It's a matter of pride to my father to restore the vine-

yards into family ownership once more. He sees it as
our inheritance. It's very important to him.'

'That may be so, but I can't say it any clearer—I
think you should hold off on those negotiations.'

Nick's steady gaze met hers. 'Jack doesn't need
you to hold his hand where business is concerned.'

A glint of steel came into Katie's eyes. 'I have to
disagree with you on that one,' she said. 'And this
is definitely not the right time to be pursuing it with
him.'

Nick frowned. 'That's another matter, of course.
We both saw how ill he was today.' He poured more
iced tea into her glass. 'You think your father needs
to be cosseted but he takes it on himself to take care
of business matters, and then it becomes a matter of
pride for him to see things through.'

So, no matter what she said, he wasn't giving up
on his plan to secure her father's land. She drank her
iced tea and studied him over the rim of her glass.
Clearly, his family was not going to be satisfied with
the empire they had built up. They would go after
whatever they wanted. Forewarned was forearmed.

Nick's phone bleeped, and he glanced down at the
screen briefly. 'It looks as though the workmen have
finished installing the hot tub,' he said. 'Shall we go
down and take a look?'

'Yes, of course.'

She followed him down the stairs and out to the
courtyard, where the workmen waited, standing by
their handiwork.

'We're all done here,' the spokesman said. 'I think

you'll find everything's in order. Just turn these controls here to adjust the jets.' He began to point out the various buttons and fittings. 'This is your filter…and here's where you change the heat settings. We've left it set to around midway. Neither too hot nor too cold, but of course it's all a matter of personal preference.'

'That's great,' Nick murmured. 'It looks perfect. Thanks for all your hard work.' He turned to Katie. 'Stay and enjoy the courtyard for a minute or two, will you, while I go and see the men off? There's an ornamental fishpond that you might like to look at, over there in the corner. I'll be back in a few minutes.'

'Okay.' She watched him go, then turned and walked towards the far side of the courtyard, an attractive area, laid out with a trellised arbour and rockery. A gentle waterfall splashed into the pond where koi carp swam amongst the plants and hid beneath white waterlilies.

She gazed down at the green fronds of water plants drifting with the ripple of water from a small fountain and lost herself for a while in a reverie of a past life.

'Sorry to have left you,' Nick said, coming back to her a short time later. 'I think the men did a good job. They sited the tub perfectly and left the place looking neat and tidy. Didn't take them too long either.'

She nodded. 'I expect you'll appreciate your new tub for a good many years to come.' Turning back to the pond, she added, 'This is beautifully set out.

The water's so clear, and the plants are perfect.' Her voice became wistful. 'I remember having one in our garden when I was a child…but it was never as good as this. I suppose you have to keep on top of things—make sure the filter is kept clear, and so on.'

'That's true. I tend to check it every so often. The pond is a hobby of mine. I find it totally relaxing, something you need so that you can wind down after a day in Emergency.' He sent her an oblique glance. 'Did your father set up your pond…or was it something that came with the house, so to speak?'

'It came with the house. My father was interested in it, but he wasn't around for long enough to take care of it, and the work fell to my mother.'

'And she wasn't that keen?'

'She was keen enough when my father was with us, but after he left to go and live here in California she fell apart. She lost interest in everything.'

He frowned. 'I'm sorry. That must have been hard.' He scanned her face thoughtfully. 'I've known Jack for some eighteen years, ever since he pipped us to the post and bought the vineyard from its previous owner. In all that time I had no idea he had a daughter back in the UK.'

'No. It seems he kept it quiet.'

'I suppose you had to take a lot of the burden on your shoulders—how old were you when he left?'

'I was eight. As to any burden, I must say I didn't really understand what was going on at the time. It was all very confusing. When I realised he wasn't coming back, I was hurt, heartbroken, and then as the years went by I became angry and resentful. There was just my mother and me, no cosy family unit with brothers and sisters to share happy times. I missed that.'

A shadow crossed his eyes. 'And that's why you never came over here until now.' He looked at her with new understanding. 'You were waiting for him to come back to you.'

She lowered her head. 'It wasn't going to happen, was it? So eventually I decided that if I was to make peace with myself, I had to come and find him and sort out my demons once and for all.'

He slid an arm around her shoulders. 'I'm sorry that you had to go through all that,' he said quietly. 'It must have been a terrible time for you.' He drew her close and pressed a light kiss on her forehead. 'It seems almost unforgivable that he should treat you that way, and yet I know Jack is a good man at heart.'

Katie didn't answer. She couldn't. She was too conscious of his nearness, and it brought up all kinds of conflicting emotions within her. Everything in her told her that this man was some kind of adversary. He was a threat to her father, and a danger to her peace of mind, and yet when he touched her like this, she was instantly lost in a cotton-wool world of warmth and comfort.

His arms were around her, his body shielding hers from all that might hurt her, and the searing impact of that tender kiss had ricocheted throughout her whole body. She didn't want to move, or speak.

Why couldn't she stay here, locked in his embrace, where the world stood still and she might forget her worries?

'Do you think you can find it in you to forgive him?' Nick murmured. 'He's very ill, and there may not be too much time left.'

'I don't know.' She gave a faint sigh. The spell was broken and she straightened, gazing down into the water of the pond. Fish darted among the green fronds, oblivious to the troubles of the world around them. If only she could find such inner peace.

She took a step backwards. 'I should go,' she said. Nick was the last person she should look to for comfort. He could well turn out to be even more of a heartbreaker than her father.

CHAPTER FOUR

'IS YOUR father really considering selling his vineyard to the Bellini family? That seems very strange
to me.' Eve Logan sounded doubtful at the other end
of the line. 'I haven't had a lot of contact with him
over these last few years, but I did gain the impression that the business meant an awful lot to him. I
wouldn't have thought it was something he would
give it up lightly.'

'No, probably not,' Katie agreed. 'When I spoke
to him the other day he said he hadn't thought it
through yet, or words to that effect. I'm wondering
if the Bellinis are putting undue pressure on him. He
isn't well, and I have the strong feeling that he isn't
up to it.'

'Then perhaps it's as well that you're over there
and able to look out for him.'

'Yes, maybe.'

Katie cut the call to her mother a few minutes later
and gazed around the apartment. She was feeling
oddly restless. Ever since her visit to Nick's home
several days ago, she had been suffering from what

she could only think of as withdrawal symptoms, and it was all Nick's fault.

That kiss had been the lightest, gentlest touch, and it surely had been nothing more than a gesture of comfort and understanding, but the memory of it had stayed with her ever since. Nick had a compelling, magnetic charm that could surely melt the stoniest heart, and she was proving to be no exception.

It wouldn't do at all. She was off men…they could string you along and lead you into thinking that everything was perfect, and then throw it all in your face with the biggest deception of all. No. Every instinct warned her that it would be far better to steer clear of Nick before he could work his magic on her. He spelled trouble and that was something she could definitely do without.

It didn't help that she managed to catch a glimpse of his house every time she headed along the main highway on her way to or from the hospital. Today had been no exception. Nick's home was beautiful, a jewel set in the golden, sand-fringed crown of the California coast.

Annoyingly, against all her better judgement, her thoughts kept straying to him. What was he doing… was he there, sitting outside on the upper deck, watching the seagulls perch on the distant bluffs?

But she wasn't going to waste any more time thinking about him. Enough was enough, and she had work to do. The dishwasher needed emptying and there was a stack of ironing waiting for her…though with any luck she could finish her chores and still have time to wander down to the beach and take in one of the glorious sunsets that were the norm around there.

She set to work, but she was only halfway through her ironing pile when the phone rang.

'There's been a surfing accident just a mile from where you are,' her boss told her. 'Darren Mayfield, a fourteen-year-old, was knocked unconscious and had to be pulled out of the water. The ambulance has been called, but you'll probably reach him before it arrives. A nasty head injury, by all accounts.'

'I'll leave right away,' she told him, unplugging the iron and heading for the door. Her medical bag was in the hall, ready for such emergencies, and the rest of her supplies were in the car.

The boy's level of consciousness was waxing and waning by the time she arrived on the beach. 'Do you know anything about what happened to him?' she asked his mother, who was waiting anxiously by his side.

'He came off his board when one of the big waves hit,' the woman said, her voice shaky. 'The board sort of rose up in the air and then crashed down on him. We had to drag him out of the water. There's a gash on the back of his head and he's bleeding… He hasn't come round properly since we brought him to shore.' Her lips trembled. 'He keeps being sick, and I thought it was just concussion, but it's more than that, isn't it? He should have recovered by now.'

'I'll take a look,' Katie murmured, kneeling down beside the boy. 'How are you doing, Darren?' she asked quietly. 'Can you hear me?' She waited, and when there was no response she added, 'Do you know what happened to you?'

He still didn't answer, and Katie began to make a swift but thorough examination. 'He's unconscious,' she told his mother, after a while. 'I'm going to put a tube down his throat, and give him oxygen, to help with his breathing, and then I need to stabilise his spine to prevent any more damage being done.' She carefully put a cervical collar in place, before checking the boy's heart rate once more. It was worryingly low, and his blood pressure was high, both signs that the pressure within his brain was rising. That didn't bode well.

Suddenly, Darren's whole body began to shake, and Katie reached in her medical bag for a syringe.

'Why's he doing that?' his mother asked in a panicked voice. 'What's happening to him?'

'He's having a seizure,' Katie answered. It was yet another indication that this boy was in trouble. 'I'm going to inject him with medication that will help to stop the fit.'

By the time the paramedics arrived, she had put in place an intravenous line so that fluids and any further drugs could be administered swiftly and easily. 'We need spinal support here,' she told the men, keeping her voice low so as not to worry the boy's mother any further. 'He has a depressed skull fracture, so we need to phone ahead and tell the trauma team what to expect. They'll most likely need to prepare him for Theatre.'

She spoke to the lead paramedic as they wheeled
Darren into the ambulance a few minutes later. 'I'll
ride along with him in case there are any more complications along the way.'

The paramedic nodded. 'You go ahead with Mrs
Mayfield and sit by him. I'll call the emergency department and keep them up to date.'

'Thanks.'

Katie looked at her patient. He was deathly pale
and she was deeply concerned for this boy as she
sat beside him in the ambulance. She had placed a
temporary dressing on the wound at the back of his
head, but it was bleeding still, and she was worried
about the extent of the damage.

The journey to the hospital seemed to take for
ever, though in reality it was probably only about
fifteen minutes, and as soon as they pulled into the
ambulance bay, Katie was ready to move. The paramedics wheeled Darren towards the main doors.

'He had another seizure in the ambulance,' she
told the doctor who came out to greet them, 'so I've
boosted the anti-convulsive therapy. I'm afraid his
blood pressure is high and it looks as though the intracranial pressure is rising.' Again, she spoke quietly
so that the boy's mother wouldn't be unduly alarmed,
but to her relief a nurse stepped forward and gently
took the woman to one side.

'We'll get an x-ray just as soon as we've managed to stabilise his blood pressure,' a familiar voice
said, and Katie was startled to see Nick appear at the
side of the trolley. He was wearing green scrubs that

only seemed to emphasise the muscular strength of his long, lean body. Her heart gave a strange little lurch.

He listened attentively to the paramedic's report and was already checking the patient's vital signs, scanning the readings on the portable heart monitor that Katie had set up. Then he looked at Katie and gave her a quick smile. 'Hi,' he said.

'Oh… I…somehow I hadn't expected to see you here.' Katie's response was muted, but she recovered herself enough to acknowledge him, and also the paramedics, who were ready to leave on another callout. She was troubled about her patient's progress, but Nick's sudden appearance had thrown her way off balance. In the heat of the moment it had completely slipped her mind that he might be on duty.

'I'm on the late shift today,' he told her, as if in answer to her unspoken thoughts, as they moved towards the trauma room. His glance ran quickly over her. 'It's great to see you again.'

'Likewise,' she said, and then tacked on hurriedly, 'I'd like to stay with Darren to see how he goes, if that's all right with you?'

'That'll be fine.' By now they had arrived in the resuscitation room and from then on he concentrated his attention on his patient, examining the boy quickly and telling the nurse who was assisting, 'We'll monitor blood glucose, renal function, electrolytes. I'll take blood for testing now and we need to consult urgently with the neurosurgeon. Given the boy's condition, it's quite likely he'll want to put him on

mannitol to reduce the intracranial pressure. Ask him
to come down to look at him, will you?'

Katie watched him work. He was remarkably efficient, cool, calm, and obviously concerned for this
teenager. He didn't hesitate for an instant, but carried
out the necessary procedures with effortless skill,
delegating other tasks to members of the team. Then,
when the neurosurgeon came to the side of the bed,
he spent several minutes talking to him about the
boy's condition.

'I'll be ready for him in Theatre in about half an
hour,' the surgeon remarked as he prepared to leave
the room. 'Let me have the CT images as soon as
they're available.'

'Of course.' Nick checked Darren's vital signs
once more, and only when he was satisfied that he
had done everything possible for the boy did he turn
back to Katie.

'Okay, we'll take him along to the CT unit. Let's
find out exactly what's going on here.'

As soon as Darren had been placed on the
CT trolley, they went into the annexe to watch the
images on the computer screen as the technician
began the X-ray. 'You're right,' Nick said, after a
few minutes. 'It's a depressed fracture, with the bone
fragments pushing down on the lining of the brain.
There's a large blood clot causing a build-up of pressure. If we don't act soon, there's a risk that the brain
will herniate.'

He spoke to the technician. 'Download the films

to the computer in Theatre, will you? Dr Kelso will want to see them.'

The technician nodded, but Nick was already striding out of the annexe towards his patient. 'We'll have to get him to Theatre just as soon as we've cleaned the wound,' he told Katie. 'By that time Mr Kelso should be ready for him.'

They went back to the trauma room and Nick began the process of irrigating the wound while Katie looked on.

'Okay, that should be clean enough now,' he said after a while. 'We'll start him on antibiotics to prevent any infection,' he told the nurse, 'and keep on with the anticonvulsant therapy. In the meantime, give Mr Kelso a call and find out if he's ready for him up in Theatre, will you?'

The nurse nodded. 'Right away.'

A few minutes later when they had the go-ahead, Nick took his patient to the lift. 'Will you be here when I come back?' he asked Katie. 'I'm going to stay with Darren until the operation's over, but it would be good to talk to you some more.'

She nodded. 'I want to see how he does in surgery. Perhaps I should go and talk to Mrs Mayfield? I know Mr Kelso has spoken to her already, but she might appreciate having someone with her to answer any questions.'

'That would be brilliant, if you don't mind. I'm sure you and she have already managed to build up rapport and it'll be good for her to have someone familiar to be with her.'

The lift doors closed behind him, and Katie walked away, heading for the waiting room where Mrs Mayfield was sitting anxiously, hoping for news of her son.

'Can I get you anything?' Katie asked, going to sit beside her. 'A cup of coffee, perhaps?'

Mrs Mayfield shook her head. 'A nurse brought me one already, thank you.' She looked near to tears. 'I've been trying to contact my husband. He was at a conference, but he's coming straight back here now.' She looked at Katie. 'Darren's in a bad way, isn't he? He was unconscious for so long. What's going to happen to him?'

'Darren was unconscious because the impact of the surfboard pushed the bones of his skull inward, causing them to break and press down on the lining of his brain. This damaged some of the blood vessels, so that a blood clot built up quickly between the skull and the lining.'

Mrs Mayfield nodded to show that she understood. 'And this operation that he's having—Mr Kelso said they needed to bring down the pressure. How will they do that?'

'The surgeon will lift up the bone fragments that are pressing down, and at the same time he'll suck out the blood clot.'

'But will he be able to stop the bleeding? Won't the clot build up again?'

'He'll use special materials to repair the blood vessels so that shouldn't happen. You can be sure that he'll do the very best he can for your son, Mrs

Mayfield.' Katie used a reassuring tone, her heart going out to this woman who was petrified for her boy's safety. She couldn't bear to think how she would feel if she had children of her own. It must be the worst thing in the world to know that they were in danger.

She stayed with her for some twenty minutes, until the door opened and Mr Mayfield walked into the room. He went over to his wife and held her tight, both of them fearful and anxious about their son.

Katie left them alone. A nurse would come by and see how they were doing in a while, and now Katie went along to the emergency room to find out if there was any news.

She knew quite a few of the doctors and nurses who worked there by now, from her work as a paediatrician and first responder. Sometimes she had to liaise with them over the phone, and occasionally, as today, she would ride along with the patient and make the handover in person.

'No news yet,' the nurse said, 'but Nick's on his way down from Theatre. He wants us to make preparations to send the boy over to the intensive care unit.'

Katie nodded. 'Thanks for letting me know, Abby. I'll wait by the nurses' station, if that's all right. I really want to know how he does.'

'Of course it is.' She smiled. 'The one consolation is that having you there from the outset must have given the boy at least a sporting chance. Too often, time drags on before people with head injuries have expert treatment. Nick reckons you did a great job.'

Katie gave a bleak smile. 'Let's hope we've all done enough to make a difference. It's such a devastating experience all round. One minute the boy's out there, enjoying the sunshine and the exhilaration of surfing the waves, and the next, in a freak accident, he's out cold and fighting for his life.' She shook her head. 'I've trained for this, but I don't think I'll ever get used to it.'

'Neither will I,' Abby said.

'You get through it by doing the best you can for your patients,' Nick commented, coming to join them. 'That way you get to sleep easier at night.'

Katie turned to face him, while the nurse left them to go and fetch linen from the supply room. 'Maybe you manage to drop off well enough,' she murmured. 'I can't say that it comes that easily to me.'

'That's a shame.' He draped an arm around her. 'Maybe I could help to remedy that?' he ventured on a husky note. 'Perhaps I could find some way to soothe you to sleep.' He lifted a quizzical brow, looking deep into her eyes.

Katie felt her colour rise. 'In your dreams,' she murmured.

He laughed. 'Well, it was worth a try, I thought.'

'Not really…and I have to say, your timing sucks.' She frowned. 'How is Darren? Did he come through the operation all right?'

His expression sobered. 'Mr Kelso managed to finish the procedure without there being any added complications,' he said. 'The boy's intracranial pressure is at a safer level now, but his blood pressure's still alarmingly high. ICU will monitor him closely, of course. All we can do now is wait and see if he can pull through. He's young and previously in good health, so that's in his favour.' He sent her an encouraging smile. 'The young are quite resilient, as you know. It never ceases to amaze me how they bounce back from even the most traumatic of situations.'

'I'll keep my hopes up for him.' She gazed around the emergency department. 'Everything seems very well co-ordinated around here,' she said. 'The staff all seem to work very well together—I expect that has something to do with the way you run things. You're in charge here, aren't you? Everyone speaks very highly of you.'

'I'm glad of that.' He looked at her from under dark lashes. 'A lot of people, the press especially, seem to think that because I come from a wealthy family I don't need to work and I'm not career orientated, but they couldn't be more wrong. I love my job.'

'I think I've seen that for myself. Though you're right…you do tend to get negative publicity from time to time, don't you?'

He sighed, leaning back against the nurses' station, crossing one long leg over the other at the ankles. 'It seems to be an occupational hazard. If you belong to a family with international holdings, I suppose you're bound to find yourself in the news from time to time.'

She nodded. 'There was a short piece about Mrs Wyatt's accident in the local press, but it was quite favourable. The journalist pointed out that you'd acted swiftly in sending for medical treatment, and that you'd helped make her stay in hospital more comfortable.'

'That's something, at least.' He made a wry smile. 'My father employs a spokesman to deal with the press. It helps to dispel any of the more outlandish stories, and gives the public our take on events.'

'Perhaps your spokesman wasn't around when the Shannon Draycott story broke?' she said softly. 'That must have caused you a few uneasy moments.'

His mouth turned down at the corners. 'I see you've been discovering my lurid past. No wonder you keep fending me off. I expect you're one of these people who believe everything you read in the papers?'

She shrugged lightly. 'Not necessarily. Though I do go along with the principle that there's no smoke without fire.' He hadn't exactly denied the story, had he? According to the papers, they had been engaged to be married—what kind of man was he that could make light of such a thing?

He winced. 'Then I'm obviously doomed.' A glint of amusement came into his eyes. 'Is there anything I can do to restore your confidence in me? I'm really one of the good guys, you know. And when I spoke to Shannon last week she seemed reasonably content with the way her life was going.'

So he was still in touch with her. The thought sounded a death knell in Katie's mind to any hopes that the stories might be a figment of someone's imagination. 'I'm glad to hear it. Perhaps she counts herself lucky to have escaped.'

'Ouch!' He clamped a hand to his chest and pretended to stagger. 'That was a well-aimed blow. I didn't realise Dr Katie Logan had such a cutting edge...though I suppose you've sharpened up your defences this last year or so.'

She nodded. 'You can count on it.' After her experience with James, she was well prepared, and on her guard, for men who had hidden secrets and a good deal of charm.

'Hmm.' He studied her thoughtfully. 'So what am I to do to persuade you that things are not as they seem? Do you think spending more time with me would help you to get to know me better?'

It was her turn to laugh. 'I have to give you eleven out of ten for trying, anyway. You're irrepressible, aren't you?'

'Where you're concerned, yes, I am.' His gaze meshed with hers. 'So how about coming along to a wine tasting at the vineyard? We're celebrating a new Pinot Noir this year, one of our finest...and you did say you'd like to see around the vineyard, didn't you? Your father's maybe, but ours is right alongside?'

'I... Um...' She thought things through. Ever since she had seen her father's land, she had been caught up in the wonder of vine culture, and now she was fascinated by everything to do with wine and wine making. She was intrigued to take a look over the Bellini land and see if it was anything like her father's. Where was the harm? It wouldn't be like going on a date, would it? After all, there would be other people around.

'A little wine tasting can be good for the soul,' Nick murmured in a coaxing tone. 'It helps you to look on life with a much more mellow attitude.'

'I'm sure that's true.' She smiled, and against all her best intentions heard herself say, 'Thanks, I think I'd enjoy that.'

. 'That's great news. I'll come and pick you up. Will you be free after work on Wednesday? I have a half-day then.'

'I will,' she murmured. 'I'll look forward to it.'

Later, though, as she waved goodbye to the paramedic who gave her a lift back to her car where she had left it on the coast road, she couldn't help wondering if she was making a mistake. Why, when every part of her knew that she should avoid getting involved with Nick, did she keep digging herself in deeper?

CHAPTER FIVE

'KATIE, Dr Bellini wants to know if you will consult with him on a young patient in the emergency department.' Carla popped her head round the door of Katie's office and waited for an answer. 'I could ask Mike to cover for you here, if you like.'

'Okay. Tell him I'll be along in five minutes.' Katie put the last suture into the cut on a small child's lip. 'There you are, young man, all finished. You've been very brave.' She smiled at the six-year-old and reached into her desk drawer for a colouring sheet and a teddy-bear badge. 'I think you deserve these, don't you?'

The boy gave a tentative nod and studied the piece of paper she'd handed him. 'A racing car!' he exclaimed in delight. 'I'm going to colour it red, and put stripes on the wings.' He looked up at her. 'Thank you.'

'My pleasure.'

She saw the boy and his mother out into the corridor, and then readied herself to go along to the emergency unit, smoothing down her pencil-line skirt and making sure that her blouse neatly skimmed the curve of her hips.

She paused, trying to make sense of her actions. Why was she doing this? Was she really so bothered about meeting up with Nick that she needed to fuss about the way she looked? Unhappily, the answer had to be a resounding 'Yes'. It gave her confidence to know that she looked okay.

A final check in the mirror showed her that her hair was the usual mass of chaotic curls, but there wasn't much she could do about that. At least it was clean and shining.

'Thanks for coming along, Katie.' Nick met her at the door of his office. His glance flicked over her, and an appreciative gleam came into his eyes. 'I'd like you to take a look at young Matthew Goren, if you will. I've asked his mother if she wouldn't mind you giving a second opinion.'

'That's okay. I'm happy to do it.'

He introduced her to the boy's mother and then to Matthew, a thin-looking eleven-year-old who looked uncomfortable and deeply troubled.

'Matt's complaining of pain in his thigh,' Nick said, as they went over to the trolley bed. 'It came on three days ago, and now he's unable to walk because of it. He has a low-grade fever, mild hypertension and slight anaemia, and he's been suffering from frequent nosebleeds in the last couple of years. Liver function, lungs and white-cell count are normal. I've done an abdominal ultrasound and an MRI of the thigh as well as X-rays, but I'm waiting on the results of other blood tests to see if they eliminate certain other possibilities.'

Nick had obviously been very thorough. This must be an unusual case or he wouldn't have brought her in on it, and she was glad that he respected her enough to ask for her opinion.

Katie gave the boy a smile. 'Hello, Matt. I'm Dr Logan. I'm sorry you're having problems with your thigh. That must be really uncomfortable.'

He nodded. 'I had it once before, when I was ten, but it went away. This is a lot worse.'

'Oh, dear.' She sent him a sympathetic glance. 'We'll have to find out what's wrong and put it right, then, won't we?' She studied his chart for a moment or two and then asked, 'Would it be all right if I examine you, Matt?'

'It's okay.'

Katie was as gentle as she could be, taking her time to assess the boy's condition. When she had finished she asked a few general questions about his symptoms.

'Has the swelling in his abdomen come on recently?' she said, looking at his mother.

Mrs Goren shook her head. 'It started just over two years ago. He says it isn't painful. To be honest, we didn't think anything of it at first—we just thought he was putting on a bit of weight around his tum.'

Katie nodded and glanced at the results of the ultrasound scan on the computer monitor. 'The spleen is definitely enlarged,' she said in a low voice, looking at Nick.

'Take a look at the radiographs and MRI films,' he suggested. 'It looks to me as though there's a patchy sclerosis in the left femoral head…and abnormalities in the bone-marrow density.'

Katie studied the films. 'That could suggest replacement of the marrow fat by an infiltrate,' she said thoughtfully.

'That's the conclusion I came to.' Nick frowned. 'This isn't something I've ever come across before, but if my suspicions are correct it could mean subjecting the boy to more invasive tests, like a bone-marrow biopsy. I'm reluctant to do that.'

'That's understandable.' She looked over the boy's notes once more then said quietly, 'You're right— this is very rare, but given the increased erythrocyte sedimentation rate, the history of nosebleeds and two separate incidents of bone pain a year apart, I'd suggest you do a blood test for glucocerebrosidase enzyme in white blood cells.'

He pulled in a deep breath. 'So you've come to the same conclusion as me—thanks for that, Katie. I was reluctant to order specialised tests on an instinctive diagnosis, but you've picked out the associated patterns of disease and helped me to make my decision. I'll go ahead with the enzyme test.'

He turned once more to his patient and spoke to the boy's mother. 'I think we'll admit Matt to hospital overnight so that we can keep him under observation and try to reduce the inflammation in his thigh. I'll arrange for a nurse to wheel him up to the ward— I'll go and organise that now—and then, once he's settled, I'll order another blood test to check for an enzyme deficiency. The sample will have to be sent off to a specialised centre for testing, but as soon as we have the results, in maybe a week's time, I'll be able to tell you more about what's going on.'

He looked at Matt. 'In the meantime, you have to rest...so that means lots of boring things like playing games on your portable computer and watching videos or TV.' He gave an exaggerated wince, and the boy laughed. 'We'll give you some tablets to take away the pain and bring your fever down,' Nick added. 'Once the leg starts to feel more comfortable, you should be up and about again—I'm hoping that will be fairly soon.'

A few minutes later, Katie said goodbye to the boy and his mother and made her way to the door. Nick excused himself and went with her, leaving the two of them to talk about Matt's hospital stay.

'Would you let me know how he goes on?' she asked, and he nodded.

'Of course.' He smiled. 'I knew I could rely on you to pinpoint the essentials,' he said as they went out into the corridor. 'You may not have been here long, but your reputation for being an excellent doctor is already hailed throughout Paediatrics and Emergency.'

'Is it?' Katie was startled. 'I'm pleased about that, of course, but I'm just doing my job, the same as everyone else.' She sent him a fleeting glance. 'Anyway, you do pretty well yourself. I thought you were brilliant with my father the other day. He hates

fuss and feeling as though he's putting people out, but
you handled him perfectly and you had him feeling
better in very quick time. I was impressed.'

He smiled. 'We aim to please.' Then his expression
sobered and he asked, 'How is Jack? Is he coping all
right with his new medication?'

She nodded. 'On the whole, it's been working well,
but I think he had a bit of a setback earlier today. He
wasn't feeling too good first thing, apparently.'

Katie recalled the phone conversation she'd had
with her father that morning. She'd sensed he'd been
holding something back, but, then, he probably kept
a good deal of his thoughts hidden from her. He
wouldn't want her to know the full extent of his dis-
ability, and that saddened her. He was her father, and
yet there was so much that they kept hidden from one
another. How could she confide her uncertainties,
and how could he share his problems with her, if no
bond had built up between them over the years?

'He didn't sound quite right, and I could hear the
breath rasping in his lungs, but he wouldn't admit to
anything more than being a bit under the weather.'
She frowned. 'I know he's using his oxygen every
night, and sometimes in the daytime, too, and he
seems more frail every time I see him. Of course, he
never tells me any of his problems. He hates being
vulnerable, and it's difficult for me to reach through
to him sometimes.'

'Yes, I wondered about that.' Nick sent her an
oblique glance. 'Are you and he getting on all right?
I know it must be difficult for you. At the hospital

the other day it was fairly obvious you and he still had a lot of issues to resolve.'

She wondered how much of their conversation he had overheard. 'That's true enough.' She frowned. 'To be honest, I don't know how I feel. I've made a real effort to break down the barriers between us lately, and I think it's beginning to pay off. I've definitely grown closer to him over these last few weeks.' Even so, doubt clouded her eyes.

'Learning to forgive must be the hardest thing of all.' Nick's gaze trailed over her features, lingering on the vulnerable curve of her mouth. 'You've had to come to terms with two betrayals, haven't you... your ex's and your father's? That's why you have so much trouble contemplating any new relationship.'

'I suppose so.' She pressed her teeth into the fullness of her lower lip. 'I hope I'm succeeding with both of those. At least with James I'm beginning to see that there were already cracks in our relationship. Maybe I was too ambitious, too set on a career path... whereas James was more easygoing, taking life as it came. I'm wondering if he simply wasn't the type to settle down. He had a child, but he didn't have much contact with him.'

'Much like your father.' Nick's expression was sombre. 'No wonder your ex's weakness hit you so hard. Your father had done exactly the same thing... followed his own path and then abandoned you.'

'Yes.' She was silent for a moment, mulling things over. Could any man be trusted? Could Nick? Not according to her father.

She frowned. 'Where my father's concerned, I still don't really understand what goes on in his head. He treats me as though he's very fond of me and has my welfare at heart...but after all those years of little or no contact it takes a bit of getting used to, to believe that he cares.' And yet only yesterday he had told her how proud he was of her, how much it pleased him that his daughter was a doctor, working to save lives. 'I needed to tell you that before I pass on,' he'd said, and she'd put her arms around him and given him a hug.

'Oh, Dad, please don't say that,' she'd implored him, her throat suddenly choked up. 'Please don't talk about passing on. I'm only just getting to know you.'

He'd smiled. 'What'll be will be.'

Nick's brooding gaze rested on her, as though he sensed something of her troubled thoughts. 'I'm sure he cares very deeply for you...but unhappily something went wrong and he didn't feel able to be there for you. Perhaps distance was a problem—living out here in California meant you were so far apart that visits would be infrequent, and he might have thought it would be less painful for you if he didn't visit at all. You would be able to settle to life without him, rather than be hurt all over again every time he went away.'

'Then again,' she pointed out, 'he could have chosen to stay in England. What was more important...his family or the job?'

He seemed to hesitate. 'That's something you must

ask him yourself. I can't answer that one for you. But knowing him, I'm sure he had his reasons.'

'Did he? I've no idea what they were. All I know is that he condemned us—me and my mother—to a lonely life.' Her expression was bleak. 'Some people may like being an only child, but I wasn't one of them. I always felt there should be something more.'

He was solemn for a moment, his lips parting as though he was about to say something, but apparently he thought better of it. He laid a hand lightly on her shoulder. 'I'm sure it will all come right for you in the end, Katie. You've taken a huge step, coming out here, and you're making great headway. Just give it a little more time.'

He glanced at his watch. 'I'm off duty in a couple of hours. I'll come and pick you up from the apartment and we'll drive over to the vineyard. Perhaps that will cheer you up.'

She nodded. 'Okay. I'll be waiting.' A day or so had passed since he'd made the suggestion, and already she was beginning to regret agreeing to it. What had happened to her plan to avoid him at all costs, to steer clear of getting involved with him in any way? Working with him was proving to be a hazard in itself. It seemed that he was there at every turn…and it was impossible for her to get him out of her head.

She was beginning to realise that there was so much more to him than she had at first imagined. He was caring and perceptive and even though that made her want to get to know him a whole lot better, she was desperately afraid of the consequences. Little by little, though, he was drawing her into his electric force field and she was powerless to resist.

The vineyard, when they arrived there some time later, was bathed in late-afternoon sunlight. Nick helped her out of the passenger seat of his gleaming silver saloon and waited as she stepped out onto the wide, sweeping drive. Katie looked around. She couldn't explain it, even to herself, but just the simple fact that he was there beside her made the breath catch in her throat and in spite of herself filled her with a kind of delicious expectation. He was wearing casual clothes, a deep navy shirt, open at the neck, teamed with dark trousers, and just looking at him made her heart skip a beat.

'Let me show you round the place,' he said. 'From a high point in the gardens you can see for miles around.' He slipped an arm around her waist, his hand coming to rest on the curve of her hip in a gentle act of possession that brought heat surging throughout her body. 'I'm sure you'll love it out here,' he murmured. 'We have a beautiful day for it…the sun's shining and the vines are heavy with grapes.'

She nodded, and tried not to think about that casual touch that was so much like a caress. It only fogged her brain and left her confused and distracted.

He led the way through the house, a pretty French château-style building that had steeply pitched roofs and round towers with turrets. Painted white, it was a gem set in the middle of the Carmel Valley, and Katie fell in love with it on sight.

The gardens were exquisitely landscaped, with trees and shrubs in full bloom so that there was a mass of colour all around. Nestled among the various arbours and flowering trees there was an elevated hardwood deck, and Nick started to head towards it.

'From up here on the deck you can see the vineyard in all its glory. It's a great vantage point,' he said, mounting the wooden stairs and walking over to the balustrade.

Katie followed him and turned to gaze at the distant Carmel Valley Mountains. 'I didn't realise that you had so much land,' she murmured. 'Are all those vines yours, or do those slopes belong to another vineyard...my father's, perhaps?'

Nick followed the direction of her gaze. 'They're ours. Your father's land is a little further to the west. We've terraced the slopes here in order to grow certain types of grapes, and then we have more vines spread along the valley floor. We're incredibly lucky in this area because there's such a long season. The grapes ripen slowly and that helps to intensify the flavour.'

She nodded, trying to take it all in. In the far distance, the verdant slopes of the ever-present Santa Lucia range added to the sense of lush, rich farmland all around. 'It looks heavenly,' she murmured, 'like an Eden where everything is in harmony and the fruit is bursting off the vines.'

He smiled. 'At least, that's how we hope it will be. A good year will produce a premium vintage, but we can't rely on that. If we get too much rain at the wrong time it can cause all kinds of problems, like mould, rot or mildew. Then again, the weather one season can be too hot and another too cool. It all helps to produce a variety of flavours and different qualities of wine.'

'So you can't simply sit back and leave things to nature?'

He laughed. 'I wish! But, no, definitely not...we have to take steps to compensate for adverse conditions.' He laid an arm around her, his hand splaying out over her shoulder and sending a thrill of heat to course through her veins. 'Over the years my family has put a huge amount of effort into building up a reputation for producing quality wines...and it all came about because of my great-great-grandfather's drive and ambition.'

She was thoughtful for a moment. 'He certainly managed to pick out a piece of prime land. He must have been an astute man—and I dare say a wealthy one, too.'

Nick shook his head. 'His family were immigrants, dirt poor, and they had to scrape a living for themselves. They came out here hoping for a better life, but it was a struggle, and I think Joseph, my great-great-grandfather, made up his mind that he would carve a path for himself, come what may. He worked at all kinds of jobs, day and night, determined to earn as much money as possible. He was thrifty, too, and put aside a good part of his earnings until, after about fifteen years or so, he had saved enough money to buy this vineyard.'

'That was a huge accomplishment.'

He nodded. 'It was. But the hardest bit was turning the vineyard around. When he first took it over they were producing inexpensive table wines, but Joseph had other ideas. He had a certain vision and he wanted to make big changes. Quality was everything to him and even though people told him he was making a big mistake, he went ahead with his plans to produce grapes that would provide superior wines. Then he had to convince the buyers that this was a product they wanted, and it all took tremendous hard work and a lot of money.'

He frowned. 'Over the years, when wine consumption declined and harvests were poor, the vineyard suffered losses that could have ruined everything for us. That's why my grandfather had to sell off a third of the land…the piece that Jack owns now. He needed the money to go on running things in keeping with Joseph's ideals.'

'And now you want it back,' Katie said flatly. 'That's why you've been asking my father to sign papers that will turn the ownership over to you once more.' She looked at him directly. 'He should have his solicitor look them over before he does anything, shouldn't he? I think I should get in touch with the law firm that deals with his affairs.' It was a subtle warning, designed to let him know that she wasn't going to stand by and see her father put under pressure. 'Only, like I said before, I don't think he's in any fit state to deal with these kinds of problems just now, do you?'

Her expression was faintly belligerent, her jaw tilted, and Nick's gaze flicked over her, taking it all in. 'I was just telling you the history of the place, that's all,' he said in an even tone. 'I don't want to get into an argument with you.'

She backed down a little. After all, she was on his territory, she was a guest here, and this was perhaps the wrong time and place to thrash out their differences.

'I'm just concerned for my father,' she said.

'I know that, and I respect you for it.' He studied her thoughtfully. 'But if you really care about him, you would probably do well to persuade him that his life would be easier if he were to offload the worries of the business onto us. That way he could relax and enjoy his remaining years.'

She stiffened. 'I think you're mistaken if you believe I'll do your deal for you.' She sent him a flinty stare. 'I haven't had many weeks to get to know him, but it's been long enough for me to begin to care what happens to him. I didn't know what it was to have a father until now, and I've started to realise that it's something precious. I never imagined I would feel this way, about him or his land—so I'm not likely to suggest that he changes anything.'

She threw him a quick glance. 'I expect you're equally protective of your parents—more so, in fact.'

He nodded. 'I'm not criticising you in any way.

It's natural that you should want to protect Jack's interests…but I'm sure he's astute enough to recognise a good deal when he sees one, and ours is far above anything he would get on the open market. Instead of trying to shield him, you could show him that it's the sensible route to follow.'

'I don't think so. I think you and your father need to back off.' She hesitated as a thought struck her. 'I don't believe you've ever mentioned your mother…'

'No.' His eyes were briefly troubled. 'She passed away some years ago…it was a virus, a nasty one that attacked her heart. The doctors did everything they could, but it wasn't enough to save her. I think she was already weak from a chest infection that laid her low.' He looked at Katie. 'I loved her dearly. She was a wonderful woman.'

'I'm sorry.' Katie pressed her lips together in a moment of regret. 'That must have been hard for all of you—your brother and your father.'

He nodded. 'Alex—my brother—was in Canada when he heard she was ill, but he came back as soon as he found out. At least we were all able to be with her at the end, and that makes it a little easier for us to bear.'

He moved away from the deck rail, becoming brisk and ready for action as though he wanted to shake off such sombre thoughts. 'Shall we go over to the winery? I said I'd take you on a tour after all.'

'Yes, I think maybe we should.' She followed him down the steps, saying, 'I was expecting some of your family to be here today—your father, maybe, or your brother.'

He shook his head. 'My father had to go into town, and Alex is in Los Angeles on business. I told him all about you, and I know he wants to meet you.'

Katie wasn't sure how to respond to that. Why would he have spoken to his brother about her? Unless, of course, he'd simply confided in his brother that a new girl had wandered in on his horizon…but perhaps she was misjudging him. It could be that her father was the factor in all this. The Bellinis were strongly allied to him through their business dealings, and it was probably only natural that they would be interested in the fact that he had a daughter—one that he had kept secret for a good many years.

They walked along a path leading from the house towards a collection of buildings some five hundred yards away. Nick pointed out a large stone-built complex where the grapes were processed, and then indicated another outbuilding where the offices and labs were housed. 'I'll show you around there later on,' he said, moving on.

She nodded. 'I know next to nothing about wine-making, I'm afraid.'

'You're not alone in that,' he murmured. He paused by a heavy wooden door set into a stone arch. 'Through here is the entrance to the cellar,' he told her. 'It has walls that are some fifteen inches thick, and it's a cool, well-ventilated environment, essential for producing good wine.'

The wine-tasting room was in a building set a little

apart from these processing areas. The outer walls were painted in a soft sunshine yellow, and there were tubs of flowers and hanging baskets facing out on to the courtyard, giving it a mellow, cottage-style appearance.

'This is so pretty,' Katie said, glancing at the winery and looking back at the chateau in the distance. 'Your father must be really pleased to live in such an idyllic place.'

'I'm sure he is. I know I loved it. I was brought up here, and it was a wonderful childhood.' He looked around. 'It might be a good idea to sample the wines out here. Perhaps a table in the shade would be best.' He indicated a table in a far corner that was bordered by diamond-patterned trellises on two sides.

'Come and make yourself comfortable,' he said, holding out a seat for her, 'while I go and fetch the wines.'

He returned a moment later, bearing a tray. 'We'll try a Burgundy-style Pinot Noir first of all. It's our pride and joy, the best vintage yet. See what you think of it. It's made from black grapes that grow on the cooler slopes.'

Once she was settled, he handed her a glass filled with dark red wine, and she took a sip. It was rich and smooth, with a hint of spice and an aftertaste of black cherry plum. Katie savoured it, letting it roll over her tongue before she swallowed it. 'I can see why you're excited about this,' she said. 'I'm not a wine buff, but I do know what I like, and this is delicious.'

Nick said quietly, 'Joseph Bellini would have been

proud.' He turned to Katie. 'This is what his hard work was all about, and nowadays we do our level best to live up to his vision. As well as this special wine, we produce our own Cabernet Sauvignon. It's stored in barrels made of French oak and allowed to mature over many years. The oak helps to smooth out the harsh tannins and introduces softer, wood tannins.'

Katie nodded and tasted the wine once more. 'Don't you have a problem if my father's vineyard produces similar wines? Doesn't that put you in direct competition with one another?'

He shook his head. 'Your father concentrates on Chardonnay. He had a really good season last year, and the result should be a superb wine.' He picked out another bottle. 'This is one of his Chardonnays,' he said, pouring white wine into a glass and handing it to her. 'Try it. I think you'll like it. It's full of fruit flavours—like pear, apple and melon.'

Katie sipped the wine and tried to forget for the moment that Nick and his family were doing their level best to pull her father's business out from under his feet. How could she be drawn to a man who would do that? He was the enemy and yet she was calmly sipping wine with him and enjoying the comfort of his home. She felt like a traitor.

She would simply have to be on her guard and watch out for Jack's interests whenever possible, she decided. Maybe she would carry out her threat and get in touch with the law firm that dealt with his business affairs. The Garcias were in the phone book, and a straightforward call might do the trick. They could advise her what to do and monitor her father's dealings at the same time.

'Mmm.' She nodded. 'This is lovely.' She raised her glass to him and then looked at the tray of wines. 'I see you have at least a dozen bottles on the trolley,' she said quietly. 'At this rate I shall be tipsy before dinner.'

Nick smiled and answered under his breath, 'I think I'd quite like to see that.' Then he pulled a wry face. 'I do have a secret stash of crackers and cheese hidden away, designed to soak up the alcohol, once we've had a taster. It's a pity that we have to eat them,' he added, his voice low and husky. 'With your senses blurred, I might have been able to persuade you that I'm everything you ever wanted in a man.' His expression was mournful, and Katie stifled a laugh.

'Give it up,' she murmured. 'I wouldn't want your hopes to be dashed.'

They tasted several more wines, including the Merlot, which her father seemed to favour most of all. It was another red wine, rich and fruity with notes of currant and cherry.

Katie was glad of the savoury biscuits and the cheese platter that Nick brought out a short time later. She had missed lunch and she was beginning to feel more than a little heady. Alongside the various cheeses, there were pizza slices and *bruschetta*— slices of toasted bread topped with *prosciutto* and tomato. He had provided a selection of nuts, too, served with slices of dried apricot.

'This has been such a great experience,' she told him. 'I've never been to a wine tasting before, and to be here surrounded by greenery and row on row of vineyard slopes has been wonderful.'

'I'm glad you've enjoyed it,' he said, giving her an appreciative smile. 'Perhaps we should go along and have a look at the processing complex, before the wine goes right to your head. You're looking a trifle flushed, and it might help if you were to stretch your legs for a bit.'

'Okay.'

He helped her to her feet, and they strolled slowly over to the stone-built production plant. Nick explained some of the processes involved—the pressing of the grapes, the addition of yeast and the many checks that were done to test each stage of the fermentation process. In each separate room there were photos and clear text descriptions on the walls to enable visitors to understand what went on there. There were photos, too, of Joseph Bellini, his son Sebastian, Nick's grandfather, Thomas, and finally Robert and his two sons. Katie stared at them in wonder. They all had the same rugged good looks, the strong bone structure, and that dark, Italian machismo.

'I had no idea such a lot of effort went into producing a bottle of wine,' she told Nick a while later as they stood by the window in the scrupulously clean barn where the grapes were poured into a giant hopper. The building's double doors were open to allow a cooling drift of air into the room. 'It must be tremendously satisfying to overcome all the hazards of production and finally taste the result—and discover that it's perfection.'

'It is. Wine-making is in our blood. It has become a part of us, much as the hills and valleys all around have become our home. I wouldn't want to be anywhere else than this small corner of the world.' He gave a crooked smile. 'My brother chose to travel, to go from place to place marketing our wines, but that wouldn't do for me. My roots are here. I love this valley and my beach house. I'm very content.'

'I imagine you are.' She gazed out of the window at the surrounding hills and then looked back at him. 'You must be very proud of your ancestors...all the dedication, strength of mind and sheer stamina that has gone into making the business what it is now. No wonder you're such a fit-looking family—what I've seen of it so far. It must be in the genes.'

He leaned against a guard rail, turning to face her full on, his dark eyes glinting. 'Fit is good, isn't it?' He slightly raised dark brows. 'Does this mean you're beginning to alter your opinion of me?' He reached for her in a leisurely fashion, his hands at the base of her spine, drawing her to him and holding her lightly within the circle of his arms. 'Perhaps there's still hope I could persuade you that I'm the sort of man you could go for?'

She laughed softly. 'There's always hope, I suppose.' She looked at him from under her lashes. 'But I wouldn't get too carried away if I were you.'

'A good thing you're not me, then,' he murmured huskily, 'because I have entirely different ideas on that score. Carried away sounds just about right to me. Carried away is a chink in the armour, and definitely something I'd like to explore a little further.'

He came towards her, his arms tightening around her waist, and as his head lowered she finally began to realise his intention. He was going to kiss her, and even though, way down in the depths of her mind, she knew she really ought to be doing something to stop him, she did nothing at all. And as his lips brushed hers in a touch that was as light as the drift of silk over her skin, she discovered the last thing on earth she wanted was to pull away.

Just the opposite, in fact. Instead, she wanted to lean into him, to revel in his warm embrace, and delight in the strength of those muscular thighs that were pressuring her softly against the cool, steel wall of the hopper. And he must have known what she wanted because he drew her ever closer until her breasts were softly crushed against the wall of his chest and she could feel the heavy thud of his heartbeat marching in time with her own.

He kissed her, tenderly at first and then with rising passion, so that his breathing became ragged and his hands began to smooth over her curves.

Katie was lost in a haze of fevered pleasure. The sun was bright in an azure sky, and for a moment or two time seemed to stand still. There was only

the sensual glide of his lips as they slowly explored
the contours of her face, her throat and the creamy
expanse of her shoulder, laid bare by the thin straps
of the cotton top she wore. And with each lingering
kiss her senses soared in response.

It was all so exhilarating, so perfect, and nothing
like anything she had ever experienced before. What
was it about him that made her feel this way? Did he
have some kind of magical touch? If so, she wanted
more, much more.

Only, as his lips began to slide lower, drifting into
unsafe territory, alarm bells started to ring inside her.
He gently nudged aside the delicate cotton strap and
ventured even further into the danger zone, trailing
soft kisses over the rounded swell of her breasts and
leading her to a heady, disturbing place where feeling and emotion were all, and logical thought was
banished.

Even so, a tiny sliver of common sense began to
filter through the mist that spread, unbidden, through
her brain. Perhaps it was the swish of sprinklers
being started up on the lawns outside that alerted
her, or maybe it was the soft flap of a bird's wings
that dragged her attention back to the reality of what
was happening. What was she thinking? How could
she have let this happen?

She struggled to get herself together. Wasn't Nick
the man who avoided commitment? Wasn't he the one
who was trying to persuade her father to sign away
his land?

And here she was, betraying every instinct she

possessed by falling into his arms at the first opportunity. She was a fool. She ought to have known better.

'Are you all right?' Nick lifted his head, depriving her of that heavenly, forbidden contact, and she tried to answer, but no words came. 'Have I done something wrong?' His voice was a soft murmur against her cheek.

'No… I… Yes…' She tried to ease herself away from him, her hands flattening against his chest as though she would put an end to his kisses. Why, then, did she feel the urge to stroke the velvet-covered wall of his rib cage and let her fingers explore the broad expanse of his shoulders? His muscles were firm and supple, inviting her to touch him and savour the moment.

Truly, she was a basket case—a woman at the mercy of her hormones and not to be trusted with the slightest task. 'I don't think I'm ready for this,' she said huskily. 'I shouldn't have let things get this far.'

'Are you quite sure about that?' His hands caressed her, and his tone was soft and coaxing, inviting her to drift back into the shelter of his arms once more. 'Life could be so much sweeter if only you'd allow yourself to taste it.'

She pulled in a shaky breath, willing herself to resist temptation. 'I'm sure…absolutely sure.' Even as she said it she wondered if she was trying to convince him or herself. She straightened and took a step away from him. 'I don't know how you manage to do this to me,' she said huskily, her gaze troubled. 'I need to feel good about myself, and none of this is helping. I'm very confused. I need time to think.'

'Okay.' He gave a soft, ragged sigh and moved to lay his forehead gently against hers. 'But I can't help thinking that you'd do better to throw caution to the wind. Life isn't easy. It's full of what-ifs and might-have-beens, and if you thought hard about all of them you might never experience the good side of things. I know you've been hurt, but sometimes you have to get back into the fray if you're to have another chance of happiness. Sometimes you simply have to go with your instinct and trust in people.'

Slowly, he released her, and then stood with his hands to either side of him on the guard rail, so that she finally began to breathe a little easier.

He straightened. 'I'll walk you back to the court-yard.' He gave a crooked smile. 'You'll be safe there.'

CHAPTER SIX

KATIE placed the consultant's letter back in her tray and tried to steer her thoughts towards work. 'Good news there, at least,' she told Carla, the desk clerk, indicating the sheet of headed notepaper. 'My young patient who was rushed to hospital from here a few weeks ago is back home and on the mend.'

'The child with kidney problems? I remember his mother was so upset.' Carla gave a relieved smile. 'It's good to know he's pulled through all right. I've been worrying about him...about the poor boy with the head injury, too.'

Katie nodded. 'Me, too. Last I heard, they were thinking about moving him from the intensive care unit. I was hoping I might find time to ring and check up on him some time today, but the time has simply rushed by.' She frowned, straightening up and easing the slight ache in her back. Earlier today she had rung her father to find out how he was doing, but things weren't good, and that was playing on her mind. His nurse, Steve, was worried about his condition.

She dragged her mind back to work. 'Do I have

any more patients to see this afternoon? There's nothing on my list and the waiting room's empty.'

Carla glanced at her screen once more. 'No, but there was a message from Dr Bellini. He said Matthew Goren was coming in to hospital as an outpatient today. He thought you might like to be in on the consultation with him. His appointment's scheduled for four o'clock—that gives you a quarter of an hour to get over there.'

'Right…thanks, Carla. I'd better run.'

She hurried over to the emergency department. She wasn't at all sure how she was going to cope with seeing Nick again—his scorching kisses had seared a memory into her brain that would last for all time. It made her feel hot and bothered even now, just thinking about it. And she had also been mulling over his words of advice… 'Sometimes you have to go with your instinct and trust in people.' Could she do that? Was she ready to put the past behind her and accept that she might be able to find happiness in his arms?

She went along the corridor in search of his room.

'Katie, I'm glad you could make it.' Nick's voice was deep and warm, smooth like honey drizzled over caramelised pears. He gave her a quick smile and invited her into his office. 'I thought you might like to be in on this one. The lab results are back, and this is the last appointment of the day so there will be time to break the news to the boy and his mother without having to rush things.'

'Break the news—it's what we thought, then?'

He nodded. 'Gaucher's disease. Fortunately, even though it's rare, there are treatments for it, so it isn't as bad as it might have been some years ago. And Matt has the mildest form of the disease, so that's another point in his favour.'

He accessed the boy's notes on his computer, and they both took time to sift through the various test results and read the letter from the consultant. When the clerk paged them a few minutes later, they were both ready to receive mother and son with smiles of greeting.

'I know you're anxious to hear the results of the tests,' Nick told them after he had made some general enquiries about the boy's state of health. 'As you know, I was concerned because Matt's spleen appeared to be enlarged and because he's been having pain in his joints. We discovered there was also some slight enlargement of the liver.'

Mrs Goren nodded. 'You took some blood for testing, and he had an MRI scan.'

'That's right.' Nick brought up the film of the scan on his computer monitor and turned to Katie. 'Do you want to explain the results?' he asked.

Katie nodded, and looked at the boy. He was a thin child, slightly underweight, with cropped brown hair that gave him an elfin look. He was looking at her now with large eyes and a faintly worried expression.

'What we discovered,' she said, 'was that you have a fatty substance in your liver and spleen. It shouldn't be there, and so we needed to find out what was going on inside you that would have caused it.'

Matt nodded, but looked puzzled and, picking up on that Katie said quickly, 'I want you to feel free to ask me questions at any time, Matt. If there's anything you don't understand, or anything you'd like to say, just go ahead.'

He frowned. 'Have you found out what caused it? Is it something I've done? The boys at school tease me.'

Katie gave him a sympathetic smile. 'No, it's nothing that you've done, and I'm sorry that you're being teased. Perhaps when you explain to the boys what's wrong, they'll understand a bit better and stop making fun of you.'

She glanced at his mother. 'Matt has a condition called Gaucher's disease. Basically, it means that he was born without an enzyme that breaks down a substance called glucocerebroside.' She turned to Matt. 'Because you don't have this enzyme in your body, the fatty substance isn't broken down and has to find somewhere to go. Unfortunately, when it finds a home in places like your liver, your spleen or even your bones, for example, it stops those parts of you from working properly. That's why you've been having pain in your thigh, and it's the reason for you being tired all the while.'

'You're saying he was born with it?' His mother was frowning. 'Does that mean it's a hereditary disease?'

Mrs Goren's gaze flew in alarm from Katie to

Nick, and Nick answered quietly, 'That's right. You and your husband may not suffer from the disease, but it's possible that either one or both of you may be a carrier. It can go back through generations, although there may not be anyone in the family that you know of directly who has the disease.'

All at once Mrs Goren looked close to tears and Katie hurried on to say, 'The *good* news is that we do have treatment for it.' She smiled at Matt. 'There's something called enzyme replacement therapy, which helps to break down this fatty substance and should soon start to improve things for you.'

Matt's brow cleared, and his mother dabbed at her eyes with a tissue and did her best to pull herself together. She looked at Nick. 'Can we start him on this treatment straight away?'

He responded cautiously. 'I can arrange an appointment for him at the hospital. The answer isn't as simple as taking a tablet, I'm afraid, but what happens is that Matt will be given an infusion—it takes about an hour to administer, and the treatment is given once a fortnight. He'll need to stay with the treatment for life, until such time as science comes up with a better answer. It's a rare disease. Of course, he'll be carefully monitored on a regular basis, so that we can check how he's responding.'

Katie was silent, watching as mother and son tried to absorb what he had just told them. Nick waited, too, before gently asking if they had any questions for him. He was unfailingly patient and kind, and her respect for him grew. In fact, every time she saw him at work, she marvelled at his caring, conscientious manner.

Mrs Goren and Matt both remained quiet for a moment or two longer. Perhaps they had all the information they could handle for the time being. It was a lot to take in, but the consolation was that from now on they would receive masses of help from the clinic at the hospital...along with ongoing input from Nick and herself, of course.

'Will the treatment cause the swelling to go down?' Mrs Goren asked, and Nick nodded.

'You should see a great improvement.' He looked at Matt. 'And the pain will go away.'

After answering a few more questions, and doing what he could to put the mother's mind at ease, he said, 'Let me leave you with some reading material that I've printed out for you. I'm sure there will be things that you think of once you leave here, but I'm hoping that these papers will help answer any immediate queries...and, of course, you can always come and see me again if you want to talk.'

Katie glanced at Nick. That was a thoughtful touch—he had gone that one step further to give his patient everything he could, and she could see that Mrs Goren was pleased.

Nick gave his attention to Matt, and said, 'The nurses and doctors at the clinic will look after you and explain anything you want to know. Next time you come to the hospital for an outpatient appointment, I'm sure you'll be feeling a whole lot better. In the meantime, keep taking the painkillers if you have any more trouble with your thigh, and get plenty of rest. Once you get started on the treatment, I'm certain you'll begin to feel much more energetic.'

Matt nodded. 'Thanks,' he said, and gave a shuddery sigh. 'I thought I had some horrible illness that was going to make me die, but it's not as bad as that, is it?'

'No, it isn't,' Nick told him with a reassuring smile, and Katie's heart went out to this child who had suffered in silence all this time. 'And if you ever have worries of any kind,' Nick added, 'please speak up. Don't keep it to yourself. Often things aren't nearly as bad as you think, and we're here to help you in any way we can.'

After they left, Nick invited Katie to stay awhile and made coffee for both of them. 'I need to write up my notes while they're fresh in my mind—but perhaps we can talk after that?'

'Okay.' She sipped her coffee and leaned back in her chair, thinking about the day's events. From a medical standpoint at work, things had gone well, but she felt uneasy somehow. There was still that niggling worry over her father's health.

She gave a faint sigh, and then stretched. What she needed right now was a complete change of scene, a trip to the beach, perhaps or maybe even a walk through the cobbled streets of the town. But that wasn't likely to happen for a while... Perhaps she ought to go and see her father, see how he was bearing up. There might be something she could do for him.

'Are you okay?' Nick asked.

Caught off guard, Katie quickly tried to collect her thoughts. She hadn't realised he'd been watching her. 'I'm fine, thanks.'

His gaze flicked over her. 'You seem…pensive. If there's something wrong, perhaps I can help?'

She shook her head. 'I was just thinking about my father—I feel that I should go over to his place to see if he's all right. I rang this morning and he was having a bad day, according to the nurse, Steve. It's a bit worrying—apparently he was talking but not making much sense.'

Nick winced. 'That happens sometimes when the blood oxygen levels are low.'

'Yes. Even so, I asked Steve to send for the doctor to see if he would prescribe a different medication. He hasn't called me yet to let me know what happened. I suppose he's been too busy, with one thing and another, or perhaps he didn't want to tie up the phone line if the doctor was likely to call.'

'That's probably the case.' He studied her thoughtfully. 'Would you like me to go with you to see him? It's never easy when someone in the family is ill, is it?'

'No, it isn't.' She might have known Nick would understand. He had been through difficult times with his mother in the past, and it said a lot about his compassion and perception that he was offering to be by her side. 'Thank you,' she said softly. 'I'd really like it if you would be there with me.'

'We'll go as soon as I've finished up here,' he said,

becoming brisk and ready for action. 'Give me five minutes.'

A feeling of relief swept over her. She didn't know why she had involved Nick in any of this, there was no accounting for her actions, and she was working purely on instinct. All at once, though, she felt that with him by her side, she could handle anything.

They went out to his car a short time later, which was in a leafy, private space in the car park. She glanced at him. Even after a day's work, he looked cool and fresh, dressed in dark trousers and crisp linen shirt that perfectly outlined his long, lean figure. His black hair glinted with iridescent lights as they walked in the sunlight, and she gazed at him for a moment or two, wondering what it was about him that stirred her blood and made her want to be with him.

He touched her hand, clasping it within his, and suddenly she felt safe, cherished, as though all was right with the world. 'I'm here for you, Katie,' he said softly. 'Any time you need me.'

Her heart swelled with joy. The truth was, he had never been anything but good towards her. He had treated her with warmth and respect, with care and attention, and he was here now, ready to be by her side at a moment's notice and support her through what promised to be a difficult time. What more could she ask?

She stood in the shade of a cypress tree, watching him as he paused to unlock the car, and it finally hit her that she was bedazzled by him. He made her heart thump and her thoughts go haywire, and there was no knowing why it was happening. Why was she holding back? She might just as well cast her fears to one side and start living again, mightn't she?

Okay, so she had been hurt once before. Her ex had had a child by another woman and had shocked her to the core with his infidelity, but that didn't have to mean all men were of a similar nature, did it? Was she going to let that experience ruin her life for evermore?

Nick came to stand beside her, his lips curving in a faint smile, and he said softly, 'Are you feeling all right? You look different somehow.'

A faint bubble of laughter rose in her throat. 'I'm fine. I'm just so glad that you're here with me. Whatever happens, I feel as though I'll be able to cope with it, just as long as we're together.'

'That's good to know.' His voice faded on a shuddery sigh. 'I've waited a long while for you to learn to trust me, Katie. I won't let you down, I promise.'

He wrapped his arms around her and kissed her gently on the mouth. His touch was light as the drift of silk, but it sent fiery signals to every nerve ending in her body, and she wanted to cling to him, to savour that moment and make it last for ever.

Her fingers lightly stroked his arms and then moved up to tangle with the silky hair at his nape. She belonged in his arms, it felt right, as though it was the only place to be at that moment.

He kissed her again, trailing kisses over her cheek,

her throat, and then with a soft, ragged sound he reluctantly dragged himself away from her.

'Wrong place,' he said in a roughened tone, as though that explained things. 'I can think of better places where I can show you how much I care.'

Katie stared at him, blankly, her lips parting, a tingle of delicious sensation still running through her from head to toe.

He sent her an oblique glance in return, his mouth twisting a little. 'Did I go too far again?' he asked. 'I hope not, because I really wanted to do that. In fact, it's on my mind every time I see you—and even sometimes when we're apart.'

She didn't answer, still lost in that haze of delirious excitement. He'd kissed her...he cared about her... All at once the world was bright and new. Was this love?

Nick pulled in a deep breath, as though to steady himself. He held open the passenger door for her and she slid dazedly into the air-conditioned comfort of his car. Then he went around to the driver's side, coming to sit beside her.

He turned the key in the ignition, starting up the car. 'I need to get my head right,' he said. 'Perhaps we should talk about everyday kind of things for a while—like work, for instance.'

She blinked and closed her mouth, trying her utmost to bring her thoughts back down to a level plane, and he went on cautiously, 'I thought you might like to know—I checked up on Darren Mayfield this afternoon.'

'You did?' She finally found her voice. 'Oh, I'm glad of that. I haven't had time to ring the unit yet today. How's he doing? I know they were thinking of moving him from Intensive Care.'

He nodded. 'That's right. I know you've been keeping tabs on his condition over the last week or so. Anyway, he's on the main ward now and he seems on course to make a full recovery. There's some weakness in his limbs apparently, but the physiotherapist is going to be working with him and he looks set to be back to normal within a few weeks.'

Her face lit up. 'Oh, that's wonderful news…the best.'

He nodded. 'I knew you'd be pleased.' He set the car in motion and turned his attention to the road, leaving her to gaze out at the passing landscape.

'You said you'd been to see your father's vineyard,' Nick remarked as he turned the car on to the valley road. 'Of course, he doesn't live on the property— his manager is the one who stays on the premises. I expect you'll have met him when you went over there.'

Katie nodded. 'Yes, I've been introduced to Toby. He seems a very friendly and approachable man. At least he was willing to answer all my naïve questions. Like I said, I've been fascinated with the whole process of growing vines and turning the fruit into wine ever since I came over here and learned what my father was doing.'

Nick frowned. 'You could always ask me anything you want to know…anytime. I'd be only too glad to tell you. We could even combine it with dinner out or supper at one of the ocean view restaurants around here, if you like. Or a stroll along the beach if that takes your fancy more.'

Her mouth curved. 'I'll definitely think about it. They all sound good to me.'

He relaxed, a look of satisfaction crossing his face. 'Wow! I think I'm actually winning for a change! Wake me up, I think I might be dreaming!'

'I seriously hope not,' she said with a laugh, 'or any minute now you'll be crashing the car into my father's gatepost.'

They had reached her father's property, a stone-built house set in a secluded area some short distance from the coastal stretch where Nick had his home. They approached it along a sweeping drive that cut through well-kept lawns, bordered in part by mature trees and flowering shrubs.

The house was a solid, rectangular building on two storeys, with the ground-floor windows placed symmetrically either side of a wide doorway.

Katie frowned as Nick drew the car to a halt. 'It looks as though my father has a visitor,' she said. 'I don't recognise that four by four, do you?'

'It's the doctor's car. Dr Weissman—I've known him for some years now.'

'Oh, yes.' Katie collected her thoughts. 'I think I've bumped into him once or twice.' Her gaze was troubled. 'I wonder if my father's taken a turn for the worse?'

Nick was already sliding out of the car, and she

hurried to join him on the gravelled forecourt. It was a fresh, warm summer's day, but the sun went behind a cloud just then and a sudden sense of foreboding rippled through her. She walked quickly towards the oak front door and rang the bell.

Libby, the housekeeper, came to answer it, looking unusually flustered. 'Oh, Katie, there you are.' She pulled open the door and ushered them inside. 'I was just about to call you,' she said, pulling at a wayward strand of soft brown hair. 'The doctor and Steve are with your father now. Jack's been having a bad time of it all day. It's his heart, I think. At least, that's what the doctor said.'

'I need to go and see him,' Katie said, a thread of unease edging her words. The feeling of dread that clutched at her midriff since she'd arrived at the house was intensifying by the minute.

'I understand how you must be feeling,' Libby answered, worry lines creasing her brow, 'but the doctor said he would come and let us know as soon as there was any news.'

Katie frowned. 'But I'm his daughter. I want to be with him. I want to know what's going on.'

The housekeeper's face seemed to crumple, and she made a helpless, fluttering gesture with her hands, as though this was all getting too much for her, and Katie said quickly, 'It will be all right, Libby, I promise. We made up our differences a while ago, my father and I…he'll want me to be there with him. I know he will.'

Libby was still fraught with indecision. 'I should

have rung you earlier, I know I should, but I had to ring for an ambulance and try to contact the others and that took up so much time. It's been such an awful day, one way and another. And the ambulance still hasn't arrived.'

Katie frowned. What others? What was Libby talking about? But perhaps she had tried to phone Jack's friends, the people who knew him best…along with the doctor, of course. Katie might be his daughter, but she had only been in town for a couple of months at most.

Nick took hold of her arm, as though to add a helping hand, and she turned to him in gratitude. 'Thanks for bringing me here. It looks as though things are much more serious than I thought. Otherwise why would Dr Weissman have wanted an ambulance?'

'It does sound as though he's concerned,' Nick admitted, 'but let's wait and hear what he has to say.'

'I must go to my father,' she said again. She knew the way to Jack's room from the first time she had been there, when her father had shown her around, and despite Libby's distressed expression she made an instant decision and began to head in that direction.

Nick went with her, but as they came to the first floor and walked along the corridor, the door of her father's room opened and Steve walked out.

He stopped as soon as he saw them and pulled in a deep, calming breath. 'Katie,' he greeted her. 'I don't think you should go in there just yet. Let me talk to you for a while. Shall we find somewhere to sit down?' He glanced at Nick, and an odd look passed between them. Katie didn't understand it. Hadn't that same mysterious kind of glance occurred when she and her father had had dinner together and she'd met Nick for the first time?

She allowed Nick to lead her away, following Steve along the corridor and back down the stairs to the sitting room.

'Please, sit down, Katie.' Steve indicated a comfortable sofa and then turned to Nick. 'You, too, Nick,' he said.

Katie did as he suggested, feeling for the settee with the back of her legs and not once taking her gaze off Steve. Nick sat down beside her, and the nurse took the armchair opposite.

She was more bewildered than ever. Something was going on here and she had no idea what it could be. Right now, though, she wanted more than anything to know what was happening with her father.

'Katie,' Steve began quietly, 'I'm really sorry to be the one to tell you this…but I'm afraid your father passed away a few minutes ago. In the end his heart simply gave out.'

'No…' Katie's mind refused to take it in. 'That can't be… I only spoke to him on the phone this morning. How can this be happening?' For all her training as a doctor, coming face to face with the death of a loved one was turning out to be every bit as difficult for her as it was for her patients. She had no idea it could be so hard to accept.

Nick put his arm around her and held her tight.

'I'm so sorry, Katie. It's a shock—in fact, it's a shock for both of us.'

Steve pressed his lips together in a fleeting moment of sadness. 'Dr Weissman did everything he could to try to resuscitate him, but in the end it was impossible. There was nothing more he could do.'

Katie was bewildered. 'I just can't take it in. I came here thinking he was just having one of those bad days. He always seemed so stoical, so determined to get the best out of life.'

'And I'm sure he did, Katie.' Nick leant his cheek against hers. 'He was over the moon because you had come out here to see him. These last few weeks he was always talking about you, saying how well you'd done for yourself.'

'Was he?' Tears began to trickle slowly down her face. 'It seems such a waste. All these years I've waited, wanting to get to know him but always holding back because I was afraid of what I might find. It took me such a long time to forgive him for walking out on my mother and me. It was such a strange sort of life…as if it was somehow off key. And now he's gone.'

He held her close, letting her weep for what might have been, and all the time he stroked her hair, comforting her just by being there for her when she needed him most.

Libby brought in a tray of tea and quietly set it down on the coffee table. 'The doctor's gone into the kitchen to fill in his forms. He's very sad. They were good friends—your father always spoke highly of him.'

Katie glanced up at Libby. The woman was ashen-faced, struggling to keep her emotions in check.

'Perhaps you should sit down and give yourself some time,' Katie suggested softly, still shaken but subdued. 'You must be as upset as the rest of us. More so, perhaps…my father told me you'd been with him for years.'

Libby put a tissue to her face. 'I have, yes, that's true.' She wrung her hands. 'I ought to go and…' She turned distractedly, as though to go out of the door, and then changed her mind and came to sit down on one of the straight-backed chairs by a polished mahogany desk. 'I don't know what to do,' she said in a broken voice.

'Don't do anything. Just sit for a while and I'll get you some tea.' Katie moved as though to go and pour a cup, but Nick gently pressured her back into the sofa.

'I'll do it,' he said. 'You stay there.'

Steve looked towards the sitting-room door while Nick poured tea and handed it around. 'I should go and have a word with the doctor,' he murmured. 'He'll need someone to see him out…and I'd better call the paramedics and tell them what's happened.'

He walked over to the door and opened it, walking out into the hallway. The sound of voices coming from there alerted Katie and made her sit up and take notice. Had the paramedics arrived already?

'We just want to talk to Libby for a minute or

two,' a male voice said. 'There will be things to arrange.'

Steve said quietly, 'Perhaps it can wait for a while. Libby's in shock, as we all are. Do you want to go and talk to the doctor instead, in the kitchen?'

'Not just yet.' The sound of the man's voice drew nearer, and Katie looked across the room as the door opened. A young man walked in, followed by a slender girl who looked to be slightly older than him, about twenty-three or twenty-four years old. She was pretty, with auburn hair that fell in bright curls about her shoulders, but right now her features were taut, as though she was doing her best to hold herself together.

Katie stood up, dragging her thoughts away from all that had happened and making an effort to behave in the way that Jack would have expected. He would want her to politely greet his guests and make them welcome, even now.

'Hello,' she said, going over to them. 'I don't think we've met before, have we? I'm Katie. For a moment there I thought you were the paramedics.'

The young man shook his head. 'I think the doctor rang and told them there was no urgency.'

'Yes, that would be the sensible thing to do.' Katie studied him briefly. He had black hair and hazel eyes, and she had the impression he was struggling to keep his emotions under control, his face showing signs of stress, with dark shadows under his eyes and a gaunt, hollowed-out appearance to his cheeks.

'I'm Tom Logan,' he said, 'and this is my sister,

Natasha.' He put an arm around the girl's shoulders. 'You've caught us at a bad time. I expect you've heard that our father has just died. Did you know him? Were you a friend of his?'

Katie almost reeled back in shock. She stared at him. *Their father?* Surely there had to be some mistake? She felt as though all the breath had been knocked out of her and for a moment or two she simply stood there and tried to absorb his words.

'I didn't realise...' she began after a while, but broke off. There couldn't be any mistake, could there? *Logan*, he had said. How much clearer could he have made it?

'Are you all right?' Tom was frowning, looking perplexed, and his sister pulled in a shaky breath and tried to show her concern, too.

It wasn't fitting that she should be here, Katie decided suddenly. These were Jack's children, and they had the right to grieve in peace. She had to get out of here. 'Yes, I...' She swallowed hard. 'I have to go... I need to get some air...' This wasn't the time or the place to explain who she was and where she had come from, was it? They'd obviously had no idea that she existed before this.

She swivelled round, desperate to get out of there, away from all these people. All at once she felt as though she was part of a topsy-turvy world where nothing made sense any more. She needed to be alone, to try to take it all in.

'Katie's upset,' she heard Nick saying. 'This has

all been a bit too much for her. Excuse us, please. I think I'd better take her home.'

Katie was already out of the front door, standing on the drive, when she realised that she didn't have her own car there. But perhaps that was just as well. She was probably in no state to drive.

Was it too far away for her to walk home? She could always get a taxi, couldn't she? But for now she just needed to keep moving, to get away from there, to get her head straight.

'Katie, wait, please.' Nick dropped into step beside her.

'Why would I do that?' She shot the words at him through gritted teeth. 'I really don't have anything to say to you.' She kept on walking. Hadn't he known all along?

'But we need to talk this through,' he said. 'You've had a shock—a double shock, given what's happened to Jack.'

'Yes, I've had a shock—and whose fault is that, precisely?' The words came out flint sharp. 'Did you really think you could hide it from me for ever? Why would you want to do that?' She clamped her lips together. 'No, don't answer that. I don't want to hear it. You colluded with him, let me go on thinking I was the daughter he loved and cared about, when all the time he…' She couldn't get the words out. Her anger was rising in a tide of blood that rushed to her head. It made her feel dizzy, and it thumped inside her skull like the stroke of a relentless mallet.

'It wasn't the way you think…believe me…'

'Believe you?' She gave a harsh laugh. 'Why should I believe you?' She looked at him, her green eyes glinting with barely suppressed fury. 'Why should I listen to anything you have to say? I was foolish enough to think that you had some integrity, that you were different to the others…that you could be honest with me. Well, I was wrong.' She was still walking, her footsteps taking her out through the large wrought-iron gates, flanked on either side by stone-built gateposts.

'Katie, this is madness. At least stop and talk to me. Let me explain.'

'There's nothing to explain, is there? I know exactly how it went. You knew all along that my father had another family, a family he didn't want me to know about…or my mother, for that matter. How old is Natasha, do you imagine? Twenty-four? That means she was born while he was still married to my mother. How do you think I feel about that? Can you imagine? And yet I still would have wanted to know that they existed. Don't you think I had a right to know?'

'Of course you did. And he would have told you, given time. It's just that he wanted to pick his moment. You were getting along so well together. He didn't want to spoil that.'

He frowned. 'Katie, you've only just discovered that he's passed on. You're bound to be upset and not thinking clearly about things. You're emotional and overwrought, and you should give yourself time to get used to the idea that he's gone before you start dissecting his behaviour and giving yourself grief over it. You'll have a much more balanced outlook in a day or so's time.'

'Will I? I think I have a pretty firm handle on the situation right now. I might even forgive my father for his deception…after all, I've been there before. He left us back in England and eventually I managed to come to terms with what he had done. I know what kind of man he is…' her voice lowered to a whisper. 'Was.'

She stopped walking and faced him head on. 'It's you I have a problem with. You're the one who kept the pretence going. You banded together to keep me in the dark about it, about my family—my brother and sister, for heaven's sake.'

She shook her head as though to throw out all the debris of broken dreams that had gathered there. 'You knew how lonely I was through all those years after he left us,' she said, her eyes blurred with tears. 'You knew how much it hurt me to be rejected and how desperately I needed to know the reason for that. You should have told me the truth…that he had another family out here, one that he was prepared to stand by, to love and protect. It would have helped me to understand. I wouldn't have kept my hopes up that my relationship with my father could have been something more than it was.'

Her gaze locked with his. 'Instead, you let me flounder and lose my way. You made it so that I stumbled across his children at the worst possible moment. You could have stopped all that, and yet you did nothing.'

'Katie, I had to keep it from you. Jack made me promise. He wanted to tell you himself when the time was right.'

'Well, you should never have made that promise,' she told him flatly. 'Because of it, all my illusions are shattered. I thought I knew you. I thought I could trust you…but I was wrong.' She took in a shuddery breath. 'You should go back to the house, Nick. I need to be alone.'

CHAPTER SEVEN

'IF THERE'S anything at all that I can do to help you through these next few weeks, Dr Logan, please be sure to give me a call…at any time.' The lawyer handed Katie his embossed card. 'I know this must be a particularly difficult time for you.'

'Thank you.' Katie accepted the card and slipped it into her bag. She was still numb from everything that had happened over the last couple of weeks. Her father had died, the will had been read and now she had to try to pick up the pieces and go on with her life.

How was she to do that? Nick had betrayed her. The one man she'd thought she could trust had let her down, with devastating consequences. He'd once told her that she was special and that she'd shaken him to the core, and yet those had been empty words. It seemed those feelings were fragile, and he was easily diverted.

His duplicity left her feeling utterly lost and alone and she couldn't see how she was ever going to recover from this.

Even now, Nick was watching her from across the room. It was bad enough that he was there at all, but there was nothing she could do about that. She could feel his dark gaze homing in on her, piercing like a laser, but she was determined to ignore him. She wanted to avoid him at all costs. He'd known all along about Tom and Natasha, but he had said nothing. How could he have left her to find out about them that way? If he had cared anything for her, wouldn't he have told her?

'It can't have been easy for you, discovering that you had a family out here in California,' the lawyer commented.

'No,' she confessed. She'd had two long weeks to think about that awful day at her father's house, and now she was here with her half-brother and -sister, gathered together under the same roof once more, and it was every bit as unsettling now as it had been then. 'I'm finding it all a bit of a strain, I must admit. I'm still struggling to take it all in. It hadn't occurred to me that my father would leave the vineyard, the house—everything, in fact—to the three of us.' She frowned. 'I'm not sure what I expected, really...after all, I hadn't been part of his life for some twenty years.'

'The terms of the will were very precise.' His brows drew together in a dark line. 'After his second wife died, he stipulated that the property and the land should go to his children, and he named each one of you specifically. It wasn't an afterthought. He had the will drawn up several years ago. Other bequests were added later—like the monetary gifts to his housekeeper and manager.'

'And the collection of rare books that went to Nick Bellini.' That was the reason for him being there, wasn't it, on a day when she'd thought she would be safe?

He nodded. 'Jack knew that he had a special interest in them, and he wanted to thank him for his help over the years. He said Nick had always been there to advise him about matters to do with the vineyard, and lately he had looked out for him when he was ill.'

'It sounds as though you knew my father very well.' Her mouth softened. 'He must have talked to you quite a bit about these things.'

'That's true. I often had occasion to meet with him, so we got to know one another on a friendly as well as a professional basis. I had a lot of respect for your father.'

Katie's mouth made a faint downward curve. It was a pity she couldn't share that opinion. Her world had been turned upside down when she had discovered her father's secret. Now she would remember him as a weak man who hadn't had the courage to admit to his shortcomings. How much grief would he have spared his family if he had done that? Even her mother had echoed those thoughts at his funeral.

For Katie's part, she wanted to weep. What was it about her that made people treat her this way? As a child, for a long time after her father left she had felt that she was unlovable…worthless…and now those feelings of rejection and isolation were intensified.

Was there anyone she could rely on? Her ex had cheated on her, and her own father had left her so that he could be with his other family. And now Nick had hurt her deeply by keeping her in the dark about her brother and sister. If he'd cared about her at all, wouldn't he have confided in her, tried to smooth her path and let her know about something so significant as a family that was being hidden from her?

'How are you bearing up?' Nick came to join them, and the lawyer discreetly excused himself to go and talk to her new siblings. 'If there's anything I can do—'

'You could stay away,' she said, slanting him a brief, cool stare.

'I'm sorry you feel that way.' His gaze flicked over her, taking in the silky sheen of her chestnut hair, the troubled curve of her mouth, and then shifted downwards over the slender lines of her dove-grey suit. The jacket nipped in at the waist, emphasising the flare of her hips, while the slim skirt finished at the knee, showing off an expanse of silk-smooth legs. 'I was hoping by now you'd have had time to think things through…and maybe come to the conclusion that I'd acted with the best of intentions.'

'Then you'll be disappointed. I won't forgive you for holding back from me. You let me down. You betrayed my trust…my faith in you. I'd begun to think you were someone I could believe in, but it turns out you're no different from any of the other men in my life.'

His head went back at that and sparks flared in his eyes, as though she had slapped him. A moment later, though, he recovered himself and said in an even tone, 'I can see I've a lot of fences to mend. I hoped you would understand that I did what I felt was right. I had to keep my promise to your father.'

She gave an indifferent shrug. 'That's as may be. I'm not disputing that. You made your choice and you stuck by it. That's fine. Just don't expect me to agree with you. If you had any thought for my feelings at all, you would have warned me. Instead, you let me blunder on, thinking I actually had a father who loved me but who had simply made a mistake.' Her jaw clenched. 'But, of course, it turns out that *I* was the mistake. That's laughable, isn't it? The offspring who really mattered to him are standing over there, talking to his lawyer.' Her gaze was steel sharp. 'You colluded with him.' She gave an imitation of a smile. 'I must have thrown the cat among the pigeons, turning up here out of the blue.'

His mouth compressed. 'You know I'm not to blame for any of that, Katie. You're putting the sins of your father onto me. Don't you think you're mixing things up in your head just a little?'

'No, I don't. Not at all.' Her mouth tightened. 'You should have told me, and you could at the very least have persuaded my father to tell me, instead of leaving things until it was too late.'

She started to turn away from him. 'I'm going to

talk to Libby for a while,' she said, 'and maybe I'll go and help myself to something from the buffet.' She threw him a warning glance. 'I hope that doesn't mean you'll feel obliged to butt in there as well.'

A muscle flicked in his jaw. 'You're mistaking concern for interference, Katie. I only want what's best for you.'

Katie's mouth twisted. 'Whatever. I don't need your help or your concern. It's way too late for that.' She walked away from him, going over to the buffet table where Libby was standing alone, looking lost. She had to get away from him.

The truth was, she still could not sort out in her mind where everything had gone wrong. He had stolen into her heart and she had glimpsed a snapshot of how wonderful her life might be with him as part of it. She had begun to care for him and those feelings lingered on, in spite of herself. It wrenched her heart to know what a fool she had been to fall for him.

Natasha came to join them a minute or so later. 'I'm just going to grab a quick bite to eat and then I'll go and fetch Sarah down from upstairs.' She bit into a cheese topped cracker, savouring it as though she hadn't eaten for hours.

Katie frowned. 'Who's Sarah?' she asked.

'Oh, of course, you don't know, do you?' Natasha smiled. 'She's my little girl. I laid her down in the cot upstairs before you arrived. Even with the excitement of a house full of people, she was ready for sleep.' She helped herself to a sandwich. 'I thought

I heard her stirring a minute ago. She usually naps for a couple of hours in the afternoon, so I take my opportunities while I can.' She waved the sandwich in explanation.

'I'd no idea,' Katie said. 'You look so young, and I'd assumed you were single, like Tom.'

Natasha smiled. 'She's eighteen months old—I've been married for four years, but Greg and I separated a few months ago, so it's just Sarah and me now.' Her mouth flattened briefly. 'Not that she's any trouble. Lately, she just wants to sit quietly and play with her dolls. None of that racketing about that she used to do when she first started to walk.' She frowned, thinking about it. 'Perhaps I ought to take her to the doctor. She's definitely not as lively as she used to be…but, then, I don't want to be labelled as a fussy mother, and it could be that she's fretting over her father.' She crammed another cracker into her mouth, brushed the crumbs from her hands and hurried away. 'Must go and check on her,' she said.

Katie watched her go, feeling a little sad. There were so many things she didn't know about her new-found family. They had at least twenty-four years of catching up to do.

'We ought to get together over the next day or so,' Tom said, coming to the table to pour himself a cup of coffee from the ceramic pot. 'There's been a lot to take in today, and the land and holdings are all a bit complex, so we really need to iron out what we're going to do.' He looked around. 'There's no use doing it here. I can't think straight in this house…too many memories. I can see Dad in my mind everywhere I go. And if today's anything to go by, there are likely to be interruptions, with visitors stopping by to pay their respects over the next week or so.'

He swallowed his drink. 'Nick has offered us the use of a conference room at his hotel. It's quiet there, and the lawyer, Antony, has said he'll come along and talk us through things in detail. I thought Wednesday would be a good day for it—you have a half-day then, don't you, Katie?'

'Um…yes, that's right.' Katie was looking at Nick, who had somehow managed to appear by Tom's side. The last thing she wanted to do was spend time at Nick's hotel. He must surely be aware of that.

His gaze meshed with hers and in that moment she knew without a doubt that he had set this up. There was a hint of satisfaction in the faint curve of his mouth. She might run, his blue eyes were telling her, but he would always be there, in her wake.

'I ran it by Natasha, and she's okay with that,' Tom said, 'so if it's all right with you, Katie, we could go ahead and make arrangements.'

She could hardly disrupt their plans for her own selfish reasons, could she? Katie flinched inwardly, but heard herself saying, 'Wednesday's fine by me,' and Nick's mouth curved.

'Juice!' A child's voice cut into their conversation, sounding clear and sharply commanding, and Katie looked round to see Natasha crossing the room. 'Juice, Mummy.' A chubby little hand appeared from out of the blanket-wrapped bundle that Natasha was carrying, the fingers curling and uncurling as the child poked her head above the fleece and spied the jugs of orange juice on the table. Pale faced, she had a mass of auburn curls that quivered around her cheeks with her excitement at seeing the buffet table.

'There's a girl who knows exactly what she wants.' Nick laughed, glancing from the infant to Natasha. 'Would you like me to get it for you? You seem to have your hands full.'

'Would you? Thanks.' Natasha handed him the child's drinking cup. 'She's such a fussy madam, this one…and you're right, she's very clear about what she wants. She'll never settle for second best.'

'Seems to me that's a good enough way to go through life.' Nick filled the cup, pressing the lid into place before handing it to the child.

'Tanka,' Sarah said, giving him a beaming smile and sucking on the spout of the cup as though she hadn't seen a drink in twenty-four hours.

'Um…tanka?' Nick echoed, looking at Natasha for an explanation.

'I'm trying to teach her please and thank you,' Natasha answered. 'She hasn't quite got the hang of thank you yet.'

'Oh, I see.' Nick chuckled. He glanced at Sarah once more and commented softly, 'I see you made short work of that, missie. I guess sleeping made you thirsty.'

'More!' Sarah reached out and waved the cup in front of his nose, and as he gently took it from her, she lunged towards him and planted an open-mouthed kiss on his cheek, letting her face linger there as though she was testing him out for touch and taste.

'Well, that was nice,' Nick murmured with a smile, gently disentangling himself from a mound of blanket as Sarah finally retreated. 'It's good to be appreciated.'

Watching the two of them brought a lump to Katie's throat. Nick seemed perfectly at home with the child's gloriously uninhibited behaviour. Seeing him relate to her, she could almost imagine him as a father—he would be a natural from the looks of things.

Her heart flipped over, even as her mind veered away from that startling thought. Over the last few years she had wondered what it would be like to have a family of her own, but she felt totally ill equipped for the role. Perhaps with the right man by her side, it would be different. She glanced at Nick once more, this time with wistfulness in her gaze. Why did all her hopes and dreams come to nothing? First her ex, and then her relationship with her father, and now Nick had let her down. What was wrong with her that these things kept happening? Why couldn't she be happy?

Nick caught her glance, sending her a thoughtful look in return, and she quickly turned away.

'Do you have any nieces or nephews back in England?' Tom was saying, and she came out of her reverie with a start. 'You haven't told us much about yourself up to now.'

'Uh—no, I don't, I'm afraid.' She smiled briefly. 'I'm an only child—or at least I thought I was until now. I wish I'd known about you and Natasha before this. I would have liked to be part of a family—or to feel that I was, anyway. It makes me regret that I didn't have the confidence to come out here earlier. I feel I've missed out on so much.' What must it be like to know the intimacy and joy that came from having young people around, from sharing a household with siblings?

'Perhaps that's why you chose to work with children,' Nick suggested, his glance moving over her, almost as though he had read her thoughts. 'That way you get to have the contact with youngsters that was missing from your life. It isn't the same, I know, but it must help in some way.'

He was perceptive, she had to give him that…far more perceptive than any man she'd known up to now. 'I expect you're right,' she murmured. 'I hadn't thought about it that way.'

'It must be very fulfilling work, being a paediatrician,' Natasha commented. She set Sarah down on the floor so that she could toddle along to a corner of the room where Libby had set out a box of toys. 'We rely on doctors so much when things go wrong. I know when Sarah had a nasty virus a few weeks ago I was really worried, but it helped to talk things through with my doctor.'

She frowned. 'I don't do anything nearly so grand as you—I work in an office, part time, and Libby looks after Sarah for me while I'm away from home.

I don't know what I'd do without her. The job doesn't pay very well, but I didn't want to work full time and lose out on Sarah's young years.' She grimaced. 'I suppose things will be a little easier once we've sorted out the inheritance, though everything's tied up in land and property from the sound of things...and stocks and shares.' She hesitated, thinking through what she had said. 'That sounds awful, doesn't it, thinking about the estate when we've only just lost our father?'

'I know what you mean, though,' Tom said. 'I started up my business a year ago—glass manufacture,' he added, for Katie's benefit, 'but without injecting extra capital I can't see how the company will survive for much longer.'

Katie looked from one to the other. 'Did neither of you want to follow in your father's footsteps?'

Natasha shook her head. 'It was very much his thing, you know. He didn't really involve us in it, and we didn't exactly badger him to let us know the ins and outs of it. We knew when the harvest had been good, or when it had been disastrous, and I suppose that's what put me off. I couldn't give my all to something that relied on the vagaries of the weather or could be destroyed by a disease of some sort. I like to know where I stand.'

Tom nodded agreement. 'I feel much the same way. I suppose we both take after our mother. She was always the practical one, the one who wanted to do something other than work a vineyard...but it was Dad's dream, and so she went along with him.'

Natasha smiled. 'Yes. Do you remember the time when she'd planned a day out and Dad didn't want to leave because he wanted to go out and inspect the crops?'

Their conversation faded into the distance. Katie found it hard to take in this glimpse of family life. It seemed strange to hear them talk about their relationships, the way that they had been at odds with their father. And yet they had loved him, there was no doubting it. That was what her father had denied her for so long. And now Nick was also to blame.

CHAPTER EIGHT

THE hotel's Garden Room was aptly named. Patio doors opened up onto a terrace, enlivened with stone tubs that were filled with bright, trailing begonias in shades of scarlet and yellow. Beyond that was a lawned area, bordered by trees and shrubs, with trellised archways and rustic fences providing support for scrambling clematis in various hues of pink and lilac.

The room was comfortably furnished with soft-cushioned sofas and low, glass-topped occasional tables. It was the perfect setting for a family meeting, but the atmosphere was tense, and Katie was feeling distinctly uncomfortable.

'I can't believe you're doing this.' A faint scowl marred Tom's features as he turned on Katie. 'You're acting on a whim, and your idea of holding onto the vineyard is going to ruin me. My business is failing and selling the vineyard is my way out. It would be different if we could sell our individual assets, but we can't, according to the will. It's all or nothing.'

'And I'm in arrears with my rent,' Natasha put in,

'and there are so many bills to pay I hardly dare open the envelopes when they come through the door. I even tried asking my ex for help, but he's struggling, too.' She hesitated, her gaze clouding momentarily. 'But, then, that's half the reason we split up. He couldn't make a go of his business and the strain was too much for us.'

'I can see why you're both upset,' Katie answered cautiously, 'and it's true I've only just come to know about the vineyard and all it represents...but it has been long enough for me to realize that it's very important to me.' She tilted her chin. 'You're forgetting that Jack was my father, too. I was his firstborn, and that means something to me. It means that I have his genes, and now I have a heritage that I want to safeguard. I'm sorry if that causes problems for you, but it's the way I feel.'

They stared at her in stunned silence, their expressions totally hostile. She didn't want to be at odds with either of them, and a surge of guilt ran through her, but with every fibre of her being she felt she had to stick to her guns.

She had been battling with them for the last hour and at times the argument had been heated and bitter. It left her feeling shaky inside, and it hurt that they had turned on her in such a savage way. It was easy enough to understand how they felt, but this was a once-in-a-lifetime opportunity and everything in her told her that she didn't want to let it go.

Was it selfish of her to want to carry on what her father had started? He might not have been the greatest father in the world. He'd let her down, but the vineyard was his handiwork, something to be proud of, the one solid achievement that she could preserve for posterity.

Her pager began to bleep. She checked the text message and said flatly, 'I have to go. There's been a road traffic accident.' She glanced at her half-brother and -sister. 'I'm sorry…perhaps Antony can help you to come to some arrangement over finances that will help you both out…but I've made my decision. Believe me, it wasn't an easy one…but I've been thinking about it for these last few weeks and I've made up my mind. I'm not prepared to sell.'

She left the room and hurried along to the hotel foyer, but she was taken aback to see Nick standing by the reception desk. He was talking to the manageress, looking through a brochure with her, but as Katie approached he turned away from the desk and let his glance drift over her.

Katie felt her stomach clench. She had been right to push him away, hadn't she? For all his careful attention and sweet-talking ways, he had shown that he was just like everyone else.

And what would he make of her dispute with her brother and sister? Most likely he would side with them and encourage them to pressurise her into selling. It would be in his interests to do that, wouldn't it?

'You're leaving already?' Nick said with a frown. 'I'd expected the meeting to go on for much longer.'

'I have to go out on an emergency.' Her voice was terse. 'There's been an accident on the main highway, with several cars involved, and they're calling for medics to attend.'

Nick's brows drew together, and as he handed the brochure to the manageress his phone began to bleep, signalling a text message. He quickly scanned it and then said, 'Me, too. It must be a bad one.' He turned to the woman once more. 'I have to go,' he murmured. 'Change the layout as we discussed and I'll look over the copy as soon as soon as you have it.'

She nodded. 'That's fine. You go ahead. I'll deal with this.'

'We should go,' Nick said, taking Katie by the arm. 'I can give you a lift—there's no sense in taking two cars, is there?'

'I suppose not.' Katie shrugged. 'I'll get my medical kit from the boot of my car.'

They set off just a few minutes later, driving along the main road from the hotel towards the coastal highway. Katie watched the rolling hills pass by, took in the magnificent cypress trees forming silhouettes against the skyline, and tried not to think about the fact that she was in Nick's car, that her heart was encased in ice, or that her siblings hated her.

'You're very quiet,' Nick said, turning the car on to the highway. 'How were things back there?'

'Not too good. Natasha was a bit edgy—she's worried about her little girl. She said she's tired all the while, but the doctor thinks the child's just a bit run down and it will pass.'

She frowned. From her experience she knew that doctors ought never to ignore a mother's instinct. But the toddler's symptoms were vague, and you could hardly expect the physician to be too worried at this stage. 'Tom seems to think the little girl is a fussy eater, and that might have led to her problems.'

'He could be right,' Nick murmured. 'At least the doctor's given her a check-up.'

'I suppose so.'

'So, how did the meeting go? You seem quite subdued. Was it not as you expected? It's a shame that you didn't get to finish it.'

'Perhaps it's just as well we were interrupted,' she answered with a faint sigh. 'Things weren't going too well. Tom and Natasha are very upset with me, and I'm sad about that because I want to get on well with them.'

He sent her a sideways glance. 'Why would they be upset with you? You only had to talk over what you were going to do about the estate, didn't you? I would have thought that was a positive thing, albeit tinged with a good deal of sadness. It's not every day you get to decide how to manage an inheritance like that.'

'Well, there's the rub.' She made a face. 'We couldn't agree on how to deal with it.'

He frowned. 'You'll have to explain. I've no idea what could have gone wrong. I know they were very keen on selling to my father and me. It was agreed that Toby would stay on as manager, so there shouldn't be any hitches.'

'No, there shouldn't…but you see, even you believe it's all a foregone conclusion. Except that isn't how it is at all.' She shot him a quick glance. He must have been feeling very satisfied, thinking all was going to plan.

The thought depressed her. How could she have had him so wrong? She had fallen for him, been caught up in a whirlwind of emotion that had threatened to overwhelm her, and life had become bright with the intense colours seen through the eyes of new love. But it had all faded, and she'd realised that she didn't know him at all.

'Katie?' His quiet voice jerked her out of her reverie.

'I told them I don't want to sell.'

His eyes widened. 'Are you quite sure you know what you're doing?' he asked, his tone incredulous. 'How on earth are you going to handle things? You have absolutely no experience of running a vineyard.'

'Then I'll have to learn, won't I?'

'Do you think it's just a matter of harvesting the crop and sitting back while the money rolls in?' He shook his head. 'It doesn't happen that way, Katie. It takes a lot of hard work and dedication.'

Her eyes narrowed on him. 'Do you think I'm not capable of that?'

His mouth twisted. 'That's not what I'm saying.

I'm just pointing out that if you go ahead with this, it's quite possible you'll come a cropper.'

'And there wouldn't be just a hint of sour grapes in your reaction, would there?' she challenged him. 'I know how much you wanted the vineyard for yourself.'

'For my family.' The correction was brusque and to the point. 'Yes, we want it.' His eyes darkened. 'And I'm not giving up on that. The offer still stands.'

Her gaze was troubled. 'But I'm not going to accept it. Okay, I'm not at all sure I'm doing the right thing, and I really don't want to upset my family. I know they're going through a difficult time. But instinct tells me I shouldn't be making such a big decision about selling so soon after my father's death. If I let the vineyard go now, I might come to regret it some months or years down the line. I'm really keen on the idea of owning a stretch of land—my father's land— that produces some of the finest wines in California. For me, that's far more important than the money.'

'It's a huge undertaking. I think you're making a big mistake.'

'I know.' She frowned. Clearly, she was on her own in this, and if things went wrong, she would only have herself to blame. He was right. What did she know about owning a vineyard? The enormity of what she was planning to do began to crowd in on her, overwhelming her with all sorts of dire possibilities, and to distract herself she looked out of the window and gave her attention to the road once more.

They were passing through scenic countryside right now, and she could see the ocean in the near distance and she watched as waves crashed on to the rocky shore. It seemed to perfectly echo the way she was feeling right now.

A minute or so later they reached the point in the road where the accident had happened. Police officers had sealed off the area and set up diversionary routes for other drivers.

Katie looked around and then let out a slow breath. 'This is a mess,' she said softly.

Nick's mouth made a grim line. 'It looks as though an SUV turned over. From the skid marks, I'd say he tried to avoid something up ahead and everyone else piled in. You're right, it's a mess.'

'There are a couple of drivers in the cars who look to be in a bad way,' a police officer told them as they went over to the cordoned-off area and introduced themselves. 'The fire department is working to free them right now. We've led the walking wounded away to a place of safety, but there are two women in the SUV who look as though they have serious injuries. Seems the driver had to slam on the brakes when someone pulled out in front of her. She swerved and lost control of the vehicle and then ended up on the embankment at the side of the road. There are some others who are injured, but the paramedics don't seem to be too worried about them at the moment.'

'Thanks for letting us know,' Nick said. 'We'll go and check them out.'

Two ambulances were already on the scene, and

the paramedics were doing triage, trying to find out which people needed attention first.

'Glad to have you along, Doc.' The lead paramedic nodded towards Nick and then gave Katie a brief acknowledgement. The two men obviously knew one another.

'The drivers of the cars have fractures of the legs and arms,' he said. 'They're in a lot of pain and discomfort, but we're doing what we can to stabilise them right now. It's the women in the SUV who need looking at. I think one of them is going into shock. My colleague did an initial assessment and we're giving them oxygen.'

'Okay, we'll see to them.'

Nick and Kate hurried over to the SUV. It was partially on its side, having come to rest on the embankment, but at least both women were accessible, albeit with some difficulty. Katie manoeuvred herself into the doorway of the vehicle and assessed the woman in the passenger seat, while Nick attended to the driver.

'Can you tell me your name?' she asked. The woman appeared to be in her early forties, and her companion was of a similar age, she guessed.

'Frances...Frances Delaney.' She struggled to get the words out, and Katie could see that she was having trouble with her breathing.

'Okay, Frances,' she murmured. 'I'm Dr Logan and I'm here to help you. Can you tell me where it hurts?'

'My chest. It's a bad pain.' The woman tried to

point to her upper rib cage, but then she tried to look round and became agitated. 'What's happening to Maria…to my sister?' she asked. 'She's not speaking—is she all right?'

Katie glanced to where Nick was carefully examining the driver. 'She's conscious,' she told Frances. 'Dr Bellini is looking after her.'

'She's hypotensive,' Nick murmured, 'and her heart rate is low. There's a contusion where the steering-wheel must have impacted, so I think we're looking at some kind of abdominal injury.' He looked at his patient. 'As soon as I've finished examining you, Maria, I'll give you something for the pain.'

Maria tried to say something, but couldn't get the words out. Katie's strong guess was that she might be asking for Frances, but the sound was indistinct and faded on her lips. 'Try not to worry, we're going to take good care of you and your sister,' Nick told her. He must have come to the same conclusion as Katie.

He had a soothing way with his patients, Katie reflected. He was gentle and soft spoken, and at the same time very thorough and methodical. Maria was in excellent hands.

She went on with her own examination of Frances. 'It looks as though you have some broken ribs,' she said quietly. 'And as far as I can tell, your forearm is fractured in two places. I'll give you an injection for the pain and immobilise it with a sling, but you're going to need surgery to fix the bones in place.'

Frances was white-faced and it was fairly obvious

that her condition was deteriorating by the minute…
something that started alarm bells ringing in Katie's
head.

'Yes. Thank you for helping me.' The taut lines
of the woman's expression relaxed a little as Katie
administered the injection. 'It's my sister I'm worried
about,' she said, her voice husky with emotion. 'She's
always looked out for me…we look out for each other.
I can't bear the thought that…' her voice began to fail
'…that something might happen to her.'

'Try not to fret yourself.' Katie frowned. Despite
the nature of the arm injuries, it was the rib fractures
that concerned her most. Her patient was already
experiencing severe pain and breathlessness. As a
doctor, Katie knew that first and second rib fractures were often associated with damage to important
blood vessels, and if that was happening, time was
fast running out. It was imperative that Frances be
taken to hospital as soon as possible.

She set up an intravenous line so that she could
give her patient fluids, a first stage in defence against
shock and blood-pressure problems that stemmed
from traumatic injury. Nick was doing the same
for Maria, but his expression was serious, and she
guessed he was concerned for his patient.

'How is she doing?' Frances whispered the words,
straining to summon the energy from a well that was
beginning to run dry. 'I can't hear her. I need…to
know…she's all right.'

Nick's gaze met Katie's. He made a small shake
of his head. Maria had lapsed into unconsciousness

and he had secured an artificial airway in place in her throat.

'We're doing everything we can for her,' Katie said softly. 'We'll be taking her to hospital with you, just as soon as we can.'

Nick called for the paramedics to assist with spinal boards for both women, and within a matter of minutes they had stabilised the sisters sufficiently so that they could be transferred to the ambulance.

Katie went to check on the other injured people. She checked vital signs and applied dressings to stem bleeding where necessary, and when she looked around some time later, she saw that Nick was doing the same.

The injured drivers had finally been freed from their cars, and were at that moment being taken into the second ambulance.

As soon as he was certain everyone was secure, Nick started to gather together his medical kit. 'I want to follow them to the hospital and oversee things from there,' he told Katie. 'Is that all right with you? Otherwise I could arrange for someone from the hotel to come and pick you up.'

'No, it's okay. I want to go with you.' She walked with him to his car. 'I'm worried about both of them. I want to make sure that Frances has an angiogram— I'm pretty sure there's some internal bleeding, and if it isn't dealt with quickly she'll be in bad trouble.'

He nodded. 'Same here. Maria's heart rate is way too low, and her abdomen felt full and doughy when I examined her. I'm sure there's some bleeding into the abdominal cavity, and the problems with her lower rib cage make me think there could be damage to her liver or spleen. An ultrasound scan should tell us what's going on there. If we can't find where the bleeding is coming from, we'll have to do a peritoneal lavage…but whatever happens, we need to do it quickly.'

They set off, and Nick drove as fast as was possible towards the hospital, arriving there as the paramedics were unloading their patients from the ambulance.

Both he and Katie made their reports to the emergency teams, and followed the women into the trauma room. 'Is Dr Wainwright on duty?' Nick asked as a nurse, Abby, hurried to assist.

She nodded.

'That's good.' He turned to Katie. 'He's the best vascular surgeon we have. If there's any damage to your patient's subclavian or innominate artery—or both—he's the man to put it right.'

'That's a relief.' A patient could die from an injury like that if it wasn't picked up in time, or if the surgeon was unable to stem the bleeding.

Nick was talking to the doctor in charge of the emergency room. 'I'd like to oversee my patient's ultrasound scan. I hope that's all right with you?'

'Of course. Any time. You don't need to ask, Nick.'

Katie went to discuss her patient's case with the doctor who was taking care of her, and a few minutes later she watched as Frances was whisked away to the angiography suite. The woman was agitated, distressed at having to leave her sister behind, and, unnacountably, as she saw the lift doors close on the trolley bed, Katie was overcome by a sudden tide of unhappiness.

Perhaps it had come about because this was the end of a long day. She had been hard at work in the paediatric unit this morning, before hurrying to the meeting with her half-brother and -sister, and now, in the aftermath of the traffic accident, she was beginning to register the dreadful impact of tending injured people in the wreckage of vehicles that had been slewn across the highway. She didn't know what had caused these feelings to well up inside her. She couldn't explain it, but her heart was heavy and she felt desperately sad.

'I need to go and get a breath of air,' she told Abby. 'I'll be outside in the courtyard if there's any news.'

'That's all right. I'll come and find you if there are any developments.'

'Thanks.'

Katie went out into the courtyard, a quiet, paved area where hospital staff could sit for a while on wooden benches set at intervals on the perimeter. There were a couple of cherry trees out there, along with tubs of velvet-petalled petunias that provided bright splashes of colour.

She sat down and tried to sort out the bewildering thoughts that were crowding in on her. She was feeling overwhelmed and off balance, and it scared her quite a bit because she wasn't used to feeling that way.

'Are you okay?' Nick came out into the courtyard a few minutes later and sat down on the bench beside her. He handed her a cup of coffee. 'Sorry it's a styrofoam cup—the coffee machine was closest to hand. I doubt you had time to enjoy the coffee and sandwiches I sent round earlier at the hotel… you seemed to come out of the room almost as soon as the waitress took them.'

'No, you're right, I didn't.' She frowned. 'Come to think of it, I haven't had anything to eat or drink since first thing this morning.' She sent him a quick look as she sipped the hot liquid. 'We had a few difficult cases to deal with in the paediatric unit this morning and I had to stay on for a couple of hours after my shift finished to make sure everything was sorted out properly.' She took another swallow of her drink. 'This is good…thanks.' Even the delectable aroma of the coffee teased her taste buds.

He smiled. 'Are you going to tell me what's wrong, or do I have to prise it out of you? I know there's something, because you were very quiet back there and you had that far-away, hurting kind of look in your eyes.'

She hadn't realised that he'd been watching her. 'And there I thought your mind was all on your patient.' She cradled the cup in her hands and swallowed down the rest of the liquid.

He shook his head. 'You're the one who's always on my mind,' he said quietly. 'Everywhere I go.

I think about you, wonder what you're doing or
whether you're okay. And I know you're not okay
right now, so you should tell me what it is that's bothering you. What's upset you?'

'I don't know,' she said simply. Did he really think
about her all the time? She put the empty cup down
on the floor. 'I watched Frances being wheeled away
and this bleak feeling swept over me. She looked so
devastated, so torn, because she was being separated
from her sister.'

She looked up at him, her eyes troubled. 'Perhaps
that was it. She and her sister seem to be so close to
one another, and maybe I wish things could have
been like that for me. I never had any siblings until
now, and it was all I ever wanted, to share that family
feeling with people close to me. Finding out about
Tom and Natasha was a shock, but once I got used
to the idea I realised that a whole new world had
opened up for me. And then I went and ruined it by
throwing a spanner in the works. I don't think they'll
ever forgive me.'

'But you have to be true to yourself in the end,
don't you? And that means sticking by your decision.'
He put an arm around her and drew her close and she
didn't have it in her to pull away from him. The truth
was, she missed that closeness, that feeling of being
cherished. A lump formed in her throat. 'Isn't that
what your father would have wanted?' Nick asked.
'Either way you choose, you risk losing out in some
way.'

'Maybe.' Her eyes clouded. 'I suppose you were

just pointing out what I already know when you said I haven't a clue about running a vineyard. And that's perfectly true. Perhaps the enormity of what I'm taking on is just beginning to sink in. It's one thing to do it when you have back-up, but quite another when everyone who matters is against you.'

'And I'm included in that group, aren't I?' His mouth made a crooked shape. 'I don't want to cause you any hurt, Katie…but the vineyard is my heritage, mine and my brother's. Running the family business is in our blood, it flows through our veins as though it's part of our being. You're just beginning to feel something of that with this inheritance from your father.'

'And I'm finding just the thought of it a little overwhelming, as you said I would. But I can't turn my back on it. I just need to find the strength, from somewhere, to go on.'

She pressed her lips together. 'I've had to come to terms all over again with the kind of man my father was. I was hurt when I found he had another family who had been kept from me, and perhaps I overreacted.' She gazed up at him. 'It was like a betrayal, and I thought I'd done with all that. I thought I had this tough outer shell that couldn't be broken, but it wasn't so. I crumbled at the first blow. I'm every bit as weak as he was. I can't even hold it together in the emergency room.'

'You know that isn't true, Katie.' He wrapped both arms around her and folded her to him. 'You're forgetting that you've only just lost your father in these past few weeks. You can't make decisions—any kind of decisions—when you're still grieving. And you *are* grieving, even though you feel he let you down.'

His lips lightly brushed her temple and Katie realised that more than anything she wanted to nestle against him and accept the comfort he offered. 'You'd grown to love him,' he murmured. 'That's why you want to hold on to what he left behind. You see his touch in every row of vines, in every grape that ripens. That's how I feel, too, when I think about how my ancestors carved out this valley and planted their crops. We can't let it go, Katie. We're no different from one another, you and I.'

'Aren't we?' She gazed up at him, her features troubled. 'You seem to be so confident, in everything you do. I'm still struggling to find my way.'

'Then let me help you,' he said softly, bending his head to gently trace her lips with his own. 'Let me help you to forget your worries for a while.'

He kissed her again, a lingering, wonderful kiss that filled her with aching need and made her want to run her hands through the silk of his hair. She ought to have been wary of him, because she knew that he would never stop trying to make her change her mind and relinquish her inheritance. Wasn't that what he'd meant when he'd said it was the wrong time to be making decisions?

She was at war with herself. On the one hand she felt he had the power to destroy everything that mattered to her…what was there to stop him from piling on the pressure until she gave in and sold out to him?

And on the other, she wanted to drink him in, as though he was the water of life, a fount of everything that could save her from herself and make her whole again.

But the moment was short-lived. He eased back from her, reluctantly dragging his mouth from hers, and she stared at him, her senses befuddled, until she gradually began to realise that she could hear the rustle of someone approaching.

'I thought you'd like to know that your patient is back from her angiography,' the nurse said. 'Mr Wainright is going to operate. And the other lady is in a bad way, too, by the looks of things. They've called for someone from the surgical team to come and look at her.'

'Thanks, Abby,' Katie managed in a low voice. 'I'll come back in and take a look at the films.' Reality began to set in once more. She felt as though she'd had a near miss…a brush with danger…but she didn't think she'd come away unscathed. She felt as though the life was being sucked out of her.

Nick stooped to pick up her abandoned coffee cup then straightened and waited for her to come and stand beside him. 'Ready?' he said.

She nodded, but she wasn't ready at all. Far from it. After that kiss, she was more bewildered than ever.

CHAPTER NINE

THE doorbell pealed, and Katie checked her watch as she went out into the hallway. It was mid-afternoon and she wasn't expecting anyone—though there was always the slim chance that Tom or Natasha might drop by to talk things through with her. It would be a relief if they did. She desperately wanted to try to clear the air between them.

It was neither of them. Instead, she opened the door to discover that Nick was standing there, casually waiting, one hand planted flat against the wall as he gazed around the vestibule.

'Katie,' he said, straightening up. 'I'm glad I've found you at home.'

His gaze travelled over her and already her body was on full alert. He looked good, too good for her peace of mind, dressed in dark trousers that moulded his hips and thighs and emphasised the taut line of his stomach and a loose cotton shirt that sat easily on his broad shoulders.

She pulled the door open wider and waved him into the hallway. 'Come in,' she said. 'This is unexpected.

Is everything all right? Is there a problem at the hospital?' She led the way to the living room and tried not to think about the way he'd held her just the day before or the way his kisses had melted the ice around her heart.

'It's nothing like that. Everything's fine. I just thought you might want an update on the Delaneys. I know you've been asking about them.'

She nodded. 'No one was very forthcoming. I know Frances had arterial grafts to repair her damaged blood vessels, and her forearm fracture was so bad that both bones had to be fixed with metal plates and screws. She was still in a fragile condition this morning when I rang. But no one seems to be able to give me much information on Maria.'

'I think that's because the situation was complicated,' Nick explained. 'Both her liver and spleen were lacerated, but the surgeon managed to repair the damage. The biggest problem was that while he was operating he discovered damage to the pancreas. He did what he could to preserve the organ, but it's touch and go from here on.'

Katie sucked in her breath. 'Poor Maria.' Pancreatic trauma was often not detected until it was too late. Sometimes, if it was a simple contusion, it could be cleaned up and drained, but in Maria's case it sounded as though the damage was extensive. All they could do now was wait and see what happened.

'Thanks for coming here and telling me,' she said.

'I was hoping you'd follow up on them and let me know how they were doing.'

His glance touched her, moving over her features in a lingering, thoughtful manner. 'That's one of the things I love so much about you…that you care about people. They're not just patients to you, but people with families and lives outside the hospital.' His mouth flattened. 'Of course, that can be a hazard in itself. Getting too involved isn't always a good thing—not if you want to feel easy in yourself.'

Katie's gaze met his briefly. There were things he loved about her? She looked away. She'd been through too much heartache to start hoping all over again…hadn't she? How many times was she going to get up on to her feet, only to have life knock her down again?

If Nick wondered what she was thinking, he made no mention of it. Instead, he cast an appreciative glance around the room, his gaze lingering on the shelves that decorated one wall. 'It looks as though you've picked up one or two pieces from the fine-art shops around here,' he murmured.

'Yes.' She pulled herself together. 'I wasn't able to bring much with me from England, so I thought it would be good to brighten up the apartment with a few colourful touches here and there.'

He nodded, and turned his attention to the glass-ware on display. 'I like these bowls…the etchings on the glass make me think of sea life, with all those fronds and water plants.'

'They're similar to some my mother has at home.'

Her mouth made a straight line. 'She and my father brought quite a bit of glassware from Murano. She likes to collect special pieces, paperweights and so on.'

Nick's gaze flicked over her. 'Have you forgiven him yet?'

The breath left her lungs in a sudden rush. 'I don't know. Perhaps.' After all, she'd been living with her father's imperfections for some twenty years. In the end, maybe she simply had to accept that he'd had genuine feelings for her. He'd told her he was proud of her, and he'd taken the trouble to warn her against falling for Nick. Though that was probably a warning that had come too late. Wasn't she already living with the consequences?

'And me?'

Her gaze faltered. 'Where you're concerned, I just think it's safer if I try to keep my wits about me.'

His mouth twisted. 'There must be some way I can get back into your good books,' he said softly. 'Maybe I could drive you over to Jack's vineyard so that you could have another look at the place? I know you've been so busy lately that you haven't been able to go over there.'

'And you think when I do I'll perhaps decide that I've made the wrong decision about keeping it?'

He laughed. 'Well, maybe that, too.' His expression became thoughtful. 'Actually, I heard Natasha was thinking of going over there this afternoon, and I guessed it might be a good opportunity for you to talk to her again—to the manager, Toby, as well, of course. He's usually up at the house at this time of day.'

She hesitated. Why was he doing this? Was it really as he said, to try to win her over, or did he have an ulterior motive? Did he think that when she saw the vast extent of the place once more she would realise she had taken on too much?

'It sounds like a great idea,' she murmured. 'Though I don't know how Natasha is going to react to me. I'm not altogether sure that there's anything I can say to her that will put things right.'

'I wouldn't worry too much about that. At least you'll have made the effort.'

'I suppose so.' She sent him a quick glance. 'Won't I be putting you out, though?'

'Not at all. I've been meaning to see Toby about a planting programme we were talking about last month. Your father and he were thinking about trying a new variety of grape, and my father wants to try it out, too.'

'Okay, then.' She hesitated. 'Are we ready to go now? I'll fetch my jacket.'

The approach to her father's vineyard took them through a glorious green valley, with pine-clad hills that soon gave way to row upon row of vines. The fruit was lush, soft hued as it began to ripen, and Katie felt an overwhelming sense that all was right with the natural world as she gazed at the sun-dappled slopes. If only her own life could be so serene.

Toby was at the front of the house, talking to Natasha, when they arrived, but they both turned to look in their direction as Nick drove on to the forecourt.

Natasha was holding Sarah in her arms, but she set the infant down on the ground once Nick had parked the car. A black Labrador had been padding about, sniffing amongst the flower-beds, but he came to greet them, tail wagging, as they stepped out of the car.

'Hi, there, Benjy.' Nick patted the dog on the head and received a boisterous welcome in return, the Labrador's whole body moving in excited recognition. Then it was Katie's turn, and she gently stroked the dog, tickling him behind the ears.

She smiled at Natasha but received a blank stare in return. Toby, on the other hand, nodded to both of them.

'Hi, there,' he said. 'I wondered if you might drive over today.' He was a tall man in his early forties, with brown hair and a face that was bronzed from many hours spent out in the sun. 'My wife had to go out, but she made some oatmeal cookies before she left, so we can enjoy them with a pot of tea. I'll put the kettle on and we can sit outside on the patio for a while, if you like. Then I'll show you around.'

Satisfied he had made his presence known, the dog went to lie down at his feet, regarding them all in a slightly curious fashion, raising an eyelid every now and again in case he was missing something.

'Thanks,' Katie said. 'That sounds good. I wanted to talk to you for a while, about the vineyard and so on.'

His expression was serious. 'I thought you might.'

'We were just going to take a look around the house,' Natasha said, glancing at Nick. 'There are one or two maintenance problems that have cropped up—like a couple of broken fences and some roof tiles that need to be replaced. Toby said he didn't mind fixing them, but I think he probably has enough to do already.' She looked at Katie, her expression cool and vaguely antagonistic. 'I suppose the ball's in your court. You were keen to take this on, so I dare say we can leave the decisions to you. Tom and I never wanted the stress of running the business and everything associated with it.'

Katie pulled in a deep breath. 'If that's what you want, then of course I'll deal with everything that comes along. I'll keep you up to date with what's happening.' She was disappointed by her cool reception, but she could hardly have expected anything else in the circumstances. Natasha was still annoyed with her, from the looks of things, but there was no point in getting into a state about it, was there?

Sarah toddled over to Katie and stood, gazing up at her. Her bright curls quivered and shone in the sunlight. 'Pwetty,' she said, and for a moment or two Katie was taken aback, until the little girl pointed to her necklace. 'Pwetty,' she said again, and Katie smiled.

'You like it? It is pretty, isn't it?' She fingered the silver filigree necklace and crouched down so that the infant could take a better look. 'My mother gave it to me, so it's very special.'

'Best not let Sarah get her fingers round it, then,' Natasha said flatly. 'She doesn't distinguish between special or worthless. She grabs everything. One tug and it's ruined.'

'Oh, dear. Well, I'd best protect it, then, hadn't I?' Katie placed her fingers over the necklace and glanced towards Nick, wondering what she could do to distract the child.

'You can play with my keys for a while, if you like, Sarah,' he said, coming to the rescue by jangling them temptingly in front of the child's face. Her eyes widened and she turned her attention to Nick, the pink tip of her tongue coming out to touch her bottom lip as she gazed up at him. The keys were irresistible, it seemed, and she held up her hands, trying to grasp them as he gently teased her, darting them about in a catch-me-if-you-can kind of game.

It didn't have quite the effect he was looking for, though, because being thwarted proved altogether too much for her, and the toddler burst into tears.

Nick's jaw dropped, and Katie looked on in consternation. 'I was just playing with her,' Nick said. 'I didn't mean to upset her.' He turned to Natasha. 'Do you think she'll let me pick her up and comfort her?'

'You can try,' Natasha said. 'It isn't your fault, mind. She's been like this for some time now, fretful and tearful, on and off. I just haven't been able to work out what's wrong with her. I've put it down to tiredness. She's been sleeping an awful lot lately, so perhaps the doctor was right when he said she was run down. I've just been letting her rest as and when she needs it.'

Nick picked up the little girl and cradled her in his arms, offering her the keys, but by now she had lost interest in them. She sobbed, large hiccuping sobs that racked her body, and tears trickled down her face, giving her a woeful expression.

'I'm sorry, cherub,' Nick said in a soothing tone. 'I was only teasing. I didn't mean to upset you.' He was thoughtful for a moment or two, and then asked quietly, 'How about I give you a rock-a-bye swing— would you like that, hmm?' He began to rock her gently to and fro in his arms, and after a while she stopped crying and stared up at him, her face pale.

Katie watched him with the little girl and felt a pang of emotion well up inside her. He was so natural with her, so caring and gentle, so obviously concerned for her well-being.

'You definitely have the knack,' Toby said with a laugh. 'I expect Natasha will be calling on you for babysitting duties from now on.'

'Heaven forbid!' Nick looked aghast. 'I'd need a bit more practice before I took up that kind of challenge.' He looked at Katie, a questioning, odd kind of look, and an unbidden thrill of expectation ran through her. What would it be like to have his children?

Toby showed them the way through the house to the kitchen, the dog following at his heels. It was a large breakfast kitchen with glass doors to one side leading out on to a terrace. 'Make yourselves at home out there,' Toby said, waving them out towards a teak wood table and chairs. 'I'll make the tea and bring it out to you.'

Nick was still holding his precious bundle, but now he looked over at Natasha. 'Do you want to take her?' he asked. 'She looks as though she's settled now.'

'Okay. I'll put her in her buggy,' Natasha murmured. 'She can sit and watch us while we talk.'

Katie glanced at the child as she lay back in her buggy a short time later. She was white faced, her curls slightly damp against her forehead as though she was a little feverish. Her breathing was rapid, and it occurred to her that the child looked exhausted.

Toby arrived with the tea, and once he had seated himself and they had chatted for a while, Katie brought up the subject of the management of the vineyard.

'I hope you'll stay on here and run things for us as you've always done,' she said. 'I know how much my father valued your work here.'

'Thank you. I'd like that.' Toby looked relieved. 'Does that mean my family can go on living here at the house?'

'Of course. I've asked Antony to draw up the paperwork to give you a more secure tenancy.'

Natasha sent her a quick look, but said nothing, and Katie said evenly, 'I'm assuming that will be all right with you and Tom?'

Her sister nodded, and soon after that Nick began to talk to Toby about the new planting programme.

Benjy, who had been supposedly dozing at Toby's feet, was disturbed by a butterfly and decided he needed to go and check things out. As the butterfly flitted away to the flower border, he got to his feet and went after it.

'Up, Mummy!' Sarah suddenly exclaimed, looking at Natasha. 'Up.' She stretched out her arms to her mother, and Natasha frowned.

'If I lift you up, what then?' she said, giving her daughter a quizzical look. 'You'll be demanding to be set down, then, won't you?' She frowned. 'You want to play with Benjy, don't you?'

Sarah's expression was gleeful. 'Up...play Benjy,' she said, and by now her fingers were doing their familiar clasping and unclasping as if she was clutching at the air.

'Okay, then, young madam,' Natasha murmured, lifting the child out of the buggy. 'But try and stay out of trouble. No pulling at the flowers.'

'F'owers,' Sarah echoed happily. 'Benjy f'owers.'

Benjy was indeed exploring the flowers, Katie noticed. His nose was pressed up against them as he drank deeply of their scent, and a moment later he drew his head back and gave an enormous sneeze. Sarah giggled.

The dog's nose was covered with pollen, and Katie smiled. She looked at Nick and saw that he was chuckling, too. Their glances met in a shared moment of amusement.

Sarah toddled off to where Benjy was getting ready for another sneeze. She patted him vigorously in sympathy and then wandered away to inspect the scarlet begonias.

Katie watched her go, and saw how the little girl seemed to slow down and come to a standstill. It seemed that she had stopped to look at a ladybird or some such, but there was something about the way she was standing that had Katie's instincts on alert all of a sudden. Then the child's legs seemed to crumple under her and in an instant Katie was out of her seat. She hurried over to her, catching her as she would have fallen.

'What's wrong with her? What's happened?' Natasha was beside herself with worry. She rushed over and began to stroke her little girl's hair as though by touch alone she would bring her back to normal.

'She just collapsed,' Katie said softly. She used the second hand on her watch to carefully check the infant's pulse. Then she glanced at Nick, who had come to kneel down beside her. 'Her heart rate is very fast, and she's much too pale. I think perhaps she ought to have a proper check-up at the hospital.'

He nodded. 'I agree with you.' The dog came to find out what was going on, and Nick said softly, 'We should take her into the house.' He glanced at Natasha and she nodded.

'You could lay her down on the sofa in the living room,' Toby suggested. 'It's cooler in there. Maybe she had a touch too much sun.'

'It's possible,' Katie said, gently handing the child over to Nick, who lifted her into his arms and carried her into the house. 'We'll give her a few minutes to see if she comes round, but I think it's something more than that.'

'You thought she was ill earlier, didn't you?' Natasha glanced sharply at Katie as they gathered in the living room a moment or two later. 'I saw you looking at her when she was in her buggy.'

Katie nodded. 'If I'm right, I don't think it's anything too serious.'

'Tell me.' Natasha crouched down beside the sofa, holding her child's hand, letting her know that she was there with her the whole time.

'Her main symptoms seem to be the tiredness and her pallor,' Katie murmured. 'You haven't mentioned anything else that's bothering you, apart from the fact that she's been quite fretful lately.'

'That's right.'

'And you mentioned some time ago that she had suffered from a viral infection—I'm guessing that this has been going on since then?'

'Yes… I think so.' Natasha's brows drew together. 'It's hard to know exactly when it started. It's been coming on gradually. What do you think is wrong with her?'

Sarah began to stir, rubbing her eyes and shifting to a more comfortable position.

Katie glanced at Nick. 'I'm thinking some kind of transient anaemia.'

'Yes.' He nodded. 'That sounds about right. Of course, we would need to confirm it with tests.'

'Anaemia?' Natasha's voice was filled with stress.

'Is that because of something I've been doing wrong? Haven't I been feeding her properly?'

Katie recognised the guilt in her voice. Parents often blamed themselves where no blame was due.

'No, it's nothing at all like that,' Nick said quietly. 'You don't often see this, but sometimes, after certain types of viral illness in young children, their bodies stop making red blood cells for a while. That would account for Sarah's tiredness and pale appearance.'

Natasha was horrified. 'That sounds awful,' she said. 'Can something be done? Is there a cure?'

He nodded. 'Usually it sorts itself out after two or three months.'

'But she collapsed. She can't go on like that, surely? That can't be right.'

Katie laid a hand gently on her arm. 'I know this is really worrying for you, Natasha, but Nick's right. Usually this type of illness clears up of its own accord. When a child collapses, though, as Sarah just did, it's best to get things checked out. She might need a transfusion. If this is what we think it is, that will help a lot and she'll soon start to feel better... though it's possible she'll need another transfusion before she recovers completely. At some point her bone marrow will start manufacturing the cells once more.'

Natasha had a panicked look about her. 'But I need to go and get help now. I want to take her to the emergency room.' She looked around distractedly. 'I shan't rest until I find out exactly what's happening.'

'I could take you to the hospital,' Toby offered, but Nick intervened.

'I'll go with her,' he said quietly. 'You stay and show Katie around the vineyard. I'm sure you must have a lot to talk about. Natasha and Sarah will be fine with me.'

'You don't mind?' Natasha asked. 'Are you sure? I don't mean to break things up, but I'm really worried about her.'

'Of course you are,' Nick said. 'I would have suggested it anyway. Sarah needs to be checked out.' He turned to look at Katie. 'Here, take my car keys. I'll take Natasha's car, and if we're delayed at the hospital for any reason, you can drive yourself home in mine. I'll pick it up later. Don't worry if you're not around when I come to collect it, I'll use my spare set of keys.'

'Okay.' Katie wasn't at all sure how she felt about driving his beautiful, streamlined car, but she judged that now wasn't the moment to dither or argue. It said a lot about him that he'd thought of her in this moment of crisis.

Natasha hurried away to gather together everything she needed to take with her while Nick secured Sarah in her car seat. The child was still drowsy, not really taking any notice of what was going on around her.

'Will she be all right?' Toby asked as he and Katie watched them drive away a few minutes later. 'I know you said it would clear up on its own, but it sounded pretty horrific to me. Anything to do with bone marrow not working properly is pretty scary, isn't it?'

'You're right,' Katie answered. 'Normally, it would be very worrying, but I'm hoping that this is one of those instances where she'll make a full recovery. We won't really know until we have the results of the tests.'

'It's a difficult situation—a worrying time all round.'

Katie nodded. 'Yes, it is.' She was glad Nick had gone with Natasha. He would be a comfort to her, and he would be able to explain anything that she didn't understand. He was a man to be relied on, a good man to have by your side in times of trouble. Or at any time, come to think of it.

She sighed inwardly. Her feelings for Nick were complex and very unsettling. Could it be that she was falling in love with him? In fact, the more she thought about it, the more certain she became that he was the one man who could make her happy…if only she could be sure that she could put her faith in him.

'Perhaps you'd like to look around the parts of vineyard you haven't already seen while we're waiting to hear what's happening?' Toby suggested. 'I know you were interested in the vines and the type of grapes that produce the Chardonnay. We have a separate area for the new planting on the west side.'

'Thanks. That would be great.'

The hills were bathed in sunshine at this time of day, and as they walked around, Katie was glad that she was wearing a simple, sleeveless cotton dress that kept her relatively cool and fresh. Even so, she was thankful for the occasional ocean breeze that fanned her hot cheeks.

Row upon row of glorious vines stretched out ahead of her, all of them in full leaf and heavy with fruit. 'You're doing a great job here, Toby,' she said.

'I do my best.' He sent her a quick look. 'These two vineyards, the Logans' and the Bellinis', have always been interconnected and run in a harmonious fashion. That might be under threat now that Tom and Natasha have shown that they're not interested.'

She frowned. 'You're afraid it will affect the smooth running of the place?'

'I think it might. At the moment they're happy for you to make the decisions, but that might not always be the case. There could be problems.'

She thought it over. 'I can see how that's a possibility—but right now I don't see any way round the situation. I can't afford to buy them out.'

'No.' Toby was quiet for a moment or two then added, 'I know Nick has an idea for smoothing things out. I expect he's spoken to you about it?'

She shook her head. 'No, he hasn't—except to say that he'd like to buy us out? Is that what he meant?'

Toby put up his hands as though to ward off any more questions. 'I'd better leave it to him to tell you his thoughts on that subject. Anyway, he wasn't specific, and I'm only concerned for the smooth operation of the vineyard.' He gave a wry smile. 'I don't want to get involved in sibling rivalry and multi-million-dollar takeovers.'

Katie stayed silent for a while after that. Toby's words had set up a welter of turbulent emotions inside her. Was Nick intending to increase his offer for the vineyard? How could he go on with his bid when he knew how much her father's legacy meant to her? She had begun to think he might have deep feelings for her, might actually come to love her, but now all her dreams were dashed once more. Her hopes had been reduced to ashes.

CHAPTER TEN

KATIE wandered barefoot along the beach, picking her way over craggy rocks and alternately feeling the warm sand glide between her toes.

There was so much to think about, so many questions that niggled at the back of her mind. What could Nick be planning? Would he really do anything to upset her? Why hadn't he rung to let her know what had happened at the hospital yesterday?

She missed him, she wanted to hear his voice, but instead there had just been a brief note pushed into her mailbox that morning to tell her that he had come along and collected his car while she was out—and to say that Sarah was being admitted to the paediatric ward so that the doctors could do tests. When Katie had tried to phone him, there had been no answer and the service had cut straight away to voice mail.

She stopped for a moment to listen to the calls of gulls overhead and to look around at the rugged, coastal bluffs. Out in the ocean, sea stacks rose majestically, carved out of ancient volcanic rock, a playground for sea otters that played offshore, feeding off the underwater kelp.

It was somehow soothing to be at one with nature…but in the end it didn't take away her inner torment. How could it? Her life had changed so much in these last few months, and she'd had no choice but to confront her demons. Where had that left her? She was afraid and uncertain, full of doubt. And yet one thing shone clearly through the gloom—Nick had been a constant support to her, showing her how much he wanted her, gently coaxing her into loving him.

Just yesterday he had taken her to meet Natasha, and surely that was because he hoped they might somehow manage to heal the rift that had opened up between them. Would he have done all that if she meant nothing to him, if their relationship was just a spur-of-the-moment thing, a casual fling? She had to hope there was more. She couldn't go on this way.

For once, she had to take him at his word and trust in him. From now on she was going to meet life head on, which was why she walking along this stretch of sand, heading towards Nick's beach house.

Of course, she had rung Natasha. She had been desperate for news of her young niece, and at least her half-sister had recognised that she cared about the child and was worried about her.

'They're keeping her in overnight,' Natasha had said. 'It was late by the time the doctors worked out what they were going to do, but Nick was by my side all the while, explaining everything about the tests and so on. I don't know what I'd have done without him.' She pulled in a deep breath. 'Anyway, I'm going to stay here at the hospital so that I can be with Sarah. My husband—Greg—said he'd try to get here as soon as he can. He's been working away in the next county. We're both worried sick about her.'

'That's understandable,' Katie murmured. 'This must have come as quite a shock to you. I hope things turn out all right for you—will you let me know what happens?'

'Yes, I will.' Natasha hesitated. 'Thanks, Katie. I know you've been concerned for her all along and you were looking out for her. We've perhaps been hard on you, Tom and I. We both feel that we've misjudged you.'

'You've had a lot to deal with,' Katie said simply. 'You're my family. I just want to know that you're all doing well.'

It was a huge relief to know that they no longer bore her any ill-will, but the problems were still there. If she refused to sell the vineyard, they would go on struggling to keep their heads above water. What was Nick planning to do that would change all that? If things were to work out well for her half-brother and -sister, there could only be one loser.

She was overcome by doubts. If she was ever to make sense of any of this, she needed to see him, be with him…talk to him.

Katie pushed away a strand of chestnut hair that blew across her cheek in the faint breeze and walked closer to the water's edge. She paused to pick up a pebble and launch it into the ocean. It made a satisfying splash, and water droplets sprayed over her cotton dress. Waves lapped at her feet, cool, even after the heat of the day.

She halted for a moment, peering into the distance. From here she could just about make out Nick's house sheltered in the curve of the bay, and she set off once more towards it.

It was late afternoon, still warm, with the sun casting its glow over all and sundry. Surely Nick would have finished his shift at the hospital by now?

It wasn't long before she reached the smooth stretch of sand that fronted his house, and straight away she saw that he was there. He was standing outside on the terrace, beneath the overhead deck, and he was facing her way. But he didn't see her because he wasn't alone and at this moment his companion was claiming all his attention.

A young woman was talking to him earnestly, her hand resting tenderly on his arm. Katie recognised her from her picture in the paper. This was Shannon, the woman he had once been engaged to, the girl he had supposedly abandoned.

Katie couldn't move. She stood and watched them, and after a second or two she saw Nick move closer to the girl and give her a hug.

The breath caught in Katie's lungs. She felt as though she had been winded, and she didn't know how to react. There was such a wealth of affection in that embrace, and it broke her heart. She stood transfixed, her pulse racing, a feeling of despair washing over her.

What was she doing, thinking that there might be a future for her with Nick? She was wishing on a moonbeam if she thought there was any chance he might have fallen for her. Hadn't Shannon always been there in the background? He'd made no secret of their relationship, had he? And in the end, hadn't he proved to be no different from her ex, professing to want Katie and at the same time making a play for someone else?

Slowly, her mind clouded by doubt and uncertainty, she started to turn away. She would talk to him later, when she had her head together a bit more. Seeing him with another woman was way more than she could bear right now. She loved him, and knowing that he was with someone else was just one more betrayal, perhaps the biggest betrayal of all because she had finally come to realise that he meant more to her than anyone in the whole world.

Her feet sank into the sand, slowing her down, but she made a huge effort to hurry away from there, even as she saw him glance in her direction and heard him call her name. She didn't look back but kept on going, putting as much distance as she could between her and the house.

'Katie…stop…let me talk to you.'

Still she kept on going. There was nothing to say, was there? She had made a mistake, and this was one from which she might never recover.

After a while he stopped calling after her, and

even the silence was a rebuke. How could she have been so reckless as to fall for him? She meant nothing to him, did she? He had let her go without a fight. Perhaps he'd never wanted her in the first place, despite what he'd said.

She trudged on, oblivious to the call of the birds around her. She paid scant attention to the rare sight of brown pelicans nesting on the high bluffs or the black-headed terns that were searching for crustaceans among the rocks.

Minutes later, though, she stirred as she heard the drone of an engine in the distance. It was coming nearer, gaining steadily on her, the sound becoming louder and mingling with the crash of surf against the distant crags. She turned to see what was disturbing the peace and tranquillity of the bay.

'Nick!' Her eyes widened in astonishment as a dune buggy swung alongside her. 'What are you doing? Where did that come from?'

'It's mine. Hop in, I'll give you a ride along the beach.'

'No, thank you.' She shrank away from him. 'I don't think so. I really don't want to go anywhere with you.'

'Of course you do...you're just not thinking straight. Come on up here beside me.' The engine chugged to a slow, idling pace.

'I can't for the life of me think why I'd want to do that,' she muttered. 'I'd just as soon be on my own right now.' She frowned, looking the contraption over, studying the sturdy wheels and the open rails that allowed the warm air to move freely over its occupant. 'Anyway, I've never been in one of those things before. What's it for?'

He cut the engine. 'It's for catching up with head-strong young women who won't stop and take notice when they're called,' he said, reaching out a hand and grasping her by the wrist. 'Up you come. You'll like it…only hold onto the rail because the ride might get a bit bumpy around the rocks.'

She tried to resist, but his hold on her was firm and unyielding and after a while she realised that her struggles were fruitless and she may as well give in. There was no one around within shouting distance to come to her rescue, anyway.

Triumphant, he tugged her into the seat beside him. She glowered at him then settled herself more comfortably and brushed the sand off her feet before slipping on her sandals.

'Where are we going?' she asked as he started up the engine once more. 'And what about Shannon—shouldn't you be with her? I saw you together. What happened? Have you just abandoned her? I'm sure she won't be very pleased to know that you're here with me.'

'Heaven forbid that I'd abandon her. No, she had to leave. She was only there on a quick visit—all she wanted was to let me know that she'd sorted out her problems.' He sent her a quick sideways glance. 'I thought we'd head along the beach to a nice, secluded spot…you never know when people are going to come along and disturb us on this section of the beach…

and then you can tell me what's going on, why you came to see me and then turned away.'

'I decided what I had to say could wait until you were less busy,' she said in a pithy tone. 'It seemed to me that you had your hands full.'

'I thought that might be it.' The buggy gathered speed. 'You have a bee in your bonnet about Shannon, don't you?' he said, raising his voice to combat the sound of the engine. 'I keep telling you not to believe what you read in the papers. She's just a friend and she's been going through a bad time, but I guess you don't believe me, do you?'

Katie's mouth turned down at the corners. 'Perhaps it would help if you told me why she was at the hotel with you that night when the press caught up with you—and why, when I saw you with her just now, you had your arms around her?'

'Does that bother you?' He studied her thoughtfully for a moment and then turned his attention back to the beach ahead. 'Does it matter to you if I'm with someone else?'

'If it's another woman...yes, it matters.' She swallowed hard. There, it was out, she'd said it, something she'd hated to admit because it made her incredibly vulnerable.

'Good,' he said, in a satisfied tone, and she looked at him in shocked surprise. 'I hope that means you're jealous. I was beginning to think you'd never take me seriously.' He manoeuvred the buggy around an outcrop of rocks and steered it into a sheltered cove.

'I don't follow your reasoning,' she said awkwardly,

looking at him wide-eyed. 'How can you care about me the way you say you do, if you're still seeing Shannon?'

His mouth flattened. 'Shannon is just a friend,' he said. 'I couldn't explain the situation before because she wanted to keep everything under wraps. The truth is, she's in love with someone her father doesn't approve of—he decided some time ago that he was a fortune hunter and did everything he could to break up the relationship. Of course, that was totally the wrong thing to do because it just encouraged them to have more clandestine meetings. Personally, I think the man she's chosen is okay. He cares about Shannon and wants the best for her.'

He parked the buggy by the foot of a cliff. 'Shannon was upset because her boyfriend was becoming wary of what her father might do—he'd threatened to cut her out of his life. So the boyfriend was thinking of going away because he didn't want her life to be ruined because of him. I was at the hotel that night when he'd tried to break it off with her, and she confided in me. We left the hotel separately, but the press had wind she was there and caught both of us on camera. They put two and two together and came up with five.'

'And now? After all, that was some time ago, wasn't it?' Katie looked at him doubtfully.

'Now she's trying to gain command of her life once more. She's made up her mind to go ahead and marry the man she fell in love with.' He gave a wry smile. 'To be honest, I don't think her father will cut her off. He loves her too much for that.'

'Oh, I see.' Katie's green eyes were troubled.

'I hope you do,' he said. 'But either way I'm glad you came to see me. Was there something special, or was it just because you couldn't stay away?' He grinned. 'I hope it was the last one.'

She pressed her lips together, still anxious. Even though he had put her mind at rest over Shannon, there was still a huge hurdle to face. She had to know what was on his mind when he spoke to Toby.

'I wanted to talk to you this morning,' she said, 'but I couldn't get through to your mobile.'

He nodded. 'I was swamped at work. We were inundated.'

'Yes, of course, I should have known.' She frowned. 'Is there any more news about Sarah?'

'They gave her a transfusion this morning and they're waiting to see if she perks up. From what the nurse said, she seems to be improving.' He paused for a moment. 'I think the doctors were worried about the cause of the anaemia initially, but now that the test results are back it appears it's as we thought. In time, she'll start to recover naturally. They say she just needs supportive care at the moment...rest, fresh air, a balanced diet.'

Katie let out a slow breath. 'That's good to know.'

'It is...and another snippet of good news is that I think Natasha and Greg will be getting back together. They were always well suited—it was just that their money worries took over once Sarah came along. The fact that she's ill has brought them close to one another again.'

'I'm glad for them...and it's good to know that Sarah will have her father back with her.'

'Yes. It's always good when families are reunited. Which applies to the Delaneys, too, by the way. They moved Maria out of Intensive Care this afternoon. Apparently, her sister went to see her and they were able to talk for a while.'

'Oh, that's brilliant news.' Her face broke into a smile. 'That's been weighing on my mind for some time.'

'A lot of things seem to have been weighing you down lately.' He lifted a hand and gently stroked her face. 'Like this business of the vineyard. You're not happy about how it has affected Tom and Natasha, are you? I know things have been difficult between you.' His hand was warm against her cheek and she revelled in his comforting touch.

'It's worrying me,' she admitted. 'Though at least Tom and Natasha seem to have forgiven me. But I know they're going to have heavy burdens on their shoulders for some time to come, and I can't help feeling I might have done something to help them avoid that situation.'

'You still could.' He fingered the silky strands of her hair. 'If you let me help you.'

Her gaze meshed with his. 'Sell to you, you mean? I won't do that, Nick. I'm sorry. I made up my mind.'

'I know. I meant you could buy them out.'

She shook her head. 'How could I do that? I just don't have the means.'

'You could...' he paused to drop a kiss gently on her mouth, catching her off guard and setting off a flurry of warm sensation to fizz inside her '...if you'd allow me to lend you the money.'

She stared up at him, open-mouthed. 'But...but why would you want to do that?'

'Because I care about you.' He gazed down at the pink fullness of her lips. 'Because I want you to be happy. Because it's in my power to do it.'

Katie was shocked, thrown completely off balance by the enormity of his gesture. So this was his plan? To help her to keep the land that meant so much to his family? Words failed her, and her head was swimming with all kinds of thoughts, all of them leading to nowhere but utter confusion.

'I need to think about this,' she said huskily. 'I don't know why you're saying this to me. I never dreamed...'

She suddenly needed to escape the confines of the buggy. She slid down onto the sand and stared about her for a second or two, her mind in a daze. What he was suggesting was something she had never even contemplated...but why would he do such a thing?

He came to stand beside her, his arms folding her to him, his body close to hers, so close that it was all she could do not to cling to him and bask in the heady comfort of his warm embrace.

'What you're suggesting is incredibly generous,'

she said huskily, her words muffled against the velvet column of his throat, 'but I don't see how I could accept. There's such a huge sum of money involved and I've no way of knowing if I could pay you back in the short or the long term. But thank you... I'm overwhelmed that you would even make the offer.'

The palm of his hand drifted lightly over the gentle curve of her spine, stroking her as though he would memorise every line, shifting to caress the rounded swell of her hip.

'You don't need to worry about any of that,' he murmured. 'It doesn't matter to me. All that matters is that you're happy and free from worry.' He gazed down at her. 'I don't know how it happened, Katie, but I've fallen for you big time. I'm completely out of my depth for the first time in my life and there's nothing I can do about it but accept it. I realised that some time ago. I love you... I need you... But most of all I want to make sure that you're safe and secure.'

The breath caught in her throat. 'I never imagined you would ever say that to me. I wanted it so much, but there was always this doubt at the back of my mind. I was scared. I'm still scared. I tried so hard not to love you because I was so sure I would be hurt...but it happened all the same, and now I'm... overwhelmed...elated...over the moon...' She closed her eyes briefly and absorbed the moment. 'I love you, Nick.'

He let out a ragged sigh and stooped to kiss her, exploring her lips with tender passion, sparking a trail of fire that flamed in every part of her being.

'Then nothing else matters,' he said softly, his voice rough edged as he came up for air. 'I'll always be here for you, Katie. You just have to learn to trust in me. I'll never hurt you, I promise you. You're part of me now. You've found your way into my heart, and we're bound together for all time.'

He darted kisses over her cheek, her throat, the bare curve of her shoulder. 'Will you marry me, Katie? Please say that you'll be my wife.' His expression was intent, his eyes as dark as the ocean on a stormy day, and she realised that he was holding his breath, waiting for her answer.

'Yes… Oh, yes… I will,' she said in a soft whisper, gazing up at him, her heart filled with joy. She reached up to lightly stroke his face. She kissed him, running her hands along his arms, his back, wanting him, desperate to have him hold her closer, and he obliged, drawing her against him, moulding his thighs to hers and pressuring her into the safe haven of the cliff side.

'I want you so much,' he murmured, his voice husky with emotion. 'I can't get enough of you, Katie. You're everything I could ever want in a woman…so gentle, thoughtful, so considerate of everyone around you.' His mouth indented in a smile. 'When I saw you with young Sarah, holding her in such a worried fashion, I thought there was the woman I would want to be the mother of my children. You're the only one for me, Katie. I love you so much.'

She gave a sigh of contentment, her fingers roaming lightly over his chest. 'I'd like to have your children some day,' she murmured. Her gaze softened as she looked up at him. 'Of course, if we should be lucky that way, you know what it will mean, don't you?'

He shook his head and clasped her hand lightly, kissing her fingertips as though he would confirm his love for her with each tender kiss. 'That we'll face the future together as a family, come what may?'

'As a family,' she echoed. 'The Bellini family. And the name will go on through the generations, just as you wanted. Our vineyards would be linked under the same name as they were once before.'

'I hadn't thought of that,' he said. 'But, of course, it's true.' He smiled. 'It sounds like a perfect solution to me.' He wrapped his arms more firmly about her, and then he hugged her close and kissed her passionately, thoroughly, until her senses whirled and she was lost in a thrilling world of heady delight.

'I feel as though I've drunk too much wine,' she murmured contentedly. 'I feel as though my head is spinning and I'm so full up of happiness that I'm brimming over with it. Everything is turning out to be just perfect...you and me, and the solution to my brother and sister's worries. I never imagined things could turn out like this.'

'I'm glad you feel that way. I want to smooth out every glitch and make things perfect for you.' He laughed softly, running his hands over her as though to make sure she was really there, that he wasn't dreaming.

'I love you, Nick…only you. There's no other man I want in my life.'

He breathed a long sigh of relief. 'That's good. Because I really, really love you, Katie'

He bent his head and kissed her once more, and Katie clung to him and kissed him in return, loving him, loving the feel of him and wanting nothing more than to be with him for all time. For now she realised he was a man she could trust, a man who would be there for her always.It had taken her a long while to let down her guard, and finally she understood that he wasn't like other men. He would keep his promise to her, she could feel it in every part of her being, and she knew that she could look forward to a love that would last for ever.

She settled into his arms, kissing him tenderly, an ache of desire burning like a flame inside her. Why had she waited so long?

MIDWIFE,
MOTHER…
ITALIAN'S WIFE

BY
FIONA McARTHUR

First published in Great Britain 2011
Harlequin Mills & Boon Limited,
Eton House, 18-24 Paradise Road, Richmond, Surrey TW9 1SR

© Fiona McArthur 2011

ISBN: 978 0 263 88577 4

Harlequin Mills & Boon policy is to use papers that are natural, renewable and recyclable products and made from wood grown in sustainable forests. The logging and manufacturing process conform to the legal environmental regulations of the country of origin.

Printed and bound in Spain
by Litografia Rosés, S.A., Barcelona

Dear Reader

Tammy was never going to be anyone's wife. Wife meant 'love for ever', and she didn't believe in for ever, and then there was that 'obey' word. She'd always had issues with authority. Plus she had her son—the only man she needed in her life.

Then she met Leonardo Bonmarito—tall, gorgeous, a brooding Italian doctor who was never going to settle in Lyrebird Lake, and who would never allow her the freedom she thrived on. And his son placed her own in danger. So what was she doing with her hands inside his shirt?

It makes you wonder if there's anything the magical Lyrebird Lake can do for these two strong and proud people who don't know how to let go of the past.

I adored this book. There's a bit of intrigue, a bit of action, the joy of birth, and of course a love story. I loved Tammy, I loved Leon, and I loved the boys—and they all made me smile down to my toes when they interacted with each other.

While this book stands alone, I hope you enjoy your return to the setting of Lyrebird Lake, which has become a very special place for me, and that Tammy and Leon's story warms you too.

I wish you happy reading.

Fiona

A mother to five sons, **Fiona McArthur** is an Australian midwife who loves to write. Medical™ Romance gives Fiona the scope to write about all the wonderful aspects of adventure, romance, medicine and midwifery that she feels so passionate about—as well as an excuse to travel! Now that her boys are older, Fiona and her husband Ian are off to meet new people, see new places, and have wonderful adventures. Fiona's website is at www.fionamcarthur.com

Recent titles by the same author:

MIDWIFE IN THE FAMILY WAY*
THE MIDWIFE AND THE MILLIONAIRE
MIDWIFE IN A MILLION
PREGNANT MIDWIFE: FATHER NEEDED*
THE MIDWIFE'S NEW-FOUND FAMILY*

Lyrebird Lake Maternity

Dedication:

*For Rosie and Carol, my fabulous friends,
who put up with those phone calls when I'm stuck.*

CHAPTER ONE

As a reluctant best man, Leonardo Durante Bonmarito caught the unashamed adoration on the groom's face as he circled the room with his new bride, and knew his own earlier arrival in Australia would have made no difference.

Leon's intention of stopping this wedding had faltered at the first sight of Gianni at the airport because nothing would have prevented his brother from marrying this woman.

Such happiness made Leon's chest hurt and he'd never liked wedding feasts. It was even harder when he felt insulated from the joy and gaiety around him by the fact he still hadn't had a chance to talk to Gianni properly since arriving.

'Not a big fan of weddings?' The words were mild enough but the tone held a hint of quiet rebuke. Tammy Moore, chief bridesmaid and for tonight his partner, spoke at his shoulder and Leon returned to the present with a jolt. She went on, 'We're supposed to join them on the floor now.'

'*Sì*. Of course. My apologies.' Automatically he

glanced around and down and unexpectedly his vision was filled with the delightful valley between her breasts.

He swept his eyes upwards and her dark brows tilted at the flicker of a smile he couldn't help.

It was a problem but what was a man to do with a bodice just under eye level? It would be strange dancing with a woman willow-slim in body and almost as tall as himself. She felt twice the height of his late wife.

He wondered if others might think they looked good together. Little did observers know their rapport had been anything but cordial, because he feared he hadn't endeared himself to her.

Leon repressed a sigh. He'd barely talked, in fact, it seemed he'd forgotten how to be at ease with a young woman, but in his defence, his mind had been torn between the recent danger to Paulo and when he could discuss it with his brother.

Tammy tapped her foot with the music, surely not with impatience, as she waited for them to join the bride and groom on the floor and he'd best concentrate. He hoped it would not be too much of a disaster because his heart wasn't in it. 'You are very good to remind me,' he said by way of apology, but she didn't comment, just held out one slender hand for him to take so the guests could join in after the official party was on the floor.

The music wheezed around them with great gusto if not great skill, like a jolly asthmatic between inhaler puffs, and Leon took her fingers in his and held them. Her hand lay small and slim, and somehow vulnerable, in his clasp, and suddenly he wasn't thinking of much except the way she unexpectedly fitted perfectly into his arms, her small breasts soft against his chest, and her hair smooth against his face.

In fact, her hip swung against his in seamless timing as if they'd danced together to a breathless piano accordion since birth.

Such precision and magical cadence took him from this place—and his swirling, painful thoughts—to a strange mist of curative tranquillity he'd craved since not just yesterday but from the haze of time in his youth.

Where was the awkwardness that'd always seemed to dog him and his late wife whenever they'd danced? The concept deepened the guilt in his heart and also the frown across his brows.

'You sway like a reed in my arms.' He tilted his head in reluctant approval. 'You must dance often.'

He thought he heard, 'Nearly as often as you frown, you great thundercloud.' The unexpected words were quiet, spoken to his feet, and he must have heard wrong because she followed that with, 'Yes, we love dancing here.'

He decided he was mistaken, but the humility in her expression had a certain facade of mock innocence, and made his suspicions deepen with amused insight. Then he caught his son's eye as they swept past, and Leon raised his eyebrows at the flower girl standing beside him.

Paulo glanced at the young girl and then back at his father, nodded and took her hand to lead her into the dance. Tammy followed his gaze and smiled stiffly, something, he realised guiltily, she'd been doing for a couple of hours now.

She slanted a glance at him. 'Does your son dance as well as his father?'

They both turned their heads to watch the children waltz and Leon felt the warmth of pride. Paulo did well and it had not been an easy few days for him. 'I hope so. He has been taught. A man must be able to lead.'

'Emma's daughter can hold her own,' she murmured, and he bent his head closer to catch her words. Did the woman talk to him or to herself? An elusive scent, perfectly heated by the satin skin of her ridiculously long neck, curled around his senses with an unexpectedly potent assault. Without thought he closed his eyes and inhaled more deeply. This scent was a siren's weapon, yet she portrayed none of the siren's tricks.

He realised with delay that she'd continued the conversation. 'We have a bring-a-plate country dance once a month in the old hall. The children enjoy it as much as the adults.'

Leon eased back, he hoped unobtrusively, to clear the opulent fog from his mind but his voice came out deeper than he expected—deeper, lower, almost a caress. 'So dance nights are common in Australia?' What was happening? His brain seemed to have slowed to half speed as if he'd been drugged. Perhaps she did have tricks he was unaware of.

He lifted his head higher and sought out his son. The most important reason he needed his wits about him. Whatever spell she'd cast over him, he did not want it.

No doubt she'd sensed the change in him. He could only hope he'd left her as confused as she'd left him. 'To hold a dance is not unusual in a country town.' Her dark brows drew together in a glower such as she'd accused him of.

'Of course.' Thankfully, this time, his voice emerged normally, though he wondered if she could hear the ironic twist under the words. 'My brother is full of the virtues of your Lyrebird Lake.' And its incredibly fertile qualities, but he wouldn't go there.

She lifted her chin high and stared into his eyes as if suspicious of his tone and the implication he might disparage her hometown. Her irises were a startling blue and reminded him of the glorious sea on the Amalfi Coast, disturbingly attractive, yet with little waves of tempest not quite concealed and a danger that could not be underestimated. He knew all about that.

She went on in that confident voice of hers that managed to raise the dominant side of him like hairs on his neck. 'Lyrebird Lake has everything I need,' she stated, almost a dare to contradict.

He bit back the bitter laugh he felt churn in his chest. A fortunate woman. 'To have everything you want is a rarity. You are to be congratulated. Even if it seems a little unrealistic for such a young woman with no husband.'

Tammy smiled between gritted teeth. This man had created havoc in her usual calm state since the first moment she'd seen him. Too tall, too darkly handsome with sensually heavy features and so arrogant, so sure of his international power. Fancifully she'd decided he'd surveyed them all as if they were bush flies under an empty Vegemite jar.

One more dance and she was done. She felt like tapping her foot impatiently as she waited for the music to start again now the guests and not just the wedding party filled the floor.

It had been as if he'd barely got time for this frivolity of weddings, such an imposition to him, but she'd stayed civil because of Emma, and Gianni, obviously the much nicer brother of the two. But soon this last dance would be over, then everyone else would not notice her slip away. The official responsibilities she'd held would be complete apart from helping the bride to change.

No more being nice to Leonardo Bonmarito.

Though Tammy did feel sorry for Paulo Bonmarito, a handsome but quiet and no doubt downtrodden child, and she'd asked her own son to look after him. Nobody could call her Jack downtrodden.

As if conjured by the thought, eight-year-old Jack Moore, another young man resplendent in his miniature wedding tuxedo, walked up to Paulo. They looked almost like brothers, both dark-haired, olive-skinned boys with the occasional awkwardness of prepubescence. Then Jack tapped the young Italian boy on the shoulder as he and Grace waited to begin again. 'My dance now, I think.'

That wasn't what she'd envisaged when she'd said watch out for Paulo. Leon's back was to the children and Tammy frowned as she strained to hear as they stood waiting.

'You said you weren't dancing,' she heard Grace say, and the girl looked unimpressed with swapping for a boy she always danced with.

Jack shrugged as he waited for Paulo to relinquish his partner. 'Changed my mind.'

Without looking at Jack, Paulo bowed over Grace's hand, kissed her fingers in the continental way with practised ease and shrugged. *'Non importo. Grazie,'* he said, and turned with head high and walked away.

The music started and the dance floor shifted like a sleepy animal awakening. Leon's son leaned with seeming nonchalance against a flower-decked pole and watched Grace being swung around easily by Jack. Like his father, his face remained expressionless and Tammy wondered if Paulo was used to disappointment.

When the dance was over, Tammy eased her hand out of Leon's firm grip as unobtrusively as she could and stepped back. She only just prevented herself from wiping her hand down the side of her bridesmaid dress to try and diffuse the stupid buzz of connection she could still feel.

The contact hadn't been what she expected and the

dancing had increased her need to distance herself from this haughty stranger even more. It had been ridiculous the way they'd danced together as if they'd spent years, not seconds, training to synchronise. Not a common occurrence with her local partners but maybe she was imagining it just because he was taller and stronger, and decidedly more masterful, than most men she danced with.

Or maybe the strength of her disquiet about him had made her more aware. Either way she wasn't interested and needed to get away from him to her friends.

'Thank you.' She didn't meet his eyes and instead glanced around at the crowded dance floor. 'Everyone seems to be up now. If you'll excuse me?'

Leon raised one sardonic eyebrow at her apparent haste. 'You have somewhere you need to run off to?'

She opened her mouth to fabricate an excuse when the glowing bride, her best friend, Emma, dragged her smiling new husband across to his brother. 'Tammy! You and Leon dance wonderfully together.' She beamed at her husband, and the look that passed between them made Tammy glance away with a twist of ridiculous wistfulness.

'Almost as good as us,' Emma went on. 'Isn't my wedding beautiful?'

'Truly magnificent,' Leon said, and glanced at Gianni. 'Your organisational skills exceed even what I expected.'

'Nothing is too perfect for my wife.' Gianni, tall

and solid like his brother, stroked Emma's cheek, and then looked across at Tammy. He smiled. 'And your partner for tonight?' He kissed his fingers. '*Bellissimo*. You, too, are blessed, brother. Tammy is another of the midwives here. Has she told you?'

'We've had little time for discussion.' Leon leaned forward and unexpectedly took Tammy's hand in his large one again. He held it firmly and the wicked glint in his eyes when he looked at her said he knew she wouldn't quibble in front of her friend. 'I was just going to find us a drink and sit down for a chat.'

Dear Emma looked so delighted Tammy didn't have the heart to snatch her fingers free, so she smiled, ignored the restart of the buzz in her fingers and wondered bitterly if her teeth would ache tonight from all the clenching she'd done today.

The music started and Gianni held out his hand to his wife. Emma nodded. 'I'll see you back at the bridal table, Tammy, after this dance. I want to tell you something.' Then Emma smiled blithely at them, sighed into her husband's arms and danced away.

Tammy looked around for escape but there was none. Trapped by her friend. Great. Leon held firmly on to her hand and steered her off the floor towards the official table. Unobtrusively Tammy tugged at her fingers and finally he let her hand free. She leaned towards him with a grim smile and, barely moving her lips, let him have it. 'Don't ever do that again or you will get more than you bargained for.'

'Tut. Temper.' He glanced down at her, amused

rather than chastened by her warning, which made her more cross.

She grimaced a smile again and muttered, 'You have no idea,' as he pulled her chair out. She slipped into the chair and shifted it slightly so that it faced towards the dance floor and her shoulder tilted away from him.

When he returned with two tiny champagne flutes Leon was fairly sure she didn't realise the angle she gave him lent a delightful view of her long neck and the cleft below the hollow of her throat...and there was that incredible drift of scent again.

He controlled his urge to move closer. This woman had invaded his senses on many unexpected levels and here he was toying with games he hadn't played since his amorous youth.

'Drink your wine,' he said.

She turned to him and her eyes narrowed blue fire at him. 'Were you born this arrogant or did you grow into it?'

So, her temper remained unimproved. She amused him. He shrugged and baited her. 'Bonmaritos have been in Portofino for six generations. My family are very wealthy.'

She lifted one elegant shoulder in imitation. 'Big deal. So were mine and my childhood was less than ideal.'

'And you are not arrogant?' To his surprise she looked at him and then smiled at his comment. And then to his utter astonishment she threw back her head and laughed. A throaty chortle that had his own mouth curve in appreciation.

Her whole face had softened. 'Actually, I've been told I am.'

When she laughed she changed from being a very attractive but moody woman into a delightful seductress he could not take his eyes off, and when she shuffled her chair back and studied him for a change, he felt the shift in their rapport like a fresh breeze. A dangerous, whimsical, warning breeze that he should flee from.

He shifted closer. 'So tell me, Tammy, is this your full name?'

'Tamara Delilah Moore, but nobody calls me that.'

'Delilah I believe. Tamara?' He rolled the name off his tongue as if sampling it, found the taste delightful and he nodded. That suited her better. 'There was a famous noblewoman called Tamara in Roman mythology. She, too, was tall and apparently rather arrogant. How ironic.'

'Really?' She raised those stern eyebrows of hers and Leon realised he liked the way she responded fearlessly to his bait. 'What if I say you're making that up?'

The music lilted around them playfully and helped the mood stay light. 'I would have to defend myself.'

She glanced down at her hands and spread them to look at her fingertips as if absorbed in her French manicure. He almost missed her comment. 'You nearly had to defend yourself in a more physical way earlier.'

So. More fire. He straightened and met her eyes with a challenge. 'I had the utmost faith in your control. You'd exhibited control all day. It's a wonder your teeth aren't aching.'

She blinked, glanced at him with an arrested expression and then laughed again. He felt the smile on his face. A deeper more genuine smile than he'd had for a long time. It felt surprisingly good to make her laugh.

Not something he'd been known for much in the past but her amusement warmed him in a place that had been cold for too long. 'Of course I also have a slight weight advantage.'

'And I have a black belt in karate.' She picked up one of the biscotti favours from a plate on the table and unconsciously broke a piece off, weighing it in her hand before putting it to her mouth. That curved and perfect mouth he'd been trying not to look at for the past ten minutes.

Karate. He searched for an image of sweating women in tracksuits he could call to mind, or the name of the white pyjamalike uniform people wore for martial arts, anything to take his mind off the sight of her lips parting as she absently turned him on.

'How long are you staying before you head back to Italy?' she said carelessly as she raised the biscuit shard. His gaze followed her fingers, drawn by invisible fields of magnetism and, unconsciously, he held his breath. Gi. The uniform was called gi.

Her lips opened and she slid the fragment in and licked the tips of her fingers, oblivious to his fascinated attention as she glanced at the dancers. His breath eased out and his body stirred and stretched in a way it hadn't in a long time.

Then she glanced back at him and he had to gather his scattered wits. When was he leaving? Perhaps sooner than he intended if this was how tempted he'd already become. 'Gianni and Emma are away for the first few days of their honeymoon, and then Paulo and I will join them at the airport before we all return to Italy.' He was rambling.

He focused on the plans he'd finalised before he left for Italy. 'We were held up.' He paused. His grip tightened unconsciously on the glass in his hand and he looked away from her—that brought him back to earth. There was no time for this when the real world required constant and alert attention.

He shook his head and went on. 'We were held up on the way over and arrived later than expected. It will give Paulo a few days to get over the "excitement" before we have to return.' She nodded.

Jack appeared at her side and tugged on her dress. 'Excuse me, Mum. Can we go and play spotlight?'

Tammy looked away from this suddenly much more attractive man to her son and the world started again. What was she thinking? She blinked again to clear her head and swallowed the last of the biscuit.

'Who with?' she asked Jack, and looked beyond him to the milling group of young boys and girls.

'Dawn and Grace, and Peta and Nicky. And some of the older kids as well.' He glanced at Leon. 'And Paulo if he wants to?'

Leon frowned and looked across to where his son was talking to Grace and another girl. 'What is this "spotlight"?'

Tammy shrugged. 'Hide-and-seek in the dark and the seeker has a handheld torch or spotlight. The children play it all the time here when parties like this stretch into evening.'

Leon's frown didn't lighten. 'Even young girls? Without parents supervising?'

'They won't go far.' She looked at Paulo, who pretended he didn't expect his father to say no. 'Let him go. He'll be fine.'

Leon hesitated, and she wondered if he'd been this protective since the boy's mother had died. Overprotecting children made her impatient but she held her tongue, if not her expression, and then finally he nodded.

'Perhaps for a short while.' He tilted his head at his son and Paulo approached them. He spoke in Italian and Tammy looked away but she couldn't help overhearing.

She had no trouble interpreting Leon's discussion with his son. She'd been able to speak Italian since her teenage years in a dingy Italian coffee shop in Sydney, dark with dangerous men and a tall Italian youth she hadn't seen since but wasn't allowed to forget. Those memories reminded her why she wasn't attracted to Leonardo Bonmarito.

'Do you wish to play this game?' Leon said to his son.

'*Sì,*' said Paulo, and he looked away to the other children.

'Be aware of your safety,' Leon continued in his native language, and Tammy frowned at the tablecloth in front of her. It seemed a strange thing to say at his brother's wedding in a country town.

'*Sì, Padre,* of course,' Paulo said again, and when his father nodded he ran off to join the children. Tammy hoped she wiped the expression from her face before she glanced back at Leon. Listening to Leon talk to his son brought back many memories and it had surprised her how easily she slipped back into recognising the words.

'Your son has beautiful manners. Is he allowed to play with other children much?'

It was her turn to be frowned on. 'Of course.' No doubt she'd offended him. Oops, she thought without remorse.

Leon went on in a low, steely voice that made her eyebrows rise. 'He attends school. And your Jack? He appears very confident.' His eyes travelled over her. 'Like his mother.'

She shrugged. Tough if he had a problem with that. 'There's only been Jack and me together, although my father and my stepmother have always been very much a part of his life since he was born. They live next door.'

She saw his gaze drift to his brother and the planes of his angular face softened as he nodded. 'Family is important. Especially when one's family is smaller than God intended.'

There seemed a story there. She wasn't quite sure what he was getting at. Did he have plans to enlarge his family? Was he here to convince his brother to take his wife back to Italy for good? Perhaps it would be better to know one's enemy, as good as an excuse as any for plain old nosiness, but she had to admit to herself he intrigued her. 'So, both your parents are gone?'

'*Sì*.' Reluctance in the answer. 'They died when we were young.'

She should stop the questions, but maybe now a silence would be even more awkward, or that's what she told herself as she asked the next. 'To lose a parent is hard, to lose both would be devastating. Especially as I believe you are the eldest of the two of you?'

He shrugged and his voice had cooled. 'By four years. It was my responsibility to be the head of the family.'

At how old? she wondered. 'No other relatives to look after you?'

He answered almost absently as his attention was distracted by the calls and laughter of the children. 'An elderly widowed aunt who has since passed away.' He frowned again as Paulo ducked with a grin behind a dark bush.

He really did have issues with Paulo playing with

the other children, Tammy decided. 'And Emma says you lost your wife last year?'

His gaze snapped back to her and this time he raised haughty brows at her. *'Molto curioso,'* he said.

Yes, she couldn't deny she was curious. She looked at him blandly as if she had no idea what he said, until he inclined his head and continued on a different topic. 'It is good to see Paulo with a smile on his face. They have been too rare in the past year.'

The pang of sympathy for both of them reminded her of the past as well. 'And now your own son has lost his mother. It's hard to lose your mother.'

Now that brought back memories she'd rather forget but felt obliged to share as she'd been so nosy. 'Even difficult mothers. I was fifteen when I lost mine. Went to live with my mother's mother.' She laughed with little amusement. 'Who said my living there made her feel too old. Such a silly woman.'

'Perhaps it is my turn to be curious?' It seemed Leon waited for her to enlarge on the topic. Not a hope in Hades.

She said the first thing she could think of to avoid a discussion of her ridiculous past. 'Would you like to dance again?' She discovered as she waited for his answer the idea held definite appeal.

His mouth tilted and she knew he was aware of her sudden change of subject. 'I would like that very much.'

The palpitations came out of nowhere. Just started to thump in her chest as he stood—and from where she sat he filled her vision; he truly was magnificent—then drew her up, with that strong hand of his closing on hers. She felt weightless, like a feather, and a little airy like a feather too, which wasn't like her as she drifted across to the floor where the piano accordion was valiantly attempting to play a waltz.

It was okay to enjoy a dance. With a skilled partner. Nothing wrong with that. His arms came around her and she closed her eyes, giving in to the moment for once, not fighting the magic that had surprised her earlier in the evening. This was what dancing was for. She just hadn't realised she'd been searching for the right partner.

CHAPTER TWO

TAMMY missed the moment when the music stopped until Leon's arm drifted down her back to her hip and he angled her towards the bridal table. The tiny, secret smile on her face fell away with her trance. How embarrassing.

His fingers were warm on her skin through the thin material of her bridesmaid dress as he led her back to her chair.

Both of them were silent. And that serves me right for letting my guard down, Tammy thought, as she tried to think of something to say that would dispel the myth she'd been lost in his arms.

In the end she was saved by the bride. 'You two seem to be getting along *very* well.' A glowing Emma grinned at them as she and Gianni approached the table. When her husband held her chair for her Emma sank thankfully down and fanned her face. She looked from one to the other but neither spoke.

Leon murmured his thanks as he lifted his hand in a 'spare me a moment' gesture to his brother. Then he slanted a glance at Tammy, his face serious as he caught her eye, before he and his brother walked off just a few paces.

Tammy saw Leon's glance flick to the boys as they disappeared around the corner of the building but her attention was brought back to the table by Emma's excitement. 'The dancing is such fun.' Emma waved her hand some more as she tried to stir the warm air. 'Did you have a good chat with Leon before the dance? I wondered if you'd find much to talk about.'

'We talked about the boys,' Tammy said, and then she heard Leon ask Gianni, in Italian, if he thought the spotlight game was safe enough. He was back to that.

Tammy strained her ears for Gianni's answer, his affirmative clear, but then something Leon said very quietly made Gianni stop suddenly and stare and the two men moved further out of earshot, both bristling, and she had the sudden ridiculous thought that they were like a pair of wolves hunting in the night.

The darkness of a black shadow ran icy fingers over her neck and she shook the feeling off mostly because she didn't do premonitions, and secondly because it wasn't a happy wedding-day vibration at all and a far cry from the heady bubble of the dance floor.

She turned to Emma and worked to dispel the unease that lingered despite her efforts to banish it. 'So what were you so anxious to tell me that I had to sit beside your brother-in-law and wait with bated breath?'

'Poor you. Was he such a hardship?' Emma teased.

Tammy glanced towards the spot where the men had disappeared. 'It's been a long day,' she said cryptically, 'but perhaps he might not be as bad as I thought.'

Emma's brows crinkled. 'Good.' Though now there was a trace of doubt in her voice. 'Because I want everyone to get on well.' Emma looked for the men too, and back at Tammy. Then all the excitement caught up with her again and Tammy vowed to be more careful not to blemish her friend's day.

'My news?' She smiled happily. 'Well, first Leon's talking to your father about some project in Rome so he and Paulo are not flying back immediately.'

Tammy knew that, and didn't see much there to be excited about. She didn't like the uncomfortable feeling the man left her with.

Emma bubbled on. 'So Leon and Paulo are staying here until after we come back from our mini honeymoon and then we're going to Italy for a month's holiday. Gianni asked if in a couple of weeks you and Jack might like to come over and be with me while he has to sort out work commitments with his brother.'

Tammy raised her eyebrows and her friend went on. 'So Grace and I won't get bored?' Emma looked at her expectantly. 'What do you think?'

What did she think? That this was the last thing she'd expected. Did she want to go to Italy? While she could admit Emma's new husband had turned out to be a delightful and doting husband, initially she hadn't been overly impressed with his brother.

And now it was more the effect he had on her that had her squirming to find a matching excitement her friend would like. 'I guess I'd have to think about it. See if Montana has enough staff to cover at the birth centre, work out which of my birthing women are due.'

She shook her head. 'Take Jack overseas? I don't know.' To Italy of all places.

Emma nodded her understanding. 'Think about it. Oh, and I gave Leon your mobile number. Hope you don't mind. In case we're out of range and he needs something.' Emma seemed to think it was no great moment. She was still focused on the Italian trip. 'It's just an idea but I love the sound of both of us in Italy.'

Tammy could see she did. And normally she'd like the idea too. Overseas travel was something she'd done a lot of in her early teens with her parents and she'd been to Italy once. Maybe that had been the start of her attraction to Italians. She tried not to think of him having her number and then decided he didn't look like a stalker. He only had a few days to stalk anyway.

The men came back, both faces too angled and sombre for a wedding feast, though Gianni smiled at his wife when he reached her side. He held out his hand. 'Do you still wish to circulate through the guests, *cara*? I believe a few of the older guests are starting to leave.'

Emma allowed herself to be drawn up and against her husband's chest for a brief hug, as if the two of them had spent a day apart and not a few minutes, and Tammy couldn't help but wonder if she'd ever have such a love as that. She damped down the almost irresistible urge to sneak a glance at Leon's face to see what he was thinking. When she did he was looking at her and for some bizarre reason her face flamed.

Thankfully, her friend seemed oblivious to Tammy's own embarrassment as she stepped, pink-cheeked, back out of her husband's arms. 'I haven't spent much time with Louisa. Shall we see her before she goes?'

'Indeed.' Gianni smiled warmly. 'I will inquire if she thinks my brother can be as excellent a guest as when I stayed with her.'

They walked away and Leon sat down. She saw him again seek the boys out in the shadows. 'Everything okay?' Tammy searched his face but the mask he'd arrived with earlier in the day was firmly back in place. She could read nothing and it irritated her for no good reason.

He inclined his head. 'Of course.'

'So you and Paulo have settled into the old doctor's residence with Louisa for a few days?'

'She has made us very welcome.' This time he did smile and the sudden warmth in his eyes did strange, unsettling things to her stomach. Things she hadn't had a problem with for nearly ten years. Maybe she was hungry. Though that seemed unlikely as the wedding feast had more choices than a country fete.

The thought came out of nowhere. What would he be like to kiss? Her belly twisted. Great, she'd bet. He had amazing lips, like sculptured marble on a work of art. Good grief. She checked out her nails again, to hide her eyes.

He went on. 'Paulo has never had so many affectionate embraces and we have only been there since last night.'

'Louisa loves a cuddle.' It was amazing she could carry on a conversation and be so focused on his mouth. She risked a glance. 'She's a recent widow.' Yep, they still looked good.

Leon concentrated on Louisa, whom he could see behind the dancers, the little woman who'd made his son so welcome, and thankfully the tension eased. He wasn't sure where it came from but he'd felt the sudden rise between them. 'My brother told me of her loss. And that is why he asked we stay there. It is no hardship.'

He kept his eyes on his brother and his wife across the floor. In fact, even this wedding had become no hardship. It was surprising how resigned he'd become to his brother's fate. And in a few short hours, partly because no one could doubt the true bond between the newlyweds, and partly because all of the people he'd met here tonight had exuded such warmth and generosity towards him and his son.

Except this woman.

The thought made him smile for some reason, as

if the challenge for supremacy between them had taken on a new urgency. He fought the errant concept away. No. Perhaps it had been too long since he had set aside time to share intimacy with a woman. The chance of a brief liaison with this Tamara was tantalising but remote. Too much was happening.

And she would be the last to welcome him. The thought made him smile again. He'd somehow offended her, and he searched his memory for that ridiculous saying he'd heard today—he'd got up her nose. And such a delightful nose it was. He smiled again. She was not showing a warm or generous side to him at all but he perceived she had one, which in fact was lucky, because he became more intrigued every minute he spent with her.

Tammy saw him smile at the thought of Louisa. So he did have a soft spot for elderly widows. The idea dangerously thawed a little more of her reserve and she reached for another unwanted biscuit to distract her concentration from this handsome, brooding man beside her.

She felt his attention and when she glanced at him there was a sudden darkening of his eyes that arrowed that sharp sensation of hunger right back through her midsection. She felt the wave of heat between them like a furnace door opening.

'Not again,' he murmured. And then more strongly, 'If you delicately consume another biscotti I will not be responsible for my actions.' His voice was very quiet, and she realised they were alone at the table—in fact, alone at their side of the dance floor.

The children shrieked with laughter in the distance just in view, Emma and Gianni were across talking to Louisa, and suddenly she couldn't look away from him. Her stomach kicked again. She got the message.

She wasn't sure what to do now with the biscuit she didn't want, but blowed if she'd let him know he'd rocked her.

Did she look away and nonchalantly put it down or did she pull the tiger's tail? There was no choice really.

Unhurriedly, with great deliberation, Emma raised the shard of almond to her mouth. With her eyes on his she parted her lips with seductive exaggeration and slid it slowly in, and chewed. It was hard to swallow with a dry mouth but she did. Choking would have ruined the impact. To drive home her point she calmly licked the sugar from her finger. One raised eyebrow left him in no doubt of her message. *Don't dare me.*

Leon stood, took the arm that reached towards him—surely she hadn't asked her fingers to do that—and Tammy found herself whisked back into the shadows with her hand in his. In an instant she was in his arms and his body felt warm and inflexible against hers. It had all happened so fast she doubted anyone had noticed she'd been abducted.

His eyes glittered in the low light. 'You do not follow orders well, I think.' She barely heard him over the thumping in her chest as he stared down at her, and there was something primal about the tree branch casting shadows across his face. 'This night has been filled with intriguing moments. I cannot allow it to conclude without this.' He bent his dark head towards her with such intent she froze as he brushed her neck with his lips. She shivered and all the hair on her arms whooshed into an upright position on little mountains of goose flesh.

'Your scent has been driving me wild all night.' His words hummed against her ear and thrummed down her throat as his lips travelled the sensitive skin around her jaw. She'd never felt exposed and vulnerable and yet starving for more.

His mouth took flight across her cheek like a hot moth that dusted both eyes before homing in on her mouth. Every nerve in her skin seemed to lean his way for attention, drawn to the light like a kamikaze insect, and she shuddered at the delicious sensations his whispered caress invoked.

Somehow her arms had wound themselves round his neck and she could feel the sinew and muscle in his shoulders, rock hard beneath her fingers. He had the power to snap her in two and they both knew it.

Then his mouth found hers, her stomach jolted and she swayed against him suddenly weak at the knees like an old-fashioned heroine. She'd never believed this would happen to her. A swoon from a man kissing her. It was ridiculous, and crazy, and…

'It was a funny wedding,' Jack said as he drove home with his mother.

'Funny in what way?' Tammy said extremely

absently as she turned along the sweeping driveway out of the lakeside complex. When Leon had kissed her Tammy realised what she'd been missing for too many years. She'd kissed a few men, more to reassure herself she could get a man to the point, but never been enamoured enough to want to repeat the experience.

With Leonardo Bonmarito she'd wanted to do more than repeat it. She wanted next verse. Next chapter. The whole darn book and she knew where that could leave her. She prayed he hadn't realised because she'd managed to step back before she'd dragged the buttons from his shirt. But only just. So she'd stepped away further, called her son and left fairly quickly after that.

'Just different.' The childish voice beside her reminded her why she'd stepped away. 'And that kid's different too.'

'Paulo? I imagine they'd be saying the same thing about you if you turned up at a wedding in Italy.'

She glanced at Jack. Her miniature man in the house, whom she adored but had no blinkers about. 'Which reminds me, you were impolite to push into that dance with Grace and Paulo.'

He looked away from her and squirmed a little. 'She didn't want to dance with him.'

'That's not what I saw.'

Jack sniffed and avoided his mother's glance. 'She danced with him later anyway,' he muttered.

Tammy dimmed her lights for a passing car. 'I

wouldn't like to think you were rude or acting the bully to a visitor, Jack.'

'I don't like him.' More muttering.

Tammy frowned. Jealous brat. 'Even more reason to be nice to him.'

Jack sniffed again. 'Like you were nice to his father?'

Now where had that come from? Thank goodness it was dark and he couldn't see the pink flooding her neck. Little ankle biter. She certainly wasn't going there. Of course the children hadn't seen. 'Yes.' She took the easy way out. 'Did you all have fun playing spotlight?'

She caught the movement of his shoulder beside her he shrugged. 'He was scared half the time.'

The dark cloud of uneasiness slid new tendrils through her mind. Tammy glanced at her son and then back at the road. 'Why do you think he was scared?'

Jack swivelled and she could tell without turning her head that he was looking at her. 'What would you do if a man tried to kidnap me?'

Tammy blinked at the unexpected question and her hands tightened until they were almost white on the wheel. Someone take her son? Harm Jack? Threaten to kill him? 'Tear him limb from limb.' She shook the power of the unexpected passion off. Good grief, there'd been some emotional roller-coasters tonight. 'What made you ask that?'

Such a little voice from the darkness. 'He said it sometimes happens in Italy for ransom money.'

'Who? Paulo?' She'd read of it but didn't want to think about such a crime actually happening. Europe was a long way from Lyrebird Lake. 'Well, let's hope someone doesn't want to ransom you.'

Then he said it. Explained it. Let loose the cloud that turned from dark to black. 'Just before they left to come to Australia somebody tried to take Paulo. That's why they didn't get here till yesterday.'

That couldn't be true. 'What do you mean? Who did?' She slowed the car, then slowed it some more, which didn't really matter because there wasn't that much traffic around Lyrebird Lake. It would be better if she didn't run into anyone.

'They don't know. His father caught them before they could get away but they put a bag over Paulo's head and knocked him out.'

Tammy's heart thumped under her ribs and she shivered at the thought of someone attempting to steal a child. Any child. Her child.

Then she remembered how she'd been less than diplomatic about Leon's reluctance with the children's game and she winced. Every instinct urged her to turn the car around and apologise to Leon for her ill judgement. Poor Paulo, poor Leon. And the kidnappers had struck a child. 'Paulo told you this?'

Jack was losing interest. 'No, Grace did. Paulo told her.'

Good grief. No wonder Leon hadn't wanted him to play spotlight. It was amazing he'd let his son out of his sight at all. She glanced at Jack. 'If that's true, even you should understand why he was scared in spotlight.'

'I guess.' He looked at his mother. 'You'd find me, wouldn't you, Mum?'

She stretched her arm across and ruffled his hair with her fingers. The strands were fine and fragile beneath the skin of her fingertips and the sheer fragment of the concept of losing him tightened a ball of fear in her chest. 'I wouldn't rest until I did.'

Jack snuggled down in his seat. 'I thought so,' he said, and yawned loudly.

Tammy was glad to get to work the next morning. The night had been a sheet-crunching wrestle for peace that she'd only snatched moments of and this morning a rush to get a tired and cross Jack through the fence to Misty's house.

Leon Bonmarito had a lot to answer for. She'd walked straight into a birth and thankfully hadn't given the man a thought for the past three hours.

Tammy wrapped the squirming newborn infant in a fluffy white towel and tucked him under her arm like a football. Little dark eyes blinked up at her out of the swathe and one starfish hand escaped to wave at her. She tucked the tiny fingers in again and ran the water over his head as she brushed the matted curls clean. She grinned at his mother. 'I haven't seen such thick hair for a long time.'

Jennifer Ross watched with adoration as the little face squinted and frowned at the sensation in his scalp. 'He's gorgeous.' She sighed and rubbed her stomach and her son turned his head in her direction.

'Thanks for rinsing his hair for me, Tammy. I'm just not up to it.' Even in the dimly lit corner of the room where the sink nestled Tammy could see him try to focus on the familiar sound of his mother's voice.

'We'll just use water today. We'll bath Felix properly tomorrow so we don't overload his poor nose with baby bath perfume.' Tammy combed a little curl onto his forehead and smiled. 'He needs to feel secure, with your skin and his smelling the same as he remembers from inside you. It all helps with establishing breastfeeding. Like the way you waited for him to find the breast and didn't push him on for that first feed.'

'I can't believe he moved there himself.' Jen's face was soft with wonder.

'He'll do it again too. That's why it's better not to wash your own hair with shampoo the first twenty-four hours. A strong scent like shampoo has can confuse and even upset his nose during that time.'

'I'll let Ken's mum know when I ring her. She likes a heavy perfume but she's a sweetie. She'll give it a miss if I ask.' Jen reached out and touched his little hand that had escaped again. 'I remember when you told my sister only Mum and Dad should snuggle babies for the first twenty-four hours. She swears her second baby is much more settled.'

'Best practice. But sometimes it's hard to manage when everyone wants a hold.'

Jen rubbed her stomach again. 'Better to do it right. If the after pains get much worse I might not have a third one,' Jen said with a rueful smile.

'Have a lie-down. You've had a big day and there's a warm wheat pack on your bed. I'll bring Felix in when I've dressed him and check your tummy.' She cast her eye over the mum and decided she looked okay. 'Let me know if you start to bleed more heavily.'

'Thanks, I'll do that.' Jen smiled and turned gingerly with her hand holding her stomach. 'I'm looking forward to that wheat pack. Ken's so disappointed he wasn't home for the birth. And I have to ring his mother and sister as well.'

'Since when do babies wait for truck-driving daddies? Ken will just be glad you're both well. Off you go. I'll be in soon.' She narrowed her gaze as the other woman hobbled out. Tammy wished Ken could have made it too. She wanted every mother's birth to be perfect for them but sometimes babies just didn't wait.

When Ben brought Leon in to see the unit Tammy had just towelled Felix's hair dry. She was laughing down at him as she tried to capture the wriggling limbs and they'd moved to the sunny side of the room as she began to dress him. The early-afternoon sunlight dusted her dark hair with shafts of dancing light and her skin glowed.

For Leon, suddenly the day was brighter and even more interesting, although his tour of the facilities had captured his attention until now. Strangely all thoughts of bed numbers, ward structure and layout seemed lower in his priorities than watching the expressions cross this woman's face. And brought back the delightful memory of a kiss that had haunted him long into the night in his lonely bed.

'Hi, there, Tam,' Ben said as he crossed the room. Tammy looked up at her father and smiled. Then she looked at Leon and the smile fell away. He watched it fall and inexplicably the room dimmed.

'Hi, Dad. Leon.' She looked at her father. Or perhaps she was avoiding looking at him, Leon surmised, and began another mind waltz of piqued interest that this woman seemed to kick off in him. 'What are you men up to?'

'I'm showing Leon the facilities. His board's been thinking of adding maternity wards to their children's hospitals and I thought you might like to hint him towards a more woman-friendly concept.'

Leon watched the ignition of sharper concentration and the flare of captured interest. She couldn't hide the blue intensity in her eyes and silently he thanked Ben for knowing his daughter so well. So, Leon mulled to himself, he'd suddenly become a much more interesting person?

'Really?' She tossed it over her shoulder, as if only a little involved, but she couldn't fool him—he was learning to read her like a conspiracy plot in a movie, one fragmented clue at a time.

She dressed the baby with an absentminded deftness that reassured the infant so much he lay compliant under her hands. Mentally Leon nodded with approval. To handle infants a rapport was essential and he was pleased she had the knack, though it was ridiculous that such a thing should matter to him.

When the newborn was fully clothed she nestled him across her breasts and Leon had a sudden unbidden picture of her with her own child, a Madonnalike expression on her face, and a soft smile that quickened his heart. More foolishness and he shook his head at the distraction the fleeting vision had caused.

Tammy tilted her determined chin his way and Madonna faded away with a pop. 'I'll just take this little bundle into his mother and come back.'

He watched her leave the room, the boyish yet confident walk of an athletic woman, not a hint of the shrinking violet or diffident underling, and he was still watching the door when she returned. That confidence he'd first seen was there in spades. She owned the room. It seemed he activated her assertiveness mechanism. He couldn't help the smile when she returned.

She saw it and blushed. Just a little but enough to give him the satisfaction of discomfiting her and he felt a tinge of his awareness that he'd felt the need to do so.

She looked away to her father and then back at him. 'What sort of unit were you looking at?'

Enough games. 'Small. One floor of the building. Midwife run and similar to what your father has explained happens here, though with an obstetrician and paediatrician on call because we have that luxury in the city.'

He went on when her interest continued. 'It would be situated in a wing of the private children's hospital we run now. The medical personnel cover is available already, as are consulting rooms and theatres.'

She nodded as if satisfied with his motives and he felt ridiculously pleased. 'We promote natural birth here and caseload midwifery. Do the women in your demographic want that sort of service? What's your caesarean rate, because ours is the lowest in Australia.' She was defiant this morning. Raising barriers that hardened the delicate planes of her face and kept her eyes from his. He began to wonder why she, too, felt the need. *Molto curioso.*

'I'm not sure of the caesarean rate—obstetrics is not my area—but in my country most of our maternity units are more in the medical model and busy. Often so understaffed and underfinanced that the families provide most of the care for the women after birth.'

Tammy nodded and spoke to her father. 'I'd heard that. One of my friends had a baby in Rome. She said the nurses were lovely but very busy.'

He wanted her to look back at him. 'That is true of a lot of hospitals. This model would be more midwifery led for low-risk women.' He paused, deliberately, before he went on, and she did bring her gaze back his way. Satisfied, he continued. 'Of course, my new sister-in-law, Emma, is also interested and I believe there is a small chance you and your son

could come to Italy in a few weeks?' He lifted the
end of the sentence in a question. 'Perhaps the two
of you could discuss what is needed and what would
work in my country that is similar to what you have
here.'

Tammy intercepted the sudden interest from her
father and she shook her head at Ben. 'I haven't even
thought much about the chance of travelling in Italy.'
Liar. The idea had circled in her head for most of the
night. 'I won't say your idea of setting up midwife-led
units isn't exciting.' *But that's all that's exciting and
you're the main drawback.* She repeated the last part
of the sentence to herself. 'But thanks for thinking
of me.'

He shrugged those amazing shoulders of his, the
memory of which she'd felt under her hands more
than once through the night despite her attempts to
banish the weakness, and she frowned at him more
heavily.

'It is for my own benefit after all,' he said.

She remembered Jack's disclosure, and the idea
she'd had to apologise if she saw him, but it wasn't
that easy. All the time they talked, at the back of
her mind, she wanted to ask about Paulo, about the
truth in Jack's revelation, and to admit she hadn't
understood his reserve and his protectiveness. But
it didn't seem right with her father there just in case
Leon didn't wish to discuss it. Or she could just let
it go.

She owed him an apology. 'Maybe we could meet
for lunch and talk more about your idea,' she offered,

though so reluctantly it seemed as if the words were teased out of her like chewing gum stuck on a shoe. He must have thought so because there was amusement in his voice as he declined.

'Lunch, no. I'm away with your father for the rest of the day but perhaps tonight, for dinner?' His amusement was clearer. 'If I pick you up? My brother and I share a taste in fast cars and we could go for a drive somewhere to eat out.'

She did not want to drive somewhere with this guy. A car. Close confines. Him in control. 'No, thank you.' Besides. It was her invitation and her place to say where they met. 'You could come to my house, it's easier. Bring Paulo if he'd like to come and he can play with Jack.'

She had a sudden vision of her empty pantry and mentally shrugged. 'At six-thirty? I'm afraid Jack and I eat early or I can't get him to bed before nine.'

He shook his head. 'That does not suit.'

Tammy opened her eyes slow and wide at his arrogance and his inability to accept she wanted to set the pace and choose a place that would be safe.

But he went on either oblivious or determined to have his own way. 'I will come after nine. When Paulo, too, is in bed. I am away all day tomorrow and we will be able to discuss things without small ears around us.'

Tammy caught the raised eyebrows and stifled smile on her father's face and frowned. She'd never been good at taking orders. She bit back the temptation to say nine didn't suit her, but apart from being different to what she usually did, she never slept till midnight anyway.

It would be churlish to stick to her guns. This once she'd let him get away with organising but he wouldn't be making a habit of it.

She conceded, grudgingly. 'I don't normally stay up late but a leisurely after-dinner coffee could be pleasant.'

'I'll see you tonight, then.' He inclined his head and Tammy did the same while Ben looked on with a twinkle in his eye. Tammy glared at her father for good measure which only made his eyes twinkle more as they left.

Tammy could hear the suddenly vociferous new arrival in with his mother and, glad of the diversion, she hastened to the ward to help Jen snuggle Felix up to her breast. She couldn't help the glance out the ward window as the two men crossed the path to the old doctor's residence.

She'd always thought her father a big man but against Leon he seemed suddenly less invincible. It was a strange feeling and she didn't like it. Or maybe she didn't like being so aware of the leashed power of Leonardo Bonmarito.

CHAPTER THREE

LEON arrived at nine.

'So, tell me about your private hospitals. What made you choose paediatrics as a main focus?'

Be cool, be calm, say something. Leon made her roomy den look tiny and cramped. Not something she'd thought possible before. Tammy had run around madly when Jack had gone to bed and hidden all the school fundraising newsletters and flyers in a big basket and tossed all evidence of her weekly ironing into the cupboard behind the door.

She'd even put the dog basket out on the back verandah. Stinky didn't like men. Then she'd put the Jack Russell out in the backyard and spent ten minutes changing her clothes and tidying her hair. Something else she hadn't thought of before at this time of night.

But now she sat relaxed and serene, externally anyway, and watched Leon's passion for his work flare in his eyes. She could understand passion for a vocation; she had it herself, for midwifery and her clients in Lyrebird Lake.

'It's the same in a lot of hospitals in the public system. The lack of staff, age of buildings and equipment and overcrowding means the convalescing patient is often cared for with less attention than necessary. With children that is doubly tragic.'

She couldn't help but admire his mastery of English. Her understanding of Italian was more than adequate but her conversational ability was nowhere near as fluent and his occasional roll of the *r*'s made his underlying accent compellingly attractive. It did something to her insides. She obviously had a dangerous fetish for Italians.

'This has concerned me,' he went on, 'and especially in paediatrics because children are vulnerable, more so when they are sick.'

That brought her back to earth. Children were vulnerable. He had great reason to believe that after Paulo's incident but she'd get around to that. Get around to the fact she'd thought him overprotective. 'I can see what you're getting at. It's hard because of priorities with those more ill. But I agree a lonely and convalescing child needs special care.'

He sat forward in his chair and his shirt tightened impressively across his chest. She didn't want to notice that. '*Sì.*' He was obviously pleased with her. 'There is a shortage of empathetic time for those children on the mend but not yet well enough to go home. I had hoped to prevent their stay from becoming a more traumatic experience than necessary.' He glanced up to see if she agreed and she nodded.

He was determined to ensure his goals were

realised. 'This is especially important if these children are dealing with other issues, such as grief from loss of loved ones, or difficult family circumstances.'

There was an added nuance in his voice that spoke of history and vast experience. An aversion to children suffering, perhaps more personal than children he'd seen in wards. The reason teased at her mind. 'Was there something in particular that made you so aware?'

His answer seemed to come from another direction. 'In our family all sons have entered the medical profession, though disciplines were left to our personal preferences. My grandfather was intrigued by surgery, my father ophthalmology. My passion lies with paediatrics and Gianni's with emergency medicine. Paolo's area is yet to be discerned.'

That made her smile. 'Paulo's a bit young to be worrying about disciplines, don't you think? I doubt Jack would have a thought in his head about what he'll do when he grows up.'

Leon shook his head. 'In Italy a man learns at an early age that he will be responsible for others.'

'Like dancing,' she suggested. 'A man must be able to lead?'

He returned her smile. '*Sì.*'

She couldn't resist teasing him again. 'So you turned your father's eye hospitals into paediatric wards?'

He raised one stern eyebrow but something made her wonder if he was secretly smiling. 'You do not really think that I would?'

There was a lot going on below the surface here. From both of them. She shook her head. 'No.' He wouldn't do that. She knew little of him but already she could tell he would hold his father's wish to provide service to the blind sacrosanct. 'So the eye hospitals are thriving.'

There it was. A warm and wicked grin that wrapped around her like a cloak dropping over her shoulders. A cloak that enveloped her in all the unusually erotic thoughts that had chased around her head for far too long last night in bed. She was in trouble.

'*Sì*. I built more hospitals. Designed especially for children and staffed with nurses who have much to offer an ailing or grieving child.'

He leaned back in the chair and the fine fabric of his handmade shirt again stretched tight across his chest. He picked up the tiny espresso coffee she'd made for him, black and freshly ground from the machine she couldn't live without, and sniffed it appreciatively. He took a sip, and those large hands looked incongruous around the tiny cup. *'Perfetto.'*

She'd learned to make good coffee years ago and it was her one indulgence. She dragged her eyes away from his hands because down that road lay danger.

She remembered he and Gianni were orphans and the pieces fell into place. 'How did your parents die, Leon?'

She had connected with his previous statement and why she could sense and understand meanings so easily from a man she barely knew was a puzzle she didn't want to fathom. She wondered if it worried him as much as it worried her.

To her relief he didn't try to avoid her question. 'My parents drowned off the Amalfi Coast from our yacht in a storm.'

Drowned. Poor little boys. 'Storms at sea.' She sighed. 'Mother Nature's temper can be wild and indiscriminate,' she said softly. His eyes gazed off into the distance and she was with him. She could almost feel the spray in her face and hear the scream of the wind and she nodded. 'I've lived by the sea. The weather can be unexpected and fierce. My father still has a house on a fabulous beach, but even he nearly drowned one day when he was washed off the rocks.'

He was watching her, listening to her voice, but she could tell half of him was in another place. 'What happened with you and Gianni?'

He looked through her and his voice dropped. 'Gianni almost died, and I, too, had pneumonia.' She glanced at his face and couldn't help but be touched by his effort to remain expressionless.

'And you were both in hospital afterwards?' Spoken gently, because she didn't want to break the spell.

He nodded and now she understood where his empathy for those in similar circumstances had grown from because she could see the suppressed emotion, even in the careful blankness. That concept hit her hard, in mutual empathy from her early teens and the scars she still bore. 'How old were you when they died?'

Leon shrugged the pain away. 'Fourteen.' Grieving, convalescing, in a hospital that was rushed and old and unintentionally uncaring. With a ten-year-old brother he'd nearly lost as well.

She could see he knew she'd connected the dots. And wasn't happy. 'It is better in my hospitals now.' He changed the subject. 'To see what you do here, in your maternity section, is good too.'

She allowed the change of subject, aware instinctively how privileged she'd been to glimpse into the private man and sensitive to his need to close the subject. 'The maternity hospital concept is an exciting idea. I'll certainly talk to Emma about it.'

No doubt he would also be happy because it would mean his brother's new wife would be interested in staying more often in Italy. She didn't fully trust his superior motives without a thought for his ulterior ones.

He was watching her again and she wondered what he'd seen of her thoughts. Not much, she hoped.

'So you, too, have suffered the loss of a parent?' His turn to pry. 'You said you lost your mother young, also?'

Not going there. Fifteen hadn't been a good age to be allowed to run free. 'Yes.' The less said there, the better.

'And that you lived with your grandmother?' So he remembered. Deep creases marred his forehead.

'Why did you not go with your father when your mother died?'

'It's a long story and maybe another day.' She and her father would have preferred that and maybe her life would have been different. She shrugged her shoulders for something she'd no control over. Fifteen had also been a bad age to be told Ben wasn't her real father.

Rebellion saw Tammy spend many hours loitering at that Italian coffee shop. Months had passed without her father's knowledge of how little supervision her grandmother had exercised.

Rides in fast cars she later found out were stolen. Dark and dangerous men that even her boyfriend was wary of. Secret meetings she'd had to stay silent in.

The day Ben, her father in all that counted if not legally, had arrived to rescue her.

He'd picked her up from the coffee shop when she'd rung him to say she was pregnant and whisked her to Lyrebird Lake. He'd told her then they were petty criminals. Not long later she'd read that her baby's father had been sent to jail for a long time.

No wonder she'd found it all so dreadfully, horribly exciting. That risk-taking and foolish time in her life was something she'd buried when she'd become a responsible mother.

Until Gianni had arrived in Lyrebird Lake and wooed her best friend, she'd covered the Italian episode in her life. Hadn't even tried her language skills out on Gianni so she doubted there was anyone except her father, and maybe his wife, Misty, in Lyrebird Lake who knew her secret.

Emma's betrothal had been such a whirlwind affair she hadn't even mentioned it when her friend had fallen for Gianni.

But she had Jack. The light in her life. And she'd change nothing now. Except maybe the subject again.

She had other motives for asking him here and he'd stayed a while already. 'There's something I want to ask you, though you may not want to discuss it. Something that means I should apologise for my presumption without knowing the facts.'

He frowned and inclined his head.

She hesitated, because she didn't really know him or how he'd react, and then typically, she dived in anyway. 'Was Paulo almost abducted before you came here?'

His brows snapped together. 'Who told you this?'

She straightened in her seat, refusing to be cowed. 'Paulo mentioned it to Emma's daughter, Grace.' She didn't say Grace had told Jack and Jack had told her.

His hand tightened on the cup he held and for a fleeting moment she had the ridiculous thought he might crush it without realising. Surely a man's hand couldn't really do that? In the silence she imagined she could hear the porcelain creak in protest.

'This is true.' He glanced at his white fingers and carefully put the cup down, then ran his other hand through thick black curls. She glimpsed the flicker of white-hot fury in his eyes and it was a warning of what he would be capable of. Strangely she had no problem with that. She'd almost pity the men who tried to harm his son if he caught them.

'I was stupidly distracted by my wish to arrive well before the wedding and took too little care. We are not the first family to be targeted by those who wish to benefit financially from people they see as too wealthy.'

So it was true. The thought made her want to clutch at her throat but she kept her hands together in her lap as if to hold onto the pictures that wanted to rise up and fill her mind. 'Good grief. What about the police?'

He inclined his head but the movement was non-committal. 'The police do their best to capture these criminals but by then it is often too late for the one abducted. This will not happen to my son or anyone in my family. I have a private investigator and body-guards working with me full-time now. Experienced operatives whose records are impeccable and that I trust with my and my family's lives.'

There was almost an aura around him and she recognised the implacable determination that would see him succeed in whatever he set his mind to. 'So you believe Paulo is safe, now that these people work for you?'

He inclined his head. 'Already they have paid tenfold for the money I retain them with. Those responsible have been passed over to the police. Paulo is safe now. No more at risk than any other boy, but it is hard not to look into the dark for danger.'

Who were these Bonmaritos her friend had bound herself to? These superficially cultured men who hid wolves beneath their Italian suits and hired body-guards. More gangsters she'd fallen in with? Or truly philanthropic doctors merely protecting their own from a culture she didn't understand.

'This all sounds very James Bondish. Not some-thing Lyrebird Lake would ever have to worry about.' She said it firmly, and perhaps a little too quickly, but she really didn't want to think of this scenario in her own home. In the lives of people she knew. In the man opposite her she was strangely drawn to. Dark forces she never wanted to be involved with again. It was too unsettling.

'So my brother says. He does not believe I need the bodyguards here but, for the moment, it is for me. These and other reasons are perhaps why my brother and I should return to our homeland.'

Surely nothing would happen here? In Australia? She didn't like any of this conversation and regretted what she'd discovered. She wondered if Emma was aware of the more menacing undercurrents of the Bonmarito family. 'This seems a long way from dis-cussing children's hospitals and maternity wings.'

Visibly Leon forced his shoulders to relax. 'I'm sorry, Tamara. I apologise if I've upset you. I still struggle with allowing Paulo out of my sight.' But his face remained changed. Harshly angled and fierce. The face of the stranger he really was.

Her chin was up as if she needed to rise and meet the challenge of this warrior of a man. He didn't frighten her but she gave him the respect he deserved. 'And I apologise for judging your need to know where Paulo was the other night.'

He inclined his head. 'You could not know.' While the dangerous side to this handsome Italian made her uneasy, it was less upsetting when she thought of her own response when Jack had asked what she would do—limb from limb seemed pretty similar to Leon's response. 'The lives of children should be protected.'

'*Sì*. And I should go to check Paulo. It is late.' He stood and she rose also, and couldn't squash the tiny irresponsible hope he would kiss her before he left. She walked him to the door and paused as she opened it. When she turned to him some of the hardness had faded from his face but there was enough of the wolf in him to still keep her head up as she met his eyes.

He had no difficulty seeing into her mind. His brows lifted. 'Do you want to play dare again, little one?'

So he thought she was little? Danger shuddered deliciously along her veins and made her remember a time in her dim past when she'd put her ear to a train track, the early rumbles of an approaching train, the danger, the paralysing fear that screamed to move. 'Should I in this mood you're in?'

He stepped in. 'That is enough answer for me.'

This kiss was different. Harder, decidedly more dominant with her crushed against his chest, and she pulled him against herself more to keep her feet on the ground and show she wasn't subdued by him. But she was. They leaned into each other, searching out secrets, showing each other hidden facets of their souls rarely exposed like little shafts of moonlight illuminating the areas used to darkness. All the more penetrating because there was no future in it.

When he left her, she leaned her forehead against the closed door with her eyes shut and listened to his car purr away in the darkness.

'Hit by the train,' she murmured into the darkness.

The next day as Tammy worked her early shift in the birthing centre she found herself glancing out the windows whenever she heard male voices, and once she saw her father in the distance with Leon, two dark heads together. One that made her smile and one that burned her with the heat of that last hard kiss.

It was strange how Leon and Ben seemed to find a common ground and mutual respect when there was a good fifteen years difference in age. And she trusted Ben's instincts implicitly so Leon must be 'good people'.

Her stepmother, Misty, the second of the midwives to move to Lyrebird Lake Birthing Centre, arrived to take over the shift. She joined Tammy on the steps to wave goodbye to this morning's new family.

'So Gloria did well.' They walked inside together and Misty grinned down at the birth register open on the desk. 'And they finally have a daughter?'

'In the bath at 10:00 a.m. She came out in three pushes and Gloria's over the moon with how much better this birth was.'

Misty ran her finger along the page and raised her eyebrows at the baby's weight. 'Lovely. And you're dropping there after work?'

Tammy bulldog-clipped the folder she'd completed. 'I said around four. Give them all time to have a sleep. I said I'd pick up their Jimmy after school and give him a chance to meet his new sister.'

'Sounds great.' Misty glanced at her with an unusual thoroughness and Tammy felt as if her stepmother chose her words carefully. 'Your father seems very impressed with Gianni's brother.'

'I was thinking that this morning.' Tammy looked back at Misty with a smile. 'What're your instincts?' There was more to the question than seemed on the surface. By 'instincts' Tammy meant those intangible nuances Misty was known for. Or even more to the point, had Misty had any of those eerie premonitions she occasionally experienced with startling accuracy?

Tammy didn't try to understand Misty's special gift, just accepted it for the reality it was and the fact that Misty had shown on occasion how useful her premonitions could be.

'There's something happening but I'll let you know if I get worried. But I like Leon too. I think despite an illusion of aloofness he's a man to be sure of in tough times. A man's man perhaps, but I've always thought you hadn't yet found a man you couldn't walk over.

He could be one of those and I'm looking forward to the tussle with great anticipation.'

Tammy slanted a look at her. 'Not very motherly of you.'

Misty just smiled. 'You never wanted me to be your mother, Tam. I'm grateful to be your friend.'

Tammy felt the prickle of tears. Not something she did often and she impulsively hugged Misty. 'I'm the lucky one.' She stepped back and straightened. 'And I'm out of here. Jen's staying another night until Ken comes home—the truck broke down at Longreach.'

She picked up her bag. 'Trina's at home in early labour, and she missed her last two appointments while away in Brisbane, so I'm not sure of her baby's size. He was a little bigger than expected last time I saw her. She knows I'm concerned. She's ringing after five so let me know if you need a hand. I'm on call tonight. Have a good shift.'

'I understand Leon Bonmarito is visiting?' Misty's face was bland.

Tammy tilted her head. 'That was last night.'

'So it was.' Misty nodded with a smile. 'Enjoy your evening.'

CHAPTER FOUR

So TAMMY wasn't surprised when the doorbell rang at nine-thirty that night. Nor was she surprised at the identity of the caller. 'Come in. I'm guessing Paulo's asleep.'

'And Louisa is watching over him. I am learning to trust he is safe again.' Leon's strong white teeth flashed in the low light. 'I would like to take Louisa home to Italy. Perhaps a change of scenery would be good for her. Do you think she'd come?'

'No.' Louisa had been housekeeper at the old doctor's residence, a short-term accommodation house for visiting doctors and nurses for a lot of years. Her husband had established Lyrebird Lake hospital and recently passed away.

'I'm sure my brother has suggested I stay at the residence and not at the resort because he wants me to fall in love with Louisa's cooking. And her stories. Has she told you about the myth of the lyrebird?'

Tammy had never been a fan of fairytales. 'I've heard of it. In all my years at the lake I've never seen

one. Emma has, twice, once with your brother.' She
smiled at how that ended. 'You'd better watch out.'

He, too, smiled. 'I think to see a bird will not
change my life.'

'Louisa's husband used to say the lyrebird heals
those in pain.' She had the feeling Leon could do with
a spot of healing but it was none of her business.

She returned to the notion of Leon worrying
about Louisa. 'Louisa spends time with her stepson's
family.' She couldn't help but think it strangely en-
dearing that this big, quiet man was concerned for an
elderly widow he barely knew. She'd made a mental
note to visit Louisa herself in case she needed more
company. 'We won't let you steal her. We'd all miss
her too much.'

She glanced at the clock. 'If you want a coffee,
I'll offer you one now. I'm on call and I know one of
the girls has come in to birth with Misty and there's
another woman due out there.'

'Please, to the coffee.' He followed her when she
stood and moved into the kitchen and she put her
hand up to halt him at the door. He kept coming until
his chest touched her fingers, a wicked glint in his
eye that warned he didn't take orders easily either,
but then he stopped.

She shifted her fingers quick-smart and tried not to
recognise how good the warmth of his solid chest had
felt beneath her palm. She needed at least three feet
between them for her to breathe. 'If you can make
my den feel small you'll crowd my kitchen. Just stay
there and let me work.'

He lifted one brow but obediently leaned against the doorframe, relaxed but alert, and they were both aware he was capable of swift movement, if he wished.

She breathed out forcefully as she turned away. Thank goodness he'd stopped. The guy was too much of a man to ignore when he was this close and a powerful incentive to get her chore done quickly and move out of here.

Then he said quietly, as if the thought had just occurred to him, 'If you are called in to work, who is here for your Jack?' Was that censure in his voice? Disapproval?

It had better not be. Nobody disapproved of her mothering. She flicked him a glance and his face was serious. 'We have an intercom between the houses and I switch it on for my father to listen in. Jack knows he can call for his grandfather if I'm not around and Dad takes him next door.' She glared at him and pressed the button on the machine for espresso and the beans began to grind—like her teeth.

'And what if Ben is called out?' Still the frown when it was none of his business but then, suddenly, she remembered he'd had a recent fright himself. One she'd put her foot in at the wedding. She eased the tension that had crept into her neck.

Of course he'd be security conscious. She didn't need to be so quick to take offence. 'We don't do the same nights on call,' she explained. 'That's the beauty of a small town and friends who organise rosters between families.'

The aroma of fresh beans made her nose twitch with calmer thoughts and she forced herself to stay relaxed. The guy could make her nerves stretch taut like a rubber band ready to snap back and sting her.

He nodded and looked at her almost apologetically, as if aware he may have overstepped a boundary. 'I begin to see the sense of this place.'

To her further astonishment he smiled and added, 'Perhaps I am less surprised at my brother's decision to spend half his time here.'

She had the feeling that could've been a huge admission for him but she didn't pursue it. She didn't want him to think it mattered to her. It didn't. Really. Time for a subject change. The coffee spurted from the twin spouts and filled their cups and she turned with them in her hands to face him.

He didn't move initially and she realised her hands were full. He could touch her if he wished. She was defenceless. Something told her he realised it too. She lifted her brows at him and waited.

He grinned and heaved himself off the doorframe and stepped back to allow her past him into the den.

'See how I understand your look?'

She bit back her smile as she sat his coffee on the low table almost on top of another of those fundraising pamphlets. She shifted it and her eye was caught by the title.

"Wanted! Man Willing To Wax Chest For Fundraising."

She had a sudden image of Leon and the gurgle of laughter floated up like the brown bean froth in the cup.

'You find that funny?'

She shook her head and bit her lip. She handed him the flyer. 'Lucky you're not here for long.'

He looked down at the paper and grimaced. 'And a man would do this?'

She couldn't help her glance at his broad chest, a few dark hairs gathered at the neck. 'They haven't found a volunteer yet. Want to offer?'

'No.' He shook his head with a smile. 'Though—' he paused and eyed her '—it would depend on who is doing the waxing.' The look he sent her left no doubt there'd be a price paid for the privilege.

Tammy felt the heat start low down, potent and ready to flame, like a hot coal resting on tissue paper. Yikes. She snatched the flyer from him and stuffed it behind a cushion on the sofa. 'Do you have much to do with young babies in your hospital?'

He settled back with a hint of smile and left the topic, clearly amused by her pink cheeks. 'No. Neonatal surgery is too specialised and we don't have a neonatal intensive care. But perhaps we would need a special care nursery if the maternity wing went ahead.'

He leaned forward and she could tell he was weighing possibilities and scenarios. She could see the big businessman she'd mentally accused him of being before she'd known him better, before she'd been kissed by him perhaps. But she had no doubt that if such a venture could be successful, then Leon would be the man to do it.

'These are all things to be taken into consideration if we opened a midwifery service. I'm sure a lot has changed since my obstetric rotation a decade ago. At the moment of birth, I mean.'

She could talk about that all day—and night. 'You're right. Things have changed a lot.' She tried to imagine Leon as a young medical student, diffident and overawed like those she'd seen in her training, but he was too strong a personality for her to imagine him ever being daunted by setting. 'I think the biggest change here is to keep the baby with the mother at all times from the moment of birth. Not separate in a cot. With emphasis on skin-to-skin contact for the first hour at least. At birth, we try not to clamp the umbilical cord for a few minutes either, unless we really have to.'

He nodded with a little scepticism. 'If the baby requires resuscitation?'

'Sure.' She brushed the hair out of her eyes. 'Though not always. It's a little trickier but the latest studies have shown that not cutting the umbilical cord for at least three minutes after birth is beneficial, though perhaps not that long in resuscitation.'

His face said he couldn't see how that would work so she explained more. 'We can give oxygen and even cardiac massage on the bed with the mother and that allows us to keep the blood flow from the cord as well. We've had great success with it. But then all our babies that come through the centre are low risk so any problems they have at birth are usually transient and should be resolved fairly quickly.'

He looked unconvinced and she couldn't help teasing him. 'Or is this a little too radical for your maternity hospital idea?'

'I'm always willing to see and hear of new ideas.' He raised his eyebrows at her comment, so quick to respond to any negative feedback she gave him, but she had no time to go on before the phone rang.

She dug her mobile out of her pocket. It was Misty and she had to leave.

'Sorry. I'm needed in birthing. You'll have to go.' Leon's eyebrows rose haughtily and Tammy almost smiled. She could tell he wasn't used to that. A woman had to go and he would be left cooling his heels.

He stood, though to say he did it obediently didn't suit the way he complied. 'You are not in awe of me at all, are you, Tamara?'

She didn't have time for this, unfortunately. 'Should I be?' She switched on the intercom between the two houses. 'I hope I haven't jinxed us talking about resuscitation and healthy babies.'

She saw his mind switch to the medical urgency. 'What was said?'

She gave him half an ear as she scooped up her keys. 'On the phone? Misty's concerned at the delay in second stage, and there's some unease with the baby's heart rate,' she murmured as she closed the front door behind them both. 'If it was bad she'd ship them out to the base hospital, but backup is always good when the back of your neck prickles. Do you want to come?'

He shrugged. 'I'm not registered in this country but happy to advise you if needed. Please.'

'Fine. People know Gianni so they'll have no problem accepting your presence.'

He hesitated at the two cars. 'I'll meet you there. No sense leaving your car or mine here because we don't know how long you'll be.'

They met outside the hospital and she let them in through the side entrance. Trying to remain unobtrusive they drifted into the birthing room and over to Misty. The lighting was still dim but Tammy saw the heater on for the infant resuscitation trolley and the preparations Misty had made. And the birthing mother, Trina, was beside the bed and not in the bath.

There was even a flicker of relief in her stepmother's eyes when she saw Leon. Tammy's stomach tightened. With uncomplicated births the midwife called a staff member from another part of the hospital as an extra pair of hands. If the midwife was uneasy she called the on-call midwife or doctor as a more experienced backup.

Misty spoke quietly so as not to disturb the couple who were leaning over the bed together. 'Trina's been pushing for an hour and a half now and everyone's getting tired. There's good descent of the head but there's still a heck of a lot of baby to come.'

Tammy nodded. 'Do you want to transfer?'

Misty shook her head. 'Maybe earlier would have

been better but Trina didn't want to go. We're just getting a head-on view now and we don't want a difficult birth lying down in an ambulance. Trina's done an amazing job.' She eased her neck stiffness. 'Thanks for coming. I wanted some backup for the end. We'll move to all fours when the head's almost here.'

'Sure. Good call.' Tammy was peripherally aware that Leon had moved to the resuscitation trolley and was checking the drawers. Excellent. It would be much easier if he knew what they had and where it was. He shut the bottom drawer, glanced up and nodded.

She hoped they wouldn't need him.

The next pain came and the expulsive efforts from Trina were huge. Tammy could see why Misty was impressed with Trina's progress. Slowly a thatch of baby's hair could be seen and Misty helped Trina down onto her hands and knees, the position least likely to result in a baby's shoulder becoming lodged behind the pubic bone of the mother.

During the next contraction the baby's head was born. Tammy raised her eyebrows at Misty. Not a small head and the fact didn't auger well for small shoulders. Tammy glanced at the clock.

'If your baby's shoulders feel tight remember you can help by bringing your chest in close. Nipples to knees. That flattens the curve of your coccyx and allows baby an extra centimetre or two.' All calm and quiet instructions that Tammy knew Misty would have given before this stage as well.

As the seconds passed and they waited for the next contraction, the skin of the baby's scalp faded from pink to pale blue, and Tammy could feel her own heart rate begin to gallop as the handheld Doppler amplified the way Trina's baby's heart rate slowed. The contraction finally began again and baby's head seemed to try to extend but didn't move and Tammy crouched down beside Trina's ear. 'Bring your knees together as close as you can and flatten your breasts down towards your knees. You're doing awesome.'

Trina squashed down as much as she could and Misty supported the baby's head. The contraction built. 'Okay, Trina, push now.'

Trina pushed and suddenly her baby eased under the arch of her mother's pelvis and tumbled limply into Misty's hands. 'Flip around, Trina, so we can lay baby on your warm stomach and have a look at this little bruiser.'

Misty wiped the baby briskly with a warm towel and passed her baby, all cord and limbs and damp skin, back to Trina between her legs, and the new mother shifted around until she was lying on her back with her stunned baby flaccid on her stomach.

Misty used the little handheld Doppler directly against the baby's chest and the comparatively slow thump-thump-thump of the baby's heart rate made them all look at the clock.

'Over a hundred,' Leon said, 'and some respiratory effort.' He leaned down and held the green oxygen tubing near baby's face until the little body became gradually more pink.

'Thirty seconds since birth,' Tammy said, and as if on cue Trina's baby screwed her face up and began to cry in a gradually increasing volume. Except for the slight blueness in her face from the tight fit, Trina's baby was vigorous and pink all over now as she roared her disapproval of the cool air Leon was holding near her nose.

He took it away and watched Tammy and Misty exchange smiles, and Misty's shoulders dropped with relief. She slid the baby up Trina's body to her breasts and put a warm blanket over both of them.

'What do you think she weighs?' Trina's husband seemed to have missed the tenseness the attendants had felt and Misty wiped her forehead with the back of her wrist.

'I'd say at least eleven pounds.' She looked at Trina. 'What do you think, Trina?'

Trina looked away from her baby and grinned widely up at Misty. 'She's as big as a watermelon. And I'm stiff and sore but glad it's over. She's definitely my biggest—' she glanced at her husband '—and my last.'

'I'm glad you mentioned you don't cut the cord immediately,' Leon said quietly into Tammy's ear. 'Or I would have been expecting a different sequence of events.'

They'd moved back away from the birthing couple to the sink to strip off their gloves and wash their hands. Tammy nodded. 'Do you think it would have made much difference if we'd clamped and cut and moved the baby to the resuscitation trolley?'

'Not with an adequate heart rate like that.' He paused and she wondered if he was comparing this with other occasions he'd known. 'Actually, no, and I can see advantages. It is always good to see differences in the way things are managed in other hospitals, let alone other countries.'

They waved to Misty and let themselves out. The parents were absorbed in their new daughter and waved absently.

Tammy smiled at the man walking beside her. 'It was good to know you were there. If those shoulders had been more stubborn we would have had a baby in much poorer condition, and in resuscitation the more hands the better.'

'The maternal positioning worked very well. My memories of shoulder dystocia were always fraught with a dread that was missing tonight.' He smiled. 'You were both remarkably calm.'

'There's some anxiety when you see a very large baby like Trina's. But we do drills for that scenario at least once a week so if there's a delay we can move straight into the positions. Because we knew Trina's baby was larger, Misty would have spoken to her about what to do if needed and good positions to try. But it can happen with small babies too.'

He dropped his arm around her shoulders, and it was companionable, not sexual. Not something she would have believed possible earlier. 'You must be very proud of your team here.'

'We are.' His arm felt warm and heavy but not a heaviness she wanted to shrug off. A heaviness of wanting to snuggle in and encourage more snuggling. She shifted away from that concept quick-smart and he picked up the tiny movement and slid his arm away. She pretended she didn't miss it. 'And the women and their families love the centre and the choice it gives them. We've quite a clientele from the larger centres coming here to birth and then going home from here.'

They were crossing the car park to Tammy's car and Tammy suddenly realised how at ease she felt with this big, quiet Italian. How she'd just expected that if Trina's baby had been compromised by a long delay before the rest of her body was able to be birthed, that Leon would be there to help. Despite his denial that he'd had much to do with new babies, she had unshakable conviction that his skills would be magnificent.

You can't tell that, a voice inside her insisted. But just like she knew that Misty could see things without proof or concrete evidence, she knew that Leon Bonmarito would be a great asset in Lyrebird Lake. Not that there was much chance of him hanging round.

She paused beside her car to speak and he took the opportunity to open her car door for her. She frowned. No one had done that for her for years and she wasn't sure she liked the warm and pampered feeling it left her with. As if abdicating her independence. But that uneasiness didn't stop her invitation. 'Perhaps I'll see you tomorrow night. If you find yourself at a loose end after Paulo's in bed.'

He inclined his head. 'Three in a row? What will people say?' At her arrested expression he laughed softly and looked around at the sleeping town. 'Your townspeople bed early, I doubt anyone is awake to notice.'

What would they notice? There was nothing to see. She'd done nothing wrong. Nobody could construe otherwise but it was as well he reminded her. She'd vowed to remain squeaky clean and the soul of discretion once she'd had Jack. Lyrebird Lake had given her tarnished youth a brand-new, shiny start, and there'd never been any hint of wayward behaviour to jeopardise that from Dr Ben's daughter.

She looked up at him, confident she'd done nothing wrong, nothing remotely possible to compromise her good name, and her chin lifted as she peered up at him in the dimness. Unexpectedly she perceived the unmistakable glint in those bedroom eyes of his. The breath caught in her throat and she moistened her lips to make the words, at the very least, sound relaxed. 'Notice what?'

'Perhaps this?' His hands came up and cupped both cheeks to prevent her escape, not with force but with warmth and gentleness and definite intent. His head bent and his chiselled lips met hers with an unmistakable purpose that spun her away from streetlights and neighbours and petty concerns of her good name, until she kissed him back because that was more natural than breathing, more satisfying than a heartfelt sigh, and kindled the smoulder of heat in her belly he'd started with a dance two days before.

When Leon stepped back she swayed until he cupped his hand on the point of her shoulder and held her steady.

Her hand lifted to her mouth of its own accord— suddenly sensitive lips tingled and sang—and she could feel the sleepiness in her eyes until she blinked it away. She glanced at the silent streets. The only lights shining were the street lamps. And no doubt her eyes.

Where had all these feelings come from? How could she feel so attuned and connected to this man she barely knew? How could she be tempted in a way she hadn't been since Jack was conceived? The depth of her response scared the pants off her. And she knew what had happened last time she'd felt like that.

He's right, she thought with convoluted logic, this was dangerous, and she'd need to think what she was doing before she ended up as the latest discussion point at the local shop.

She moved back another step. 'I could see how people could form the wrong idea,' she said wryly, and then she swallowed a nervous laugh as she slipped past him into the car. She stared straight ahead as she turned the key. 'Thanks for the reminder and for being there for all of us tonight.' And for the kiss, but she wasn't saying that out loud.

As an exit line it wasn't bad. Showed she had presence of mind—something she wouldn't have bet on one minute ago. 'If you visit, maybe you could walk to my house tomorrow night, instead of driving. More discreet.'

As she drove away she decided the invitation had been very foolish. And not a little exciting. She was a sad case if that was how she got her thrills.

CHAPTER FIVE

LEON glanced in the oval hallway mirror beside the door and grimaced at the five-o'clock shadow that darkened his jaw. His watch said it was too late to shave again this evening. And no time to walk.

Paulo had been unsettled tonight and Leon doubted Tamara would appreciate a ten-o'clock visit. If he didn't know better he would say he was wary of upsetting her.

Little firebrand. He could feel the tilt of his mouth as he remembered the wedding and her not so veiled threats of violence to his person. And the kiss last night under the street lamp. That had been bad of him. The man in the mirror smiled. Not that he wouldn't do it again if he had the chance. The result had far exceeded his wildest expectations and the ramifications had disturbed his slumber again for much of the night. It was fortunate he'd never required much sleep.

She amused him, intrigued him, but most of all she burned his skin with Vesuvian fire whenever he touched her and that should be enough to warn him off. He couldn't deny the danger but then she was so different than the women he was used to.

There was no fawning or attempts to use guile. He laughed out loud as his hired car ate up the short distance to her house—she did not know the meaning of the word *subtlety*.

Though no doubt she'd prefer he walked and with less fanfare of his arrival, and he needed to remind himself this town was different to Rome. Even Gianni had told him that. Perhaps he would walk tomorrow if he was invited again.

Another smile twitched at his lips. That would be two days before they left and each day he was becoming more interested in the concept of his new sister-in-law bringing her friend to visit his homeland.

When he knocked quietly on the door, it wasn't Tamara who opened the door, but her father, Ben, with his grandson standing behind his back. The degree of Leon's disappointment was a stern warning of how quickly he was becoming accustomed to Tamara's company.

'Evening, Leon. Tammy said you might call. She's over in the birthing unit with Misty.'

Another crisis? 'Do they need a hand?'

Ben shrugged but there was tension in his smile. 'Haven't asked for one but you could hang around outside on standby. Misty said it was good having you there last night. Or you could wait with us?'

'Perhaps I will return to the hospital and check. It will be too late for visitors when she's finished anyway.'

'I'll give her a quick ring and let her know you're available, then.'

'Thank you.' He nodded at Ben and turned away. He could hear Tammy's son asking why he had come. Perhaps a question he should be asking himself. But at the moment he was more interested in his instinct that he be there in case Tamara needed him.

Leon had intended to poke his head into the birthing room and then wait at the nurses' station until he heard the sound of a well baby. What he did hear when he arrived was the sound of the suction and oxygen and the murmur of concerned voices. When he opened the door his eyes caught Tammy's and the urgent beckon of her head had him beside her before he realised he'd moved.

'Will you tube this little guy, please, so we can have a look? He's not responding as well as I'd like.' She had the equipment ready to hand him, the laryngoscope, the endotracheal tube and introducer, even the tape. 'I thought I was going to have to do it myself but I'd rather you did.'

Easily, but that would not help her next time. 'Then go with that thought. You do it and I'll help. Better for when I am not here.' She swallowed and nodded and he tapped the dispenser of hand cleaner on the side of the trolley and quickly cleaned his hands before handing the laryngoscope to her.

'No rush,' he said conversationally, and steadied her hand with his as she fumbled a little. 'His colour is adequate so your resuscitation has maintained his oxygen saturation but a direct vision and an airway into his lungs is a good idea if he's not responding.'

He handed Tammy the equipment in order as she gently tilted the baby's head into the sniffing position as she'd been taught, and viewed the cords with the laryngoscope.

Misty murmured background information to fill Leon in. 'A true knot in his very short umbilical cord and it must have pulled tight as he came down.' They all glanced at the manual timer on the resuscitation trolley as the second hand came around to the twelve. 'So quite stunned at birth. Heart rate's been sixty between cardiac massage, and he's two minutes old. We've been doing intermittent positive pressure since birth and cardiac massage since thirty seconds. He's slow to respond.'

Tammy passed the suction tube once when the laryngoscope light bulb illuminated a tenacious globule of blood that must have occluded half of the baby's lungs from air entry.

'That will help,' she murmured. This time when they connected the oxygen to the ET tube she slid down his throat, his little chest rose and fell and his skin quickly became pink all over.

'Heart rate one hundred,' Misty said when she ceased the chest compressions to count, and they all stood back as the baby began to flex, wince and finally attempted to cry around the tube in his throat.

'I love the way all babies wish to live,' Leon murmured. 'It is their strength.' He nodded at Tammy and gestured with his hand. 'Slide the tube out. He doesn't need it now.' He felt the pride of her accomplishment expand in his chest and smiled at her as the little boy began to wail his displeasure. 'Well done.' He nodded his approval of her skill. 'How did that feel?'

Tammy's voice had the slightest tremor that matched the one in her fingers now it was all over. 'Better now I've done it again. Thanks.'

Misty lifted the crying babe and carried him back to his mother, who sat rigidly up in the bed with her empty arms outstretched to take him.

Tears ran down her face and even her husband wiped his eyes as their baby cried and the mountain of fear gradually faded from their eyes like dye from new denim.

'Don't do that to Mummy, Pip,' the dad said as his wife's arms closed over her baby and she hugged him to her chest. Her husband's arms came around them both and their heads meshed together in solidarity. The baby blinked and finally settled to squint at his parents through swollen eyelids.

The dad looked across at Misty. 'He'll be all right, won't he, Misty?'

'He's good, Trent.' She glanced at Tammy and Leon to include them. 'A clot of blood was stuck in his throat. We'll watch him for the next twenty-four hours but Pip responded well once the airway was clear. No reason to think otherwise.'

'That was terrifying,' the mother said with a catch in her voice.

Leon smiled. 'Yes. Always. Of course this is the beginning of many frights this child will give you.'

He smiled again. 'I know. I have a son.' He bent and listened with the stethoscope to the baby's little chest. 'Your son sounds strong and healthy, and obviously he was born under a lucky star.'

His mother shivered. 'How's that lucky?'

'A true knot in the umbilical cord is dicing with danger. The knot could have pulled tight much earlier when there was nothing we could do but he waited until it was safe to do so. And in such a good place as this.'

Misty and Tammy smiled and the parents looked at each other as if to say, Thank goodness we have a clever child.

'If you excuse me, I'll leave you to enjoy your family.' He leaned across and shook the father's hand, nodded at the mother and smiled at Misty.

'I'm ready to come with you,' Tammy said as she glanced at Misty for confirmation.

'Go. I'm fine. Thanks again. Both of you.'

They left, shutting the door behind them, and when they reached the outside, Tammy inhaled the night air deep into her lungs and let it out as if her very breath had been hung with lead weights. 'I hate that floppiness in a compromised infant.' She shuddered with relief.

He could see that. Clearly. 'Of course. Everyone does. You did well,' Leon said quietly at her shoulder, and to his surprise he realised she was wiping at tears. Instinctively he pulled her gently into his chest and held her safe against him with her nose buried in his shirt. This time only for comfort and he was surprised how good it felt to be able to offer this.

But Tamara in his arms was becoming a habit. She felt warm and soft and incredibly precious within his embrace and the fragrance of her filled his head. His hand lifted and stroked her hair, hair like the softest silk, and the bones of her skull under his fingers already seemed familiar. He accepted he would find her scent on his skin when she was gone. Like last night. And the night before. And the night before that. The thought was bittersweet. 'You did beautifully.'

Her head denied his approval and her voice was muffled by his shirt. 'I should have done it earlier.'

'You could not know there was an obstruction there. To decide to intubate is no easy decision. And the time frame was perfect because he was well perfused while the decision was made.'

She unburrowed her head from his chest. Obviously she'd just realised she was in his arms again and wondering how that happened. He couldn't help the twitch of his lips.

'This is becoming a bit of a habit.' She said it before he could.

'Hmm. So it is.' He could hear the smile in his voice as she stepped back.

'I'll be more confident next time.' There was no amusement to spare in hers. His arms felt empty, like the mother must have felt before she was given her baby, but he felt anything but maternal towards Tamara. Probably better that she stepped away because his thoughts had turned from mutual comfort to mutual excitement in a less public place.

He forced himself to concentrate on her concerns. 'Do not disparage yourself. I'm impressed. Intubation is a skill that not all midwives have and very useful for unexpected moments. It was very brave of you to conquer your fears.'

She straightened and met his eyes. 'I felt better once I knew you were there as backup.'

He was glad he could help. The streetlight illuminated the delicate planes of her face, the shadows lengthened her already ridiculously long neck and his fingers tensed inside his pocket where he'd sent them to hide because he itched to cup her jaw. Already his mouth could imagine the taste of her, the glide of his mouth along that curve that beckoned like a siren, but a siren unaware of her power. He drew a low breath and looked away. 'I'm glad I was there.'

'So am I.' He felt she avoided his eyes this time and maybe it was better. 'I should get home to Dad and Jack. They'll be worried.'

He wasn't sure either of them would be worried but he could tell she was uncomfortable and maybe a little aware of the danger she was in. Her night had been stressful enough without him adding pressure. 'And I will see you tomorrow. Sleep well, Tamara.' He wouldn't.

'Tammy,' she corrected automatically. And then she smiled. 'Goodnight, Leonardo.' He liked the sound of his name on her lips.

* * *

The next afternoon Tammy and Misty stood beside Pip's wheeled cot and stared down at him as he slept. 'Lucky little guy.'

Misty shook her head. 'It's always when you least expect it. The labour was perfect, Pip's heart rate all the way was great, and then I just started to feel bad, edgy for no reason, and I had to call you.'

Tammy gave a quick squeeze of her stepmother's arm for comfort. 'Your instinct has always been terrific.'

Misty rolled her eyes. 'I did wonder if Trina's birth from the night before had given me the willies and I was losing my nerve. You know, doubting myself by wanting to call you.' She looked at Tammy. 'You were great. I'm really pleased you came.'

'Your turn to intubate next time. I'm pleased that Leon came as well. I know that if we do what we did, just keeping the oxygen and circulation going until they recover, we're going to be fine. I *know* babies want to live.'

They stared down at Pip and Tammy went on. Voicing what they both knew. 'The horrible thing is that every now and then, for their own reasons, babies don't do what we expect. On that day I want to know we did everything we could. Maybe we could ask Leon about the latest resuscitation techniques before he leaves?'

Misty nodded. 'I think everyone would be interested in a discussion and the practise too. I know your father would. We need to include it more, like we practise the emergency drills.'

That was the beauty of working at Lyrebird Lake. Everyone wanted to keep their skills top notch. Wanted to support growth and competency and faith in one another. 'We need to include new trends in Resus more.'

'Next time I see him I'll ask him.' Probably tonight, she thought with a bubbling anticipation she tried to ignore. 'It'll have to be soon because he'll be gone.' She hoped she didn't sound plaintive.

Misty missed nothing. 'Sunday, isn't it? I think you'll miss him. You okay with that?'

Tammy reached for a pile of nappies to restock Pip's cot. At least she could avoid Misty's eyes that way. 'Fine. No problem.' She didn't want to think about it. Something she hadn't been able to achieve in reality. She shrugged. 'I've enjoyed his company, but really, we barely know each other.'

And yet on another level they knew each other far too well.

Misty might have been able to read her mind but there was no pressure in her comment. 'Sometimes it doesn't take long to feel that connection.'

Tammy smiled at the pile of nappies. 'Like you did with Dad?'

She could hear the returning smile in Misty's voice. 'I can remember driving away as I tried to deny it.'

She'd heard the story many times and never tired of it. 'And he followed you to Lyrebird Lake.' Tammy stood and glanced over at her stepmother. 'I'm glad he did, and glad he brought me with him. But I can't see Leon hanging around here for me and I'm certainly not moving to Italy.'

She thought about the differences in their cultures and she thought about distance and all she'd achieved here. Then she thought about her bad run with Italians and finally the kidnap attempt on Leon's son, even though the criminals had been caught and Paulo was safe now. She couldn't imagine living a life like that.

Misty handed her some clean singlets to put under the cot. 'I'm sure your father told me once you can speak Italian?'

She didn't know why she wanted to hug that to herself. 'Only a little.'

'Does Leon know?' Tammy shook her head.

Misty smiled. 'Isn't that interesting.' She moved away from Pip's bed to change the subject. 'I'm actually glad it's my last evening tonight. Peta and Nicky want to go to the beach house on the weekend and your father says he's not going without me. It'll be good to relax.'

Tammy thought of her father and the run-around her stepsisters would give him if Misty wasn't there to gently control their exuberance. 'I don't blame him. The girls are full-on.'

Misty laughed. 'And Jack isn't?'

'Must be in the genes.' They smiled at the family joke. Though Ben wasn't Tammy's biological father they'd decided Tammy had inherited all her bad traits from him.

'Actually—' Misty paused as if weighing her

words '—I was wondering if Jack would like to come with us? Give you a weekend off.'

Tammy frowned at the sudden unease the thought left her with. All this talk of kidnapping and violence and her son away. Then she thought of her response when she'd thought Leon was coddling his own son. 'Maybe not this weekend. But another time, sure. As long as I can take the three of them some weekend and you and Dad could have a weekend off?'

'We could do that.' Misty glanced at the clock and saw it was almost time for Tammy to go. 'Has Jack been keeping Paulo company?'

She'd tried to encourage her son to visit but he'd resisted. 'Not yet. I'm not sure they get on. I have a feeling they both like being only children. Rivalry. I'm taking him around to Louisa's this afternoon to play.'

Tammy glanced at her watch. 'Did you want to send the girls around after school? Louisa would love it. The more children, the happier she is. Just until Dad gets home with Leon? I'll be there too.' Not to mention she'd be there when Leon came home. She wouldn't have to wait until late that night to see him and the thought sat warmly just under her throat.

Misty glanced at her own watch and weighed up the time she had to change plans. 'Instead of after-school care? They'd like that.'

'It was Louisa's idea for the children to visit.' And Tammy had been quick to agree. 'I've been meaning to catch up with her for a few days.'

Misty nodded as they both paused and thought

about Louisa's loss and Tammy went on. 'Leon says she's lonely. That the residence is too big and empty for her.'

Misty bit her lip. 'Poor Louisa. Maybe she needs a change of scenery to help her think of something else for a while?'

'Leon says he's trying to get her to move to Italy with him.' She was starting all her sentences with 'Leon says.' Good grief. She needed to watch that and she'd bet her stepmama wouldn't miss it either. She changed the subject. 'I wonder where Gianni took Emma for the Australian leg of their honeymoon?'

Tammy saw Misty bite back her smile as she accepted the change. 'She'll send us a postcard, I'm guessing. It's not long till they fly out.'

Tammy glanced at her watch. It was time for her to go before she said something else she'd regret. 'Yep. Imagine—Italy on Sunday.' She didn't look at Misty as she left. Just waved and stared straight ahead.

'I don't want to play with him. I'm not a little kid, Mum, you can't make me.' Tammy glanced across and checked that Jack had done up his seatbelt before she started the car. Stinky pulled against his dog restraint and panted longingly at the window.

'Sure I can.' She ruffled Jack's black hair. 'So stop acting like a baby and be nice. The girls are coming too. The poor kid's probably bored out of his skull not being able to go to school.'

Jack screwed up his nose. 'Poor Paulo. Imagine not having to go to school? How terrible.'

'Don't be sarcastic. It doesn't suit you.' Tammy tried to keep a straight face. There was a lot of muttering going on under Jack's breath and she thought she heard, 'I'd kill to not have to go to school.' She could remember thinking the same thing a lot of years ago.

She parked outside and walked the path of the old doctor's residence and up the stairs onto the verandah. Tammy knocked and opened the door. The residence was always open and Louisa would be out the back in the kitchen.

The tantalising aroma of fresh baking wafted down the hallway and she sighed philosophically about her new jeans that were a little tight already. Louisa's scones were legendary.

'Hello, Jack.' Tiny Louisa held out her snuggly-grandma arms and smiled hugely as she enveloped him in a big hug. Louisa was the only person he'd suffer a hug from and the sight made Tammy smile too.

Jack emerged pink cheeked, grinned shyly, and he leaned up and kissed Louisa's cheek. 'Hello, Aunty Lou.'

'You need fattening up, my boy. You and Paulo are like two skinny peas in a pod.' She glanced fondly over at Paulo, who sat beside the window with an open book in front of him. 'Paulo's been forcing down my scones. Haven't you, Paulo?'

Paulo smiled shyly at Louisa and kissed his fingers. *'Delizioso.'*

Tammy stepped in for her own hug, and she

squeezed Louisa's waist which suddenly seemed smaller than she remembered. She frowned. 'You losing weight, Louisa?'

Louisa patted her round tummy. 'Oh, I'm not cooking as much, though I've put on a pound or three since two more gorgeous Italians moved in.'

Tammy felt slightly reassured but decided she'd mention Louisa's health to her dad next time she saw him.

She noticed Jack had wolfed down his scones by the time Peta and Nicola arrived. Misty and Ben's girls were both fair-headed like their mother and Nicola stood half a head taller than her sister.

More hugs and more homemade strawberry jam and freshly whipped cream to be piled onto disappearing scones and then the children all trooped off to play outside. Tammy felt Paulo dragged his feet a little and she frowned after him.

She glanced at Louisa. 'Maybe I should ring Montana? Paulo seemed happiest talking to Grace at the wedding.' Grace was staying with Montana and Andy's daughter while Gianni and Emma were on their first few nights of the honeymoon.

Louisa laughed. 'She'll be here soon. She and Dawn have been over every afternoon after school. The three get on very well.'

Tammy nodded, and helped Louisa carry their tea to the verandah. The women sat looking out over the green lawns, talked together easily while the children played and drank tea.

The sun shone on the red roof of the hospital

across the road and fluffy white clouds made magical shapes in the blue of the sky. The breeze from the lake helped keep the temperature down and Tammy decided the two boys seemed to be getting on well enough.

The children's games started simply, though even to a casual observer the boys competed for most stakes. They always seemed to be the last two to be found in hide-and-seek and were the fastest at finding people. Both were better than the girls at shooting hoops and it quickly became apparent how important it was to be the boy with the best score. Tammy shook her head as Jack whooped when he won the latest game.

The afternoon sun sank lower and Louisa went back inside to start dinner while Tammy flicked through a magazine as she watched them play.

Leon would be home soon, and her thoughts returned to the man who had erupted into her life with a compelling force she wasn't prepared for.

She'd already seen his concern for Louisa but what was he like while he stayed here? Was he tidy and thoughtful? Did he wait to be served his meals or jump up to help? Was he a good father, attending to all Paulo's needs? At the last thought she pulled herself up. It didn't matter what the answer was to any of these questions, he was leaving on Sunday. And she was not going to waste her time wondering about things that didn't concern her.

She called out to the children to suggest they finish off their games and come in. Stinky barked as he tried to join in and the sound echoed over the quiet, tree-lined street.

Tammy glanced at her watch again. He'd be here soon. The questions she'd asked herself itched like a raised rash at the back of her mind and she gave in to the urge to search out Louisa for some of the answers before it was too late.

Her mind wandered to whether or not Leon would visit her house tonight as well.

Wandered to the night after he left for his home country and how empty her den would feel.

Wandered to whether the tension she could feel heating between them could be contained to prevent an inferno, a conflagration that could damage them both as they went their separate ways in the very near future.

Her hip buzzed and she reached for her phone. It was Misty and she opened it with a smile.

Her smile fell at the unease plain in her stepmother's voice. 'I've got a bad feeling.' Misty sounded shaky and Tammy felt her stomach drop. Misty went on. 'Where's your car?'

Tammy frowned into the phone. 'Outside. Why?'

'I'm coming over.' Misty hung up.

Outside, the girls were happy to quit but the boys had one more point they wanted to settle and the ultimate test was Jack's idea.

'Just one last race. A longer one. I'll race you past the last tree and around that car down the end of the road and back. No stopping.'

Paulo looked at the distance, pondering the slight incline in the hill over the rough stones and the fact that they both had bare feet. He'd always run well in bare feet. And he was fast.

'*Sì*. Then we must go in, for my father will be here soon.'

'You're on.' Jack looked at the girls. 'Grace? You be starter.'

Paulo looked confused and Grace whispered, 'I say, "Ready, set, go." On "go" you run like the clappers.'

Paulo nodded. He understood 'go'.

The other girls were silent as Grace counted. 'Ready. Set. Go.' The two boys took off like deer in the bush, along the path, down the hill, and Stinky ran with them, barking the whole way. The girls cheered as the two distant figures ran neck and neck and then split each side of the car as they came to it and turned for the return journey. Then a strange thing happened.

The car doors opened wide and two men got out and suddenly the boys disappeared. Almost as if they were sucked into the vehicle. Both of them. The doors shut and the car pulled away on the road out of town in a skid of gravel and the roar of an engine even the girls could hear.

All that was left was the dust and the tiny four-legged figure of Stinky chasing the black sedan down the road.

Grace blinked and looked at Nicky and Peta and

then she spun on her heel and raced into the house. 'Tammyyyyy. Someone's taken them!'

Grace ran full pelt into Tammy, who'd just shut her phone and was staring at it as if trying to understand. She steadied the girl against her chest. When she realised Grace was crying, dread curled like a huge claw in her chest and she looked at the empty lawn. Where were the boys?

She thrust Grace aside into Louisa's arms and rushed out into the street. A white car backed out of a driveway down the road and drove away; otherwise, the road was deserted in every direction. No Jack. No Paulo. Just Nicky and Peta with their arms around each other in fright outside the door.

Tammy spun on her heel. 'Who took them, Grace?' Her brain searched for a reason. More kidnappers? 'What did they look like? It wasn't a white car, was it? What were they driving?'

Grace sniffed valiantly and her mouth opened and closed helplessly. Louisa hugged the little girl into her side as the older woman, too, tried to make sense of what had happened.

Grace swallowed a sob that blocked her throat. 'It was a black car.' She sniffed hugely and then the words tumbled out. 'It was parked down the road. The boys had a race and, when they ran past, men came out of the car and pushed them inside and drove off. Stinky's run after them.'

Tammy grabbed the keys to her own car off

the table. 'Mind the kids, Louisa. I'm going after them.'

'Is that wise?' Louisa's vice trembled. 'It could be dangerous.'

'Dangerous for them,' Tammy snarled. 'Ring Dad to find Leon. Let Leon ring the police if he wants to.' Tammy was having trouble seeing through the thick fear in her head. How dare they take her son? And Leon's.

'They had black shirts and black trousers on,' Nicky said suddenly.

'And it was a car like Grandpa's,' Peta added.

Tammy's brain was chanting Jack's words over and over. *You'd find me, wouldn't you, Mum?*

Peta's words sank in as she threw her bag over her shoulder. 'A Range Rover?'

Peta nodded. 'Sort of. A big black four-wheel drive.'

'Right, then.' And Tammy was gone, running for her car and roaring away from the kerb as she fumbled with her seatbelt. They probably only had about three minutes head start on her and she knew the road. Misty's phone call came back to her. 'Where's your car?' And here she was in her car. She hoped to hell that Misty's premonition had seen a good end to the scenario.

The winding road into Lyrebird Lake could be treacherous for those who didn't know it. But then if they were Italians as she expected they were, they'd be used to driving on treacherous winding roads. Damn them. She pushed the pedal down harder and

she flew past a gliding Maserati she barely recognised coming into town. A minute later her mobile
phone rang and she snatched it up and didn't even
consider it unusual she knew who it was. 'I can't drive
and talk.'

'Put it on speaker.' Leon's order was calm, yet
brooked no refusal. She flicked the speaker on impatiently and his voice echoed in the cabin. 'Stop your
car, Tamara. Do not chase these people.'

Her foot lifted off the accelerator and then pushed
down again. 'No. I won't stop.' She hung up and
pushed the pedal down harder. And nearly ran over
Stinky, who appeared as she rounded a bend.

She skidded to a halt, reversed, leaned over to the
passenger's side and opened the door. She breathed
deeply in and out several times. She wasn't surprised
when she looked in the rearview mirror and Leon's
car was behind her.

Stinky's tongue was hanging twice its length as he
gulped air. 'Get in, Stinky.' Stinky leaned his paws
on the frame and sighed. Such was his dedication
to chasing the boys he didn't have the energy left to
jump in.

Tammy pulled on the handbrake, opened her door,
dashed around the car and picked up the little dog,
but before she could bundle him in, Leon pulled up
behind her. He was out of his car in a flash.

'Do not follow them. That's an order. You do not
understand and will cause more harm than help.'

His words dashed over her like a bucket of cold
water and she didn't reply as he went on implacably.

'Your son will be safer if you do not confront them.'
His voice lowered. 'And so will mine.'

Her footsteps stopped beside her car, as did the
frozen focus that had consumed her, and she slumped,
horrified again at what had happened and chillingly
aware of how the fear in her chest was almost choking her. She turned and leaned her face on her arm
against the roof of her vehicle and then she felt Leon's
hands as he pulled her back into his body.

She almost sank into him until she remembered
he'd brought this on her. They'd taken Paulo and now
he'd brought this agony to her when they'd taken Jack
too. He wrapped his arms around her stiff body, but
there was no yielding, no relief he could give her.
Nothing would help the cold that seeped into her as
if she were being slowly submerged in an icy blanket
of dread. Her son had been abducted.

Her chest ached with the spiralling fear started by
Misty's call and the empty yard.

And they sped away further as she stood here. She
yanked herself free of his embrace. He was letting
them get away. 'I could have caught them.' She threw
her head back and glared into his face. 'Seen where
they went.'

His voice was flat. Cold. Implacable. A stranger. 'I
will know where they went. Those who follow them
are better prepared to apprehend than you or me. I
told you I had people protecting my family.'

Great. That was just great. 'And what about mine?
Whose protection does my son have?'

'My protection too, of course,' he ground out. Her

eyes flashed a deep fear at him that tore at his faith
in his men and his belief he'd done the right thing
to stop her. He'd done this to her. Why had he left
Paulo again today? He'd created a pattern. The first
rule of prevention. So much for his belief the threat
had passed. So much for his efforts to not be too
protective of his son. Now his nightmare had spilled
over onto Tamara.

But he hadn't believed they'd follow him here. It
didn't make sense. Why would they do such a thing?
Was it not easier to wait until he returned to Italy?
Even Gianni had thought danger in Australia highly
unlikely. But thinking these thoughts brought no
solace at this point.

She was waiting for a crumb of reassurance and
he was too slow with it. 'Of course he will be safe.
You have to trust me.'

She stepped back, further out of his arms, and
spun away. 'You're asking a lot,' she threw over her
shoulder as she paced. 'To trust you with the most
important person to me in the world.'

He knew it was such a huge thing she entrusted
to him. Her shoulders were rigid with it. 'I know,' he
said.

She narrowed her eyes as she turned to face him.
With her arms crossed tight across her breasts as if
to hold in the fear, she searched for a hint of unsure-
ness or ambivalence on the rightness of his actions.
He hoped there was none.

Did she trust him? It was achingly important she
could. Her chest rose and fell in a painful rasping

breath full of unshed tears that tore at his own pain like the claws of a bird.

He saw the moment she accepted there was nothing physical she could do. He'd taken that away from her but he'd had to, for her own safety, and for the boys. She sagged back against her car. 'What happens now, then?'

'We go back home and wait.'

She shook her head angrily at the passiveness of the action, then threw herself off the car and back into action. 'I'm going to see Misty.'

CHAPTER SIX

'MY MUM'S going to rip your arms off!'

'And my father will see you in hell.'

Both boys looked at each other and nodded. The captors, three dark-clothed Italian men, laughed as they drove.

Jack screwed up his face at the men and patted Paulo's leg. 'Don't worry, Paulo. She'll come.'

Paulo hunched his shoulders. 'It is my father who will come. And these dogs will pay.' The bravado was wearing a little thin but it still helped the fear that crept up their arms and settled around their tight little bellies as they sat wedged between two burly men. Two small boys in a situation they shouldn't have had to deal with.

'How have we two of them?' The Italian accent was coarser than Paulo's dad's and his partner shrugged.

'Didn't know which to take. We can get rid of the other one.'

In the back the boys huddled closer together.

* * *

Tammy parked her car outside Louisa's house and left the door gaping as she ran straight into Misty's arms. Ben came out of the house to meet them.

Leon heard Misty say, 'I feel they're fine. Honestly,' and he grimaced at the strange comment. He passed Tammy's open car door and shut it with tightly leashed control before he followed her in.

He felt suspended above himself, detached and icy cold as though he were peering down a long tunnel when all he wanted to do was find the people who had taken their sons and crush their throats. But he needed to stay calm for Tamara—and for the boys. He'd been speaking to his bodyguards and they had caught up with the car but were keeping distance between them. They had to find a way to stop the vehicle and keep the boys safe.

When he entered the residence it seemed the room was full of people. Louisa, her lined face white and shaking, stared at him as if she didn't understand. Kidnappings and violence were not in her life and Leon moved swiftly across and folded her in his arms. He stroked her hair. Nothing like this would have ever happened before in Lyrebird Lake.

Leon remembered his hope he wouldn't need to call on his brother's help for just such a situation. Gianni wasn't here but it seemed he'd get as many people as he needed. But for the moment he had to trust his own men and, now that he'd just contacted them, the Australian police. They would ring him if he could do anything.

And past his fear for his son was Tammy, and

her son's kidnapping, leaving Leon devastated he'd brought this on her by association, and regretful of her pain. His own agony was like a gaping wound in his chest and no doubt it would be as bad if not worse for a mother. Louisa shuddered in his arms and he rested his chin on the top of her grey head. Poor Louisa. Poor Tammy. And what of the boys?

The afternoon stretched into evening and then to night. Six hours after his return to the lake Leon stood tall and isolated in Tammy's den. He searched her face for ways to help but he knew she wasn't able to let herself relax enough to take the comfort he wanted to offer.

He carried the coffee he'd made her from the machine in the kitchen and the strong aroma of the familiar beans made him think of home. At home he would have more access to resources.

His arms ached to pull her against him and transfuse the strength she needed in the closing of this tumultuous day. Her distress left him powerless in a way he wasn't used to and he placed the cup on the mantel, then sighed as he reluctantly lowered himself to the sofa to watch her. 'I stay until we have them back.'

Tammy heard him. The coffee aroma drifted past her nose. She was glad he'd finally sat down. It gave her more room to pace and her eyes closed as she processed his words. *Until we have them back.* 'I want my son.' She wanted to wring her hands. 'I want Jack now. I don't want you.'

That wasn't strictly true. She'd driven everyone else away—her father, her stepmother—but she'd been unable to evict Leon from her presence. He'd flatly refused to leave her. And she needed him near her so she could know she was kept in the loop. Despite her wall of pain she seemed to be able to draw some strength from Leon which seemed absurd when he was the reason she was going through this.

She reached for the cup and took a sip. It was strong, and black, as she liked it. She'd drunk her coffee that way since she'd been that impressionable teen who'd fallen for a man similar to this one. Or was that unfair to Leon?

What was it with her and men that attracted trouble and danger?

At sixteen Vincente Salvatore had taught her to love his language, his country, all things Italian, with a heady persistence that endeared her to him. An Italian with trouble riding his shoulders, hot-headed and hot-blooded. Then he blew it all away with a reckless abandon for right and wrong that left her with the realisation of just how dangerous his lifestyle was. She swallowed a half-sob in a gulp of coffee. Maybe Vincente's friends could find Jack.

How on earth had she embroiled herself and her son in trouble without realising it? But she would have to deal with that. It was her fault. She couldn't believe she'd been so irresponsible as to let the children out of her sight. Couldn't forgive herself for daydreaming her way to negligence. Such stupidity could have cost Jack his life. And Paulo his.

It wasn't as if she hadn't known of the possibility of danger. Even though Leon had said it was past. And what had she been doing? Daydreaming about a man. Following Louisa for titbits of gossip about his presence at the old residence. Anything to feed her growing fascination for Leon.

Well, it would all stop. Now. She would promise anyone who would listen that the risk of danger to her family far outweighed any fleeting attraction this dark Italian held over her.

A bargain.

Jack and Paulo back safe and she'd never think of the man again. Honest.

She should have learned that she was destined to be brought down by her heart, and the menace of these Mediterranean men, her nemeses. Now their sons had paid the price.

Unfortunately, at this moment, it was hard to keep those thoughts clear in her mind because her shattered emotions were torn—torn between guilt for her negligence, spiralling fear for the outcome and the gnawing need for comfort from the very man who caused it all.

Louisa had been gathered up from the residence by her stepson and whisked away. And Leon was here, the only barrier to the emptiness of this house.

It was eerie how she could imagine the outside of her empty house, dark and forlorn in the moonlight, and she glanced out the window to the shifting shadows in the street outside. Strained her ears for imagined sounds and then turned abruptly from the window and put the cup down.

She even ran her fingertips along the mantelpiece as if to catch dust and at least do something useful. Her mind was fractured into so many fear-filled compartments and what-ifs she couldn't settle.

She wanted both boys asleep in Jack's room, with Stinky's head on his paws as he watched his master—glancing at her every time she went in as if to ask if he could stay.

But the blue room at the end of the hall stayed empty like an unused shrine.

And Leon watched her.

It had taken until midnight for Tammy to decide she couldn't stay at her father's house. She'd said she wanted to be near Jack's things. Leon had refused to allow her to go alone and he was still glad he'd come. But as he watched her, she glittered like glass in moonlight with nervous energy. Every sound made her jump, every creak of the polished floorboards made her shiver, and Leon ached for the damage he'd caused to this sleepy town and to this woman.

He patted the sofa beside him and held out his hand. 'Come. Sit by me. Let me help you rest for a few moments at least.'

She turned jerkily towards him. 'I can't believe he's not here.' Staccato words stabbed the air in the room like little knives, tiny steel-tipped blades of guilt that found their mark on him.

'They will have them by morning. My men have promised me.' Leon rose to slide his arm around her stiff shoulders and pull her down to sit beside him so their hips touched. She was so cold and stiff and he nudged more firmly against her hip, offering comfort to both of them, and a safe place to rest if only for a moment, and if only she could.

'Your men?' She sniffed. 'If they were so good the boys would never have been taken at all.'

'Nobody expected this here. We were lucky they were still with us.' Leon had his own demons. Paulo gone and he didn't know if he was alive. Or Jack. Surely they would get them back.

There had been no demand yet. Would they discard the boy they didn't need? Would they leave him alive? It had been his choice to delay the police while his men followed the trail initially.

The trail Tamara had wanted to chase. His first sight of her face as she drove past him like a woman possessed still affected him. Her little car pushed to its limits to the point where his more powerful motor could barely catch her. His throat tightened. 'I can't believe you pursued them in your car.'

She brushed the hair out of her eyes impatiently. 'Why would I not?' Her eyes searched his. 'I could still be chasing them if you hadn't stopped me. What if they've disappeared and we never find where they went? What, then?'

He shook his head at the thought. No! It would not be like that. He had to trust what his operatives told him. Tomorrow in the early morning, it would be okay. 'I was terrified for you as well. What were you going to do if you caught them?'

Her eyes burned. 'Whatever I had to. They have my son.'

And mine. She had no idea. And he did and should never have brought this on these people. He knew what loss and guilt did to people. 'What you did was too dangerous.'

Another swift scornful search of his face. 'For them?'

'For you and for the boys.'

She shook her head. 'For the first time in a lot of years I don't know what to do. You tell me to wait. But how long must I wait? I want him now.' Her shoulders slumped and slowly, like the deflation of an overstretched balloon, all the fight leaked out of her and she sagged against him as she buried her face in his shoulder.

He smoothed her hair. Had to touch her and try to soothe her agitation as she went on. 'There's never been such hard waiting. I've never had such fear. Make me forget the horror I can't shake. Talk to me. Tell me something that helps.'

He pulled her onto his lap and hugged her, still smoothing her hair and whispering endearments she wouldn't understand. Assuring her the boys would be returned. That he knew she was scared. That he was scared.

His hand travelled over her hair and his mind seemed to narrow its focus, the room faded until only the sheen of silk beneath his fingers existed. Rhythmically he stroked as he murmured until suddenly he began to speak more easily.

In his own language, not hers. All the things he'd bottled up for years but never said.

He said he knew how scared she was. How scared one could be in that moment of loss. He could taste his first moment of absolute fear and horror, all those years ago on the ocean, at fourteen, not yet a man but about to become one.

The storm upon them before his father realised, the sudden wave that washed he and his brother overboard, and his father throwing them the lifebuoy just as the boom smashed him and his mother into the water after them.

He'd grabbed Gianni's collar and heaved him against his chest so his head was out of the water. He could remember that frozen instant in time. Them all overboard, Gianni unconscious and only he with something to cling to. He couldn't let go of his brother and, screaming out against God, he'd watched his parents sink below the surface.

So alone in the Mediterranean under a black sky. It had grown darker as the night came; Gianni awoke, and he'd had to tell him of their parents' fate.

Such fear and swamping grief as they'd bobbed in the dark, imagining sharks and trying not to move too much, chilled to the core, fingers locked to the rope of the buoy. Knowing they would die.

Their rescue had been an anticlimax. A fishing boat pulled them in. Then the week in hospital alone and grieving, with visits from lawyers and one old aunt and her change-of-life son who'd hated them both.

He'd vowed that day he would be strong. And he had been.

He'd married Maria as his parents had betrothed them, and finally they'd had Paulo. His heritage safe again.

Then Maria had died and Paulo had been almost taken. He'd realised his life could fall apart again any moment and he'd needed to see his brother, his only family.

He, who'd never spoke of anything that exposed his soul, poured it all out to Tammy. It eased the burden of guilt he carried to tell her how he felt, without the complication of her knowing. From somewhere within it was as if the walls he'd erected around his emotions began to crumble, walls he'd erected not just since Maria's death, but since that lost summer all those years ago when he'd felt he failed his parents. Walls that prevented him being touched by feelings that could flay him alive.

He continued to murmur into her hair as her softness lay against his chest. His native tongue disguising the compromise and giving freedom to express the beginning of something he hadn't admitted to himself as he held her warmth against his heart. Her healing warmth. The way she touched his soul. He told the truth.

How sorry he was to have brought this on her. How the lure of her physical attraction for him had begun to change to a more complete absorption. How she made him feel alive as he hadn't felt for years, even if sometimes it was with impatience or frustration when she thwarted him.

How beautiful she was, how she'd captured his attention after their first dance at his brother's wedding, how he'd never felt that connection before with another woman, even his wife, and that made him feel even worse.

How these past few days he couldn't stay away, spent his mornings and afternoons dragging his thoughts away from her so he could concentrate on business—something he had never had trouble with before—when in fact he was waiting for the evening when he could call on her.

The lonely nights dreaming of her in her house a street away, staring out through the window all night so he could start the whole process again.

How he'd glimpsed the promise of what could have grown between them, but now that had changed. Had to change. Once the boys were returned he would sit on a plane and watch the ground fall away beneath him, knowing she was still in Australia. So she and Jack would be safe, apart from the danger that followed him.

Knowing the distance of miles would not be the only distance that grew between them every second. But he would. Because she would be safe. Her son would be safe. His life was too complicated for this, the ultimate complication, but he could never regret these past few days. And he would never forget her.

Tammy listened. Her head on his chest, the regular beat of his heart under her cheek as his liquid words flowed over her. Some words and phrases she didn't catch but most she did, like the honesty in his voice and the gist of his avowal. The sad acceptance of his promise brought tears to her eyes.

When she lifted her face to his, he saw the tears and softness in her eyes and he could no more stop himself from kissing the dampness away than he could stop himself drawing breath. Her arms came up around his neck and her face tilted until she lay suspended below him, mute appeal his undoing.

He stood with her in his arms, cradled against him, and strode to her room, a dim and disconnected haven from the reality which they both sought to escape.

To hide in each other, buffer the pain of their fears with the physical, the warmth and heat of each other's bodies. At the very least the release might let them sleep.

Tammy knew she would regret this. But there were so many huge regrets—this tiny one was nothing if it gave her some flight from the pain, and comfort to them both.

He lowered her feet to the floor until she stood next to him, beside the bed, eyes locked as slowly they peeled away each other's clothes, layer by layer, like the emotions Leon had peeled away for her, until she was as bare as him.

She stepped forward until her breasts brushed his chest and with a muffled groan he crushed her to him. And she knew it was her turn to comfort him. She needed to comfort someone because she couldn't comfort Jack. Her hands curved around his neck and she pulled him closer so she could wrap herself around him, and draw his pain into her. In some unexplained way it eased her own suffering as they stood locked together in a ball of consolation that slowly unravelled into something else.

It started with a kiss, a slow gathering of speed. Kissing Leon was like running beside the wolf she thought him, down an unexpectedly steep hill, barely able to keep her feet. The momentum grew and her heart shuddered and skipped as she was swept alongside the rush of Leon, the heat of his chest, his powerful hands, his eyes above her, burning fiercely down as he searched her face for consent.

She reached up and pulled his mouth to hers again and she could feel the need in her chest and belly and in the heart of her as he gathered her closer, stroked her, murmured soft endearments of wonder in Italian which deepened the mist of escape and made her want to melt into him even more.

His hands slid down her back, marvelling at the smoothness of her skin, curling around her bottom and lifting her until her weight was in his hands. When he lifted her higher she rose against his chest. She'd never felt so small and helpless, dominated yet so safe and protected. She ran her cheek against the bulge of his arms, savouring the tension of steel beneath her skin from this mountain of a man who made her feel like a feather, as effortlessly he carried her until she felt the wall behind her. Then the nudge of him against her belly.

In a moment of clarity that came from the coolness

of the wall on her back, she told herself she shouldn't do this, didn't deserve to experience this man at this moment in this way, would not die if she didn't. But she didn't really believe it.

She did believe she'd always regret not taking the gift of solace they offered each other in their darkest hour. And soon he would be gone.

He stilled, as if sensing her thoughts, and when she looked again into the midnight of his eyes, she knew she could stop this. Her heart felt the tear of denial, the breath of resolution and the tiniest lift of her skin away from his but something inside her snapped. No. She needed this for her sanity because with that one millimetre of distance between them, the outside world pummelled her and the pain made her wrap her legs around his corded thighs, hook her ankles and implore him to save her.

Afterwards, they lay together on the bed, entwined, her head on his chest as he stroked her hair and, against her will, against any conviction she'd be able to, she fell into a dreamless sleep and rested.

Leon listened to the slowing of her breathing and his arm tightened protectively around her. How would he forget this woman? What had happened between them was something he hadn't expected and he certainly hadn't foreseen the severity of the impact of their collision.

More barricades had tumbled under her hands, barriers he'd closely guarded and never planned to breach. He would regret this night and yet could not wish it undone. His eyes widened in the dark when he realised what else he'd done. Or not done.

His sins compounded. Not only had he not protected her son, he'd not protected her.

The flash of light on his silenced phone was muted by his shirt pocket on the floor but he saw it. He buried the enormity of that other problem for another time as he slipped his arm out from under her head. She snuggled back into him and he paused until her breathing resumed before he slid from the bed.

His brow creased as he read the message, then he gathered his clothes swiftly and left the room.

CHAPTER SEVEN

SHE was woken by ringing as he came back into the room. He leaned over and switched on the bed lamp before he reached for the phone beside the bed and gave it to her. 'Yes,' she listened, mouthed, 'the police' at him and then said, 'I understand.' She listened again and then nodded, her eyes closing with relief. He could read it in her face. She put the phone down. 'They're safe.'

He didn't tell her he'd known already. Just turned her into his body and hugged her. It was her he needed to hug and not just because of the boys. Crushed her into his chest and closed his eyes as if blotting out all the terrifying pictures his mind had been filled with before his bodyguards had rung him.

Tammy pulled back and her tear-streaked face looked up into his. Searched his eyes, searched his face. 'They wouldn't have made a mistake. Would they?'

He shook his head. 'They're on their way home now.' He didn't tell her there had been a gunfight. Between two groups. Coming on them his men had scooped the boys from the confusion, had been fortunate one unidentified man had thrown himself in front of the boys to save them and been badly wounded. They'd left the dead and dying where they were for the police. He didn't say his bodyguards wanted to know what enemies he had that they knew nothing of.

Perhaps it wasn't over yet. It was an unexpected nightmare he'd dragged her into and he would never forgive himself. How many people were after him in his life? But there was much he didn't understand.

She searched his face and pulled away a little. 'There's more, isn't there?'

How could she tell? 'The boys aren't hurt.'

Still she watched him. Closely. 'Your people?'

He shook his head. 'No.'

Her head lifted as if she could scent danger. 'Then something went wrong with the kidnappers. So it's not finished.'

He squeezed her shoulders tight beneath his hands. 'It will be finished.'

She moved out of his embrace and her narrowed eyes flicked over him and away. 'You can't promise that.'

'I promised the boys would be returned.'

She looked at him and slowly she nodded. 'You did.' He could feel the distance grow between them. Despite what had passed only an hour ago. Or perhaps because of it. He thought briefly of a subject they hadn't broached but she went on.

'And I trusted you. But I don't know if I could do

that again with my son's life.' And there was more there than was spoken and they both knew.

He inclined his head. 'I understand.'

She moved to slide out of the bed and he laid his hand on her shoulder to stay her. 'There is another thing we must discuss.'

She wrinkled her forehead. 'Yes?'

'I did not protect you when we made love. What of those chances?'

She shook her head. 'I'm meticulous.'

'Then there is nothing else you need to worry about.'

'Or you,' she confirmed.

The Saturday night before they left was so much harder to have Leon in the house, Tammy reflected with a sigh, thanks to a moment of weakness.

When she'd finally held her son safe in her arms that morning, Jack had asked if Paulo and his dad could stay their last night with them. Of course she'd said yes. She understood Jack's need and would have given her son anything he desired in that moment, that precious, arm-filling, flesh-and-blood hug of her unharmed child.

Both boys hadn't wanted to be separated after their ordeal and the day had been spent quietly watching over them as they slept and feeding them when they were awake. Leon had spent hours with the police.

How could she say no? What could she say, that she needed as much space as she could get from Leon now that she knew the man? Knew him with a depth and intensity and physical knowledge that scared the living daylights out of her.

Had heard his deepest fears exposed, had wept for the young orphan, had seen a little of his growing feelings for her. During her darkest hour those things had immeasurably comforted. Now they would both pay the price and tonight was incredibly awkward. And on top of it all was the guilt that Leon didn't know she'd understood his words.

Then there were the secrets he held. Where had he been when she'd been woken by the phone? Certainly not beside her in a state of undress. Plus the fact that two quiet men were outside, somewhere watching over her house and the people inside. She felt as if her world was spinning out of her control. She, who prided herself on control.

Leon had been reluctant to confirm their presence, but she'd seen them leaning on the tree across the road, and another out the back against her father's fence. His bodyguards.

Again she thought of Vincente and his cronies and the secrets and murky dealings she'd learned more of each day, and it hardened her resolve to stay aloof from this other dark man. But she needed all that resolve to not seek the same comfort she knew she could lose herself in.

The boys were finally asleep for the night. She'd been in and checked on them so many times she was almost dizzy with it.

Leon circled her, wary of intruding on her space, wary of her, as he should be. She was afraid of herself, her thoughts, her dilemmas that loomed large in the emotionally fogged compartments in her brain.

He came closer until he stopped in front of her. Lifted his hand and brushed the hair out of her eyes.

She shrugged and shifted out of his reach because she knew how easily she could have thrown herself back into his arms and that was the last thing she wanted communicated to him.

For Leon it was confirmation that she didn't need him. She had her son back. He was just prolonging her embarrassment. He watched her turn away again and search the room for the peace she obviously hadn't found next to him. 'The boys are safe now,' he said.

'Are they?' She sighed. 'Really? I have to bow to your superior knowledge, there, don't I?'

It was his fault. Letting her guess it was all not finished. He laughed without humour. Still she didn't trust him. 'Why don't I believe you could bow before anyone?'

Her eyes pinned him. 'Well, what if these criminals do come back to hurt the boys?'

He ran his hand down her arm. His aim had been to gentle her but all he seemed to achieve was to reinforce her agitation and his own aching feeling of loss. In the past twenty-four hours he'd changed.

Making love with Tamara had changed him. Had cost him something he hadn't wanted to give, ever again. But now was not the time to rail at himself for something he'd had no control of. Later he would sift what could be salvaged from the wreckage. He said again, 'The boys are safe.'

'You don't know that.' She looked at him. 'You can't lie that you aren't frightened they'll come back for Paulo.'

He sighed and he fought the dark pictures away. The way he'd only just caught them last time, Paulo pale and almost lifeless in his arms, the panic at the airport. The sickness of dread. And now again, unexpectedly, in this far-off land, and the fact that no ransom had been demanded. 'But there was no reason to take Jack.'

'There wasn't yesterday.' Tammy shook her head. 'But now he knows what the men look like.'

He raked restless fingers through his hair. Nearly all the men had been caught. With one close to the end when last he'd heard. 'What if it was not Paulo they were after?'

She shook her head. 'I don't understand.'

Neither did he. 'Is there any reason somebody would want Jack?'

Her hand flew up as if to brush aside the idea. Vehemently. 'Of course not. They were after Paulo.'

He watched her, narrowed his eyes as he tried to understand the nuance he was missing. Something that didn't ring true, though she'd never given him cause to disbelieve her before. It was hard to pinpoint his unease. 'My bodyguard was told they were delivering Jack.'

She shook her head. 'They made a mistake.'

He heard her words but this was what he couldn't

understand. There had to be a connection. 'What about his father?'

She avoided his eyes. 'He's never seen his father.' He'd been in jail for all of Jack's life, but she didn't want to share that delightful pearl of information. She shook her head again. 'Jack knows I haven't seen or heard from his family since Ben moved me out of Sydney eight years ago. Before Jack was born. Jack's father was not someone I'm proud of falling in love with.' And I'm not making the same mistake twice.

Leon sat and pulled her down next to him. 'How old were you, Tammy?'

She stood again and walked away. She didn't want to talk about this now. When she had her back to him she answered, 'Does it matter?'

Leon persisted and she didn't understand why. 'Does anyone in this man's family know about Jack?'

She shook her head but she didn't even know that. She'd been pregnant, fifteen, with belly quietly bulging under the bulky clothes she'd worn. Her grandmother had panicked and her father had arrived. Thank goodness for the love of Misty and her dad. She was fairly sure Vincente was working himself up from a petty gangster and she would have been in the thick of it.

'I guess his mother knew I was pregnant because she worked for my grandmother, but whether or not she knew who the father was, I'm not sure. The whole world knew when I left.'

'So perhaps they could know?'

What was he getting at, digging through this old history? That horrible black trepidation was creeping over her again and she hated the feeling. Mistrusted it more than ever after yesterday.

She felt cold and she rubbed the goose flesh on her arms. It wasn't a cool night. 'This has nothing to do with the fact your son was kidnapped and mine was taken as well. Don't try and blame this on me. Our life was normal before you came.'

'I'm sorry.' He thrust his fingers deep through his hair. 'You're right. Unless he was Italian there can be no connection.'

Tammy's breath jammed in her throat and she hoped Leon didn't hear it stick. Another shiver ran through her as her heart slowed and then sped up twice as fast. She could feel her blood trickling coldly in her chest as she tossed that idea around like a hard lump of ice. No way.

Leon crossed to her. Her face gave away the turmoil he'd caused. He was a fool and a thoughtless one. 'Forget I asked. Please, Tamara, forgive me.' And he could do little else but gently draw her into his arms and kiss her.

She was so soft beneath him. Her cheek like satin against his face, her hair fluid under his fingers in that way he would never forget. How could he cause her more distress? He stroked her arm. 'Come lie down with me. Just to hold you. Nothing else. Let me keep you warm.'

She wanted to. So badly. It was a great theory to just hug and wrap themselves around each other and drift off to sleep but she doubted it would end that way.

She shivered again. 'I am cold.'

Was it wrong to want to lie with this man? To experience the immersion in another human being, to feel the power of her inner woman that she'd only just discovered because he'd shown her? She wanted to lose herself in him, or perhaps truly find herself, and in doing so maybe gain some peace. Why did this man, a man leaving tomorrow, have to be the one who had shown her that? The only man she'd ever sought peace from. Why was that? Why did everything go so wrong?

She wrapped her arms across her chest and attempted humour. 'If you took me to bed I don't know if I could keep my hands off you.'

The worried crease across his brow jumped and the tiniest twinkle lit his eyes. 'Perhaps I could sacrifice myself to your needs. If that should happen I would forgive you. Medicinal purposes, of course.'

No. They couldn't. There was the chance of the boys wandering in. 'I don't think so.'

'I could stay on top of the bedclothes.'

'And how would you warm me, then?' Perhaps that would work. She was so tired and cold and miserable and the thought of leaving her troubles for him to mind while she rested was beyond tempting.

'I'll be out in a minute.' She dived into the bedroom and shut the door. She imagined his face when he saw her in her too-big, dark blue striped, flannelette pyjamas.

But when she returned he didn't comment. Just took her hand and led her to the bed. She doubted he wanted to risk her changing her mind and making him sleep in the den. When she stood before him he took both her hands and kissed them.

'Tonight will look after itself.'

Sometime in the night she awoke, her pyjamas strangling her. Her arm had little movement where she lay on the ungiving fabric and she felt trapped. Trapped and claustrophobic by the material and ripped off by the thought that tomorrow Leon would be gone. The bare skin of her feet had wormed between his legs and soaked in his heat and his hand had slipped between the buttons of her shirt and rested like a brand to cup her breast.

She lifted her free hand up to move his fingers but instead she stroked the back of his hand. He kissed her neck.

So he was awake also. *'Stai bene?'* Then, 'Are you okay?'

She almost said *sì*. 'I'm a little uncomfortable.'

'Your pyjamas?' She could hear the laughter in his voice and the sound was more precious than she expected.

'Yep.'

'I have a solution.'

'I'm sure you do.' The solution was delightful.

The next morning dawned clear and bright. Unlike her head. Tammy still felt fogged with the twists and turns of the past few days, let alone the disaster of sleeping with Leon again. Her face flamed in the privacy of the bathroom. Goodness knows how she was going to face the boys. At least Leon had been up and dressed before either boy had appeared.

Today they left for Italy. She was still telling herself his leaving was a good thing.

Emma and Gianni returned to Brisbane today from their honeymoon and Montana was also driving up with Dawn, taking Grace to meet up with her mother and new step-father, before they all flew out.

Leon had taken the boys to the shop while she showered, to buy bread rolls and cold meats for brunch, a last-minute attempt to create some normalcy from Paulo's trip to Australia. A family picnic by the lake before they left.

She'd told Jack they weren't seeing them off at the airport. It was the last thing Tammy wanted—a long, drawn-out goodbye in front of strangers or even to sit opposite Leon at a small café table and make small talk in front of their sons. The picnic would be hard enough but at least it was private.

Tammy was meeting them back in the kitchen in half an hour to make the hamper. When they'd gone she slipped next door in search of her father.

Ben was painting the bottom of his old rowboat down the long yard that backed onto the lake. No trip to the beach this weekend. The ghost gum towered into the sky and shaded the grassy knoll above the water where he worked. The boatshed was where her father came when he was stressed.

She'd spent months of lazy summer afternoons with Ben and Misty here, watching swans and ducks when Jack was a baby. She realised time, peaceful and trouble-free time, so different to now, had drifted by like the floating leaves from the overhanging trees.

'Hello, there, Tam.' Her father looked up with a smile and his piercing blue eyes narrowed at the strain in her face.

He wiped the excess paint off the paintbrush and balanced it carefully across the top of the open paint tin before he stood. 'How are you? How's Jack? What's happened was huge. Bigger than anything we've had to cope with before.' He came closer. 'You okay, honey?'

She watched one large drip of red paint slide down the end of the brush and fall onto the grass like a drop of blood. A spectre of foreboding. But she didn't have premonitions—that was Misty's way. She shivered. She was here for a reason. 'I'll be fine when Leon's gone and Jack's safe.' As if to convince herself?

Her father's dark brows, so like her own, raised in question. He slid an arm around her shoulders and drew her to sit beside him on the circular iron stool that ringed the trunk of the biggest gum.

'You think the two go together, do you? Leon and trouble?'

'Of course.' So quickly she could say that but still there was that tiny seed of doubt planted last night, an illogical but still possible seed that maybe the trouble had come from her.

She wasn't sure how to broach a subject everyone in her family had left alone for more than eight
years.

'Do you remember when you came for me that
last time at Grandma's?'

Ben's black brows rose in surprise. 'Of course.'

'Did you ever learn much about Jack's father?'

Ben's arm slid away and he straightened and gazed
across the lake. 'Yes. A little.'

She wouldn't have been surprised if he'd said,
'No—nothing,' so the other answer made her curious.
She couldn't read his face. 'What could you know? I
didn't tell you much.'

Still he didn't look at her. 'I found out what I
needed to. To be sure you were safe when I took you
away. To be sure Jack was safe.'

She really didn't want to hear those words. *To be
sure Jack was safe.* Her stomach plummeted as she
watched his profile. 'I think Vincente was involved
with the mob on a small scale.'

Ben winced. 'I believe he was. I spoke to his
mother and he was betrothed to a woman in Italy so
he was never going to marry you.'

'Do you think there is any reason they'd want Jack
now?' She'd said it. Out loud because she needed
her father to deny, say it was nonsense, because she
couldn't say it to Leon, whom she needed to tell.

Ben looked away again and didn't meet her eyes.
Her stomach sank and she didn't want to think about

the ramifications of that. He hesitated but then he said, 'Can't think of one.'

Tammy sighed with relief. 'Of course not.'

CHAPTER EIGHT

THE picnic had been Jack's idea. The boys kicked a soccer ball between them as they walked down to the water along the shaded path and every now and then Jack cupped his hands around his mouth and called, 'Coo-ee,' across the lake. Paulo would imitate him. The echoes bounced off the hills across the lake and rolled back over the water and Tammy could hear the boys giggle up ahead as they trickled the ball between them.

Somewhere to the right a kookaburra laughed at nothing in particular and she drew the moment in with the breath of freshly mown grass that drifted across the street. It was good to remember what normal felt like.

Not that it was normal to have a gorgeous Italian man by her side. 'The hamper not too heavy, Leon?' Tammy glanced across as they strode down the leaf-strewn path.

Leon swung the hamper as if it was filled with fluff and nonsense but Tammy knew it must have weighed a ton. 'It's fine.'

Like heck it was. She'd put cans of soft drink, a thermos of freshly brewed coffee, mountains of savoury mini quiches, cold sausage rolls and a full bottle of tomato sauce in with the meat and rolls. Small boys could eat man-size portions. Then there were the sweets on plates Misty had forced on her.

As she walked she kept glancing at his bulging biceps and, becoming more noticeable, the veins in Leon's right arm. She clamped her lips on the smile that wanted to spread across her face. She could tell there was a little strain adding up. He swapped to the other arm.

By the time they'd reached one of the picnic tables under the trees she could've put a drip in his veins with a garden hose. She waited for the sigh as he lifted the bag onto the table and wasn't disappointed. She had to laugh.

He slanted a glance at her. 'And what amuses you?'

'How useful a man's arm is when you need it.' She grinned down at the hamper. 'I'm afraid I loaded the food up. On my own I'd have put it in the car and driven it down.'

He smiled and said cryptically, 'It kept my hands busy.'

Just one little comment like that and a dragon unfurled inside her stomach. He could seduce her in an instant in an open park with children a few feet away. How did he do that?

When the soccer ball came out of nowhere and almost hit her in the head, it put paid to the dragon and she stumbled back. Leon's hand speared out to knock the ball away, then caught her arm to help her balance. He turned and raised his brows at the boys.

'Oops. Sorry, Mum.' There was a pause and then Jack added, 'Sorry, Mr Bonmarito.'

'Perhaps you could aim for those trees behind you,' Leon suggested mildly, but the boys immediately spun to face the other way.

'You're proving handy this morning.'

'*Sì.*' Very quietly, under his breath, she heard him add, 'And sometimes at night.'

Tammy fought the tide of colour away from her cheeks and just managed to keep it in check as she began to unpack the hamper. Change subject. 'What time do you meet Gianni and Emma at the airport?'

'Five. Our plane leaves at eight.' Leon reached across and took the heavy thermos and weighed it in his hand. He raised his brows at her. 'Could you not find a house brick to place in the bag as well?'

She grinned. He made her smile and she sneaked a look at his handsome profile as he gazed across the lake. She'd miss him. More than a little. She couldn't remember ever being so at ease with a man on one hand and so supersensitised on the other.

Leon reached in and stole a juicy prawn wrapped in lettuce and she offered the tiny plastic container with seafood sauce.

He smiled and dipped, then took his time raising it to his mouth, a teasing light in his dark eyes and

she couldn't help but follow it. He was laughing at
her but it was nice. She watched him indulgently as
he closed his eyes in pleasure. But when he licked
those glorious lips, capable of such heat and hunger,
last night flooded back and she wished she'd just
given him the sauce and run away.

'Your seafood is amazing.'

'Ah.' Brain dead. Wake up. 'Yes. I love it.' She replaced the lid on the sauce in such a hurry it splashed
over her hand, but before she could wipe it clean he'd
taken her wrist and brought it to his mouth. A long
slow sip of sauce and she was undone. Her dragon
breathed a spurt of fire as her belly unfurled and
there was no hope of keeping the pink out of her face
this time. She glanced hurriedly at the boys but they
were running and whooping between the trees with
the ball.

She rushed into speech. 'Misty's excelled herself
in sweets. It's almost embarrassing.' She opened the
folded cloth to offer the plates with plastic film dis-
playing their contents. 'Let's see,' she garbled. 'Oh,
Lamingtons.' Bite-size Lamingtons, chocolate eclairs
oozing creamy custard, tiny swirls of meringue with
tart lemon sauce in the middle. And another squat
steel thermos jammed with homemade ice cream and
some waffle cones to hold the ice cream which helped
restore her sense of humour. With the crockery and
the thermos she'd bet that weighed a ton too.

Leon wasn't seeing the food. He would miss her.
His hands stretched in his pockets where he'd thrust
them away from her. He wanted to pull her into his

arms and lose himself and could feel the tension between them stretching. Perhaps he should kick the ball with the boys as a more useful outlet for unexpected action. 'Do you need help setting out the food?'

She shook her head. 'A bit of space would be great.'

He grinned to himself. 'Always so complimentary. It is fortunate my feelings cannot be hurt.'

'Or mine,' she retaliated, and he turned away with a shake of his head. She could be stubborn and blunt to the point of offence, but despite her efforts he could see through the independent facade she insisted on showing him. He had the impression it was he that brought out this harsher side of her and he acknowledged she had reason to distance him.

'Kick me the ball, Paulo,' he called, and the boys whooped as he joined their game. Fearlessly Jack attempted to tackle and when Leon sidestepped him Jack fell laughing to the ground.

Paulo swooped on his father while he was distracted and stole the ball and the three of them were bumping and pushing one another as they fought for possession. It was no surprise that soon they were all laughing and wrestling on the ground.

The immaculate Leon Bonmarito rolling in the grass with two grubby boys. It hurt too much to watch. This was what she couldn't give her son, though Ben had the same man-versus-man mentality that boys seemed to love. She didn't understand it but could see that Jack was delighted with the rough and tumble.

Leon looked and acted so big and tough and yet he was so good with the boys. She wished she'd been spared this memory. Jack was sent rolling away and Paulo dived on his father. She was sure someone would be hurt soon. Then it would all end in tears. The table was ready, almost groaning under the table-cloth full of ham and silverside rolls and the mountains of cold savouries she suddenly didn't have the stomach for.

She called to the boys. 'Come and eat.'

It took a minute for her voice to soak into the huddle on the ground but then they brushed themselves off and walked back towards her, all smiling and filthy. She pointed to the wipes she opened at the edge of the food.

'You can all wash your hands.'

'Yes, Mama,' Leon said as he shook his head at the spread. 'I think we need to put out a sign and invite people to share.'

She began to pour drinks. 'That happens. If you see anyone, wave them over.'

Leon believed her. This past week had shown him a town full of generosity and warmth and the concept of sharing was in every connection he made. He bit back the tinge of jealousy that wasn't worthy of him. His own life was different, and he wasn't able to function like this self-sufficient small town could. He had responsibilities, people depending on him and his family business to continue to grow to provide a service for those in need.

He was glad they had the chance today to do something normal. Though the taste of this magical interlude would no doubt come back to haunt in his and Paulo's emptily spacious apartment in Rome.

By the time they'd finished what they could, the boys were groaning and tottering back to their ball and Leon had subsided with a sigh onto the picnic rug.

'Had enough?' Tammy teased, and she looked over at him with satisfaction. When you don't know what to do with a man, you could always overfeed him.

Before she'd been foolish enough to sleep with him he'd taken up a huge portion of her day even when he wasn't there in person. Now, with so many memories in all dimensions, he would be everywhere.

Tonight he would be gone and the long nights ahead promised little rest at all. She was such a fool. But the opportunity for further foolishness was drawing to a close and when he invited her with a questioning look, she eased down beside him on the rug until their shoulders touched. She had no problem imagining more. Her ears heated with the need to tell him her secret.

Last night, in the dark, after he'd warmed her in a way she would never forget, he'd whispered again to her in his native tongue and the burden of her deceit had grown impossible.

He'd whispered softly how being able to hold her

in his arms had been the only thing that had kept him sane while the boys were missing.

That his guilt for drawing her into this mess had been very hard and her forgiveness so precious.

How hard it would be to fit back into his life as he remembered the feel of her weight against his chest and how much he savoured the little time they'd had together and the gift she'd given him.

All soul-exposing statements he didn't know she understood.

Maybe it could have been different if he didn't live on the other side of the world. She could never leave the lake, take Jack from his grandparents, leave her friends and her work and, if she was honest, her independence, and just move in with Leon. Not that he'd asked her.

But she knew she'd be unable to go to Rome and not be in his arms again.

'Do you think you will come to Italy next month? For the maternity wing.' It was as if he'd read her mind without looking. He shifted his attention back to her and it was her turn to look out across the water.

The smile fell off her face. 'Perhaps.' No, she didn't think so.

He slid his finger beneath her chin and turned her face towards him. 'You do not seem too sure.'

She met his eyes. 'I'm not. I need to think about the idea when my head isn't full of kidnappings and work crises and other—' she grimaced '—emotionally charged events I'm not sure what to think of.'

He nodded and let her chin go. 'I won't pressure

you. Though I'd like to. Perhaps you will think about it. I know my new sister-in-law would be pleased.'

Bring in the big guns, why don't you, Tammy thought with a sigh. Emma would understand though.

She looked back across the lake so he couldn't read her eyes. 'We'll see.'

The boys returned and fell down beside them. She saw the glances they exchanged at the closeness between Leon and herself and she ached for their naiveté. She'd wondered if Jack would be wary of Leon but he seemed to accept that the big man had a place in his mother's attention. Maybe because he knew that place had come to an end?

In the few minutes they all lay there before packing up, the simple pleasures of the morning rolled over them. Even the boys were silent and peace stole over their blanket.

The blue sky through the leaves overhead hurt her eyes it was so bright—or that's what Tammy told herself, why her eyes stung—and small puffy clouds skittered and were reflected in the lake that stretched away through the trees.

It was a perfect day for their overseas visitors to see before they left. The thought bounced around like an echo in her head. That's what they were. Visitors. Tammy felt the emotion and the hopelessness of the dream overwhelm her.

She heard the sharply indrawn breath of Leon beside her, and turned to see a small brown bird poke an inquisitive head out of the bush across from them.

A lyrebird, his beady brown eyes unblinking, tilted his beak at Leon and then stepped fearlessly out into the open less than ten feet from where they lay. The boys froze and covered their mouths with their hands, their little chests almost bursting with suppressed excitement.

The lyrebird lifted his brown, curved tail until it stood behind him like a fan, then shivered and shifted his feathers, until the upright display was to his satisfaction.

Only then did he strut and pivot in a stately dance to show them his glory.

When he opened his mouth the unexpected sound poured out. 'Coo-ee.' The notes from the lyrebird soared across the lake and bounced back at them. Strong and sure and perfectly mimicked on the boys earlier. 'Coo-ee,' the lyrebird trilled again, and he stared at them all as if he'd just given them a very important message. Then his tail fell and with regal disregard for politeness he disappeared back into the bush.

Tammy felt the air ease from her lungs, and the collective sigh almost lifted the paper napkins into the air. Jack whispered, 'A lyrebird. Grandpa told me about them.'

'It copied our call.' Paulo, too, was whispering.

'That's what they do. They imitate noises,' Tammy said quietly. 'They can copy anything. Even a baby crying.' She felt like crying herself it had been so magical. She sighed and somehow the load seemed a little lighter. 'We'd better pack up.'

Leon stared at the bush, his mind strangely less cluttered by the past. But no doubt that was because the present had been so chaotic. The bird had looked at him, and of all the memories of this place he would take with him today, that bird, and these people spellbound by his dance and song, would remain with him.

It was time for the Bonmaritos to leave. They'd said goodbye to Ben and Misty and Louisa already.

The fierceness of Paulo's hug surprised Tammy, as did her own in return. The lump in her throat grew as she hugged him back.

Paulo's beautiful dark eyes, so like his father's, so serious and young, seemed dreadfully in need of a mother. Her heart ached for him, and for Jack, and the loss of what could have been.

She tried to imagine how this quiet young boy felt, all he'd gone through, even worse than Jack because he'd been taken twice. She hugged him again. Paulo had to feel nervous.

She stroked his shoulder. 'Your dad will mind you.'

'*Sì.*' He nodded, but the concern stayed in his eyes. 'And who will keep you and Jack safe?'

'We'll be fine, honey.' She hugged him for the last time. 'Have a good flight and look after Grace and Aunt Emma for me.'

'Until you come?' He searched her face. 'Jack wants to come.'

'We'll see.' She glanced across to Leon, who seemed just as embroiled as she, with Jack. 'I'll think about it.' Not on your life was she going anywhere near Leon Bonmarito. Hopefully by the time he came back to visit his brother she'd be over this infatuation that had rocked her nice tidy little world.

Jack returned to her side, looked at Paulo and shook hands and then threw shyness to the winds and hugged the other boy, who hugged him fiercely back.

'You guys got over your mutual dislike, I see,' she teased, and they broke apart, both pink-tinged in the neck.

'He's okay,' Jack said gruffly.

'Too rrright, mate,' Paulo said with a stiff upper lip and a fine attempt at Aussie slang. His accent rolled the *r*'s and made them all laugh.

Then Leon stood beside her. So big and darkly handsome...and so ready to leave.

'*Arrivederci*, Tamara.' His arms came around her for a brief hug and he kissed her in the Italian fashion on both cheeks. Nowhere near her mouth.

It was as if they both knew it would hurt too much. With his head against her hair she heard him say, '*Addio, amore mio.*'

Ciao, Leonardo, she whispered soundlessly into his shirt and then she stepped back. 'Safe trip.'

'Come,' Leon said to Paulo. 'You have forgotten nothing?' Paulo shook his head and Leon closed the boot on their luggage. They would leave the rental at the airport.

It was time. He lifted his hand in salute, no last chance for a kiss goodbye, Tammy thought with an ache she'd have to get used to, but surely it was better this way.

With Jack by her side she watched them drive away and as they walked back into the suddenly empty house, Tammy felt a gaping emptiness in her chest that made tears burn her eyes.

'I'm going to my room,' Jack said gruffly, and she nodded. She wanted to go to her room too, and crawl under the covers for the rest of the day, maybe the rest of the year.

Five minutes later Jack was back. 'We'll have to see them off now.' When her triumphant son reappeared, brandishing Paulo's backpack like a glorious trophy, she had a ridiculous urge to laugh out loud.

Then common sense stepped in. 'No, we don't. We can post it to him.'

Jack shook his head decisively. 'It's got everything in it. His MP3 player, his phone, diary—' he paused for effect '—his mother's photos.' Jack knew he had the winning hand. 'What if all that gets lost in the post?'

Tammy rubbed her forehead and ignored the stupid leap of excitement in her belly. She'd have to take it. They'd have to take it. Jack wins.

'Maybe we'll catch them. It's three hours to Brisbane and a real pain.' Not that she'd planned anything useful today except feeling sorry for herself.

Tammy grabbed her keys with a heart that was lighter than it should have been. This was not good. She'd have to go through the whole painful farewell routine again and this time she was bound to cry. But if she had to do that, she was darn sure she was at least getting that kiss. A real one. To hell with the consequences.

Her eyes narrowed for a moment on Jack. 'You and Paulo had better not have cooked this up between you. I won't be impressed if we catch them and Paulo's not surprised to see us.'

They didn't catch them and half an hour into the drive Tammy accepted it was a dumb idea to try. Once she thought a police car was following her and she slowed down even more. She wished she'd remembered to bring her phone so she could have called Emma.

The plane didn't leave for another five and a half hours so she wasn't worried about missing them. Leon was meeting Emma and Gianni at the International Departure gates at 5:00 p.m. As was Montana with Grace. She had plenty of time. It was only one-thirty now.

By the time she took her parking ticket from the machine at Brisbane airport Tammy had reached a definite point of regret for her decision to come.

And they'd all, especially Leon, think her mad to chase across the country to give back a bag she could have posted. She could have sent it registered mail, for crying out loud. It was Jack's fault.

Her mood wasn't improved when she realised that

she and Jack were in such a hurry they'd forgotten Paulo's bag in the car and they'd had to race back and get it.

Dragging her son through the terminal, she wished herself home until finally she spied the signs directing her to the departure lounge entry. And there, towering above the crowds, big and dark and brooding with his broad shoulders lovingly encased in his grey Italian suit, stood Leon. Her steps slowed and her hand tightened on Jack's as she came closer.

Leon turned, as if sensing her, and his eyes widened with surprise and a warmth that almost had her fan her face.

Jack eased his hand out of hers and ran across to Paulo brandishing the bag. The two boys hugged and Tammy and Leon looked back at each other with raised brows.

Her feet slowed but Leon stepped past the boys without a word and walked straight up to her. *'Ciao, bella.'* His head bent and he stared into her face as if still not sure that she was real.

Her cheeks warmed under his scrutiny. *'Ciao, Leonardo,'* she said. It was safe enough to echo, and of its own accord her hand lifted to brush his cheek. 'You didn't kiss me goodbye.'

His eyes darkened and roamed over her. *'Sì.* For good reason.'

'And what reason would that be?' Her belly kicked with the heat in his scrutiny and suddenly they weren't in a crowded airport. They were alone, in a mist of vision that narrowed to just Leon's face.

'I believe that's a dare.'

Wasn't that how they started? 'It's been done before.'

His head lowered further and just before his lips touched hers she heard him whisper, 'But not like this.'

She should have realised how dangerous it was to challenge this man. Or maybe she was very aware of the consequences. That was the glory of it. When he finally stepped back, the hard floor of the terminal seemed to sway beneath her feet and he kept one hand cupped beneath her elbow until she balanced again. Some kiss.

He lifted her chin with his finger. 'Why are you here?'

Still vague and dreamy she answered absently, 'Paulo forgot his bag.'

They both turned to the boys, forgotten in the heat of the moment, a few feet away only minutes ago, but the place they'd occupied stood vacant. Two older men moved with a leisurely intent to stand and chat there instead.

Leon craned his neck around the men, and frowned heavily. 'Now where have they gone?'

The boys were running. A vague and nebulous plan had formed in the few moments their parents had ignored them. What if they ran away? Together. Somewhere safe, of course, just long enough to miss the flight, and ensure their parents had more time together. More chance to stay longer in Lyrebird Lake for the Bonmaritos.

A family in front of them were heading for an arriving bus, pushing luggage and laughing, and the boys followed them and two older ladies onto the bus.

'What is Long-Stay Parking?' Paulo whispered as they sat unobtrusively behind the noisy family.

'Don't know, but sounds like a good place to sit while we wait for the plane to go,' Jack said.

The bus filled quickly with those returning from holidays and trips to their cars parked in the furthest part of the terminal. 'My father will be very angry,' Paulo whispered, regretting their daring already.

'So will Mum, but they'll get over it.' Jack's voice wobbled only a little. 'It's for their own good.'

'What if we get lost?'

'You've got your mobile in the bag. We'll ring your dad. Which reminds me, you'd better turn it off now.' He looked at Paulo. 'In case he rings?'

Paulo paled and hastily dug in his bag. '*Sì.*' He flipped open the phone and held down the key until the screen changed. They sat there and stared as the light dimmed and disappeared. Both gulped.

The bus revved and moved off. The trip seemed to take a long, long time. When it pulled up, the jerk thrust them forward in their seats while all around them people stood and lifted bags and shifted in a line towards the exit and a huge area with rows of parked cars. In every big square of cars, a brick waiting room sat on edge of the bus line, to provide shelter in case of rain.

'We could sit in that shed,' Jack said, less sure of the brilliance of his plan now that they were there.

Paulo didn't say anything but he followed the other boy with his head down, his backpack bumping on his shoulder like the weight of the world.

Both boys' eyes lit up when they saw the snack vending machine in the corner of the waiting room. 'You got money?' Jack said.

'*Sì.*' Finally Paulo smiled.

'I can't believe this.' Tammy felt sick and frightened and most of all incredibly angry and disgusted with herself. And the man beside her.

Leon was reaching for his phone. A muscle jerked in his cheek and his mouth had thinned to a grim line. 'This, I think, is a trick thought up by your son.'

The possibility had crossed her mind. A bit like the suddenly found backpack of Paulo's. But she couldn't admit that. Surely Paulo had some say. 'Why does it have to be my son?'

Leon's hand tightened on the phone. 'Because mine is aware of consequences.'

Not true but she wasn't going to fight about it now. She was too scared to have lost Jack again. 'Where are your clever bodyguards? What if someone's taken them again?'

'One has left to organise our safe arrival and the other I gave leave for a few minutes. He approaches now.'

Leon launched into a flood of Italian and Tammy battled to keep up. It seemed the bodyguard had gone

to buy a drink and also not seen the boys disappear.
So Leon wasn't discounting the chance of abduction. Tammy turned to the elderly men beside them.
'Excuse me. Have you seen two little boys, dark hair,
about eight years old?'

One of the men shook his head and the other
stroked his chin. 'I might have, actually. Did one
have a backpack?'

'*Sì*,' Leon broke in. 'Did you see where they
went?'

The gentleman lifted his hand and waved.
'Running towards the exit. I thought it strange but
they caught up with a family and I assumed they were
with them. I'm sorry.'

'Thank you. You've been very helpful.' Leon gestured to the bodyguard and the man jogged quickly
towards the exit. He slanted a grim I-told-you-so
glance at Tammy.

Tammy's head ached with the beginning of a tension headache. How could the boys have done this
to them? They knew how frightened she'd been. She
couldn't believe this was happening and all because
they'd brought a stupid bag to the airport. When
would she learn that this man was trouble? Where
were Jack and Paulo?

Leon flipped open his phone again. Then he swore
in Italian. Graphically.

'Don't swear,' she said—anger was the last thing
she needed—and rubbed her face.

Leon blinked. '*Scusi*. Paulo has switched off his

phone.' He narrowed his eyes at her. 'And how did you know I was swearing?'

Good grief. She didn't have time for this. She shrugged and avoided his eyes. 'I didn't really. It just sounded like swearing.'

His eyebrows raised but he said nothing more. 'I will try the washrooms. Perhaps you could check the shops.'

She nodded but the fear was forming a monster in her throat. 'And what if we can't find them?'

'Then we'll check with the police.'

The next hour was fraught with false leads, and small boys that for a moment made her heart leap, and then ache with growing fear. The police had faxed through the photos of the boys to airport security and the inspector in charge of the previous kidnapping was on his way.

Tammy slumped against a pole outside the terminal and searched out groups for small boys. 'I can't believe we've lost them again.'

Leon ran his hand through his hair and glanced at his watch. 'Nor I. There will be retribution for those responsible.' The underlying menace in his voice made Tammy shiver and for a second she almost hoped for Jack's sake that they'd been kidnapped.

Leon glanced at his watch again. 'I must meet the inspector and Gianni should also soon be at the departure gate. And Montana with Grace. Do you wish to come with me or remain searching?'

What? And stay here by herself, imagining the worst? 'I'll come.'

When they returned to the terminal again only Emma and Gianni were there. Leon broke into a flood of Italian and when he said to his brother that no doubt it was a hoax dreamed up by Tammy's son, Tammy shot him a look of such pure dislike, he paused midsentence.

Leon held his hand up to his brother and turned to Tammy. Her heart thumped at his comprehension. He searched her face, took her arm above the elbow and steered her away from the others.

His grip was more than firm. 'You understood everything I said?' The question came in Italian.

'*Sì,*' she spat back.

He dropped her arm as if it was suddenly dirty. 'This we will discuss later.'

'Or not,' Tammy replied, and closed her eyes as he walked away. She felt like burying her head in her hands but it wouldn't help. He'd never forgive her. But it didn't matter. Nothing mattered. The boys were the important thing.

The inspector arrived accompanied by his constable. 'I do not think they have been taken by the same people.'

'Why are you so sure?' Tammy had to ask.

The inspector shrugged. 'We have all except one of the men responsible for the kidnapping in custody or in the morgue. It seems the shootout was between two warring Mafia gangs. They planned to hostage the one man's son for the location of stolen property.'

Leon's brow furrowed and his impatience with this diversion was plain. 'What has this to do with my son?'

'Nothing, I'm afraid.' The inspector scratched his ear. 'It's the other boy. Our informant believes Miss Moore's son was the illegitimate child of one Vincente Salvatore. Mr Salvatore was killed in the battle. It is believed he protected the boys with his life.'

Tammy felt the look of incredulity Leon shot at her and she shook her head. Vincente was dead. He'd saved the boys. She looked at Leon but he didn't hide his contempt for more lies. She hadn't known Vincente knew. How could she have known that Paulo's abduction had been mistaken identity? All this fear and danger her fault—for a hidden heist. And all the time she'd blamed Leon for the boy's danger. 'I'm sorry.'

'I wonder what else I do not know,' he said quietly in Italian, and she could tell he didn't care if she understood.

The inspector went on. 'There's still one man at large so we will be keeping an eye out. Might be prudent to be careful, Miss Moore.'

The airport security chief arrived at that moment to join the inspector and Tammy turned still-stunned eyes on him. 'We've isolated the video coverage in the time frame the boys went missing. It seems there's a chance they boarded the long-stay car-park bus.

We're waiting for a patrol car now so we can check that out.'

Leon's phone rang. He glanced at it with an arrested expression and closed his eyes with relief. 'Paulo?'

He paused as the boy spoke. *'Sì.'*

He looked at first Tammy and then the police inspector. 'We will come,' he said in English. 'Long-stay car park. It seems they have run out of money for the vending machine.'

'I'll go,' Tammy said quickly. 'My car's just outside.'

There was an awkward pause as they all looked at Leon. The security chief pulled a pad and pen from his pocket. 'Give me the registration and they'll let you through.' Tammy wrote down the number.

'I, too, will come.' Leon's tone brooked no argument and Tammy was too emotionally exhausted to care. It was her fault the boys had been kidnapped. Vincente's fault. The fact rotated in her mind like a clothes line in the wind. Around and around. Leon's words sank in. It was a wonder he'd travel with her but she guessed he'd handed his own car in. 'Feel free. What the hell.'

'Don't swear,' he mocked as they walked away together. She gave him the keys in the hope he wouldn't get out of the car when they first saw the boys. At least driving back to the terminal would give them some cooling-off period.

Leon glared down at her as they walked. 'So, all this time it is you who has placed my son in danger—not, as I thought, my imposition on you. You should have told me his father was a criminal. And Italian.'

She ignored the part she had no defence for. 'It was more than an imposition to almost lose the lives of two children,' she said wearily, 'and I had no idea that Vincente knew about Jack.' That wasn't strictly true. She'd *hoped* Vincente hadn't known about Jack.

'Is that the truth or more lies?' He didn't believe her. Couldn't say she blamed him.

She rubbed her aching temples. 'Nothing warned me the Salvatores, or their enemies, knew of my son's connection to their family. As far as I was aware, there was no connection.'

Leon strode forward more quickly when he spotted her car. She had to almost run to keep up. 'It is well there is still time to leave today because I find myself wanting to shake you for destroying my trust in you. That you speak my language.'

She wasn't happy being in the wrong either. 'I know. If it's any consolation I'm embarrassed I didn't let you know earlier. But the longer I left it, the harder it was to tell you.'

He speared a glance at her across the roof of her car. 'So I have told you what is in my heart, my most inner secrets, and you are the one to feel embarrassed? My sympathies.'

He came back to her side and opened her door, and his courtesy while he waited for her to get in was an insult.

His sarcasm flayed her and she could feel the

tears she refused to let fall. Would this horrible day never end?

She'd witnessed his utter emotional devastation, and for a proud man who barely showed emotion normally, of course it must be mortifying. He'd never forgive her. 'I can only say I'm sorry. And that I wish I could have told you myself before you found out.'

It seemed she could look forward to years of distrust and dislike whenever he visited his brother in Lyrebird Lake. At least there was no decision now about visiting Rome.

It wouldn't matter how hard she tried to re-establish their mutual trust after this.

CHAPTER NINE

LEON drove with icy precision.

They followed the signs to the long-stay car park and the operator at the booth magically waved them on when their car appeared.

Two small and forlorn boys stood sheepishly outside the brick shelter, little white faces pointed to their shoes as Leon and Tammy pulled up beside them.

There was silence until Leon spoke very quietly. *'Arrivare,'* he said to his son. 'Get in,' he said to Jack. Then he glanced at Tammy. 'Or does your son understand Italian too?'

'No.' Tammy didn't offer anything else. The silence stretched and remained in the car until Leon reparked in the terminal car park.

They all heard his deep breath. 'I do not want to know whose idea this was—' his cold glance brushed them both '—but I wish you to appreciate how frightened and upset both Tamara and I were when we found you gone. This has been a difficult week for everyone and I would prefer if no further problems arise.' His voice remained low but every word made Tammy wince. 'Or there will be retribution.'

Paulo held back his tears. '*Sì, Padre. Mi dispiace.*' He looked at Tammy. 'I'm sorry.'

Jack sniffed and nodded, then he, too, took a deep breath. 'It was my idea, Mr Bonmarito. Not Paulo's. I'm sorry.'

'It is to your mother you owe an apology, Jack.'

She watched her baby struggle to hold back the tears. 'I'm sorry, Mum.' Tammy just wanted to hug him but she couldn't risk him thinking he could run away ever again. And if she was honest, she was a little nervous of Leon, in the mood he was in.

'Thank you, Jack. And Paulo.' She fought back her own tears. 'Let's just get you Bonmaritos on that plane.'

They all climbed out of the car and walked silently back towards the departure gate. Incredibly there was still time for boarding. Tammy was so emotionally punch-drunk she couldn't wait to make her own exit.

She saw Gianni and Emma up ahead and it was like a seeing a drink machine in the desert. They had Grace so Montana must have been gone. Emma, her best friend—a welcoming face, thank goodness, from a world she understood and felt comfortable in, a face from home. Her steps quickened and she threw herself into Emma's arms and hugged her fiercely.

Emma hugged her back. The loudspeaker called another flight and reminded them all that time was running out and they hadn't been through customs yet. Emma searched Tammy's face and then looked to Leon and gave her friend one last hug. She blinked back the tears and glanced at her husband before she took her daughter's hand and they moved through the departure gate into customs. One wave and then they were gone from sight.

Which left Tammy with the thundercloud, two subdued boys and a goodbye that never seemed to end.

'Say goodbye to Tammy,' Leon said quietly to his son, and perversely Tammy wished Leon had called her Tamara.

'Goodbye.' Paulo moved in against her as she held open her arms. She cradled his dark head against her chest and her heat ached for him. *'Ciao, Paulo. Hanno un buon volo.'* Have a good flight. She may as well tell everyone she could speak it if she wanted to. Now.

Paulo's eyes widened at her faultless Italian and then he smiled. A beautiful smile. *'Sì.'*

Leon took the insult on the chin. She was mocking him. It seemed she had always mocked him. He'd made a fool of himself with her deceit. Did she have no shame? How had he allowed himself to be fooled by her smile? And yet he was tempted to throw everything to the winds and demand to know if she cared for him a little. He bit the impulse stubbornly back. Did he have no pride? Did he want to lower himself again? He was a Bonmarito! 'Goodbye, Jack. Look after your mother.' He inclined his head and it should not have been so hard to brush past her and walk away. But it was.

Tammy watched Paulo follow his father, his eyes shadowed as he waved one last time to Jack and her. Then it was too hard to see because her eyes were full of tears. But still she couldn't look away from the broad back that finally disappeared through the gate.

He'd gone. Leon's gone. She'd tried to apologise in the car, but maybe she should have tried again before he left. Of course she should have. Should have thrown herself on his chest. Should have made him see she hadn't meant to continue the lie, but opportunities had slipped away. And in those last few seconds, she'd only alienated him more. With her pride. Lot of good that would do her now.

The fact slapped her in the face. She loved him. Loved Leon. And she should have told him she loved him. At least then they would have both been exposed. The fact stared her mockingly in the face as she watched strangers disappear into the void that had taken the only man she should have fought for.

And she'd been too stubborn and too cowardly to beg him to forgive her. Too proud to share the same thoughts and emotions he'd shared with her more than once. She felt the tearing in her chest as she realised her loss. The tears welled thicker and her throat closed.

Jack tugged on her hand, then jerked hard, and she brushed her hand across her eyes and turned back to look. What was the boy doing now?

She looked again. A man with a barely hidden wicked-looking knife had taken Jack's other hand and was pulling him away from her. Again. They were trying to take her son again.

A red haze crossed her vision; all thought of self-defence she'd learned for years flew out the window in this recognition of danger and she raised her handbag like a club and rushed at him, threshing at his face and head until he let Jack go. She kept hitting him until something hot and yet chilling struck her chest.

People stopped and stared as Tammy blinked at the sudden heat in her chest and the last thing she heard was Jack's scream. She fell as the air seemed squeezed out of her lungs and a steel band tightened slowly and relentlessly across her chest. The world went dark.

Leon made it to the first checkpoint, clicked his pen to complete the departure form and suddenly a word leapt out. *Departure*. His hand stopped. His fingers refused to write a letter and he'd grabbed Paulo's hand and spun back towards the entry.

Making their way backwards through the crowd had taken agonising seconds and he prayed she hadn't gone far through the terminal. He didn't know what he was going to say but leaving without a kind word because of stupid, stubborn Italian pride would not happen. He'd made the gate just as Jack had been accosted. His heart exploded in his torso as he'd pushed past people to where he could see Tammy flailing at the man. He saw it happen with a horror he would never forget, the awfulness of the knife, and seeing her eyes close as she fell.

He hit the man once, with a force that snapped the man's head back, and the knife flew into the air and then clattered to the ground. The assailant slid to the floor where he lay unmoving and for a few seconds Leon hoped he was dead. Then he fell to his knees beside Tammy and slid his hand to her neck to feel her pulse. 'Can you hear me? Stay with me, Tamara. You'll be okay.'

He found her pulse. It was there, beneath his fingers, rapid and thready, as the bright red blood poured from the wound in her chest. He pulled his handkerchief from his pocket and tried to staunch the flow, glancing around for help.

'She's alive,' he said to Jack, beside him, and then Paulo was there too. 'Look after Jack,' he said to his son, and white-faced Paulo nodded and put his arm around his friend as both boys looked on in horror.

A security guard arrived and Leon snapped orders at him. 'He's stabbed her. I'm a doctor. Call for an ambulance.' All the time his brain was screaming, *No, not Tamara. Not here. Not now. Not ever.* Wrenching his mind away from the unthinkable he clinically assessed her. With one hand he lifted her eyelids and no flicker of recognition eased his fear. 'Stay with me, Tamara,' he said again. He rechecked her pulse, still fast but it was her pallor and the unevenness of her breathing that terrified him.

Then he saw it in her throat. The sign of imminent death. The tracheal shift from internal pressure within her chest. The veins in her neck began to bulge as the pressure of one lung expanding from within its layers squeezed the air out of the underlying lung and crushed her heart.

Gianni and Emma arrived, pushing though people who crowded around them. 'Thank God.' Leon gestured from where he was crouched. 'He's stabbed her lung.'

Without a word, Gianni took over holding the wound as Leon rolled her gently to check there was no exit wound.

'Where are the paramedics? There is very little time to decompress her lung.'

Emma fell to her knees and put her arms around both boys. 'What happened?'

Leon spoke across Tammy's body. 'He stabbed her. An ambulance is on its way.'

Jack sobbed and Leon grasped his shoulder to give him strength. 'Move the boys away, please.'

The paramedics arrived and they all moved back. Except Leon. 'I'm a doctor. Tension pneumothorax. It needs releasing. Now.'

The paramedics, young and a little unsure, gulped, looked at each other and nodded. With barely controlled haste they opened their kit and removed their largest cannula normally used for rapid infusion of intravenous fluids.

The paramedic wiped the area with a swab but his hand shook so that he dropped the swab. The bleeding sped up. He hesitated. The gauge looked huge and Leon could feel the sweat bead on his brow as her veins stood rigid from her neck. Come on, he thought.

Still they hesitated, perhaps unsure, and Gianni leaned across his brother. 'Here.' He pointed to the precise spot. 'Between the second and third intercostal space.' Of course his brother had dealt with this many times in rescue from flying debris and it was enough to galvanise Leon.

He ripped Tammy's shirt where the knife had gone in and her skin looked alabaster in the artificial light of the terminal, with a slash of sluggish blood. Her low-cut lacy bra was stained a garish red and he pulled it down further with one hand. Her collarbone lay round and fragile and he slid his finger along halfway, then down, one, two spaces between the ribs.

He glanced at her face, her beloved face, and she had the blue of death around her mouth. Leon snatched the cannula from the man and slid it with precision between her ribs and through Tammy's chest wall. The hiss of air escaping made him want to cry. He who never shed a tear could barely see.

Leon sat back and the paramedic, spurred on by Leon's decision, apologised for his slowness and hastened to remove the stylet so that only the thin plastic tube remained in her chest. 'Sorry. Never done it before, sir.'

His partner handed the tubing that would connect the indwelling catheter to the Heimlich valve that stopped the air from leaking back in and immediately the blueness began to recede from around her mouth.

Leon felt the weight ease in his chest. Slowly her chest began to rise and fall with inflation as the air between the layers in her lung escaped and allowed the tissue beneath to expand.

Her breathing became more rapid and the blueness faded more. 'We'll cannulate before we move her, sir.' The paramedic was all efficiency now and Leon winced for his love when they inserted the intravenous line in her arm. Seconds later the cardiac monitor assured them all her heart was beating fast but in a normal rhythm. A few more seconds and she was on the trolley and they were all moving swiftly towards the ambulance.

Still she didn't regain consciousness. Leon's fear escalated. 'How far to the hospital?'

'Brisbane Central. Five minutes, tops.'

'We'll follow and take the children with us in Tammy's car,' Emma said, and she clutched Tammy's bag so fiercely it was as if she was holding her friend's life in her hands. They peeled away with Grace and the boys.

By the time they had her settled in the ambulance, Tammy's pulse was still rapid but appeared stable.

Leon took her hand and leaned down near her ear so she could hear him over the sound of the siren. 'I'm here, Tamara. It's Leon. I need you to listen to me. Jack is fine. We're all fine. We need you to hang on.'

He didn't know what he was saying. He just knew he needed to make sure she could hear his voice. Unconsciously he switched to Italian and he didn't care that if she woke she would understand every word. He ached for her to do so.

'I love you, Tamara Moore. The thought of you dying right there, in front of me, will live with me for ever. Why did I think I could go and leave you when it is plain to see you need me around you all the time?' He smoothed the hair from her still-pale features. 'I adore you with all my heart, my love. I need you. You must get well and we will plan our life together. If you will have me.' He rested his face against her cheek and to hear her breath was all he needed to keep going.

They kept him from her in Emergency, but after beginning one tedious form he brushed them off and at his most imperious he cornered a doctor and gained entry to her side.

He oversaw them insert the underwater sealed drain that would keep her lung from collapsing again, and watched the colour return to her face with bags of blood they replaced.

He followed her to the intensive care unit and supervised her transfer into the bed. The only person he couldn't bully was the specialist nurse who stared him down and told him to step back.

'She's my patient. When she's stable you can have her back.' And to the surprise of the other medical staff he did back down. Because, he thought with a wry smile, how like his beloved Tamara she was.

When Tammy woke up, she saw him asleep in the chair pulled up to her bed. His dark hair was tousled, his five-o'clock shadow heavily marked around his strong jaw. He was a disgustingly handsome wreck of a man as his cheek rested on her bed. She'd done this to him.

'I've been meaning to tell you,' she whispered, and the air stirred between them. He shifted in his chair and opened his eyes. The warmth that poured over her brought the heat to her cheeks. No one had ever looked at her like that. As if her presence had brightened his whole world. As if the sun had just risen with six words.

His hand tightened where it still held hers and he raised it slowly to his mouth and kissed her palm.

'Meaning to tell me what, *amore mio*?'

'That I speak Italian. Have done since I was a teenager.'

'So we discussed,' he said, but he was smiling. 'But now you have told me yourself and I am glad you can.'

She searched his face. 'What you said in the ambulance. Was it true?'

'You heard me, then?' Such love shone from his eyes she couldn't doubt him.

'I was trying to stay away from the light,' she only half teased.

He squeezed her hand and kissed it again. 'Nothing I have told you is not true.'

She closed her eyes and relaxed back into the pillow. 'In that case, yes, I will you marry you.'

'Sleep, my love. And when you wake I will ask you properly.'

CHAPTER TEN

LEON BONMARITO allowed the blessing to flow over him as the priest joined him and Tamara Delilah Moore in holy matrimony. His heart filled with the joy he'd once avoided on his brother's face and he thanked God again for allowing him to find and keep his love.

He had no doubt that somewhere ethereal above them all his parents were smiling down at them.

The tiny family chapel on the hillside at Portofino, filled with the scent and delicacy of flowers, held smiling people most important to them both.

Their two sons, dressed again in their tuxedos, tried hard to contain their mischief in the front row with the flower girls but he had no doubt Tamara's parents would quieten them if they exploded.

His brother and his wife, her pregnancy just show-ing, stood at the altar as their attendants but could not keep their emotion-filled eyes off each other.

His housekeeper and her husband, who had served the Bonmarito family all of their lives cuddled up to

Louisa, who had come for a holiday and to share their happiness.

There would be a party at Lyrebird Lake when they returned but this day, far away from the magic of the lake, was for them. To savour the solemnity of their vows and celebrate their love in front of a special few in a special place.

Afterwards, Leon took Tammy to honeymoon at the Hotel Macigno in Ravello. Their suite of rooms perched high above the cliffs where at night, when the boys were asleep, he showed her how much he truly adored her.

In the blue-skied days the boys flew kites under the watchful gaze of the nanny Leon had insisted on so they could relax, and the nanny was watched by Louisa.

As Leon and Tammy walked the cliff paths hand in hand, the spectacular Amalfi Coast shimmered below them and he pointed out traditional fishing villages and the reflected blue of the Mediterranean.

Nearby Amalfi, Positano, Capri and Pompeii beckoned for day trips and the boys flourished in the warmth of love that radiated from both parents as they played in the sea and explored the ruins of ancient cities.

Gradually Jack began to call Leon Dad, and though Tammy had told Paulo he could always call her Tammy, the boy asked, diffidently, if he could call her Mum. 'That is different to *Madre*, if that is okay?' And slowly their family melded, became one with a solidarity Leon thanked God for every day.

EPILOGUE

One year later

'WE DON'T have to go to hospital. You could call Misty and Emma and they could look after me here.'

'*Cara*, I would give you anything. But what is the use of following your every wish for the centre and then you choose to birth at our villa in Rome?'

Tammy shook her head stubbornly. 'I don't want to get out of this bath.'

Leon perched on the edge of the tub and regretted he'd made it so large. Large enough for two but not for two and the birth of his child. 'They will have the pool ready for you at the centre. I promise. They're dying to have someone use it. You could be the first.'

'Misty and Emma have to be there.' She sounded plaintive and he wanted to smooth the worry lines from her face.

'Of course.' He'd agree to anything. He was confused and anxious and totally bewildered by the sudden change in his calm and level-headed Tamara.

The boys were with Gianni and what had begun as a slow romantic day before the birth of their child had suddenly turned into a mutiny he hadn't expected.

He smoothed the hair from her forehead. 'Come, *cara*, I will lift you out.'

She sighed and he watched her gorgeous shoulders sink below the surface of the water as if savouring the last pleasure to be had from the day. 'I'm sorry, Leon.' She gazed up at him and he saw the flicker of uncertainty in her beautiful eyes. 'I think I had a panic attack when I realised today was the day.'

She reached for the handles at the edge of the bath and quickly he lent down to take her hand. She smiled with relief as she slipped her hand into his and prepared to climb out. 'Which is silly. Because I've done it before, and I know I'm designed to do this.' He didn't know if she was talking to herself or to him so he nodded encouragingly, trying not to pull her up so fast she'd realise how scared he was she'd change her mind.

She went on musingly now. 'But for a minute there I didn't want to admit that the time is here.'

She stood, her magnificent roundness running with water and bubbles and acres of shiny taut skin that made him bless the magic day he was allowed into her heart.

'You are such a beautiful Madonna with child, my wife.' His words came out gruffly, filled with bursting pride and a smattering of fear for the unknown.

He needed to have her and their baby safe and then all would be fine.

The drive to the hospital was accomplished with typical Italian chaos but, for once, traffic parted before the assertiveness of an extremely worried father.

Their journey from the front door to the birth room was faster than the speed of light so that Tammy felt quite giddy in the chair Leon had cajoled her into. 'Slow down, for goodness sake, before all my endorphins run for the hills.'

He slowed, just, and she chuckled to herself at this man, her husband, this anxious, gruff, darling man who was so unsure of the next few hours that his usual calm had been totally misplaced.

Her own moment of doubt was long gone. She knew all would be well. She knew her baby was waiting to meet them with the same anticipation she felt.

The ripples of conversation followed them. The Bonmarito baby was coming. No doubt there would be a hundred people in the waiting room when the boys arrived. It wasn't her problem. Her husband would sort that out.

They were through into the birth suite now. The eggshell blue of the rounded walls greeted her like a long-lost friend. She'd spent hours pouring over designs and new innovations to create the perfect birth space. No angles or corners, just soft and rounded curves and a welcome like a mother's arms.

The pool water lapped gently, waiting for her

arrival, and against the large window overlooking the shifting branches of a huge tree outside, Misty and Emma also waited. Both women smiled in understanding at the harried look on Leon's face when he came to a halt in front of them. He looked down at his precious cargo and began to smile sheepishly. 'I may have panicked for a moment there.'

'For only a moment,' his wife murmured with a smile as she lifted herself out of the chair and was embraced first by Misty and then by Emma. She glanced at Leon. 'Perhaps you could ask someone to take the chair away, darling, while I get organised.'

Leon nodded and hurried away. The three women laughed softly until Tammy began to sway as the contraction built and they stood holding her as she leaned against them. She breathed in deeply, her belly pushed low with the breath in her lungs, and then a downward out breath full of power and rightness.

Misty held the Doppler and they listened to the steady clopping of Tammy's baby's heartbeat as the contraction faded away and was gone. Then a quick rest back on the couch while Misty ran her gentle hands over the smooth mountain of Tammy's stomach, finding the baby's head well fixed deep in the pelvis, baby's back to the right and all as it should be for the final descent.

'The bath, I think,' said Misty.

Tammy nodded and her loose sarong fell to the floor with her underwear. Before they could move, the next pain was upon her and her two attendants smiled at each other and glanced at the door.

'I want Leon.' Barely had the words left her mouth and he was there. Kicking off his shoes and snatching at socks, shedding his trousers and plucking off his shirt until his powerful shoulders rippled freely as he leaned down and lifted her back against him for a moment before he stepped easily into the bath with Tammy safe in his arms. 'I am here, my love. Lean back against me.' And they sank into the water.

Tammy lay back against her man, safe and secure, surrounded by the warm cradle of buoyancy and her husband's arms. The bath gave the ease of movement she hadn't wanted to leave at home and the ability to move her cumbersome body to each new position with a gentle shift of her arm. As the next pain rolled over her she closed her eyes and breathed. The water rose and fell and her belly heaved with the life of her baby within.

She knew Leon's arms held safe around them both. Her fellow midwives would watch over them all until the journey was complete, and her heart was calm.

When Tammy's baby entered the world she was born into the silence of warm water, the welcoming hands of her mother about her, and lifted gently to the surface to breathe her first breath under the awestruck eyes of her family.

Perfetto. Except her father was crying.

Paulo and Jack Bonmarito scowled at the visitors. The new Lyrebird Wing of the Bonmarito Cura Nella Maternitá postnatal wing in Rome was crowded with well-wishers and they couldn't get near the door to their new baby.

'It'll be a boy. For sure,' Jack muttered, and Paulo nodded glumly. With three boys the new one would have to be favourite but neither said that out loud.

The boys looked at each other and shrugged and searched for Leon in the crowd.

'Who are all these people?' Jack asked.

Paulo chewed his lip. 'Acquaintances of my father. Business partners, patients, relatives of people from our village.' He shrugged. 'They will go soon.'

'Jack?' Paulo tapped his shoulder to attract his stepbrother's attention. 'I do not understand how the baby is born.'

Jack looked at him. He had a hazy idea but didn't really think about it. Or want to. 'Ever been to a farm? Seen animals give birth?'

Paulo nodded and then paled. 'You are serious? Who told you this?'

'Mum. That's what she did at Lyrebird Lake. What all the midwives do. Usually in the bath. People go there to have their babies. Mum catches 'em and cleans 'em up when they come out.'

Paulo had trouble getting his head around that. 'Does it hurt, do you think? For the woman?'

Jack shrugged and packed away the deep fear he'd been fighting with all morning. What if his mother died like Paulo's mother had? 'I've never heard a cat or dog complain. What about you?'

Paulo shook his head weakly. 'I feel sick.'

Jack grinned, suddenly glad his new brother

shared his fear. It was amazing how much better he felt when he realised he wasn't the only one afraid. 'And you're going to be a doctor? Let's find Dad.' In the end it wasn't hard to find him because the door opened and their father towered over everyone else in the room.

Leon gestured to the boys and they pushed their way through. 'Come, boys. Come and meet your new sister.' Jack and Paulo looked at each other and a slow, incredulous smile mirrored on both faces. Jack fisted the air. 'Yes!'

Leon swept them in and they saw Tammy. Serene and smiling, sitting calmly in a recliner chair, not looking like she'd done much at all.

Jack sighed with relief. She was okay. Mum was okay. That hard lump in his throat was going away. Well, he guessed all she'd done was catch a baby of her own in the water.

Nestled in Tammy's arms, curled like a kitten, was a tiny, pink-faced baby, with dark, soft curls piled on her head. She had the softest, rounded arms and tiny starfish hands that fisted up to her chin and mouth. She blinked at them.

'Look at her eyes,' Jack whispered, and he peered over Tammy's arm at the baby and Isabella blinked as if desperate to focus on her new big brother.

Paulo nodded. 'And her fingers,' he whispered back. 'She's got tiny fingernails.'

And across their heads, Leon and Tammy exchanged loving smiles full of promise and pride and wonder at the blessings that surrounded them.

MILLS & BOON®

are proud to present our...

Book of the Month

Walk on the Wild Side
by Natalie Anderson

from Mills & Boon® RIVA™

Jack Greene has Kelsi throwing caution to the wind —it's hard to stay grounded with a man who turns your world upside down! Until they crash with a bump—of the baby kind…

Available 4th February

Something to say about our Book of the Month?
Tell us what you think!

millsandboon.co.uk/community
facebook.com/romancehq
twitter.com/millsandboonuk

SUMMER SEASIDE WEDDING
by Abigail Gordon

Dr Amelie Benoir plans to spend the summer healing her bruised heart—not falling for the impossibly handsome Dr Leo Fenchurch!

REUNITED: A MIRACLE MARRIAGE
by Judy Campbell

GP Sally Lawson is shocked that her ex, Dr Jack McLennan, still makes her pulse race… But Jack is a changed man and he's fighting for a second chance. It might take a miracle, but he wants Sally as his bride!

THE MAN WITH THE LOCKED AWAY HEART
by Melanie Milburne

There's definitely chemistry between the mysterious new cop Marc Di Angelo and local doctor Gemma Kendall. But can Gemma release his tightly guarded emotions before he leaves town for good…?

SOCIALITE…OR NURSE IN A MILLION?
by Molly Evans

Spanish doctor Miguel Torres isn't convinced new nurse Vicky has what it takes. Vicky is determined to show him that behind her socialite reputation lies a heart of gold—a heart that's rapidly falling for her gorgeous new boss!

**On sale from 4th March 2011
Don't miss out!**

0211/03b

ST PIRAN'S: THE BROODING HEART SURGEON
bY Alison Roberts

Everyone at St Piran's hospital has fallen under Dr Luke Davenport's spell, except Anna Bartlett, who is certain the ex-army medic is hiding something. She should remain professional, but Anna's longing to be the one to save Luke from his nightmares—if only she can reach out to the man behind the brooding mask…

PLAYBOY DOCTOR TO DOTING DAD
by Sue MacKay

Arriving in Nelson to run the A&E department temporarily, gorgeous Kieran Flynn is greeted with a few life-changing bombshells—including Abby Brown, the woman he spent a magical night with two years ago…

**On sale from 4th March 2011
Don't miss out!**

2 FREE BOOKS
AND A SURPRISE GIFT

We would like to take this opportunity to thank you for reading this Mills & Boon® book by offering you the chance to take TWO more specially selected books from the Modern™ series absolutely FREE! We're also making this offer to introduce you to the benefits of the Mills & Boon® Book Club™—

- **FREE home delivery**
- **FREE gifts and competitions**
- **FREE monthly Newsletter**
- **Exclusive Mills & Boon Book Club offers**
- **Books available before they're in the shops**

Accepting these FREE books and gift places you under no obligation to buy, you may cancel at any time, even after receiving your free books. Simply complete your details below and return the entire page to the address below. You don't even need a stamp!

YES Please send me 2 free Modern books and a surprise gift. I understand that unless you hear from me, I will receive 4 superb new books every month for just £3.30 each, postage and packing free. I am under no obligation to purchase any books and may cancel my subscription at any time. The free books and gift will be mine to keep in any case.

Ms/Mrs/Miss/Mr _____ Initials _____

Surname _____

Address _____

_____ Postcode _____

E-mail _____

Send this whole page to: Mills & Boon Book Club, Free Book Offer, FREEPOST NAT 10298, Richmond, TW9 1BR